the
Florence
Letter

BOOKS BY ANITA CHAPMAN

The Venice Secret

ANITA CHAPMAN

the Florence Letter

bookouture

Published by Bookouture in 2024

An imprint of Storyfire Ltd.
Carmelite House
50 Victoria Embankment
London EC4Y 0DZ

www.bookouture.com

ISBN: 978-1-83525-649-7
eBook ISBN: 978-1-83525-648-0

For Liv and Fred

PROLOGUE

MARGARET

MARCH 2013

Margaret Anderson sat at the desk, her dear cat, Mr Emerson, curled up in the basket on the floor beside her. Sliding open the top drawer, she took out a sheet of cream writing paper of the highest quality, along with a matching envelope. Usually someone who was careful with her pennies, she made an exception now and again, and stationery was not to be scrimped on. Through the bay window, she paused to admire the magnolia tree outside St Andrew's Church opposite, its hot-pink flowers on the cusp of being in full bloom, bringing a splash of colour to a grey drizzly day. Spring was always a joyful time of year, a season of hope, after months of her aches and pains being exacerbated by colder temperatures.

Refilling her fountain pen from the pot of ink, she positioned her hand ready to begin, arranging thoughts in her mind. The pen leaked so much the royal-blue ink ran all over her fingers, but she liked to use it whenever she could. During the war her aunt used the pen to write diaries for the Mass Observation, and so it had sentimental value. Taking a handkerchief from the pocket of her slacks, she did her best to remove the excess ink from her fingers.

Margaret had written a different version of this letter twice before. Initially in 1993, and again in 2003. This was one last attempt to fulfil her old friend's request. Now, at the ripening age of ninety-one, time was running out. Who knew how long one had left? She was managing all right but took pills for arrhythmia, and the old arthritis flared up every now and again. The recent cataract operation had gone well – to her relief, because reading books and writing letters were two of her favourite pastimes. She picked up the book that she liked to keep on her desk: *A Room with a View* by E.M. Forster, and ran a hand over the cover. Smiling to herself, she took a moment to reminisce before putting it back down again.

And then, Margaret put pen to paper.

Dear Sir/Madam,

I am writing to ask if you might assist with a query. I'm looking for a person associated with Gatley Hall during the Second World War. Her name is Tabitha and she lived at Rose Cottage...

Would someone reply this time? She'd placed a series of telephone calls, to no avail, in the 1990s. Various members of staff had promised to hunt down her letter and 'get back to her', but they never did. Now, had she remembered to include all the relevant information? Her memory wasn't what it was and she sensed a vital piece of information was missing, but for the life of her, however much she racked her brain, it failed to reveal itself. Well, that would just have to do. Gently, she pressed a scrap of blotting paper over her carefully constructed words. Maybe it would be a matter of third time lucky. She wrote out the address for Gatley Hall and stuck on a stamp. The bells at

St Andrew's chimed a quarter to five, and if she made haste, she'd catch the last post. Margaret got up from the desk and put her chair underneath, then went to get her mackintosh off the stand in the hall. She wrapped a silk scarf round her head, doing her best to tie a knot under her chin, checking her appearance in the mirror above the console table. Mr Emerson, noting her leaving the study, had made his way into the kitchen and was happily munching on biscuits in his bowl. Opening the front door, Margaret stepped onto the pavement and made her way to the postbox.

CHAPTER 1

CLAIRE

As I passed through the black and gold gates, many of Gatley
Hall's Sunday visitors were driving in the opposite direction as
it was nearing closing time. The drive was bordered by grass
verges lined with trees and beyond the hedgerows were the
rolling Surrey Hills and a patchwork of fields as far as the eye
could see. The house came into view and although I'd seen it
when attending my interview, I slowed down the car in order to
take a proper look. Gatley Hall was majestic, with big white
columns at the front like a Roman villa. Following the Association of Treasured Properties sign to the staff car park, I found a
space and lifted my suitcase out of the boot. It would take a few
journeys to and from the car to unload all my stuff and I'd come
back later, after a cup of tea.

Rosalind, the house manager, had shown me Rose Cottage
with its charming white picket fence after my interview but
didn't have a key with her at the time, so I hadn't seen inside.
Being desperate for somewhere to live, I wasn't going to be
choosy. My dad had died only days before my thirtieth birthday

and this was followed by my break-up with Miles the day after the funeral. I'd moved out of his flat in Wimbledon, wounded after he revealed his vision for our future. My mother, or Deborah as she liked to be called, put me up, reluctantly, at her home in Richmond upon Thames. Being an actress, she could be rather self-involved, and she'd dropped regular hints about *how good* it would be for me to have my own space again. So I'd agreed to live at Rose Cottage without seeing inside, and despite the prospect of living alone in the countryside.

I wheeled my suitcase over the gravel path, sighing as white dust from the stones covered my most expensive piece of luggage. As I passed the back of the cafeteria's kitchens, the smell of food came through an extractor fan, reminiscent of school dinners and mixed with the odours emanating from two rather large and stinky refuse bins. But as I continued, a fairy-tale world came into view, fields in shades of green ranging from lime to pistachio to emerald, and punctuated by woodland. Smoke rose from the chimney of a farmhouse in the distance, and a tractor chugged nearby. To my left stood Gatley Hall, viewed from the side, a vast lawn descending to a lake.

Seeing the sign for the rose garden on my right, I lifted the latch and pushed open the cast-iron gate. Rosalind had informed me that the rose garden, enclosed by a red-brick wall, was Edwardian. An arch covered the main path and there were numerous flower beds filled with a variety of roses, divided by paving stones, some of them a little loose in places. A curved white bench filled one of the corners and it would make a nice spot to read in during warmer months. Passing through the gate at the other end, I dropped the latch back into place, and there was my new home: Rose Cottage. Rosalind said the cottage had been divided into two for staff members at some stage. 1A would be mine and 1B was where the head ranger lived. At first, I hadn't relished the thought of living on the property on my own, but the idea of someone living next door had put my mind at rest. I pictured him as a middle-aged outdoorsy type who could be relied upon if anything broke, and it was a comfort to know he'd be there at night.

Reaching the cottage, I searched for the key in my bag. A rose bush was sprawled over trellis attached to the wall between matching green front doors and I imagined the cottage would look pretty in the summer when the roses were in bloom. Being a born and bred Londoner, I felt like Cameron Diaz in *The Holiday*. The countryside was new to me, my only remotely rural experience being walks in Richmond Park growing up and strolls on Wimbledon Common with Miles when the flat got hot in the summer. Was I doing the right thing, leaving the world I knew for this place? It was beautiful, but would I be lonely? Perhaps I'd become inspired by my new surroundings and take up art again. Dad's death had brought some kind of urge to be creative in recent weeks. Being a film director, he'd always encouraged me to nurture my creative side, telling me I had real talent.

Unlocking the front door, I found myself in a small living room with a sofa to sink into, a couple of mismatched armchairs and a pine coffee table with spilt-drink stains all over it. It was clear that no one had lived there for a few weeks, the temperature chilly, and I needed to switch on the heating. There was a bay window with a large sill, perfect for plants and candles, and a Victorian fireplace complete with mantelpiece, and it was flanked by bookcases. A set of tools made from brass took up one side of the hearth, but having no idea how to build a real fire, I couldn't imagine using them. The furniture had a musty smell, and the cottage needed a good airing as well as a thorough dusting and vacuuming. I followed the hall to a small kitchen with a round table, and two stools tucked under a worktop running across the centre. The floors were wooden, and my boots clumped as I went up the stairs to explore further. On the landing, I spotted the programmer for the heating, and switched it on, hoping to warm the cottage up before bedtime.

The main bedroom at the front of the cottage overlooked the Surrey Hills and a box room faced the back, with a view of the cafeteria bins. A wardrobe took up most of the space and a tired-looking mattress was propped against the wall. It wasn't as if I was expecting any overnight visitors. Looking out of the window, I saw a patio area with table, chair and umbrella, and a makeshift barbecue made from bricks. A few terracotta pots were dotted around, the plants dried up and dead. A small bathroom was tucked in between the bedrooms, with a bath and shower. There was limescale in between the tiles and around the sink. I'd need to give everything a good scrub. The cottage certainly needed a bit of TLC and perhaps it would be good to have a project to keep me busy.

Back downstairs, I found a handful of tea bags in a canister by the kettle, but when I opened the fridge it was bare apart from old stains. Yuck. My phone said four thirty, and I hoped the cafeteria was still open so I could get something to eat. Heading back through the rose garden, I followed signs to the cafeteria – called The Stables – and as it was getting late, the staff were packing food on display into plastic containers. I bought a small quiche to take away. In the shop opposite, I looked for something exciting to drink, but the only alcohol to be found was a bottle of ginger wine on sale. Imagining long quiet evenings, I scanned the book selection, searching for something that would help with research for the Below Stairs exhibition I'd be organising as research and exhibitions officer. I found *Mrs Field's Diary*, written as part of the Mass Observation during the Second World War.

Back at the cottage, I poured a generous measure of the ginger wine into a tumbler, mentally adding wine glasses to my shopping list. I tucked into the quiche at the kitchen table, delicious, but quite rich and creamy. Although the ginger wine tasted a little acidic, I carried on drinking it, craving some kind of kick as the near silence struck me. The only sound was a bird tweeting outside. In Wimbledon, there was almost always passing traffic, as well as the murmur of people talking as they walked past the house. Living in the countryside was a shock to the system for someone like me. Could I adjust to this way of life? Opening my laptop, I played a smooth playlist on Spotify – I'd have to get my speaker out of the car when unloading the rest of my stuff later.

A key turned in the lock of the front door. I heard it creak open and then footsteps across the floor as someone approached through the living room. My heart raced. Who had a key to my cottage? As I stood up and grabbed the bottle of ginger wine, ready to smash it over the intruder's head, a man appeared at the open doorway to the kitchen. I shrieked, ready to strike until I saw he was bare-chested, with a royal-blue towel wrapped round his waist. What on earth was a half-naked man doing in my house?

CHAPTER 2

MARGARET

19 SEPTEMBER 1940

Breakfast of a stale slice of bread with some of that horrid margarine did nothing to alleviate my exhaustion after another sleepless night, and I tripped down the last of the steps leading to the pavement, clutching the gatepost to steady myself. Me and the other girls from the boarding house had spent the night in the basement as what seemed like hundreds of planes droned over London, the thud, whizz and bang of bombs dropping only a cat's whisker away while our landlady, Mrs Puddleton, invited us all to join hands and pray. After that, my room-mate Betty passed round a bottle of whisky bought from under the counter at the corner shop because the owner was sweet on her. We splashed it generously into our mugs, singing 'Knees up Mother Brown' and all the other songs in our repertoire as we dragged on cigarettes. Remaining calm was a struggle, although some managed more easily than others. Betty said she found the experience exciting, and Mrs Puddleton scolded her for finding joy in people being downright murdered in their homes.

The clear blue sky mocked my tiredness. Fumes from the

incendiary bombs made their way into my throat, making me cough, and I pulled a handkerchief from my pocket to cover my nose and mouth while crossing Great Portland Street. I took a left and headed towards Oxford Circus and then turned right onto Oxford Street. As I observed the devastation left by the Hun overnight, my eyes fell upon part of a piano and clothes scattered all over the place. My stomach turned when I saw an arm, complete with a man's hand, a gold band on his wedding finger, just lying there next to a gramophone. I looked away, trying my best to shut the image out of my mind, but it was too late. This vision would remain embedded in my memory for the rest of my days, revealing itself at unexpected moments. This wasn't the first time I'd witnessed such horror, and it was a concern that I might become hardened to this sort of thing until it meant nothing at all. Would living through the war turn me into a cold, heartless person?

Several buildings had been destroyed and fires caused by the carnage continued to burn. The smoke was intoxicating; the handkerchief at my mouth doing little to protect me. Despite this, commuters emerged up the steps from Oxford Circus tube station, seemingly undeterred by the events of the previous night, and swarmed along the pavement, no doubt doing their best to reach places of employment, as I was. Regardless of the devastation, if we didn't turn up for work we wouldn't get paid, and money was needed for rent and food – if we could get hold of anything decent to eat. I stepped around broken glass blown from a shop window, almost bumping into a man wielding a broom as he swept it into neat piles by the gutter. Two men roped off the area around a crater in the middle of the road, and red double-decker buses queued to pass, stuffed with passengers, some hopping on and off. All I could do was share everyone's optimism and carry on as if we weren't living through a blitzkrieg.

As I neared Taylor and Stone, my chest tightened as I saw

the fire engines that lined that side of the road, and firemen battling as best they could to put out the flames. Thank goodness no one was likely to have been in the building overnight. A crowd had formed on the pavement opposite the devastation at my place of work, and I recognised colleagues amongst them, who presumably like me had no idea what to do. Watching my beloved department store burn down broke my heart, but my only option was to stand and watch. After fighting so very hard to persuade Mother that I'd remain in London and be a shopgirl, my lifelong dream was now in tatters. Despite her letters, pleading with me to get away from the nightly bombardments, I'd insisted stubbornly on staying, assuring her that I always carried my gas mask – a broken promise as it was rather cumbersome.

My friend Geraldine, who worked in hats, was nowhere to be seen and I hoped she was all right. The manager of my floor, Mr Hicks, at six foot three towered above the throng, and I approached him.

'What are we supposed to do now, Mr Hicks?' I said.

He looked down at me and let out a sigh.

'We'll have to find other means of employment, Miss Bartlett. That's all one can do, as well as be grateful to be alive,' he said, shaking his head. He took a packet of cigarettes out of the inside pocket of his jacket and offered me one, but I declined. I'd smoked far too much the night before in the basement, and the fumes were already making my throat drier. He lit one for himself using a book of Taylor and Stone matches and drew on it deeply. Turning his head to one side, he exhaled a cloud of smoke. 'I'm sure you'll make a success of whatever path you choose to take, Margaret. Good luck to you.'

All I could do was nod and smile, and say, 'Thank you, Mr Hicks,' hoping he was right. Unable to see anyone else I knew, and eager to escape a scene that saddened me, my only option was to return to the boarding house and write to Mother to reas-

sure her I was all right. No doubt she'd hear about Taylor and
Stone on the radio soon enough and jump to conclusions about
my welfare. She'd write back by return of post, urging me once
again to get in touch with Aunt Edith, who lived in a humdrum
village in the Surrey Hills. Being a London girl, the thought of
decamping to the countryside where I was bound to be bored
didn't appeal to me. Aunt Edith was the widow of my father's
brother, Uncle Reg, and she'd been offering to find me a means
of employment locally for some time. Now I had no choice in
the matter.

That night we huddled together once again in the basement
at the boarding house, the cotton wool in our ears doing nothing
to lessen the din as the Hun bombed our dear city throughout
the night. The others were determined to stay as they still had
jobs to go to, but I was well aware of my fate. My letter crossed
with one from Mother that arrived the next morning. She was
staying with my older sister, Mildred, in Brighton.

> *5 Bridge Road,*
> *Brighton.*
> *19 September 1940*

Dear Margaret,

*I was sorry to hear about the horrifying air raid on 18
September and it sounds as though London took quite a bash-
ing. They said on the radio that your place of work has been
destroyed, and now I urge you once again, and hopefully for
the last time, to get in touch with your Aunt Edith in Surrey
who has offered to take you into her home. Being the widow of
a vicar, she is well connected in her local village of Gatley and
she'll secure you a paid position within no time. I hope you'll
now see sense and write to her straight away.*

All my love,

Mother

What was the alternative? Mrs Puddleton needed rent, paid weekly, and I was no longer in a position to pay it. The destruction of my beloved place of work had me more shaken than I cared to admit, and so it seemed my destination was Gatley, a place not visited since I was a small child. Memories of the village came back to me – it was pretty with buildings dating back to the eighteenth century and even Tudor times. While Gatley had a certain charm, it wasn't the most exciting destination for a young woman; but it seemed I was destined for country life after all.

CHAPTER 3

CLAIRE

The intruder didn't seem too threatening, dressed only in a towel, and he grinned at me as if I ought to know who he was. Around my age, his hair was a light-brown colour and stubble covered the lower part of his face. He mopped his brow with a hand, as if he'd just been immersed in some kind of sweat-inducing activity.

'You must be Claire,' he said. His voice was deep and husky and fitted his appearance perfectly.

'I am indeed.'

He raised his eyebrows. 'Claire with an "i"?'

'I don't see how that's relevant, but yes.'

'Are you planning to smash that bottle over my head?' he said.

'Seeing as I have no idea who you are, it's a strong possibility, yes.'

Leaning forward and reading the label, he said, 'It would be a terrible waste of... oh, it's that rancid ginger wine from the shop. You must have been desperate for a drink.'

Feeling like an idiot, I placed the bottle on the table,

keeping my hand gripped round its neck. He seemed harmless, but still.

'I'm Jim from next door, by the way.'

'Jim, the ranger?'

He nodded. 'That's me.'

So he wasn't middle-aged after all.

'And you're the curator from that fancy art gallery in London?'

'Yep.'

Despite his looks, he was kind of annoying.

'Anyway, what are you doing in my house?' I said.

'What do you mean?' he said.

'I don't recall the contract saying half-naked strangers can wander in whenever they like.'

'I'm sure there's a clause in there somewhere. You must have missed it.'

Admittedly, he was quite funny. Squashing a smile, I said, 'Aren't you a bit cold?'

'Does that worry you?' he said, adjusting the towel round his waist.

Struggling not to picture what lay beneath, my face warmed. No doubt my cheeks were the beetroot colour they tended to go in such situations. An awkward silence hung between us but he refused to move his eyes away from mine. They were a deep blue like the Med on a blistering-hot day. Releasing my grip on the bottle, I looked away, sliding my hands into the back pockets of my jeans.

'Hardly a stranger, am I though, being a colleague?' he said.

He was a little intimidating. I bit my lip.

'Mike, your predecessor, let me use the shower as mine is broken.' He wasn't leaving without getting his wash.

'Oh, right,' I said, defeated.

'Look, Claire, it's quiz night for the volunteers down the Stables, and I'm hosting, so if you don't mind.'

He stepped out of his flip-flops and placed them neatly by the wall, one in front of the other, before disappearing through the door and up the stairs. *If you don't mind.* What a cheek. How could I allow this person to intimidate me in my own home? Fired up by this thought, I followed and called after him.

'Just because Mike didn't mind doesn't mean I don't,' I said, the words coming out as a tangled mess. So many negatives – what had I even said? As I repeated the sentence to myself under my breath, he appeared on the landing and folded his arms.

'Claire, I understand you're a bit flustered with me barging in, but I've been out on the land all day, working my arse off, and I need a wash before this damn quiz night. The sweat is literally dripping off me. If you were standing any closer, you'd be aware that I absolutely stink. Are you saying I can't use your shower?' he said.

'Not exactly, but I mean, how long is it for?'

He shrugged.

'Five minutes, tops.'

Why was this man having such an effect on my ability to make myself understood?

'No, I meant when will your shower be fixed? Having you barge in like this whenever you feel like it is a bit much.'

'The plumber is booked for next week.'

'Okay, then,' I said, turning my back on him.

'You may want to put the hot water on for a bit longer,' he called after me before going into the bathroom. He closed the door behind him, the lock clicking into place.

With a sigh, I made my way to the landing. Already the shower pump hummed, the sound of water splashing into the bath. I put the hot water on for an extra hour, ready for a bath before bed. Back in the kitchen, I sprayed the worktops with disinfectant, giving them a thorough wipe, then made a start on the shelves in the fridge. Jim was burly enough to fend off any actual intruders, and that was a comfort at least. The sound of running water came through the ceiling while I washed up, studying the patio through the kitchen window. It would be a nice place to sit on a warm day with a glass of wine. I could plant new flowers in the pots, maybe some herbs too.

Jim came back into the kitchen. 'Err, Claire...' he said, his tone more friendly now. His thick hair was wet, and he ran a hand through it.

'Yes?' I said, drying my hands on the back of my jeans.

He pulled out a chair and gestured for me to join him at the table. He certainly wasn't lacking in confidence. I sat down.

'It must have been a shock for you when I let myself into your house.'

'So now it is my house?'

He smiled and nodded. 'And I'm sorry.'

'I guess this is as exciting as evenings get round here.'

'Where did you live before?'

'Wimbledon.'

'Ah yes, a bit more lively perhaps, but you haven't experienced quiz night yet.'

I laughed.

'Why don't you come along? You'd probably be the only person apart from me under the age of seventy, but they are a nice bunch, and we ordered a few bottles of Rioja in especially.'

'I start my new job tomorrow, so...' I said.

'There's always next month.' He leant across the table, proffering a hand. 'No hard feelings?'

'Sure,' I said, shaking it. His grip was firm, and he fixed his eyes on me once again. Really, he needed to stop this. But I ought to stay on good terms with him, being a colleague. And he'd be good at fixing things, no doubt – apart from his own shower.

He pushed his chair back and stood up. I went to put my glass by the sink.

'So, you don't mind me keeping hold of these keys, then?'

I shook my head. 'No, but perhaps cover yourself a bit more next time.'

'Too much?' he said.

Definitely too much.

'I'll give you a set of my keys as well, just in case I lock myself out, if that's okay?'

'Okay,' I said.

'See you later, Claire with an "i".'

'Bye.'

He slipped his flip-flops back on and left, shutting the door carefully behind him. Once again, I was alone. Knowing Jim would be there while I slept that night was reassuring, at least, and I couldn't help thinking that living next door to him might liven things up a bit.

Picking up my keys, I went to unload the rest of my stuff from the car. As I carried boxes into the cottage and upstairs to the bedroom, it occurred to me that this was the beginning of a new era. Putting the cover on my duvet, my thoughts returned to all I'd been through in the past couple of months. This was my chance to make a fresh start and find the time to process all that had happened. I made a cup of tea and took it upstairs with my laptop, ready to snuggle up in bed and watch Netflix while the water heated up for my bath.

CHAPTER 4

MARGARET

The postman brought Aunt Edith's reply the next morning and she urged me to pack immediately and make my way to Gatley, that very same day if I were able. She was quite surprised I'd remained in London for so long. At midday, I took the train from Waterloo station. Mrs Puddleton was not happy about my departure as she'd need to find a replacement, but said, reluctantly, that she understood the position I found myself in. The train carriage was crammed with passengers who presumably, like me, were displaced due to the bombing. Once I'd put my suitcase in the luggage rack overhead, I was grateful to get a seat, although it was next to a group of noisy children. They were being escorted by a rather fierce-looking woman clutching a clipboard. A pair of glasses rested on her nose, and she called out their names and they answered, 'Yes, miss,' in return. On the other side of the carriage sat a middle-aged man, wearing a bowler hat, his head buried in *The Times*, and he didn't look too pleased when the woman directed a couple of the children to the seats next to him. Everyone seemed to be relocating and they all looked as miserable as I was to be forced out of our beloved London.

We passed through Clapham Junction, and I looked out of the window at the rows of houses going up the hill, thinking back to better times when Mother, Father, Mildred and my other sister, Joan, had all lived together in a terraced house near Battersea Rise. When Father died, Mother encouraged Mildred and Joan to marry – as she was concerned about their financial security – and they did so, rather too swiftly for my liking. After they left, it was only Mother and me until the war began and I missed their company. Not long after the blitzkrieg started, she sold the house and decamped to Brighton to live with Mildred, offering to help look after the children while her husband was away fighting.

The signs had been removed from all stations in order to confuse the Hun if they did indeed manage to invade, and so I counted them one by one until we reached the tenth, shortly after Epsom. When I got off the train, so did many of the other passengers, and it took a little time for everyone to move along the platform as they organised themselves and their luggage. The fierce-looking woman led the children, who continued to chatter loudly, up the steps and over the footbridge. They moved at a snail's pace, which didn't bother me too much as I wasn't desperate to reach Gatley in a hurry. I looked across at views of the Surrey Hills, and it was all very scenic with not a building in sight; but still, I was a city girl at heart. All I could do was accept my fate – the war was driving me to the country-side, and there was nothing I could do about it.

I crossed the footbridge and, while descending the steep staircase on the other side, I studied the platform from where the trains ran to Waterloo. Hesitating for a moment, I consid-ered buying a cup of tea in the cafeteria and waiting to board the next train back. Clocking the payphone on the platform, I thought about calling my aunt to say I'd changed my mind.

The people ahead of me made their way towards the gap in the wall marked 'Exit' and the station became quiet, the only sound birdsong, the murmur of two women sitting on a bench on the other platform, the clippity-clop of horses and the distant hum of a motorcar. It was tempting to get back on the train to London, but where would I live? Mrs Puddleton wouldn't let me back into the boarding house if I had no money to pay rent. And what job would I do now Taylor and Stone had burned to the ground? It could take weeks to find another means of employment. Besides, Aunt Edith was expecting me, and Mother would be livid if I didn't turn up. My only option was to proceed as planned. I could always return to London in due course, once I was able to afford it. Aunt Edith seemed certain of her ability to secure me a job, so I could put some money away, build a nest egg.

As I approached the exit, someone coming from the other direction bumped into me and knocked me for six. My nerves heightened by recent events, I found myself physically shaking from the shock, tears pricking my eyes. Looking at the ground, I was horrified to see the contents of my suitcase spewed across the platform, and a brassiere draped over the impeccably polished shoes of the man who'd made it happen. Looking up, I noted he wore a chauffeur's cap and a charcoal-grey jacket with gold buttons.

'Look what you've done, you clumsy oaf,' I said, but instantly regretted my words as he studied me with kind eyes.

'I am very sorry, miss. Are you quite all right?'

'I'm fiiine,' was all I could muster, my voice wavering while I fought to stop myself from crying. I wasn't one of those women who used tears to manipulate and gain the sympathy of others, but the past few days had almost broken me, and there was more uncertainty to come. He bent down and picked up the brassiere as discreetly as was possible, his lips upturned as if he were trying not to laugh, and dropped it into the suitcase.

'You don't need to do that,' I said, looking away as he rolled up a pair of stockings. Ignoring me, he continued to collect the rest of my belongings, and I allowed him to.

'Thomas, is that you over there?' A voice came from the other platform, and one of the women sitting on the bench, who wore a beautiful green hat with a wide brim, rose to her feet. He stopped what he was doing and stood up. 'Do hurry up, young man,' she said. Her knee-length coat was cream with a black collar and matching buttons, and she reminded me of the well-to-do women who'd come into Taylor and Stone with their husbands' money to spend. I'd always been glad to see a woman of her ilk approach the counter, but knew how demanding they could be. They were used to getting what they wanted and often could be condescending towards me, a mere shopgirl. The woman in the hat made her way towards the bridge, the heels on her shoes clicking, and her companion, presumably a maid, followed.

'I'm sorry, milady,' Thomas shouted across to her in reply. 'The Standard didn't have enough petrol and I had to get the Rolls out of the garage. You know it's not easy, what with the fuel rationing.'

'Oh Thomas, really, you know I prefer to be collected in the Standard.' She shook her head. 'Never mind.'

He looked down at me. 'That's my mistress, Lady Violet. I do apologise for running into you like that. As you can see, I was in a bit of a hurry – her ladyship does not like to be kept waiting,' he said, raising his eyebrows. He squatted once again and clicked my suitcase shut, before standing up and passing it to me, our hands brushing as we did the exchange.

It was an accident after all, and he seemed a good sort. 'It seems that you were indeed in a hurry,' I said. 'Thank you for your apology.'

'Do make haste, Thomas, really. Stop talking to your lady friend.' Lady Violet was now halfway up the steps on the other side.

He headed for the footbridge, then stopped, turning to look over his shoulder.

'I didn't catch your name, miss?'

'Margaret, although most people call me Mags.'

'Mags it is,' he said. 'Most people call me Tom. Hope to see you again.'

'Oh, I don't intend to stay in this place for long. I'm a London girl.'

He laughed. 'That's what they all say.'

He broke into a jog as he approached the steps, as if suddenly realising his mission, and ran over the footbridge to the other side, where he picked up Lady Violet's bags. She and her maid, who wore a rather dowdy brown dress that hung off her slender frame like a farmer's sack – highly inappropriate for a lady's maid, I noted – followed him. Not wanting to encounter them all, I left the station through the gap in the wall marked 'Exit' and found myself alone. The horses and carts and motorcars had gone, apart from the Rolls that Thomas had mentioned, gleaming as if recently polished. A trail of passengers from the train stretched ahead along the country lane – towards the village of Gatley, I assumed. There were no signposts, just like there were no signs at the stations, and in unknown locations we all had to guess where we were going. It was a damn nuisance, but a necessity. The country lane was bordered with hedgerows and most of the fields beyond looked as though they were being used for crops. The scenery was rather cheering and the air noticeably cleaner than in London, a consolation at least.

Carrying the suitcase was tiring and I stopped and sat on it to rest, longing for a glass of water and a bite to eat. The Rolls passed and, as Tom threw me a discreet wave with a gloved hand, I wondered whether we'd see each other again. Summer lingered despite it being nearly the end of September, and I removed my mackintosh, tied it round my waist, and blotted the film of sweat on my forehead with a handkerchief. Conkers from a sweet chestnut tree lined the ground, and I picked one up and turned it over in my hand. It was so shiny and clean, and I marvelled at how nature produced such beauty. I slid it into the pocket of my dress for luck and watched a tractor plough the field beyond the hedge, with what seemed to be a woman driver, a land girl no doubt. The way it moved up and down was soporific and, while studying the furrows created, I imagined working as a land girl. Wearing scruffy clothes and trudging through manure and mud didn't appeal much, although driving a tractor might be fun. But you were right out there in the open while enemy planes passed overhead and who knew if a stray bomb might fall on you? I shuddered at the thought.

One day, when the war was over, I would go back to London and pick up where I'd left off. In the meantime, all I could do was inhale the country air into my lungs and do my best to keep on going.

CHAPTER 5

CLAIRE

The next morning my phone alarm went off at seven, over an hour later than in my Frampton Gallery days, and I put on my favourite grey trouser suit with a white shirt. Did I even need to dress up in this place? Everyone had been wearing jeans and ATP fleeces when I came in for my interview, apart from my new boss, Rosalind, who wore a skirt suit. Being well dressed at work had always given me confidence, though, and as it was my first day I wanted to make a good impression. I slipped on a pair of kitten heels and grabbed my handbag, hoping the café would be open to pick up a coffee before work.

The night before, I'd been able to hear Jim moving about next door as he got ready for bed. His bedroom seemed to be next to mine and the wall was paper-thin. I'd fallen asleep quite quickly but was woken up by a fox screeching outside. After that, I lay there for a while, thoughts pushing through my mind, processing the past few months. Dad dying days before my thirtieth birthday lunch, the only time he made the effort to see me, had set wheels in motion. The cancer he'd beaten years earlier had returned, spreading to his lymph nodes, and he had only lasted a matter of weeks. When I went to say goodbye to him in hospital, he took my hand and apologised for playing such a small part in my life. Not only did I have to deal with losing him, but I was heartbroken that we'd never got to know each other as a father and daughter should.

In the car after his funeral I asked myself, what was I doing with my life? I was permanently exhausted by my high-powered job and a boyfriend who wouldn't give me answers whenever I brought up our future. It took my father dying for me to pluck up the courage to give him an ultimatum. Miles finally admitted he didn't want to have children with me. His teenage son, conceived on a one-night stand in his twenties, was enough and he wasn't prepared to give up any more of his money, time and affection.

Locking the door, I spotted a bottle of Rioja next to the step and an envelope addressed to me. Opening it, I pulled out a note from Jim.

C with an i,

Here are my keys.

And to make up for barging in, here's a bottle of Rioja, on me – or the ATP, anyway.

You missed a great night (next time).

J

I couldn't help smiling to myself. What a charmer. At least I'd have something decent to drink that evening.

I made my way to the Stables for breakfast. Walking through the rose garden in kitten heels wasn't easy as they kept catching in the gaps between the paving stones, but I was still determined to wear them. After ordering a cappuccino and a croissant, I settled at a table in the corner and lifted *Mrs Field's Diary* from my bag. I'd read a few chapters in bed the night before, realising I knew little about the home front during the Second World War. The diary was written as part of the Mass Observation. Audrey Field was not her real name; no one seemed to know who she really was, according to the introduction. Her words were compelling, and I found myself moved by what she and her friends and neighbours lived through. Being in Surrey, between London and the English Channel, Gatley had experienced some devastation as planes made their way back and forth, and the village had been descended upon by people evacuated from London because of the Blitz. I longed to find a mention of Gatley Hall, but hadn't found the house referred to yet. I had become completely engrossed, and didn't notice Jim pull out the chair opposite until he said, 'Good morning, Claire,' in a chirpy voice as he sat down.

I needed a bit of time and at least one coffee before conversing with anyone in the morning, and he'd caught me before I was ready. Looking up, I saw he was dressed this time, a couple of buttons undone on his navy-blue ATP polo shirt and a matching hat bringing out the colour of his eyes. He removed the hat, which had a brim, and placed it on the table. My insides danced a little and I put it down to eating the croissant too quickly.

'Hello, Jim,' I said.

'What are you reading?' he asked, gently prising *Mrs Field's Diary* from my hands. He glanced at the front cover, then turned the book over and skimmed the blurb on the back. Raising his eyebrows, he handed it back to me.

'Looks interesting, if that's your thing.'

'It is, and you've lost my page now,' I said, in a mock huff, and he grinned as if delighted by my reaction. He reminded me of the boys at school who'd wind me up in the library during sixth-form study periods. 'You work in this place but don't want to know about life here during the war?'

He shrugged. 'Sure, a little. My grandfather fought at Dunkirk and came back in one piece, but I'm more invested in what's happening now in the countryside around us, about protecting the wildlife, and conservation, and how to stop fly-tipping on the South Downs Way.' He took a sip from his ATP reusable cup, navy blue with the logo in hot pink splashed across one side. 'I'm happy to lead a simple life, whereas *you*, having worked at that stuck-up gallery in London, aren't cut out for it.'

He was probably right, but I wasn't going to let him know that.

'Where on earth do you get that idea from?'

'This isn't the place for a fancy suit, Claire. You need to relax a bit, adapt your wardrobe to fit in. I could take you shopping at Country Fit in Guildford with my discount card if you like?' He chuckled to himself as he buttered his toast.

Doing my best to keep a straight face, I said, 'I'm not looking for a personal shopper, Jim. What's wrong with my suit exactly?'

'Haven't you seen what the staff and volunteers are wearing?'

'If I was dressed like you, my brain wouldn't work properly.'

'My brain works perfectly well, thank you. You won't find a fleece warmer than the ATP one, and Gatley Hall has its own microclimate – you'll find it gets pretty cold round here in these winter months. And there's talk of snow before Easter. What you're wearing today isn't going to help much in that situation – it gets inches deep, and the temperature drops to well below zero. Do you even have a winter coat?'

He bit into his toast with a crunch.

'Of course I do. How do you know so much about where I used to work, anyway?'

'I knew about you before you even set foot in this place.'

For some reason, this gave me a warm feeling. But I did my best to hide it, suppressing a smile.

'You did?' I said.

'Rosalind showed me your CV, and I helped compile the shortlist.'

'Why would a ranger be involved with my job application?'

'As head ranger, actually, I'm part of the house management team, so involved with decisions impacting the future of Gatley Hall and its land.'

Great, so he had the power to get me sacked. Perhaps I ought to play the game with him a bit more, although the thought of being obliged to do this grated. At the Frampton Gallery I'd been part of the management team, and fairly senior too, but wasn't I here to get away from that? All the responsibility and worrying about other members of staff as well as myself had been exhausting at times.

'Oh,' I said.

Wiping his mouth with a napkin, he said, 'I read about the work you've done on those exhibitions, and that blog post you wrote about Van Gogh – you had me reading right to the end, and I'm not even into art. You're a good writer.'

His compliment was a boost, and I found myself wanting him to admire my work. Why should his opinion matter so much?

'It was me who said you should be on the shortlist, despite being overqualified and the salary here being nowhere near what you were getting. No wonder you have all those fancy clothes.'

He threw me a look. Not only did he know what my salary was, but also how much I'd been making before. Wasn't he abusing his position a little?

'I assumed you'd be full of yourself, especially as you are the daughter of Deborah and Dickie Bell, but it was about who could do a good job at the end of the day.' He scrunched up his napkin and dropped it onto his plate. 'And you were the best candidate by far. You actually have me to thank as I made the deciding vote to bring you in. Some of the management team said you'd think the job was beneath you.' He lowered his voice. 'So, you could say that you're here because of me.'

I didn't like people knowing who my parents were as they'd often assume I was spoilt and had a lot of money when the reality had been very different. My father had directed a hit film that had been nominated for an Oscar in the seventies – his only real success. Deborah had acted in it, but these days she mostly performed in pantomimes and appeared on C-list celebrity TV shows. Those first few weeks after his death had been particularly hard with Dad being in the public eye. His picture had been on the front of newspapers and his films had been shown on television along with chat show interviews going back to the 1970s. I'd watched it all with a box of tissues by my side. Jim had hit a nerve and I blinked back tears. This wasn't like me, but I was feeling especially vulnerable after recent events.

'My, you have done your homework,' I said, struggling to mask the waver in my voice.

'I am sorry about your dad, by the way,' he said, gently. Clearly he meant it, by the way he scratched his head and pressed his lips together. I did wish he hadn't brought up my recent loss though. It was still far too raw. He looked away. This was the first time I'd seen him appear to be uncomfortable.

Attempting to pull myself together, I inhaled. 'And were you right in your assumption?'

'About what?'

'About me being full of myself.'

He shuffled in his chair. 'You were a bit last night, but you seem to have mellowed this morning. Is it only safe to approach when you're drinking coffee?'

Now he was attempting to recover the situation.

'You barge into my house half-naked and expect me to welcome you with open arms?'

'Good point.' He took a phone out of his pocket and glanced at it. 'You're not going to get me sacked for trespassing, are you?' Laughing, he leant to one side as I pretended to throw my book at him. 'I'd better get going.' Putting on his hat, he stood up, and frowned as he picked up my disposable cardboard cup. Shaking his head before putting it down again, he said, 'You are a bad girl.'

'What have I done now?'

'You need one of these,' he said, holding up his ATP cup as if he was in an advert. 'They're complimentary for staff, I'll pick one up for you later.'

'You've already given me a bottle of Rioja this morning.'

Putting his hands on the back of the chair and leaning towards me, he said, 'Ah yes, but how many presents is too many?'

'I can hardly wait,' I said.

CHAPTER 6

MARGARET

I got up off my suitcase and continued to walk. The rest of the passengers had now disappeared round the corner, and I reached a sunken lane with the roots of the trees visible. Their branches blocked out the light, creating an eerie atmosphere, the gurgle of a nearby stream running over rocks the only sound. When I reached daylight once again, the road curved round to the left and Gatley's church spire came into view. My stomach rumbled, and this spurred me on to quicken my pace, as I longed for a cup of tea and piece of cake or at least a biscuit on my arrival. Reaching the high street, I passed the sweet shop where Uncle Reg used to buy me barley sugar twists as a child. Shops lined either side of the street and I passed a butcher, a baker and a grocer. Opposite were a haberdashery and a milliner amongst others. Church Road was on the right before the church, St Andrew's, a grand old Norman building, and number fifteen was near the end of a row of white terraced cottages. The door was red with a semicircle of stained glass above. We'd visited my aunt and uncle at the rectory – a grand Georgian house with lush gardens bursting with flowers and

trees that produced beautiful colours in autumn and spring –
but this was the first time I'd seen her new home. When I gently
rapped the brass knocker, a girl around my age opened the door,
presumably Aunt Edith's maid. She wore a black dress with
matching white collar and sleeves and had an apron tied round
her waist. My aunt, whose grandfather had made his fortune in
shipbuilding, would never live without help.

'Hello, I'm Margaret and my aunt is expecting me,' I said.

'Do come in,' she said, taking my mackintosh and hanging it
on the coat stand. I put my suitcase on the floor underneath.
'She's just waking up from her afternoon nap and will be down
in due course. Would you like a cup of tea while you wait?'

'Yes, please.'

The maid showed me into a sitting room where a fire roared
in the hearth and a grandfather clock tick-tocked in the corner.
A portrait of Uncle Reg hung on the wall above the mantelpiece, and a black cat was curled up in an armchair. A vase of
white roses decorated the vast sill created by the bay window
with a view of the church opposite.

Aunt Edith entered the room. A few years had passed since
I'd seen her as, after Uncle Reg died and then Father a few
years later, we'd stopped visiting. Approaching seventy, my aunt
wore her grey hair in a neat bun, a handful of grips keeping
everything in place.

'My dear Margaret, how was your journey?' she said, taking
my hands in hers and giving them a squeeze.

Aunt Edith had always been kind to me, although she could
be overbearing. Mother found her a little condescending at
times and they'd never got on particularly well. However,
Mother, being a practical sort, was always prepared to overlook
her opinion of others when it was to our advantage.

'As good as can be expected. I hadn't realised the station
was so far from the village.'

'Oh, that's my fault. I should have arranged for someone to pick you up. Please forgive me, dear.'

She lowered herself into an armchair and gestured for me to take the one opposite. The maid appeared, adjusting the cushions behind her.

'This is Lilian,' Aunt Edith said.

'How do you do,' I said.

Lilian and I exchanged a polite smile.

'Will you bring us some tea and a small bite to eat, my dear?' Edith said.

Lilian nodded and left the room.

'There is no way I could manage without her help, what with the arthritis in my hands, which makes it tricky to do things in the kitchen. And more recently the gout in my knees has become quite unmanageable at times.'

'I'm sorry to hear that,' I said.

Shrugging, she said, 'Such is life. So, Margaret, your beloved shop was bombed and burned to the ground, I hear?'

'Sadly, yes.'

'But you're still in one piece, and that's all that matters. Your mother is relieved you have at last come to your senses.'

'Thank you for allowing me to stay,' I said.

'Well, it won't be for long.' What did she mean? 'You'll have to sleep on an old mattress on the floor in Lilian's room, I'm afraid, as we are short of space and I can't exactly turf her out of her own bed. Billeting officers and evacuees from London have been knocking on the door all week, asking for a bed. It broke my heart to turn them down, but I've done my best to help place some of them by asking acquaintances at the Auxiliary Territorial Service canteen and in the WI.'

Lilian brought in a tray with a teapot and cups and saucers and a plate with two fingers of shortbread. She set it all on the trestle table and poured cups of tea for us both. So hungry by now, I took a finger of shortbread and wolfed it down in a rather unladylike manner. It was melt-in-the-mouth delicious, better than anything consumed in London in weeks. Aunt Edith cast a frown in my direction.

'I see you're enjoying the shortbread. Mrs Saunders from the WI dropped it round this morning.'

'How kind,' I said.

'It's a very close-knit community here in Gatley and we all look after each other rather well.'

After taking a sip of her tea, she placed the cup back into its saucer, and said, 'Now let's get down to the reason you're here. You'll be delighted to know I found a position for you this very morning.'

Unsure whether I was ready to start a new job straight away, what with my nerves being dented by recent events, I said, 'Already?'

'The Dowager Countess of Elmbridge, who happens to be my cousin once removed, is looking for a lady's maid for her daughter-in-law at Gatley Hall. Lady Violet's current lady's maid has gone to work in a munitions factory. Being only nineteen years old gives you an advantage over other candidates as there's the constant fear of one's employees being taken away by the government. I'm confident she'll give you the position as long as you don't make a hash of the interview.'

Lady Violet from the railway station. I could not believe it. She had seemed quite demanding, but now it made sense that the girl I'd seen wasn't dressed as well as a lady's maid should be. Clearly she'd been filling in for someone who had already left. Being a shopgirl at heart, with the dream of having my own establishment one day, working as a lady's maid didn't appeal to me. Mother had worked as a lady's maid in a house in London – that was where she'd met Father, who worked there as a carpenter. Mother had been eager for me to follow in her footsteps, ensuring I remained at school until the age of sixteen. She also arranged elocution lessons to get rid of my South London accent. When I went to work at Taylor and Stone, she was put out at first, but came round to understanding that working in a department store gave me more freedom than servant life.

My old room-mate Betty had told me about her experience working as a scullery maid in a grand house in Mayfair. Servants got no time off compared to shopgirls – one of the reasons why the upper classes were struggling to recruit as they once had. Besides, women were also being encouraged to do their bit. In recent years, it seemed, young people had discovered they didn't have to give up everything for their employers. Many servants, especially in London, now lived out, enabling them to have a life of their own. But I'd be expected to live in at Gatley Hall, and devote every waking moment to Lady Violet, with little time to see friends. And Betty had told me even friendships were monitored. In the big country houses you could only be friends with servants on the same level as you, and relationships with men were downright forbidden. Not that I was looking for any of that.

I didn't seem to have any choice about attending the interview for this position. Although it wouldn't be difficult to make a mess of it, that wouldn't be fair to Aunt Edith.

'That's kind of you to go to so much trouble,' I said.

'Not at all. We shall visit the dowager countess tomorrow, late morning. I hope you have something appropriate to wear, but do bear in mind that, as a prospective lady's maid, you must be prepared to not outshine your mistress. Lady Violet isn't much older than you and she is exceptionally beautiful, but still one must be careful.'

It had been impossible to see Lady Violet's face under the wide brim of her hat, but she had moved with the air of an attractive woman who was born into wealth. The thought of having to dress down grated as I was proud of the wardrobe I'd built up over the past few years, most of the dresses made myself from discounted material purchased at Taylor and Stone.

'I'm sure I can find something suitable,' I said.

CHAPTER 7

CLAIRE

Jim seemed about to say something else when a woman in her fifties with hair greying at the roots came over, an ATP lanyard round her neck. She was carrying a tray with teapot, cup and saucer, and wore jeans and a bobbly red jumper, with the collar of a floral blouse showing. She gave me a warm smile. Her aura was a positive one and instantly, I sensed an ally.

Putting the tray on the table next to me, the woman said, 'Hello, Jim,' in a tone implying she knew what he could be like but tolerated him.

'Helen, this is Claire, the newbie and my next-door neighbour.'

'Pleased to meet you at last, Claire,' she said.

'Hi,' I said.

Looking across the table at me, Jim said, 'Helen's a volunteer and she does a bit of everything, don't you?'

'Yes, I've been at Gatley Hall for over ten years,' Helen said, lifting her lanyard, proudly.

I leant forwards, to see the number ten and a big pink star on it.

'I'm a steward when the house is open from March until Christmas, otherwise I help Wendy with PR. During busy times, I get involved with the gardening too. Last year, I helped set up the staff allotment scheme and planted bulbs in the herbaceous border. Jim's even had me move fallen trees – not single-handedly, I might add – and check on abandoned lambs. Are you going to leave then, Jim, so I can get to know this interesting young woman?'

'All right, I get the hint,' he said.

'Do you mind if I take Jim's seat, Claire?'

'Please do.'

Helen moved her tray to my table, sat down, poured tea into her cup and added milk, giving it a stir with a teaspoon.

'So, how are you settling in?' she said.

'It's going okay, thanks.'

Jim stood there, using his thumbs to tap out something on his phone.

'See you later, Helen. Claire,' he said, throwing me a look. The way he said my name was provocative, and he winked at me over his shoulder while walking away. I couldn't help enjoying our interaction. Miles had no idea how to flirt and didn't know the meaning of the word banter. Without realising, I watched him walk away, studying his firm backside in those khaki chinos. Helen caught my attention by waving from the other side of the table, the corners of her mouth raised in a knowing smile.

'Everyone likes Jim,' she said.

I laughed. 'He can be a bit much sometimes though, can't he?' I said, instantly realising, as Helen raised her eyebrows, that I was talking about a colleague and being hugely unprofessional. The caffeine hadn't kicked in yet, and I ought to be more careful on the first day of my new job.

'Sure, he can,' she said, now grinning. 'So, you've replaced Mike at Rose Cottage. How is it?'

'Mike left it in a bit of a mess and allowed Jim to wander in and use the shower whenever he felt like it,' I said.

'Oh, has he done that with you then?' Helen said, her eyes lighting up.

'He let himself in, dressed only in a towel wrapped round his waist, and I thought he was an intruder.' I told her about almost knocking him over the head with the wine.

Helen laughed. 'Sounds like a meet-cute to me,' she said.

'What?'

'You know, like in romcom films. I'm a romantic novelist so I know all about that kind of thing. Ooh, might have to use that one.' She took out her phone and tapped into it. 'My phone notes are full of random bits of information like this,' she said.

'You're a romantic novelist?'

'I am indeed. Published thirty-five books with Hunt and Mellor.'

'That's impressive,' I said. 'Do they have rude scenes in them?'

She laughed. 'They're a little on the spicy side, one might say. So, is there a man in your life, Claire?'

'I recently split up with my boyfriend.'

'Were you together long?'

'A few years.'

'Oh, well, I'm sorry to hear that. I don't expect it will be long before you meet someone new.'

'I'm not sure I could handle seeing anyone right now.'

'Fair enough. Jim couldn't wait for you to start working here, by the way. He's a bit of a fan of your father's films, I think, especially that one that got nominated for an Oscar.'

'*The Monopoly?*'

'That's it. I am sorry for your loss, by the way.'

'Thank you.' Not wanting to talk about Dad once again, I said, 'I ought to get to the office. It is my first day, after all,' but my attention was drawn to Jim, beyond Helen's left shoulder as he talked to a well-turned-out woman with blond hair knotted in a high ponytail. She was slim and dressed in skinny grey jeans with zips at the ankles and a baby-blue polo-neck, her ATP lanyard resting on perfectly pert boobs. She used her hands to express herself while speaking – her nails were painted a deep-red colour – and she touched his arm every now and again. He clearly enjoyed her attention, his face fixed in a beam.

'Who's that talking to Jim?' I said.

Helen turned round, as indiscreetly as was physically possible, but Jim and the woman were so engrossed in their conversation, it didn't matter.

'That's Samantha,' she said, in a tone of voice that implied she was bad news.

'And what does she do?'

'She's a volunteer. Used to work in PR. The ex-husband was loaded – he invented one of those fancy hand driers they have in public loos. She lives in a mansion with her five kids – the kitchen itself is bigger than my whole house – over in Winsham. At Christmas, she invited staff and volunteers over for drinks. Champagne was free-flowing and there were waiters with canapés. Rumour has it Jim stayed the night and they've been seeing each other ever since.'

While watching them interact, I couldn't help disliking her and knew that was unfair. I was someone who liked to judge people as I found them rather than from what others told me. But she was all over him and he was loving every single second. Jim's radio buzzed and he lifted it from his pocket and spoke into it. He gave Samantha a wave as he left, and she fixed her eyes in our direction. She started to walk towards us.

'Oh wait, she's coming over,' I said.

On reaching our table, she leant forwards and proffered a hand. 'You must be Claire,' she said.

'That's me.' I shook it.

'Samantha,' she said.

Helen glanced over her shoulder. 'Hello, Sam.'

'It's Samantha, actually. You should know that by now, Helen.'

Across the table, Helen smiled to herself.

'So, you're organising the Below Stairs exhibition, I hear,' Samantha said.

'I am,' I said.

'Well, good luck, and let me know if you need any help. It was originally my project, after all.'

'Will do,' I said.

'Jim's got my phone number, if you have any questions. I hear you're neighbours?'

'Yes, we are.'

'How cosy.' Samantha threw me a nod before turning and walking away.

'Why would he get involved with her?' I said. 'From what you've said she probably uses half the energy in her local area, and he's massively into the environment.'

'Sex, what else.' Helen winked, and I sensed she'd be fun to hang out with, despite being closer in age to Deborah than to me.

She sipped her tea. 'Anyway, just a heads-up – she did apply for your job and was extremely miffed when she didn't get it. Almost handed in her notice as a volunteer, but Rosalind persuaded her to stay by giving her a little promotion to make her feel important. Now she helps Wendy with press releases.'

'Ah, I see.'

'Of course, you should get to know her yourself before making up your mind, but being someone who would rather like a person than not, she is rather bad news, I'm afraid. She got Larry sacked as a steward when he left the library unmanned while chatting to Sidney in the saloon. This place was Larry's whole life, the poor man is seventy-eight years old.'

'Oh dear,' I said, standing up and pushing my chair underneath the table. It seemed Samantha was someone to look out for.

'So, are you looking forward to working on the Below Stairs exhibition?' Helen said.

Pressing the lid onto my coffee cup, I said, 'Yes, it's going to be interesting, I'm sure.'

'Nice to meet you, Claire. Let me know if you need anything,' she said.

'Thanks, Helen.'

Reaching up and giving my arm a squeeze, she said, 'Really, I mean that. It doesn't sound like things have been easy for you lately, and if you need someone to talk to, just ask.'

'That's very kind of you.'

Standing up, she said, 'I'd better get going as well.'

Helen dumped her tray on the trolley by the kitchen, and I threw my coffee cup into the general waste bin, feeling a bit guilty after what Jim had said.

'At the moment, I'm in the office above the stables with Wendy and the rest of the PR team. Why don't you come to the Old Fox on Thursday night, and get to know everyone?'

The idea of going out with loads of people I didn't know seemed overwhelming, but I could hardly pretend I was busy.

'Sounds good,' I said.

'I'll see you then?' Helen said. 'Bye, Claire.'

I'd need to get out of those drinks and, running through the usual excuses in my mind, a migraine was likely to be the most realistic option.

CHAPTER 8

MARGARET

Later, once Lilian had prepared the house for blackout, Aunt Edith and I ate at the table in the kitchen. Lilian had cooked our meal of liver with boiled potatoes and green beans. She served us, then said, 'I need to go and get changed now, Mrs Bartlett. See you in the morning.'

'Off to the Old Fox with the Canadian chap, are you, Lilian?'

She blushed, and said, 'Yes, Ted's going to treat me to supper tonight.'

'Lucky you,' Aunt Edith said.

Lilian headed for the stairs. 'Don't forget there are baked apples under the grill.'

Aunt Edith gave her a nod as she closed the kitchen door behind her, then said in a low voice, 'Lilian has been courting a Canadian soldier, stationed nearby at Netley Park. Very handsome apparently, and he provides her with silk stockings and cigarettes.'

'Oh right,' I said.

Aunt Edith lowered her voice. 'She cast the butcher's son, Martin Chester, aside for the Canadian chap, sadly. The poor lad was devastated to discover their romance when he came home unexpectedly on leave. Saw them kissing down at the Old Fox. Martin always thought he and Lilian would get married one day. Childhood sweethearts they were.'

Mother had never approved of the way Aunt Edith liked to spread gossip, and as a result didn't tell her anything that mattered. Often, when we'd visited, Aunt Edith would reveal the deepest secrets of people who considered her to be a friend.

'How unfortunate. These potatoes are very good,' I said, not wanting to get drawn into a discussion of her maid's love life.

'Lilian drops a sprig of mint into the saucepan when boiling them. Makes all the difference. We are fortunate to have a good crop of spuds from the vegetable patch,' Aunt Edith said. 'And those beans were picked this very morning, fresh off their stalks.'

'Mother says it's nice to have more space for planting vegetables now she's in Brighton,' I said.

'Indeed, I couldn't manage without Mr Foster, who used to tend the garden at the rectory. He comes once a week to keep it all going and downright refuses to charge me a penny. Does it for Reg, he says. I tell him to take whatever he wants from my garden, within reason, and his wife is always grateful. She goes to the trouble of writing thank-you notes; not necessary at all, but there you are.'

When we'd finished eating, I cleared the plates and got the apples from under the grill. We ate them with evaporated milk from a tin.

'These apples are from Mrs Patterson next door. We did an exchange, apples for potatoes. She has a tree that produced a big crop earlier in the month. They're all stored beautifully in her shed, and Mr Patterson is making cider with some of them, that's when he isn't doing wonderful work as an air raid warden. Poor man spends half the night walking around spotting fires and arranging for them to be put out. Mrs Patterson does worry about him so, but he insists on doing all he can to help the villagers.'

The apples were delicious, and they dissolved in my mouth, leaving an aftertaste of cinnamon and sugar. After we'd finished eating, I offered to wash up the dishes.

'Thank you, dear. I'll go and listen to the news on the wireless.'

When I'd washed and dried the dishes and put them away, I went into the sitting room and sat opposite Aunt Edith. She was writing, using a fountain pen, on sheets of paper resting on a book in her lap. The news announcer talked about the usual, bombs being dropped all around the country, especially in London and the south-east. Listening in wasn't particularly uplifting, but one felt the need to stay informed.

'Are you writing letters?' I said.

'No, I'm taking part in the Mass Observation, a new endeavour taken up in recent weeks to exercise my writing muscles. Keeps the brain sharp.'

'And what is that then?'

'I write diary entries and send them off by post, and they'll be filed for future reference. If at any stage they're published, my name will be changed unless I give permission for it to be used.'

'That sounds interesting.'

'Writing a diary entry has become part of my daily routine, and it's a way to deal with what we're living through. A moment in history, Margaret. Doing this makes me feel of some use. Today, I'm recording your arrival in Gatley, but don't worry, I've changed your name.'

'Thank you,' I said, unsure whether I wanted to be written about. 'What to?'

'I thought Penelope rather suited you.'

I nodded.

'Don't worry, dear. I'm not writing anything personal. Only

facts. It's all quite bland really. I note what is happening with no room for thoughts or feelings. It's more of a journal than a diary really.'

'That's a relief,' I said.

'Do you keep a diary, Margaret?'

Shaking my head, I said, 'No, I don't.'

'Writing down thoughts and feelings does one the world of good at times like this. I suggest you start one, for the sake of your sanity if nothing else.'

It hadn't occurred to me to write a diary, but I could see the benefits. 'I can imagine it would help,' I said.

Aunt Edith continued to write, and I wasn't sure what to do with myself. My evenings would usually be occupied with sewing projects, but I didn't have one on the go. I could write to Mother, but wanted to wait until after the interview so as to deliver the latest news. The grandfather clock chimed, startling me. There were nine slow dongs and then the church bells opposite started to do the same. They were out of sync with each other, and it was rather nauseating to listen to. And then the sound of planes droned overhead en route to London, ready to cause more destruction. Mother was right; I was best off out of it, but from what Aunt Edith said I wasn't exactly out of the woods in Gatley either. Seeing that the fire had almost gone out, I got up to add another log, using the poker to get it going again.

'Thank you for doing that, Margaret. You must be tired after your journey. Why don't you make us some cocoa, then you can get an early night to be fresh for the interview?'

'All right,' I said, standing up, feeling dismissed. Still, it had been a long day.

'Make mine lukewarm please.'

I went into the kitchen, and it didn't take long to find what was needed. I filled two cups and took Aunt Edith's into the sitting room, placing it onto the trestle table beside her.

'Thank you, my dear. It's nice to have your company. Lilian

goes out most evenings and comes back late. I'll tell her to be careful not to wake you when she comes in.'

'Thank you,' I said.

Aunt Edith lowered her glasses and looked up at me. 'If it's a particularly bad night out there, we'll all end up in the cellar with a bottle of brandy and cotton wool in our ears, of course. Let's hope not. Goodnight, Margaret,' she said.

'Goodnight, Aunt.'

Taking the stairs, I considered how easy it would be to mess up the interview. But with no proper bed for me at Aunt Edith's house, where would I live? All the spare rooms in the area were taken up with evacuees from London. My only choice was to pursue a live-in position and working at Gatley Hall seemed to be the answer.

CHAPTER 9

MARGARET

Aunt Edith and I walked up Church Road, past St Andrew's, then crossed the high street to the other side. We'd spent the previous night in the cellar along with Lilian as planes passed overhead, and we were immensely tired. All of us had tried to sleep on the assortment of cushions Aunt Edith kept down there, but the cotton wool in our ears had done little to drown out the racket. A loud bang had shocked us all – it had sounded close enough to be in the back garden. My nerves were as shattered as they'd ever been. The impact of the blitzkrieg was almost as bad in Gatley as it was in London. When I'd looked out of my bedroom window that morning, there were wisps of smoke coming from a fire in the field beyond St Andrew's. No doubt the Auxiliary Fire Service volunteers had battled throughout the night and were continuing to do their good work.

We passed through a gate to a large white house built in Georgian style with an in and out driveway, its small roundabout filled with lavender bushes. A shiny black Rolls-Royce was parked outside the front door. I'd dithered over what to wear and decided on a knee-length green dress with white collar, tightened at the waist by a narrow belt in a darker shade of green. Hopefully, this was an appropriate choice for the interview.

Overcome by all the grandeur, butterflies engulfed me as we approached the front door, and I said, 'Do you think I'm qualified for this role, Aunt Edith?'

'You worked in ladies' fashion at Taylor and Stone, did you not?'

'Yes.'

'And before you were on the shop floor, you worked as a seamstress?'

'I did.'

'Therefore, not only do you know about fashion, but also you're able to design and make dresses, as well as repair them. Besides, your mother was a fine lady's maid, and so it's in your blood.'

I nodded. I was as qualified for this role as anyone could be without having actually worked as a lady's maid.

'And you remained at school until you were sixteen years old, a sensible decision on your mother's part. You are educated, well spoken, and capable of making polite conversation when required?'

'Yes, I am.'

Aunt Edith rapped the knocker. 'Your mother told me you speak a little French, although your prospective mistress won't be visiting France any time soon. Don't forget to only speak when spoken to, and remember to address the dowager as "your ladyship".'

A butler opened the door and greeted us without smiling. This did little to ease my discomfort about being in such lavish surroundings. He led us to a vast drawing room, where we sat down on armchairs covered in gold velvet. The walls, painted in a deep blue, were crammed with portraits in a variety of sizes. Presumably the young woman with a faint smile on her lips above the fireplace was the dowager herself. Expensive-looking objects were dotted around the room: enormous vases, filled with flowers, white marble busts and glass cases, which no doubt displayed a collection of treasures. I longed to get up and study it all, but such comportment would have been unseemly. Although a fire crackled and popped in the hearth, the tall windows and high ceiling meant it was still rather chilly.

The dowager entered the room, her presence instantly evident, and we stood up to greet her. She was probably a little older than Aunt Edith, and the skirts of her dress, made from grey silk, swished as she moved in our direction.

'Bring me a gin and tonic, Slater, will you, my good man? And whatever my guests here require,' she said to the butler.

He approached us, and Aunt Edith asked for the same for us both. A ruby pendant decorated the dowager's neck, and her immense pile of grey hair was styled into a bun. Her lady's maid had no doubt spent a great deal of time and care dressing her.

Aunt Edith dipped her head slightly, and I followed her lead.

'Good afternoon, dear Edith, and this must be the niece you've told me so much about.'

'Yes, Clarissa. Margaret, this is her ladyship, the Dowager Countess of Elmbridge.'

'How do you do, your ladyship,' I said.

'Delighted to meet you,' she said, casting me a glance as she lowered herself onto the chaise longue opposite us, arranging the skirts of her dress around her. We sat back down. Mr Slater brought in our gin and tonics, and I took mine and sipped it. It was rather strong, especially for late morning, and I placed the glass on a coaster on the trestle table beside me.

'Can you get the fire going, please, Slater?'

'Certainly, milady.' He approached the fireplace and picked up a pair of bellows.

'Do tell me about yourself, Margaret,' the dowager said.

As I repeated what Edith and I had discussed en route, the dowager looked at me blankly as if her mind were elsewhere, then raised a hand to indicate that I should stop talking.

'You speak very well. Have you had elocution lessons?'

'Yes, your ladyship,' I said.

'Very good. You are less plain than one would like when selecting a lady's maid, but the pool is rather limited, currently.'

Surprised that my appearance was being commented upon during what ought to be a discussion of my capabilities, I merely nodded. She drew in her breath. 'Evidently, you know about fashion, but I suggest you wear duller colours to avoid outshining my daughter-in-law. It needs to be blindingly obvious that you are the servant and she is your mistress.'

She took a cigarette out of a silver case and placed it in a holder, and Mr Slater leant forwards to light it with a match. He then went to stand by the door, hands behind his back, face without expression.

'So, what do you think, Clarissa?' Edith said.

'What do I think?' The dowager took a drag of her cigarette and exhaled. 'Margaret is the best we shall find under the circumstances. I did not expect the government to call up our servants and can understand the middle classes are able to do without help, for they are more capable of looking after themselves. We, on the other hand need a number of employees to run our households smoothly. Thank goodness Slater here is too old to go and fight.' She looked at me. 'Although you have no experience, I'm sure Mrs Willis, the housekeeper, will bring you up to speed.'

She turned to Aunt Edith and they made small talk about the weather and the war. The dowager explained that billeting officers knocked on the door every day. She'd taken it upon herself to give up a wing of the house to mothers and their young children from the East End of London.

'How very kind,' Aunt Edith said.

'Their cockney accents are so strong, no one can understand a word they are saying. Thank goodness for our kitchen maid from Whitechapel, who acts as a translator when needed. Lady Violet has been kind enough to take in two mothers and their children, who will reside above the stables at Gatley Hall,' the dowager said.

'Generous indeed,' Aunt Edith said.

'One hopes it won't be too long before she has children of her own,' the dowager said, drawing on her cigarette. It was clear an heir was expected, and soon, and I didn't envy Lady Violet for being put in such a position. 'Her two predecessors have failed in their endeavours, and my son is becoming rather anxious about my nephew superseding him. Well, we all are.' She sighed.

The dowager seemed to be divulging more information than appropriate, especially in my presence, and Aunt Edith nodded.

'And did you hear about the vicar's wife, Mrs Whitby experiencing the misfortune of coming across a German parachutist while walking her dog across a field?' Aunt Edith continued.

'Yes, Slater keeps me informed of all the local news. He gathers up all the gossip in the servants' hall and delivers it directly to me,' the dowager said.

'Poor Mrs Whitby couldn't remember any of the German she'd been taught in order to deal with such a situation. Thankfully he spoke English, his leg was broken and he couldn't get very far without being captured and sent to a prisoner of war camp.'

As they continued with this tittle-tattle, I studied a white marble statue in the corner – it appeared to be a Greek god, no less. No doubt Gatley Hall would be like this house but on a larger scale. The dowager stubbed out her cigarette in an ashtray on the trestle table and put a hand over her mouth as she coughed.

'You must excuse me, dear Edith, for I have been battling

with a cold and am rather fatigued,' she said. Looking directly at me, she said, 'I shall instruct Slater to telephone Mrs Willis and say you'll commence work with immediate effect.'

'Thank you,' I said. Aunt Edith nudged me in the ribs. 'Your ladyship,' I added, wondering why Lady Violet wasn't involved in the recruitment process. Did she even know this interview was taking place? I would have appreciated a little more time to mentally ready myself, but at least there would be a bed for me to sleep in that night – presumably.

'We are most grateful for this opportunity,' Aunt Edith said.

'Slater, will you see my guests out?'

'Certainly, milady,' he said.

The butler led us out of the drawing room and into the hall, opening the front door, without making eye contact or uttering a word. We walked back to Aunt Edith's cottage, the September air lukewarm, and there were people wandering up and down the high street, looking bewildered.

'Poor things, bombed out of their homes, no doubt,' Aunt Edith said, as we passed a man carrying a battered suitcase. 'You must be delighted to find a role so quickly, Margaret?'

'Thank you for arranging the interview,' I said. 'Shouldn't I have met Lady Violet before accepting the offer?'

'I'm sure the two of you will get along just fine,' Aunt Edith said. Taking a key from her coat pocket, she unlocked the front door and, once we were both inside, I went upstairs to pack.

It didn't take long to gather up my belongings and, as I placed a brassiere in the suitcase, I was reminded of the moment I'd bumped into the chauffeur, Tom, at the station. The prospect of him being below stairs at Gatley Hall was reassuring.

When I came downstairs with my suitcase, Aunt Edith was in the sitting room, reading the newspaper.

'I have something for you, Margaret.'

She got up and went over to her desk, retrieved a notebook

from the drawer and handed it to me. It was made from black leather, and probably worth a few bob.

'Promise me you'll start a diary. I guarantee that it will help you on those days when the black dog rears its ugly head.'

'This is very generous of you, Aunt Edith. Thank you.'

'I always keep a few spare. There is nothing worse than being without pen and paper. I would be grateful if you accompanied me to St Andrew's on Sundays, when you are able.'

'Of course, if I can get permission from my new mistress.'

'They can't stop you from going to church, I'm sure,' Aunt Edith said. 'I shall call Mr Foster and ask him to take you to Gatley Hall.'

This new world I was about to enter was sumptuous and impressive to an outsider, but at the same time rather formal and cold. The thought of working as a lady's maid filled me with dread. Adapting to life as a servant with little, if any time off would be a hurdle to overcome, no doubt. All I could wish for was that Lady Violet would treat me with respect and that I'd get along with the other servants. I hoped Tom at least would be kind to me.

CHAPTER 10

MARGARET

Mr Foster took me to Gatley Hall in his horse and trap. We approached the grand eighteenth-century house, built in Palladian style, from a long, twisting drive lined with trees, their leaves a golden colour. On either side of the drive sheep ate grass on the verges and, beyond the hedgerows, fields extended as far as the eye could see. Apart from Buckingham Palace, I had never seen such a grand house before – it was rather intimidating to someone like myself, a young girl from a working-class family. A wave of nausea overwhelmed me. Would I be all right in this place in the middle of the countryside? What if I couldn't remember all the rules, many of them unwritten? One would no doubt be expected to know what was what. Would I get a moment to myself? All I could do was attempt to be grateful to Aunt Edith and to the dowager for giving me this opportunity, as well as Lady Violet, who I doubted had played any part in my appointment. What if she were miffed that I'd been recruited by her mother-in-law? That would not be the best start for me.

Mr Foster dropped me off at the servants' entrance and I thanked him for his kindness. The door was unlocked and I entered the house and followed the passageway to the house-keeper's parlour. When I tapped on the door, no one answered, and so I continued to the servants' hall, where I could hear chattering and laughter. The door was slightly ajar, and I peered through the gap to see a vast room with a long table where servants were seated, eating luncheon. Pushing the door open, I made myself known with a cough, and felt rather silly as many of them stared at me with blank looks on their faces.

'Apologies for interrupting your luncheon,' I said. 'I'm Margaret Bartlett, the new lady's maid.' No one uttered a word. 'Ready to report to Mrs Willis,' I added. Never had I felt so small.

To my relief, I spotted Tom, the chauffeur – how glad I was to see a friendly face! He put down his knife and fork. 'Mrs Willis is indisposed, presently. Mags, isn't it?'

I nodded.

He leant across the table and addressed one of the girls, who wore a black and white maid's uniform. 'Aren't you going to show the young lady to her room, Elsie?'

Elsie turned to look at me over her shoulder, then pushed back her chair, scraping the flagstone floor. She seemed greatly inconvenienced by my arrival, understandably, as I was interrupting her meal.

Getting up, she said, 'You'd better follow me.' I smiled, but Elsie didn't reciprocate. Her face was familiar, and I tried to place her as she led me out of the servants' hall. Then I recalled that she'd been the one filling in and assisting Lady Violet at the station – that was why she hadn't been dressed as a lady's maid usually would be. No doubt she'd be demoted once more now I had arrived and wouldn't be best pleased.

Elsie approached the servants' staircase, not speaking to me at all. We went up a floor and the stairs were very steep. It was rather tiring, especially while carrying my suitcase. Many of the steps were crumbling and desperately in need of repair, so I trod carefully in order not to slip. She pushed open a door and we came out onto a carpeted landing, on our left a grand swirling staircase with portraits decorating walls painted a deep-red colour. I followed her to the end of the corridor, where she took a set of keys from the pocket of her apron and unlocked a door. We entered a bedroom twice the size of the upstairs of the terraced house I'd been raised in. Putting down my suitcase, I studied the room. There was a large fireplace with basket of logs, and three vast windows – two of them faced the lake and the other had a view of a walled garden. Each window had blackout curtains. The bed was large enough for two people. I'd only ever slept in a single bed before. Various pieces of antique furniture were dotted around.

'This room is all mine?' I said.

'Yes,' Elsie said. 'It was mine until this morning.'

'Oh, I'm sorry,' I said. She must have been sleeping there while covering the lady's maid position.

She sighed. 'I'll have to go back to being a lowly housemaid and share a freezing cold room with the kitchen maid, Dot, and she's a snorer. We don't get logs to go with our tiny fireplace. Seems I'm not posh enough to be a lady's maid all of the time, just when milady can't find anyone better. Like yourself,' she said, her voice dripping with bitterness. Although I understood her reasoning, this attitude didn't bode well for me. No doubt she'd do her best to make my life difficult.

Elsie opened a door and gestured for me to follow.

'These are her ladyship's quarters,' she said.

She showed me a bedroom even larger than mine. It had a four-poster bed with gold curtains acting as a centrepiece. A room fit for a princess. More doors led to a private bathroom with a marble suite, and another room with wardrobe, Georgian chest of drawers with animal feet, and a dressing table with looking glass, facing the window.

'This is her ladyship's boudoir,' Elsie said. 'Here you will prepare her clothes for the day and help her get dressed if she needs assistance.' She opened the wardrobe and squatted to lift a piece of red velvet off a box that was fixed inside. 'This is her safe, containing her expensive jewels. It will be your responsibility to look after her jewels when you travel together,' she said.

We went back into my bedroom and, before I could say anything else, Elsie left me alone, closing the door behind her. 'Thank you, Elsie,' I called after her. Although she couldn't be more unfriendly, my only option was to be polite towards her. I couldn't let her childish comportment impact mine. Should I unpack now or later? Was I expected to report to Lady Violet that afternoon, or the following morning? Where was Mrs Willis, who was supposed to tell me what to do?

Overwhelmed by it all, I sat on the edge of the bed to compose myself. This welcome was reminiscent of my first day as an apprentice seamstress at Taylor and Stone. The other women didn't give me the time of day at first, and it had taken weeks to settle in. But before long I'd made friends. Remembering this gave me hope, at least. Despite my luxurious accommodation, working as a servant did seem like a step backwards after what I'd achieved as a shopgirl. But who knew how long the blitzkrieg would go on for? Some of the staff at Taylor and Stone were convinced the Hun would manage to invade, and such an idea didn't bear thinking about.

I opened my suitcase and hung the dresses in the wardrobe. When time allowed, I'd find an iron and press out the creases. While arranging my belongings, I recalled them being scattered across the station platform. Tom had come to my assistance once again during that uncomfortable moment in the servants' hall. We were on a similar level when it came to rank, and the thought of having an ally in this place was reassuring. Deciding to unpack the rest later, I made my way back to the servants' hall, hoping Mrs Willis might now be in a position to explain my duties to me.

CHAPTER 11

MARGARET

When I reached the servants' hall, everyone had left apart from a young lad. He had a full plate of food in front of him, and I guessed he'd been running an errand while everyone else was eating.

'Hello, I'm Mags,' I said.

'Sam,' he said, pushing a fork into his stew.

'Do you know when Mrs Willis will be back?'

He said with a mouthful of food, 'She went to visit Mrs Marshall on the farm.'

'Oh,' I said. He didn't intimidate me, being younger and with an earnest manner. I pulled up a chair opposite him and smiled.

'She'll be back shortly, I'm sure,' he said.

'Who should I report to then?'

He pulled a face. 'Elsie, I suppose.'

'She didn't do much to help me, I'm afraid,' I said, but regretted the words as soon as they came out of my mouth. The past few days had been exhausting both physically and mentally, but I should know better than to talk about one employee in front of another, especially on my first day. They could be firm friends for all I knew.

'That's because she was after your job, and got turned down, didn't she? It's understandable really.'

'Yes, it was rather awkward.'

He shovelled the stew into his mouth as if it were his last meal. Nobody seemed to have taught him table manners and he was bound to end up with indigestion.

'What do you do?' I said.

'I'm a hallboy. I run errands, pick up after everyone else. You know how it is.'

'Yes. My father was a hallboy once, before he became a carpenter. How old are you?'

'Fifteen.'

'Do you like working here?'

'My parents are poor and what with rationing and Dad's health problems leaving him unable to work, it helps if I live here and get proper meals.'

'I expect they miss you though?'

He nodded, wiping gravy from around his mouth with a handkerchief. 'And my brother has gone to fight in the war, so my mam has been feeling sad without her boys.'

'I'm sorry to hear that, Sam.'

'I cycle into the village to see them on days off.'

'Do hallboys really sleep on a mattress in the hall?' I recalled my father telling me about this and how cold he'd been at night.

'I was doing that but, when Mr and Mrs Willis got married last year and moved into Rose Cottage, I got the butler's pantry at night because Mr Willis wanted me to guard the silver. It's nice and warm in there what with plenty of logs for the fire. Mr Willis has been good to me.'

I had my own luxurious room and my tasks were bound to be

less physically demanding than Sam's. Sometimes hearing about another person's life made one grateful for their situation. Especially when that person seemed so happy with their lot, as Sam did.

'Mr Willis sounds like a kind man. Why is everyone so unfriendly towards me, Sam?'

'We don't usually mix with the likes of you, miss,' he said.

Despite having been warned about servant hierarchy by Betty, I hadn't expected it to be entirely true.

'Oh?'

'Her ladyship's old lady's maid only spoke to the senior servants and looked down on the likes of us.'

'I won't be like that,' I said.

He lifted his eyebrows. 'You're up there, and we're down here, and that's that,' he said, using a hand to make his point.

Pouring myself a glass of water from the jug on the table, I said, 'I used to be a shopgirl, and am not used to such nonsense.'

'My cousin says shopgirls think they're better than us servants.'

There was no winning this game. We sat there in silence until Sam finished eating and then he got up and put his plate on the side.

'Time to report for duty,' he said, heading for the door. 'I'll see you later, miss. Oh, look, Mrs Willis is back. I'll tell her you're here.'

Mrs Willis came into the servants' hall, and I stood up.

'You must be Margaret,' she said.

'Yes, ma'am.'

'Why don't you come with me.'

I followed her into the housekeeper's parlour. It was a cosy room with a round table and a window looking onto the gardens behind the house. A fire roared in the hearth. I could only aspire to having a room of my own like this one day, although my ambition was not to be a housekeeper. I didn't want to work in service for any longer than I had to, especially as most female servants ended up as spinsters. Although Sam had said Mrs Willis was married to the butler, which sometimes happened. She gestured for me to sit by the fire, taking the chair opposite.

'So, Margaret, you're Lady Violet's new lady's maid. You'll report to me, and the usual standards of behaviour are expected here at Gatley Hall.'

'I understand.'

'That means no friendships with lower servants, no relations with male servants, including those who are visiting with their masters. You know the drill,' Mrs Willis said.

I nodded.

'I understand Elsie has shown you to your room?'

'Yes. It was rather awkward,' I said.

Mrs Willis sighed. 'Such is life. Unfortunately for Elsie, you are more qualified for the role. Let's go and meet her ladyship, shall we, Margaret?'

Mrs Willis led me along the passageway and through a door into the main house. We came out in a cloakroom, off a grand hall, and the marble flooring was most impressive, with black and white tiles. The fireplace was imposing, with a mantelpiece decorated with a pair of blue and white vases and candles, a portrait of a man whom I presumed to be Lady Violet's husband, Charles Wentworth, the Earl of Elmbridge hanging above. We passed the sweeping staircase and Mrs Willis led me along a corridor to a library with walls crammed with books, and tables dotted around, covered in framed photographs. Lady Violet sat by the fire, protected by a screen, reading a book with a glass made from crystal in her hand.

'Miss Bartlett is here, your ladyship.'

'Do come in and sit down,' she said, gesturing for me to sit opposite her. Mrs Willis left the room, and we were alone.

'Thank you, your ladyship,' I said, attempting a curtsey as I wasn't quite sure what was expected from me.

'You will address me as milady, and I shall call you Maggie.'

I preferred Mags or at least Margaret, but wasn't in a position to argue.

'My mother-in-law seems to have appointed you without consulting me, but, seeing as we are working with a limited pool currently, I shall not make a fuss about it. From what I've heard regarding your experience at Taylor and Stone, and judging by your well-turned-out appearance, I shall hope for the best.'

'Thank you, milady,' I said.

'This afternoon I'm hosting drinks for people in the local community, and you'll need to select suitable attire for me to wear; elegant and smart but, at the same time, understated. You can start preparing while I finish reading this chapter. Mrs Willis will assist.'

'Yes, milady.'

I went to find Mrs Willis, who led me up the main staircase, a privilege indeed, and along a corridor to Lady Violet's bedroom. From there we entered her boudoir. She helped me select a cream silk blouse and navy-blue pencil skirt with black shoes.

'Milady will give you a key to the safe and ask you to select any jewellery required.'

Mrs Willis left me alone and, before long, Lady Violet came into the boudoir. I laid out her clothes on a chair and she dressed. She was a beautiful young woman with blond hair and a slender yet curvaceous figure; what one would call an English rose. It was evident that she was well aware of this as she admired her appearance in the full-length looking glass on the wall, turning to study her reflection from different angles, pressing her lips together.

'This outfit needs something else. Be a dear and get my emerald brooch from the safe, will you, Maggie?' she said. 'It's in a red box from Ellis and Son.' She opened a drawer in her writing table and reached inside for a few moments before taking out a key. Pressing it into the palm of my hand, she said,

'There's a false bottom in that drawer and if you ever need the key in my absence, just press the button at the back.'

I went to the wardrobe and located the safe under the piece of red velvet shown to me by Elsie earlier, and found the red box from Ellis and Son, the writing in gold letters, amongst a heap of other jewellery boxes. Lady Violet had plenty to choose from, as was to be expected for a woman of her rank. Lifting the lid, I gasped on seeing the most beautiful oval-shaped brooch with an emerald in the centre, encircled with tiny diamonds. It must have been worth a small fortune. I passed her the brooch, and she pinned it to her blouse.

'This is my favourite piece, and I have jewels worth far more. It was a gift from my mother on my wedding day and so it has sentimental value. My grandmother wore it when she met Queen Victoria. My grandfather owned a railway company and his friend, Prince Albert, would visit with the queen on occasion.'

It was a beautiful brooch and with a lovely story to go with it. I doubted I would ever own anything so exquisite. Girls like me simply didn't acquire such items.

'It is very beautiful, milady,' I said.

'Maybe one day I might let you borrow it for a special occasion, as I did for my former lady's maid at a servants' ball. I shall miss dear Sophie, poor thing having to go and work in a factory. This war is obliging us all to do things out of the ordinary.'

Lady Violet's daily life didn't seem to be impacted by the war and I doubted she was suffering much. I couldn't imagine her lending me any of her jewellery to wear.

'Indeed.' I gave her back the key to the safe and put away the clothes she'd been wearing before getting changed.

When I'd finished, she said, 'That will be all for now, Maggie.'

'Very well, milady,' I said.

Dismissed, I left her boudoir and took the servants' staircase back to the below-stairs quarters. Mrs Willis brought me some mending to work on in the laundry room; a combination of items with a button to be sewn on a footman's uniform, and a rip in one of her aprons to be repaired. This was to keep me occupied until her ladyship provided me with things to do.

Later on, Mrs Willis invited me into her parlour to eat supper with her, Mr Willis and the cook, Mrs Downside. Nobody spoke while we spooned vegetable broth into our mouths, and the thought of spending every mealtime with these people, who were perfectly pleasant but the same age as my mother, was a daunting prospect. Would I get to spend time with any of the younger servants? After supper, I carried on with the mending until Lady Violet dismissed her guests at midnight. Then I was summoned to put her clothes and jewels away, and brush her hair before styling it into a plait. I selected a silk nightgown, as directed, and passed it to her. A white blouse needed pressing as she would be taking tea with the dowager the following morning. I took the blouse down to the laundry room and used the iron before carrying it back upstairs to keep in my wardrobe until the morning.

It had been an exhausting day, adapting to my new surroundings, and I was still coming to terms with Elsie's attitude towards me. If she had any influence on the opinions of the other servants, then life could be difficult for me at Gatley Hall.

CHAPTER 12

CLAIRE

After leaving the Stables, I took the tree-lined path towards my office. The air was cool and fresh, the breeze brushing my face, and the only sound was birdsong. It was one of those crisp January blue-sky days. Back in London, my commute had been very different, involving rushing to the station by seven thirty in the morning. Usually there would be scrunched-up beer cans and cigarette butts on the pavement, and a queue of cars, buses and taxis stuck in traffic. The exhaust fumes would get in my throat, and I'd hold my breath while waiting to cross the road. I'd worn earbuds for most of my journey, shutting out the world around me. Although there would always be a book in my handbag, I'd usually end up skimming the news and scrolling social media on my phone instead.

Now, it struck me that this hadn't been the healthiest way to live, neither physically nor mentally. I'd thought that I thrived in that fast-paced, noisy environment where everyone did their best to avoid each other's gazes on the commute. I'd be lucky to get a seat on the train, then the tube was always jam-packed, and I'd go up the steps at Piccadilly Circus in denial of the knot in my chest. Working in a capital city was exciting, but I'd rarely taken a moment to breathe properly. Was this a better way to live, and should I be taking more time to appreciate nature and the simple things in life?

My office was in the old servants' quarters on the ground floor of Gatley Hall. Rosalind had shown it to me after the interview. I'd be sharing with her, but she apparently spent a lot of time in meetings. The sound of banging and drilling came from the rooms towards the end of the corridor, and I recalled Rosalind saying that the ground floor was being renovated in preparation for my Below Stairs exhibition. A sign on the door said HOUSEKEEPER'S PARLOUR.

'Morning,' I said to Rosalind, putting my bag on the floor next to my new desk. The computer monitor looked ancient.

'Hello, Claire.' Rosalind swivelled round on her chair to face me. 'You're looking very smart. You know you can wear jeans and, well, whatever you like really?'

'You're not the first person to tell me that,' I said, smiling.

'And a hot tip – coming from a woman who likes her designer shoes, I wouldn't bother with heels round here. You never know when you might need to walk to the other side of the property. I damaged a rather fine pair of Jimmy Choos getting the heel caught in a paving stone last summer. Never again,' she said, shaking her head.

Understanding her pain, I pulled a face. Perhaps I'd have to reconsider my wardrobe after all.

'Have you settled in at Rose Cottage?' Rosalind said.

'Yes, thanks.'

'And you've met Jim?'

'I have indeed.'

'Right, I have a few meetings this morning, so you see the bottom drawer in your desk?'

'Yes.'

'In there, you'll find correspondence from people connected with the house over the years.'

'Oh?'

I slid the drawer open. It was filled to the top with envelopes and pieces of paper. What a sight. I closed it again swiftly.

'Where did all this come from?'

'We've found that when servants or descendants of servants, villagers, labourers who worked on the farm, even a land girl, thought they were about to die, they'd get in touch and tell us stories linked to the house as they didn't want the information to be forgotten.'

'How interesting,' I said, and it was, although the prospect of going through that drawer was quite overwhelming.

'Some of it goes back to the late nineties, but we've had more correspondence since we were on that TV show, *Objects from the Past*.'

'What do you want me to do with all this?'

Rosalind shrugged. 'I'm hoping you might find some gems to use in the Below Stairs exhibition. The board is very interested in this project and wants Wendy in PR to try and get some articles in the mainstream press if she can, to encourage ATP membership, which has been flagging in recent years. Feel free to ask one of the volunteers if they're able to help you, once you get to know everyone.'

'Sounds good.'

'Right, I have to go, so will catch you later,' Rosalind said, getting up and closing the door behind her.

'Bye,' I said.

Had I got ahead of myself, thinking life here would be better? I could still be working for one of the most prestigious art galleries in the world and my assistant would be doing the admin. But after Dad died, hadn't I wanted an easier life in order to process the grief? Would I have taken the job if Rosalind had shown me this drawer during the interview? How

would I get to know the volunteers? So far, I'd only met Helen.
Maybe she'd be able to help me.

All I could do was give this place a chance. Besides, Rose
Cottage was tying me to Gatley Hall, and, if I decided to leave,
where would I live?

Sliding open the drawer once again, I saw envelopes
addressed to Gatley Hall in the cursive handwriting of a lost era
and scraps of paper in various shapes and sizes with notes
written on them. The letters had already been opened and I
placed them into a pile. Many were illegible, and the ink had
faded in some of them. One was dated 1998. Sifting through
them, I couldn't find much of any interest, although I could
probably use the information in a display to give an overview of
Gatley Hall during the war. Stories from the 1940s about holes
in boots and not being able to find batteries for torches. A
liaison between a housemaid and a Canadian soldier training at
Netley Park, nearby.

One letter caught my eye. It was written in fountain pen,
the ink a rich royal-blue colour. The paper was thick, of good
quality and cream and it was the beautiful, cursive handwriting
that drew me to this letter, in particular.

> 15, Church Road
> Gatley
> 1 March 2013

Dear Sir/Madam,

*I am writing to ask if you might assist with a query. I'm
looking for a person associated with Gatley Hall during the
Second World War. Her name is Tabitha and she lived at Rose
Cottage. Her maiden name was Willis, if that helps, and after
she got divorced (her married name was Dobson) she probably
changed it back to that. Although I can't be certain of whether*

*she married again. I was employed as a lady's maid for Lady
Violet during the Second World War and would be grateful if
you were able to tell me where Tabitha is now. It is most
important that I find her as I'm not getting any younger, and
you are my last hope.*

Yours sincerely,

Margaret Anderson

So, Tabitha had lived in my cottage. But who was she and
what was her connection to Margaret? Why did Margaret want
to find her now? I remembered seeing a photo of the servants in
the Gatley Hall guidebook when preparing for the interview. I
took a copy from the shelf above me. Flicking through the pages,
I found the black-and-white photograph, taken in 1941 in front
of a Christmas tree in the grand hall. I scanned the servants
from left to right, back to front. A butler, footmen, hallboy,
chauffeur, housekeeper, cook, lady's maid – could she be
Margaret? – and a few housemaids in black dresses, white
aprons and white caps. Names and roles were typed on a
double-page spread, along with snippets of information about
some of them.

The lady's maid was called Margaret Bartlett, and she was a
slim and pretty young woman. Surely this had to be her, and
Bartlett was her maiden name? She stood next to the cook, a
Mrs Downside – a buxom, stern-looking middle-aged woman.
Margaret wore a dark-coloured dress with a collar and long
sleeves. The expression on her face was serious. None of the
servants were smiling, and I guessed it wasn't what people did
then when posing. Besides, they were probably standing there
for a while so it would be difficult to maintain a smile, even if
they wanted to. The butler, a tall, broad man wearing a morning
coat, was called Mr Willis, and the housekeeper, who stood on

the other side of the cook, was Mrs Willis. The butler and housekeeper must have been married, as sometimes happened, like Mr Carson and Mrs Hughes in *Downton Abbey*. Margaret was looking for Tabitha Willis – she had to be their daughter. Why did she so desperately need to find Tabitha?

My curiosity was piqued and perhaps this letter would give me something to get my teeth into as it would be good to keep my mind busy. My eyes filled with tears as I thought about how losing Dad had heightened my awareness of mortality. I wanted to help Margaret fulfil her quest before it was too late. In turn, selfishly, I hoped doing this might ease my grief. I put the other letters back in the drawer. This was the one that would get Wendy in PR her story, my gut told me so, and I felt that helping Margaret would be a good use of my time.

I photographed the letter with my phone before sliding it back into its matching envelope and placing inside my work diary. Why had Margaret waited so long to look for Tabitha? The first of March 2013 was almost two years ago. Would Margaret still live at the same address, or might she be in a care home? Would she even be alive? She looked around twenty in the photograph of the servants, so now she would probably be in her nineties.

All I could do was hope Margaret was alive and of sound mind.

CHAPTER 13

MARGARET

The next morning, Elsie woke me up at half past six.

'Mrs Willis sent me to get you up, Margaret,' she said.

When I opened my eyes, she was standing over me.

'You can call me Mags,' I said.

'Margaret will do.'

Using my full name seemed rather formal from a colleague. Did anyone want to respect my wishes regarding my name in this house?

She left the room, and I put on a grey dress and went down to the servants' quarters. Being so tired the night before, I'd slept rather well despite the cold – the fire doing little to heat the vast room – and the bed was comfortable with a firm mattress. And, for the first time in a while, I had not been woken up by planes. Mrs Willis was in the housekeeper's parlour. I joined her and poured myself a cup of tea. Dorothy, the kitchen maid, came in with a plate of bread and butter, and I helped myself.

'You'd better go up and see her ladyship when you've finished eating, Margaret, no later than seven thirty. Dorothy will give you her breakfast to take up on a tray.'

'All right, thank you, Mrs Willis,' I said.

As instructed, I took the tray upstairs and knocked on Lady Violet's bedroom door.

'Come in,' she said.

On entering the room I said, 'Good morning, milady,' and put the tray on her lap. She was sitting in bed, propped up by pillows, still in her silk nightgown.

'Thank you, Maggie,' she said. 'A boiled egg. Cook has excelled herself. Now, I did ask you to select a blouse and skirt for today but, seeing as there is not a cloud to be seen in that beautiful blue sky, I've changed my mind about this morning's activities. Rather than have tea with the dowager, I shall take Jack out.' She took a sip of her tea.

As she didn't have children, I had no idea who Jack was. A dog perhaps?

'Who might I ask is Jack, milady?' I said.

She laughed. 'Jack is my favourite horse. You'll need to select my jodhpurs and white shirt, with my tweed jacket. Ask the groom to get Jack ready and one of the servants will find my riding boots.'

'What time shall I tell the groom, milady?'

She glanced at her clock on the nightstand.

'Nine o'clock. And please ensure a message is despatched to the dowager. I'm sure she'll understand.'

Having met the dowager, I wasn't sure she would. It was more than likely that Lady Violet was avoiding her mother-in-law.

'Certainly, milady.' Without thinking, I added, 'And how should I occupy myself while you are out riding?'

'Do whatever you like, Maggie. In my absence, I do not care what you do as long as you complete your tasks. Make do and mend, or whatever it is lady's maids do with their time. Tell Mrs Willis I'll expect luncheon to be ready in the library at one o'clock.'

'Very well,' I said, thinking that I might explore the grounds.
'You are dismissed,' she said.

I went downstairs and passed on the information to Mrs
Willis about sending a message to the dowager. After Sam had
found Lady Violet's riding boots, I took them upstairs, before
going outside to the stable yard. Searching the stables, I couldn't
see a groom, but noticed Tom was polishing the Rolls-Royce
outside the garage opposite. Seeing his friendly face lifted my
mood.

'She's a beauty, isn't she?' he said.

'Yes, she is,' I said.

'So, you might be staying in Gatley for a while after all,
then?' he said with a smile.

Shrugging, I didn't want to divulge that my aim was to get
out of this place as soon as was feasible.

'Were you looking for a groom?' he said.

'Yes, her ladyship wishes to take Jack out.'

'Stuart was called up yesterday, so now being a groom is one
of my jobs.'

'A chauffeur and a groom. Thank you, Tom. She would like
Jack to be ready at nine o'clock.'

'I also help out old Mr Carter with the gardening and work
as a footman when there are visitors.'

'A jack of all trades,' I said.

'Some might say a master of none,' he said with a wink, and
I hoped he hadn't taken offence. 'And how are you finding it
here at Gatley Hall?' he added.

'As good as can be expected,' I said.

Two young boys, both around ten years old, came out of a
door next to the stables.

'Are they the evacuees?' I said.

'Yes, they're staying in the apartments above the stables
with their mothers.'

I recalled the dowager telling Aunt Edith this during my

interview. They started to kick a ball around the stable yard. It couldn't have been easy for them having to uproot their whole lives, but at least they were accompanied by their mothers, I supposed.

'And where, might I ask did you work before?' Tom said.

'I was a shopgirl in London.'

'Oh?' he said, raising his eyebrows as if he were impressed. 'And you left because of the air raids?'

'My department store, Taylor and Stone, was bombed by the Hun the other night.'

'I'm sorry to hear that. Well, I'd better get Jack ready. See you in a jiffy, Mags.'

'Bye, Tom.'

I found Lady Violet in the boudoir, sitting at her dressing table.

'Is everything organised, Maggie?'

'Yes, milady.'

'Jolly good. Let me talk you through your morning routine. First, you will need to brush my hair for exactly half an hour. I have my clock here to measure the time. And then I'd like you to fashion my hair into a low bun for riding.'

She handed me the brush and, after taking out the plait I'd done the night before, I brushed her hair. It was terribly long, running to the base of her spine. Standing behind her, I could see her face in the looking glass as she sat at the dressing table. She was looking out onto the gardens, the lake and surrounding hills. It was a stupendous view indeed, but, looking up into the sky, I could see the now familiar black dots in a formation – the Hun passing over us as they once again did their best to destroy London. The sight of them triggered the now familiar nerves that plagued me every time I was reminded of what we were living through. The sound was so loud as they passed and usually I'd put a hand over my ears, but couldn't stop brushing Lady Violet's hair. Neither of us acknowledged these planes – it was as if they weren't there at all. And after they'd gone, I shut them out of my mind, pretending the war wasn't happening, that we were living in a normal world after all. My arm ached as I continued to brush, but one could be doing far worse things for a living. And one could be about to be killed by a bomb dropping from one of those planes. I was grateful to Aunt Edith for saving me from that fate and counted my blessings. After half an hour had passed, Lady Violet said, 'It is time to style my hair now.'

Me and my sisters had spent much of our childhood practising different styles on each other's hair, and so I performed this task with confidence. Lady Violet directed me to select her riding attire from a drawer and the tweed jacket from the wardrobe. She changed into her undergarments behind a screen and then put on her jodhpurs and shirt. I assisted with the jacket, holding it as she pushed each arm through a sleeve. She sat on the edge of the bed while I rolled on her knee-high socks and pushed on her riding boots.

'Very good,' she said, standing up and checking herself in the mirror. 'Let's go downstairs, Maggie.'

We took the main stairs and, on reaching the grand hall, Mr Willis greeted Lady Violet with, 'Good morning, milady,' before opening the front door. Lady Violet went down the steps and, as I followed, Mr Willis called after me.

'Margaret?'

'Yes?'

Lady Violet started to walk down the path leading to the stable yard.

'Mrs Willis asked me to pass on a message. Samuel's brother is home on leave and so he has asked for a few hours off. Therefore, would you be so kind as to go and collect supplies from Home Farm this morning?'

'Certainly,' I said. The thought of negotiating unknown fields with enemy planes flying overhead didn't appeal very much, but what else could I say? 'How will I find it?' I said, hoping for a way out. Couldn't Mrs Willis send Elsie?

Mr Willis said, 'Thomas will point you in the right direction. Mrs Willis could send one of the maids but, seeing as her ladyship will be out riding, it would be an opportunity to introduce yourself to Mr and Mrs Marshall, and to meet the land girl who lives there – she's around your age and Mrs Willis thought you might enjoy each other's company.'

'How very kind,' I said. 'Thank you, Mr Willis.'

He nodded and closed the door behind me as I went down the steps and caught up with Lady Violet.

In the stable yard, Tom stood holding reins attached to a horse, presumably Jack, complete with brown leather saddle and bridle.

'Good morning, milady,' he said in a cheery voice.

'Morning, Thomas,' she said.

He gave her a leg-up and she settled into the saddle and stroked Jack's neck.

'I'll meet you in my room before luncheon, Maggie,' she said, squeezing Jack with her calves before trotting out of the stable yard. More planes passed overhead and, looking up, I could see the swastika on their undersides. I shuddered at the thought of what Londoners had coming, and during the daylight as well.

Tom threw me a look. 'Not the best sight,' he said.

'I can't help thinking of the people who are about to lose their lives.'

He nodded. 'What will you do now?'

'Mrs Willis asked me to go and get the supplies from Home Farm, seeing as Sam isn't around this morning.'

'Will you be all right?'

'What do you mean?' I said, not needing to be reminded of how anxious I was.

'It can be dangerous.'

'I couldn't very well say no, could I? I'll be fine,' I said. 'Can you point me in the right direction?'

'Go down to the lake, take a right and go over the stile into Long Meadow. Keep walking straight ahead over the hill and you'll see the farmhouse in the distance.'

'Thank you, Tom.'

'Shall I go on your behalf?' he said.

He was certainly a gentleman.

'That's a generous offer, Tom, but Mrs Willis wanted me to introduce myself to Mr and Mrs Marshall, and to meet the land girl who lives there.'

'All right, well do be careful,' he said.

'I'm more than capable of taking care of myself, but thank you for your concern,' I said.

Tom had only been trying to help and walking away, I regretted using that tone of voice with him. The prospect of going to Home Farm alone was rather daunting but I hadn't wanted him to think that I was a coward.

CHAPTER 14

MARGARET

Tom did seem like a nice fellow, and it warmed my heart that he cared about my welfare. His words had heightened my fears about being out alone in the countryside, but I was obliged to fulfil Mrs Willis's request. I made my way along the path to the lake and approached the stile. I gathered the skirt of my dress using one hand and held on to the fencepost with the other to steady myself. Planes continued to drone above and, shuddering, I told myself that they were merely passing through en route to London and didn't intend to harm me. As a distraction, I attempted to appreciate the beautiful scene, a patchwork of fields, and I inhaled the clean air, free of the smoke fumes that engulfed London. A train clattered on tracks somewhere nearby. The golden leaves on trees edging the field shone as the bright sun captured them. Piles of leaves lay on the ground underneath the trees and I went over to kick them with my boots. A huddle of Jersey cows, their coats a light-brown colour, gathered under a big old oak tree in the centre of the field, tails thumping from side to side.

Nearing the top of the hill, I made out the farmhouse, smoke wisping from its chimney. A tractor engine chugged nearby, and I climbed over a stile into the next field. Here, sheep chewed the grass. This field was rather steep and, as I climbed the hill, my legs aching and my breath shortening, a white shape near the brow caught my eye. What on earth could it be? As I got closer, my heart raced as I registered what it was – a parachute. Did it belong to a German spy – and, if it did, where was he now? The Walls Have Ears posters came to mind. Perhaps he'd already made his way into the village. Who should I inform about this? Tom would no doubt know what to do. A sudden urge to reach a place of safety consumed me. Gatley Hall was my only option. I must get back in case the German parachutist was close by.

A shout came from behind me, and I turned round to see three men only a few feet away. One of them was Tom. Another had dark hair and wore farming clothes, shirtsleeves rolled up his forearms. He and Tom were fighting a blond man, presumably the German parachutist, who brandished a knife that shone in the sunlight. Had it been meant for me? My chest tightened as they continued to battle with the man, who was giving as good as he got. The German attempted to stab Tom, but the farm labourer punched the attacker in the face. The knife flew towards me and I ducked, falling to the ground, as it went past me and dropped onto the grass, where it lay, gleaming in the sunlight. Tom went to pick it up. The German man lay on the ground, blood on his left cheek, his eyes closed. Tom crouched beside him and felt his pulse. The man wasn't dead, I hoped, even though he'd been planning to kill me only moments before.

'He's unconscious, but I don't know how long for,' Tom said.

'Are you all right?' the dark-haired man said to me in a foreign accent that was difficult to place. Surely he was an ally as he'd just saved my life as well as Tom's? Looking up, I noted he was incredibly handsome, with a chiselled jaw; an even better version of Jimmy Stewart with his thick dark hair, big brown eyes and eyelashes to die for. His shirt was undone a few buttons, displaying thick dark hair on his chest. He took my hand in his, squatting down to my level, for I was lying on my back. His touch sent a thrill right through me.

'What is your name?' he said, his eyes locking with mine.

'Margaret, I mean Mags,' I said, getting lost in those eyes as he studied me. I wondered what he saw. Did he find me beautiful?

He let go of my hand and stood back up.

'I am Luca.'

Before I could answer, Tom approached, sliding the knife into the inside pocket of his jacket.

'That was a close call. Thank you, Luca.' Tom patted his shoulder, and they shook hands.

'Are you all right, Mags?' Tom said.

I stood up and used a hand to brush the grass off my dress. 'Yes, thank you.'

'You know each other?' Luca said.

'Mags here just started working at the house,' Tom said. 'When she said she was going for a walk, I had an inkling something wasn't right, you know, and felt the need to check up on her.' He turned to me. 'Luca is an Italian prisoner of war on Home Farm, Mags.'

'Oh, I see.' He was Italian. That explained his dark hair and eyes.

'Yes, I am lucky to work for the Marshalls, who are good to me. We must go before the German wakes. Help me carry him, Tom.'

'All right. You look rather pale, Mags. Why don't you come with us and Mrs Marshall will give you a cup of tea with some sugar for the shock. Maybe she'll have a cake or something too. Besides you need to pick up the supplies.'

'Would she mind if I have a sit down for a bit? I don't feel ready to walk back to the house yet.'

'She is nice lady,' Luca said. 'Come on, let's go.'

Luca and Tom picked up the man between them, and I followed as we crossed the field to the other side. When I opened the gate to the farmyard, I noticed my hand was shaking. Geese honked in the yard and a sheepdog approached, barking at us. The front door was wide open, and a man came out.

'Mr Marshall,' Luca said.

'What have we here, lads?' he said.

They laid the man on the ground. 'This German parachutist just tried to stab Mags here in the Dairy Field. Almost killed me too.' Tom removed the knife from the pocket of his jacket.

'My goodness! Are you all right, dear?'

I nodded, unable to speak for I was rather tongue-tied.

'She's a bit shaken, and I was hoping Mrs Marshall could make her a cuppa,' Tom said, and I was grateful to him for communicating on my behalf.

'Of course she can. Tom, you take Mags inside while me and Luca sort out this chap. Help me put him in the back of the truck, will you, Luca, and we'll take him down to the Home Guard.'

Tom took me into the house, through a porch filled with muddy boots and shoes, and we went into a kitchen, where a woman stood at the stove, an apron tied round her waist.

'Tom, how nice to see you. And who is this young lady?'

'This is Mags, the new lady's maid at the house.' He explained what had happened.

'You must have had a terrible fright. Do sit down, Mags, and I'll make a fresh pot of tea.'

She filled the kettle and put it on the stove. Tom and I pulled up chairs at the table and, before long, the kettle whistled and Mrs Marshall placed a teapot on a mat and gave us cups and saucers and slices of fruit cake. She joined us and filled our cups.

'Make sure you have plenty of sugar in that tea, Mags. It's good for shock.'

'Thank you,' I said, quietly.

'How are you finding it up at the house?'

Not wanting to say the wrong thing, I said, 'I'm settling in.'

'She only started yesterday, didn't you, Mags?' Tom said. He seemed to be taking responsibility for me, and I was thankful.

'I'm sure you'll feel at home before long,' Mrs Marshall said. 'Where are you from?'

I explained about what happened in London and my reason for leaving.

'You have been through the mill, haven't you, dear?' She finished her tea and stood up. 'I have to pop into the village now and post some letters, but it's lovely to meet you, Mags. Do drop in for a cup of tea whenever you like. I'm always grateful for the company.'

'That's very kind, thank you, Mrs Marshall.'

'Mags was on her way here to collect the supplies as Sam is indisposed,' Tom said.

She opened the door to a pantry, retrieved a bag and handed it to Tom. 'There you are, dear. Now, you two make yourselves at home and finish your tea. Just close the door on the way out so the geese don't wander in, the little blighters.'

'All right. Thank you for your kindness, Mrs Marshall,' Tom said.

She undid her apron and hung it on a hook underneath the sink. 'I'll see you both again soon, no doubt,' she said.

We both said goodbye.

After she'd left the room, Tom looked at me across the table. 'What a morning, eh?'

'My nerves are certainly suffering,' I said.

A tall and stocky woman came into the kitchen, dressed in brown trousers and a dark-green jersey.

'Why, hello, Tom,' she said, approaching the sink and filling a glass with water. Leaning on the counter, she said, 'Mr Marshall explained what happened just now. Aren't you going to introduce me?'

'This is Mags,' he said.

'Oh, Sam told me you're the new lady's maid. Poor you.' She leant forward and shook my hand. 'I'm Pam, resident land girl.'

I recognised Pam as the woman driving the tractor when I was walking into Gatley from the station that day. She downed the water and filled the glass once again, then cut a slice of bread and joined us at the table.

'Pleased to meet you, Pam,' I said.

She slathered the bread with butter and ate it as if she were absolutely famished. She must have been exhausted from doing physical work. I was grateful that, although my hours were long, the work was hardly arduous in comparison. Pam finished wolfing down the slice of bread and got up to cut another.

Looking up at the clock, I saw it was ten minutes to eleven. The thought of not being at the house on Lady Violet's return was a concern, especially as this was my first full day working at Gatley Hall. I had no idea how she'd react to me not being there when needed.

'We should get back to the house before Lady Violet does,' I said.

Tom glanced at his watch. 'Goodness, I didn't realise the time. I'll have to sort out Jack. Let's go, Mags.'

He cleared the table, putting the cups, saucers and side plates by the sink.

'Off already?' Pam said, returning to the table.

'We need to get back for her ladyship,' Tom said.

'Well, that's an awful shame. It's my birthday on Friday and a few of us are going down the Old Fox for a few drinks and a sing-song. Bert will be on the piano. Please say you'll come; the more the merrier.'

Would I be allowed to take the evening off?

'I should be able to as there aren't any events on at the house this weekend. Mags will probably need to ask for permission,' Tom said.

Nodding, I said, 'I'll ask Mrs Willis and let you know.'

We said our goodbyes and went back outside into the farm-yard. I found myself not wanting to walk through the Dairy Field, as Tom had referred to it.

'Is there a different way back to the house?' I said.

'There is, but it would take too long, I'm afraid. Don't worry, Mags, I'll look after you.'

His words were reassuring, but I had come face to face with death less than an hour earlier. My stomach still twisted and churned, and I was struggling to catch my breath as we walked. Despite my anxiety, thoughts of Luca filled my mind as we crossed the fields. Picturing the way he'd studied me with those dark-brown eyes, I couldn't wait to see him again.

CHAPTER 15

CLAIRE

The week dragged by, with Jim dropping in for post-work showers and leaving swiftly afterwards. Perhaps he didn't want to impose after my reaction to him barging in that day. In the office, I couldn't find any letters that grabbed me more than the one written by Margaret. I thought about visiting the address in Gatley to see if she still lived there. But should I try to find out more about her and Tabitha first? I'd learnt the hard way that it was best to prepare properly before embarking on a work-related meeting. That's if she was still alive, and her memory hadn't deteriorated since writing the letter. In the meantime, I created a document about the Below Stairs exhibition, using information from the guidebook as a starting point and selecting which photos should be blown up.

On Thursday after work, I sat in my kitchen with a second glass of Rioja from the bottle Jim had left on the doorstep. Chilled music played through my speaker. Gatley was certainly a calming place to be, and I had more time on my hands in the evenings. There was the sound of a key turning in the lock of the front door and Jim came into the kitchen, wearing a navy-blue dressing gown.

'Hello there, Jim,' I said, feeling a little tipsy from the wine.

'Evening, Claire. You may have noticed I'm sporting a new dressing gown.'

'That's considerate of you.'

He tightened the belt. 'I popped into Dorking earlier and treated myself. Thought I'd stop putting you off your dinner.'

I laughed.

He placed an ATP reusable coffee cup on the table. 'A gift,' he said.

'Oh, how thoughtful. Thanks,' I said, a hint of sarcasm in my voice. It wasn't the most exciting design and now I'd have to use it when there was any chance of seeing him.

'My pleasure,' he said. 'No more disposable cups for you.'

He smiled, but I had a feeling he'd get cross if he caught me using one again.

'Any update on the plumber?' I said.

'He's booked for early next week. Is that all right?'

'Sure.'

'Thank you, Claire,' he said, rather formally, as he slipped off his flip-flops and lined them up neatly by the wall before heading upstairs. Just being in his presence lifted my mood.

My mobile vibrated. It was Miles. What did he want? Answering, I said, 'Hello, Miles.'

'Claire?'

'Yes?'

'Everything all right?'

'Why are you calling?'

'I have some post for you. Shall I bring it over or would you prefer me to forward it on?'

He was making an excuse to see me, surely?

'Forwarding it should be fine.'

'Miss you though,' he said, in the voice he used when he wanted something. Did he mean this, or was he testing the water?

'You do?'

'Of course. Do you miss me?' he said.

I shrugged, pointlessly as he couldn't see me. He wasn't a fan of FaceTime, probably because he didn't think it made him look that good. I'd given up trying to get him to use it whenever one of us was away on business. Did I miss him, or the life we'd shared and a warm body next to me at night? In hindsight, I'd stayed with him for way too long, partly due to the fear of upheaval. Our life together had been comfortable and easy. Did he regret letting me get away?

'Your silence speaks volumes,' he said.

'What do you expect me to say?'

'Can I come and see your new place tomorrow night and check you're okay? I've been so worried about you, you know.'

He hadn't seemed too worried when he allowed me to load my car alone. He'd picked up his keys from the dish by the door and headed off to the pub to meet a friend, giving the excuse that he hated goodbyes. Later that evening, no doubt inebriated, he'd sent a message, signing off with one large kiss – something he'd done rather than adding a cute emoji when we weren't getting on.

Sorry things didn't work out. Good luck with everything X

'Sorry things didn't work out' rather than 'Sorry, I messed up'. How passive-aggressive, I'd thought at the time as I sat on the sofa in Deborah's living room, alone because she was playing the wicked stepmother in *Cinderella* at Richmond Theatre.

'Sorry I led you on for years and years, allowing you to think we had some kind of future.' That's what the message should have said. The night before, he'd finally admitted he never intended to have children with me. Until then, Miles had allowed me to think this might be a possibility sometime in the not-too-distant future.

One evening after work, while staying at Deborah's, I had flicked through the pages of *What's Up, Surrey!* magazine and there it was, an ad for the job at Gatley Hall, complete with a cottage to rent. On a whim, I'd applied that very night.

Jim's footsteps clumped down the stairs out of nowhere. Had he been eavesdropping?

'Look, Miles, I can't really talk. There's someone here,' I said, not knowing how to answer his question. If I allowed him onto my new territory, would he tarnish my attempt at a new start when it was all going quite well?

'Thanks, Claire,' Jim said, far more loudly than was necessary, as he waved from the kitchen doorway. I pointed to the phone next to my ear. 'Sorry,' he mouthed, making for the front door. But speaking to Miles had made me crave some company and I wasn't ready to see him leave yet.

'Do you have a man there?' Miles said, a hint of jealousy in his voice.

'Just my neighbour. I have to go. Bye, Miles.'

Hanging up, I found myself following Jim out of the front door, and caught him as he turned the key in his lock.

'Jim, wait.' My phone rang. It was Miles calling back. Jim raised his eyebrows, his face serious, as he ran a hand through his thick wet hair. It seemed I'd misread that he wanted to interact with me. Pursuing him to his doorstep had been a mistake.

'Aren't you going to get that?' he said.

Pressing decline on my phone screen, I shook my head.

'Is everything okay, Claire?' he said, in an exasperated voice.

His change in tone towards me hurt. My chest tightened and I took a moment to breathe.

'Yes, but you can't walk into my house whenever you feel like it.' My voice wavered, but I couldn't control it. Exhaling, I said, 'That was supposed to be a private conversation and it was obvious you were listening in.' What was I even saying? Miles had triggered negative emotions, and now my phone vibrated as he tried again to call back. Pressing the decline button firmly, I looked at Jim and bit my lip to stop myself from going any further, embarrassed that he was getting to see me like this.

Slipping his keys into the pocket of his dressing gown, he stepped into his cottage and leant on the front door. He sighed, and said, 'Your mundane life doesn't interest me, Claire, and, as I said before, the plumber is coming next week.'

'You think my life is mundane?'

My voice continued to waver. How was Miles managing to mess up the new life I was building from afar?

'No, I didn't mean that,' he said, gently. 'You just got my back up, that's all.'

My eyes started to well up. Jim was right. My life was mundane, and his brief appearances had been the only spark to look forward to. And now I'd gone and fallen out with him. What was I thinking, speaking to my only friend here like that?

'Whoever that was on the phone has clearly upset you. Are you all right?' he said.

The world seemed to be caving in. I'd done my best to forget Miles since arriving at Gatley Hall, but now he'd caught up with me.

Sniffing, and in need of a tissue, I said, 'I'm fine,' dismissing Jim with the wave of a hand before turning to go back inside, but a breeze had blown the front door shut behind me. This really was not my day. 'Damn, I've locked myself out now.'

Jim pressed his keys into my hand, and I unlocked the door.

'Thanks.'

'Claire,' he said as I handed them back to him.

'Yes?'

'Why don't you come to the drinks for the volunteers at the Old Fox tonight?'

The drinks Helen had mentioned. Caught off guard, I wasn't ready with a viable excuse, and so I spoke the truth.

'I'm not really feeling sociable.'

'Everyone's friendly enough. What do you have to lose?'

Picturing a lonely night ahead trying to get over the phone call with Miles, I said, 'Okay. When are you leaving?'

'Ten minutes?'

'So soon?'

'There's no need to dress up. I'll knock and we can go together.'

Walking into the pub with Jim would be a lot easier than arriving on my own.

'Thanks.'

I ran upstairs to change my clothes and apply a bit of make-up.

CHAPTER 16

MARGARET

Tom escorted me back to the house and explained everything to Mrs Willis, who lent a sympathetic ear and said she regretted sending me to Home Farm. Before long, I was called back to Lady Violet's side to help her dress for luncheon. Afterwards, she took a nap and I seized the opportunity to spend time alone in my room, with encouragement from Mrs Willis, who said I should try to take it as easy as possible when not required by her ladyship for the remainder of the day. We didn't tell Lady Violet about the parachutist – she wouldn't wish to be bothered with trivial matters relating to servants, but also Mrs Willis was concerned it would worry her when she went out riding.

'Best keep this to ourselves,' she said.

She also gave me permission to attend Pam's birthday drinks at the Old Fox. Tom would escort me there and back, and he promised to return me home in time to get Lady Violet ready for bed.

When Friday came, I was exhausted, both mentally and physically. The parachutist incident had impacted me more than I cared to admit and my days working for Lady Violet were often long, as she was a woman who liked to burn the candle at both ends. Sometimes, I wouldn't go to bed until one o'clock in the morning, and then I'd lie awake, listening to the planes, the distant thud of bombs dropping rather unsettling. My imagination would run away with me and I'd visualise a bomb dropping directly onto Gatley Hall. We could all so easily be killed while sleeping without feeling a thing. It would be worse to survive and be buried in rubble for hours or even days while Auxiliary Fire Service volunteers did their best to find us. To die like that would be tragic. Or what if one survived but lost a leg or an arm or some other body part? In bed at night, I'd repeat the Lord's Prayer in my head over and over, hoping he might be listening, that this small gesture would protect me in some way.

Every morning, I collected Lady Violet's breakfast from Cook, Mrs Downside – often a boiled egg and toast with butter along with a pot of tea – at seven thirty, regardless of whether I'd slept or not. Lady Violet existed on only a few hours' sleep, but her days were to do what she wished with, and she usually indulged in an afternoon nap – not a liberty I was able to take. Although many of us would have liked to be in her position, her daily life seemed rather mundane. The people she mixed with were more acquaintances than friends, and she spent a great deal of her time sitting around drinking tea, or often brandy if it was after eleven o'clock. Her husband, the earl, was a member of the House of Lords, and so he was in London dealing with important matters relating to the war.

My nerves affected by recent events, I'd often need to remind myself to inhale and exhale properly. A moment alone at Gatley Hall was to be cherished, and I would seek peace and quiet in the laundry room. Sam was often to be found polishing boots in there. He'd make me laugh with his silly jokes and anecdotes about servants and villagers. I had to be careful though, as he was close to Elsie. One afternoon, Sam told me he and Elsie were second cousins and she'd helped him get the job as a hallboy. And so I needed to watch my words when talking to him, presuming that everything could be passed on to Elsie. On occasion, I would find the two of them gossiping in the laundry room about something or other – usually another servant – and they'd stop talking as soon as I entered. This made me uncomfortable, and Elsie would never be a friend of mine, she'd made that abundantly clear.

On Friday evening, Tom and I set out for the Old Fox. He took his bicycle, and I borrowed Sam's. Tom led the way and I followed as we progressed up the twisting and winding drive towards the black and gold gates and into the village. Apart from a sliver of moon, the night was pitch black and I found it difficult to see where we were going. We weren't allowed to use torches due to the blackout. It was a starry night though, and I could make out the Plough. The drive was riddled with potholes, and this made for a bumpy ride and the strong likelihood of getting a puncture. Plane after plane passed over us, making it impossible to converse as we cycled. I tried to shut the visions of buildings in flames and belongings and body parts scattered around the streets out of my mind. We had to do our best to remain strong in the face of adversity in order to survive the horror we were living through. Sometimes, I liked to pretend it was all a dream or a film at the pictures.

When we at last reached the village, we left our bicycles outside the Old Fox and went through the front door and into a room bustling with people. It was cosy, with a log fire burning and the atmosphere a joyous and lively one. When we arrived, the pianist, presumably Bert, was playing 'Roll out the Barrel', and a few girls were leaning over the piano, singing along with great enthusiasm. Every table was taken and people stood at the bar, talking and laughing. Going to the pub was a way to escape, to act as though we were living in normal times. Pam sat in a corner with Mr and Mrs

Marshall and said hello as we pulled up chairs and joined them.

It was then that I spotted Luca opposite Pam. He was so handsome and he was causing quite a stir. Girls were stealing a glance whenever they had the opportunity. I even caught Lilian staring at him, despite being with her Canadian soldier Ted, who looked rather handsome himself, dressed in uniform. Tom bought me a beer along with one for himself. Luca was talking to Pam, using his hands as he spoke. How I wished Luca thought about me as much as I did about him, but it couldn't be possible. For, although I scrubbed up well when putting on a nice dress and a spot of rouge, I was no beauty, with hair Mother often referred to as unruly and difficult to tame. Luca did throw me a look though, and I wondered, nay hoped, he might find me attractive after all. I smiled at him, and he came to sit in the chair next to me. This unexpected move produced a fluttering in my gut.

'How are you, Margaret, after what happened?'

'Oh, I'm all right, thank you. Stiff upper lip, and all that.'

He scrunched up his forehead, clearly not understanding. 'Margaret, I wonder if you like to have picnic with me?'

'I'd be delighted. It would have to be when her ladyship is lunching though, and I wouldn't have very long.'

'All right. I send you message.'

He went back to the other side of the table and, when Tom looked over, I hoped my face wasn't the colour of beetroot. Had Luca really asked me to meet him?

The evening turned out to be fun, reminding me of drinks with my Taylor and Stone colleagues at the Running Horse. But when I went to buy a drink for Tom in return, Ted bumped into me as I was carrying the glasses back to the table. It wasn't his fault – he'd been edging his way around some girls singing along to 'My Old Man's a Dustman' and waving their arms around, and so didn't notice me trying to squeeze past. Some of the beer splashed onto the floor and, before I knew it, Tom was standing before us.

'What do you think you're doing?' he said to Ted.

'I'm sorry, man. I didn't see her,' Ted said.

'She has a name and it's Mags. How dare you disrespect her like that! And you spilled some of my drink in the process.'

'It was a mistake and I apologise,' Ted said.

'You Canadians, taking our women while their men are fighting a war. Well, Martin Chester is my best friend, and he was ready to marry our Lilian.'

Ted ran a hand through his hair, awkwardly, and I felt sorry for him.

'Nothing to say, *man?*' Tom said, in a mocking voice.

Lilian came over and said, 'What's going on?'

'Nothing, darlin', just go and sit down. I can handle this,' Ted said.

'You can, can you?' Tom said, his face reddening.

I was shocked to see Tom being so aggressive.

'It's not his fault,' Lilian said. 'Me and Martin were never going to get married.'

'That's not what he thought,' Tom said to her. Then, turning to Ted, he said, 'Taking over our village, and giving our girls silk stockings. Who do you think you are?'

'I'm sorry, man, I really am,' Ted said, attempting to walk away.

Tom raised his fists. 'How dare you walk away from me when I'm talking to you! Come on, then, why don't you show me how tough you really are. Taking a girl from her man while he's fighting for his country.'

'I don't wanna fight you,' Ted said.

'Don't want to or are you too scared? All bravado, are we?' Tom raised his fist and jabbed Ted's arm.

'Come on, then. Let's see who's a better man. I'll fight you on behalf of my friend. Kick your head in, I will.'

Me and Lilian looked at each other. I wanted to stop Tom but didn't know how as his eyes were filled with such fury. Ted was much taller and broader than him.

Bert had stopped playing the piano and everyone in the room was watching. Mr Marshall stood up and came over, took Tom gently by the arm.

'Come on, Tom. It's not worth it, lad. It's time you went home.'

'I'm not finished here though, Mr Marshall,' Tom said.

'Oh yes, you are,' Mr Marshall said. 'Go on,' he said to Ted, 'you and your girl go and sit over there.'

Ted and Lilian went over to the far corner. She was sobbing.

'It's not fair what happened to poor Martin, but she's made her choice, and you need to stay out of it,' Mr Marshall said.

'Let's go, Mags,' Tom said with a sigh.

Seeing this side of Tom both horrified and disappointed me. Although I could empathise with his point of view, he shouldn't be starting a fight. I put it down to him being angry about the betrayal of his friend, but still his behaviour was unacceptable. We left the Old Fox and cycled back to Gatley Hall in silence and I replayed the argument in my head, quite shaken. Then I thought back to my conversation with Luca. How I hoped he'd keep his word about sending a message to me.

Tom held the door open to the servants' entrance, and said, 'I'm sorry you had to see all that, Mags. Martin Chester is a mess because of that Canadian chap stealing his girl.'

'I did find the whole experience rather upsetting, but I suppose you were sticking up for your friend,' I said.

He threw me a look as if he were a little ashamed, and I said, 'Goodnight,' as I went up the stairs. I just wanted to forget about it all and hoped our friendship wouldn't be impacted by this awkward exchange.

'Goodnight, Mags,' he said.

After agreeing with Lady Violet what she'd wear the next

day – thankfully, she didn't have guests, so was earlier than usual that evening – I went to bed. Feeling restless, I thought back to what Aunt Edith had said about writing a diary to help get one through on darker days.

Getting out of bed, I removed the diary she'd gifted me from the drawer of the writing table. I started to write with my fountain pen, recording what happened that day out in the field and how it had made me feel. When I'd written a couple of pages, I instantly felt better. The last thing I wanted was for anyone to read my private thoughts, and so I put the diary under my mattress. And then, to sleep, my head filled with a vision of me in Luca's arms with him kissing me as if I were the only girl in the world.

CHAPTER 17

MARGARET

The next morning, Lady Violet asked me to carry a few items to the gamekeeper's cottage. The earl had gifted it to her to use as an art studio when the gamekeeper was called up. I carried a canvas and a cloth bag filled with tubes of paint. Lady Violet wanted to start painting again after a period of feeling uninspired, and she blamed the war for this. Her life wasn't affected greatly by the war. Food rationing didn't apply to her or his lordship, or to us servants, and for that I was grateful. Regular supplies of milk, butter, cheese and meat came daily from Home Farm. And Mr Carter, the old head gardener, kept the kitchen garden ticking over with help from Tom and Sam, providing us with vegetables of the season. The orchard supplied apples all year round as they were stored in a cellar, and there was an abundance of wild blackberries to be picked from the surrounding land. The kitchen maids would make jams, preserves and pickles in the still room to ensure nothing went to waste. One experience Lady Violet could not escape – and she complained about it daily – was the sound of the planes and the whizz, bang and thud of bombs being dropped around us. She seemed oblivious to the devastation they caused, and her view of the war was rather blinkered compared to us servants.

We walked down to the lake, designed by Capability Brown in the eighteenth century – Lady Violet had told me one morning while we discussed the view as I brushed her hair – and it was complete with folly, grotto and waterfall. The leaves on the trees surrounding the lake were red, orange, yellow with the advance of autumn, and they reflected in the water. We climbed over the stile onto the grass, the morning dew dampening my ankles above the line of my boots, and entered the bluebell woods through a gate. Leaves, pine cones, conkers and acorns covered the ground. Gunshots could be heard coming from Netley Park, where the Canadian soldiers were based. Birds called out to each other and there was the occasional squawk from a pheasant. We passed a pillbox, one of many installed in the area in case the Hun succeeded in their plan to invade. Lady Violet led me along a narrow path, pushing the undergrowth aside with a big stick until we reached a cottage straight out of 'Hansel and Gretel'. It was built from red bricks and complete with chimney and two windows with floral curtains on either side of a door. Removing a key from her pocket, Lady Violet unlocked the door, and we went inside to a sitting room, dominated by a vast fireplace and a basket of logs. The floor was covered with a beautiful Persian rug with a red-and-white pattern. There were two armchairs, a chaise longue, a table in the corner and a small stove. A door led to a bathroom with water closet and sink. In the corner of the living room stood an easel with a half-finished painting of a bowl of fruit, and there were brushes and palettes and a number of tubes of paint scattered around. I unpacked the paints and brushes from the bag, placing them on the trestle table beside the easel.

'What will you paint next, milady?' I said.

'I must confess that I've always wanted to paint a portrait,' she said, her eyes lighting up.

'Of whom?' I said.

'That is the question, Maggie.'

'You don't know who to paint?'

'No one in this place inspires me. Servants are all rather bland to look at in their plain uniforms and I have no desire to paint you, despite your impeccable taste in clothes. No offence.'

This didn't bother me as who wanted to sit still for hours on end?

'What about your guests?' I said.

'Oh there isn't time to paint them what with all the fun activities we could be partaking in.'

'You could invite someone to the house especially in order to paint them?'

'I could indeed, but no one springs to mind, Maggie. I'm used to being in London, and Gatley is a rather dull place with equally dull people, don't you think?'

As she was being especially unkind, I felt obliged to set her straight. 'You're talking to a London girl, so I can see what you mean about it being quieter here. But it would be unfair to refer to the local community in that way.'

She rolled her eyes. 'Well, I suppose you do have a point, Maggie. Where will I find my muse in this place?'

I shrugged. 'Hopefully someone will turn up. In the meantime, you could paint a vase of flowers?'

'Boring.'

'Or a country scene?'

'Maybe.'

That evening, when I was ironing a blouse for Lady Violet, Sam brought me a note.

Meet me tomorrow at 1 o'clock on bench under willow tree by river in Gatley. I bring picnic.

Luca

My heart soared. Luca had kept his word.

'When did Luca give you this?' I said.

'I just went to Home Farm to get milk and butter, and he asked me to give it to you. I wrote it for him as he doesn't know how to write in his own language, let alone in English.'

'That's good of you,' I said.

Aunt Edith had asked me to accompany her to St Andrew's the following morning for the Sunday service. The other servants went to the chapel at Gatley Hall most Sundays, but Lady Violet had given me permission to go into the village. I had planned to walk but, if I met Luca, the time it would take to get back would make me late for Lady Violet after her morning activities.

'I promised to take my aunt to church in the village tomorrow, but I won't get back in time for Lady Violet if I meet Luca after the service.'

'Why don't you borrow my bicycle again?' Sam said.

'That would give me plenty of time. You are a good egg, Sam. Thank you.'

I couldn't wait to see Luca again, and wondered whether he'd try to kiss me. As I took Lady Violet's blouse upstairs, it struck me that it wouldn't be long before Sam told Elsie about my rendezvous with Luca – if he hadn't already – and then the other servants might find out as well. What if I became a laughing stock? Although this thought concerned me, my feelings for Luca were so strong that nothing was going to stop me from meeting him. I'd just have to take the risk and hope for the best.

The following day, I cycled into the village, called on Aunt Edith, and together we crossed the road to St Andrew's.

'You are a dear, Mags, accompanying me to church,' she said.

Throughout the service, I was so excited about meeting Luca that I sang each hymn with great enthusiasm, especially 'Morning Has Broken', my favourite hymn of all.

Afterwards, I dropped Aunt Edith home before going to the river to meet Luca. He hadn't yet arrived and so I leant the bicycle on a low wall bordering the towpath and sat down, my heart beating faster than usual. I could almost hear it thumping, and a queasy feeling lurked in my stomach, reminiscent of when I'd been excited growing up about my birthday or Christmas Day. On the opposite bank, leaves on the trees were beginning to turn, and clusters of them floated down the river towards the bridge. A cloud of midges flew into my face, and I swatted them away with a hand, spitting out a couple and wiping my mouth with the handkerchief from my pocket. A couple of ducks larked about, quacking loudly. Planes in a V-formation passed overhead, the now familiar sound ominous. Villagers walked up and down the high street, popping into shops, and the ATS canteen across the road, where Aunt Edith volunteered, looked especially busy, with a queue of people at the counter. A man trudged past with a suitcase, his head hanging low, yet another London evacuee no doubt. A horse and trap passed, the clippity-clop of hooves soporific, the sound taking me back to when Mr Foster had taken me to Gatley Hall only days ago. So much had happened in that short space of time. I'd almost been murdered, and had become infatuated with the man who saved my life. And now we were about to be alone together for the first time.

Luca appeared ten minutes or so late, and propped his bicycle against the wall next to mine, his rear wheel resting on my front wheel. He removed a brown paper bag from its basket. On seeing me, his face broke into a big smile, and he looked more dashing than ever. He wore the clothes of a farm labourer, with a hole in the sleeve of his jersey, but this didn't matter to me one bit.

'Ciao, Mags,' he said.

'Hello, Luca,' I said.

He leant down and kissed me on one cheek and then the other – it was traditional where he came from, I understood – before joining me on the bench.

'I have egg sandwich. Mrs Marshall made.' Opening the paper bag, he took one out and handed it to me.

'Thank you,' I said.

'Prego,' he said, taking one out for himself.

We ate. My sandwich was delicious. No doubt the eggs had been collected that very morning. It was uplifting to sit outside by the river and watch life go by.

'In Italy we say, "Dolce far niente",' Luca said.

'What does that mean?'

'The sweetness of doing nothing.'

'That is a lovely saying,' I said. 'Where in Italy are you from?'

'Firenze,' he said. 'Florence, the English say.'

I had heard of Florence, of course. 'Oh really?' I said.

'My family has bakery, the best in the city.'

'And you know how to make bread, and cakes?' I said.

'Certo,' he said, and I assumed this meant certainly.

'What is Florence like?'

'It is a city of art. There is the Michelangelo statue of David and you can go to the Uffizi gallery with Botticelli pittura of Venus, the goddess of love.'

When he said the word love, I looked away, my face warming, for it would be embarrassing if he knew how quickly I'd fallen for him. It wasn't the done thing to allow a man to know how besotted you were.

How I longed to go to this place with all its art and to eat the bread and cakes from Luca's family bakery. If only it were possible to speak to him in his language. Although I spoke a little French, Italian was different, the words more rounded and voluptuous. And the way these words rolled off Luca's tongue was mind-boggling. How did he get his tongue to make that sound? As he told me about this faraway, dreamy place, I imagined visiting one day. He must be sad to be so far from home, away from his family as well as his own traditions and culture. Being in England must be a culture shock for him, and I hoped that the war would end soon so he could go home. This would take him far away from me, but I couldn't imagine that we had any kind of future.

'There is Ponte Vecchio – a pretty bridge with houses – and the River Arno where in summer you go' – he made a breast-stroke movement with his arms and I said,

'Swimming?'

'Swimming, yes. Or...' He then used his arms to show he was rowing.

'Boating?'

'Esatto. In Italy, summer is hot, and we try to stay cool. We go to countryside, the mountains, the sea. My family has house in the hills.'

Luca's command of English was competent, but could be improved upon. I wondered whether I should offer to teach him more. Would he be offended or delighted by such an offer? When we'd finished eating, he leant towards me and kissed me on the lips. Although he smelt of a strange mix of cologne and dirt from the farm, it was a kiss I'd never forget as long as I lived, tender and loving. He pulled away from me and looked into my eyes and I saw how long his lashes were.

'You are beautiful, Mags,' he said. 'Ti amo.'

'What does that mean?'

He brushed my face with his fingers, sending a tingle right through me. 'Love,' he said, softly. 'I love you, Mags. You are so bella, beautiful.'

Overwhelmed by his words, I didn't know what to say. He loved me? And so soon after our first meeting? How could he know? I was certain that I loved him, so it was possible. Perhaps we were soulmates, and we'd known each other in a previous life or something. Was that how we both knew so quickly?

South London boys didn't waste time on saying nice things before or after kissing you, like Luca did, despite having a far broader vocabulary available to them. He leant forward and kissed me again, this time for much longer, pushing his tongue into my mouth in the most expert way, and I didn't care about passers-by throwing disapproving looks in our direction. When I looked up, an elderly woman in a red hat shook her head and tutted in our direction. Luca threw her one of his beautiful smiles and she scuttled off along the pavement, and then he put his arms round me and pulled me to him, and I inhaled the scent of him. Never had I wanted to be with a man so much. This was a dangerous situation, though as falling pregnant was far too easy. Mother's words sprang to mind; all those warnings about being careful that I'd shrugged off, not expecting ever to feel like this about anyone. My hormones had a mind of their own, and they were directing my decisions, rendering me powerless. I was completely and utterly entranced by him; one might say obsessed in an unhealthy way. Mother had been right; when you were overwhelmed by strong feelings for a man you'd allow him to take you in his arms, because all you wanted was to be with him, to feel his skin against yours. Luca's confidence and swagger gave away that he'd made love to many women. All he had to do was ask me to meet him somewhere quiet where no one would find us, and I'd give myself to him without a second thought.

For now, I needed to go back to Gatley Hall, to complete my sewing tasks, and prepare for Lady Violet waking up from her afternoon nap.

'I have to go,' I said.

'We meet again next Sunday, same time?' he said, as if reading my mind.

Thrilled by his suggestion, as it fitted in rather nicely with taking Aunt Edith to church, I said, 'All right.' Although waiting for a whole week seemed like an awfully long time.

We kissed again, and he wrapped his hand round mine, stroking my fingers in the most seductive way. Reluctantly, I pulled away and went to fetch my bicycle, releasing my wheel from his. It was impossible not to be aware of him watching my every move even though I had my back to him. Sure enough, as I turned to face him and gave him a wave, he was studying me intently, almost unbuttoning my dress with those big chocolate eyes of his. The anticipation of our next meeting sent a tingle right through me as I cycled back to Gatley Hall, unable to wipe the smile from my face. For I was madly in love.

CHAPTER 18

MARGARET

The next day was fairly uneventful, but thoughts of Luca helped me to pass the time while completing routine tasks. Then, on Tuesday, when Lady Violet woke from her afternoon nap, she asked me to accompany her on a walk. We went down to the lake and crossed Long Meadow, heading towards the Dairy Field where the parachutist incident had occurred. Lady Violet still had no inkling of what happened that day, and revisiting the scene made me apprehensive. What if we came across another parachutist, and this time he succeeded in killing one or both of us? My mind running away with me, I pictured newspapers reporting us being murdered with photographs of Lady Violet on the front pages. However, I was on cloud nine after my rendezvous with Luca, and I attempted to use this morale boost to relieve my anxiety.

'Where are we going?' I said.

'To seek inspiration, Maggie. I need to create a spectacular work of art, and I thought if you accompanied me on my quest you might have an idea. You are rather creative, after all, with all those dresses you've made for yourself.'

'All right,' I said.

The beauty of the hills did soften the blow of being stuck in the countryside somewhat. Fields stretched ahead for miles with no sign of human life whatsoever. A rabbit hopped out of a burrow by the hedgerow, saw us and disappeared back to where it had come from rather swiftly. A plane passed over, the swastika evident on its underside, and I hoped a German spy hadn't jumped out with his parachute somewhere nearby.

'Should I bring an easel out here, Maggie? Do you think I could do the countryside justice? I would rather like to paint a rabbit like the one we just saw, but how on earth do I get it to come out of its burrow and stay still for long enough? Or a squirrel with its bushy tail. How about a fox, a beautiful red fox? Impossible to paint a wild animal, unless it were stuffed, of course.'

I winced at the thought of this. 'The lake is rather beautiful. You could try painting the folly or the waterfall,' I said, hoping to entice her away from the Dairy Field and the bad memory associated with it.

'That doesn't interest me,' she said.

We progressed over the stile and into the Dairy Field. As the vision of the white shape from that awful day came to mind, a man appeared over the brow of the hill. Even from a distance, there was no doubt the man was Luca, and once again my heart raced at the sight of him. Our next encounter could not come soon enough. He moved with the self-assured gait of a man who knew how to please a woman. Luca, my Luca. But in Lady Violet's presence, I would have to pretend we were merely acquaintances.

Lady Violet clutched my arm. 'Who is that man?' she said. The war made us all suspicious of strangers, and her reaction to seeing him was understandable.

'It's Luca, an Italian prisoner of war who works on Home Farm.'

He threw us a friendly wave and walked towards us. How

would I manage our interaction in Lady Violet's presence? I reassured myself with the fact that she wouldn't want to speak to a farm labourer, especially one from a country we were at war with.

As he got closer, she used a hand to shield her eyes from the sun, and gasped.

'What a beautiful man, Maggie. He is the answer to what we have been discussing. I must paint him as soon as is physically possible. Just look at him.'

This wasn't what I'd expected, at all, and a sudden fear filled my whole being.

When he reached us, he removed the flat cap he was wearing and gave us both a nod, and I said, 'Lady Violet, this is Luca.' It struck me that I didn't know the surname of the man I'd shared a kiss with only a couple of days earlier.

'Buonasera, Luca,' she said.

'Piacere, signora,' he said. 'Luca Mancini.'

Lady Violet was being given privileged information and they'd only just met. He proffered a hand and, as she shook it, he looked her in the eye and then, rather obviously, studied her entire physique, those brown eyes running up and down her long slender legs and settling on her breasts, perfectly packed into the fitted white silk blouse that I'd selected the previous evening. For she was a vision for any man, no doubt, and, standing next to her, I was bound to look rather plain. She reciprocated, eyeing him in a way a woman of her class really shouldn't. Jealousy filled my every pore and I clenched my teeth. If I'd known Luca was going to appear out of the blue like this, I would have found a way to take Lady Violet somewhere else for our walk. And she spoke his language? This meeting did not bode well for me, and I longed to turn back the clock, ensure that it didn't take place. But it was too late.

'You speak Italian?' I said to Lady Violet, quietly.

'Just a little,' she said, as if it were nothing, while continuing to smile at Luca. They could not take their eyes off each other. 'I spent some time in Tuscany with my governess when I turned eighteen. Of course, there's no possibility of visiting while this damn war is on.'

By now, I was used to Lady Violet referring to the war as an inconvenience.

'Oh,' I said.

They exchanged a few words in Italian, I had no idea what they were saying, and felt like I was playing gooseberry as they interacted. Seeing my Luca look at my mistress in this way hurt me a great deal. Meeting him had given me some hope of being happy in this place. How could he treat me like this when we'd kissed only two days earlier? As a POW working at Home Farm, which was owned by Gatley Hall, he needed to be civil. But this was taking courtesy further than was strictly necessary. I looked away, tears pricking my eyes.

Lady Violet, no doubt oblivious to how I was feeling, nudged me with her elbow. 'Well, this is a stroke of luck. Maggie, you may go back to the house. Luca will accompany me to the studio this very moment and I'll do some preliminary sketches. He'd be delighted to sit for me.'

And so, I was dismissed.

'All right,' I said, and quietly mumbled goodbye. Neither of them replied as they continued to converse in Italian. I headed in the direction of Gatley Hall, pulling a handkerchief from the pocket of my dress to wipe my eyes as tears ran down my face, at full throttle now there was no one to hide them from.

As I walked past the lake, I told myself to be strong, despite my broken heart. Would our encounter still take place the following Sunday? Did I want it to when, clearly, Luca had eyes for other women?

Surely there was no chance of romance blossoming between an Italian POW and a countess? Besides, she was married and would certainly not succumb to his advances, if he dared to make them.

I convinced myself that she merely wished to paint his portrait, but after witnessing the chemistry they had with each other, envy had taken up residence in my gut.

CHAPTER 19

MARGARET

When I reached the stable yard, Tom was polishing the Standard outside the garage. Not wanting him to see how upset I was, I composed myself. He spotted me instantly, and waved, and I went over to him. After what happened at the Old Fox, we'd seen each other a handful of times and I was thankful that things weren't awkward between us. I couldn't bear to lose my only friend at Gatley Hall.

'Good afternoon, Mags, what are you up to?'

'Hello, Tom. I was just out on a walk with her ladyship. She was looking for inspiration for a painting.'

'What's she working on today, then?'

'Well...' I said, unable to say that she'd be all alone with Luca in that cosy cottage – for hours, no doubt. I couldn't bring myself to tell Tom how they'd looked at each other.

'Are you quite all right?' he said.

It was no use. I burst into tears once again. The strain of the past few weeks had caught up with me.

Tom took a handkerchief out of the pocket of his trousers and handed it to me. 'What's the matter?' he said, looking at me, his eyes softening.

'I'd rather not say,' I said, through my sobs.

'Well, how about we take your mind off whatever it is? One of the tyres on the Standard keeps losing air and I need to go to the village garage. We can take a little drive – it might cheer you up?'

I hadn't been in a car for months, not since my friend Geraldine drove me to see Mother and Mildred in Brighton the previous summer. Petrol rationing had put a stop to any further trips taking place.

'Do you think I'd be allowed to accompany you?'

'Your mistress doesn't need you until later, does she? And you can always tell Mrs Willis you had to get something from the haberdashery.'

'All right.'

'Let's go on a little adventure, Mags,' he said, opening the passenger door and gesturing for me to get in.

Stepping down into the low seat, I saw the Standard was beautiful inside, all brand new with the sweet earthy scent of leather upholstery. Tom got in and slid a key into the ignition. The engine started, the *brmmm* sound it made rather thrilling. This wasn't a car that people like us would normally get to be in. We really were going on an adventure, albeit only to the end of the drive, but my mood soon lifted. The car purred as Tom turned out of the stable yard, doing his best to avoid the potholes. As we progressed up the drive, I admired the row of trees, their leaves shimmering in the sun like gold coins.

'It's only a short drive, but we can have a cup of tea at Sally's while we wait, if you like?' Tom said.

Turning to him, I said, 'I'd like that, thank you, although I don't have any money with me.'

'I'll take care of that, don't you worry.'

Being with Tom made me feel looked after, a relatively rare feeling. Since Mother had gone to live with Mildred, I'd been alone in London, bold on the outside while slightly scared on the inside. Although I'd had colleagues and the girls at the boarding house, no one had been there for me on a bad day.

When we reached the village we drove along the high street, and, as we were in the Standard, passers-by stopped to look at us. He pulled up at Hart's Motorcars.

'I won't be a minute,' he said. 'You stay here, Mags.'

He got out of the car and went into the small hut that served as an office, and a few minutes later reappeared with a man in a boiler suit, sleeves rolled up and black oil smudges on his forearms. They squatted by the front tyre on the driver's side and exchanged a few words, before standing up and shaking hands.

Tom came to open the passenger door. 'Let's go and get a nice cuppa. We'll have to leave the car here overnight, so hope you don't mind if we walk back to the house?'

'The exercise will do us good,' I said.

We went to Sally's and took a table by the window. Tom ordered a pot of tea for two and a slice of Victoria sponge to share. The waitress brought it all on a tray and we tucked in.

'This is a treat,' I said. 'Thank you, Tom.'

'You're welcome. It's nice to have someone to share a slice of cake with.'

'Don't you have any friends at Gatley Hall?'

'Well, I get on with everyone, but haven't been to Sally's with any of them.'

'Who is your favourite person there?' I said.

'Sam is a nice young lad.'

'He is indeed,' I said. 'Although I do worry about the way he gossips with Elsie.'

Tom raised his eyebrows.

'They are related and you can't be surprised if they do tell each other everything. What can they possibly have on you though, Mags?' he said.

I couldn't tell Tom about my meeting with Luca, but sensed he might know already.

'I try to give Sam a bit of big-brotherly advice sometimes, you know, what with him being so young. I was the hallboy before him and a footman took me under his wing.'

'Oh, you have done well,' I said.

'Mr Willis promoted me to footman rather quickly and then, when the chauffeur was called up, he gave me the job. It was a real honour – I'm only from a humble background.'

'The war, despite its horror, does bring opportunities,' I said. 'I can see why Mr Willis promoted you.'

'Why's that?'

'Because you're reliable and hard-working as well as cheerful to be around, and I expect Mr Willis could see that as well.'

'Thank you, Mags. I do want to make something of myself. My father has been a cobbler all his life, and his father before him, and so on. But I don't want to be a cobbler. The world is changing, and, as you say, the war is bringing opportunities to spread one's wings a little.'

'How old are you, Tom?'

'I'll be eighteen on Christmas Day. I want to be an RAF pilot, although someone like myself might have to start off doing admin.'

'A pilot, gosh, Tom. You would be spreading your wings, quite literally.'

He smiled. 'My uncle was a pilot at the end of the last war, and he told me stories. Every year, on my birthday, he used to give me a model aeroplane and we'd make it together. I've wanted to be a pilot for as long as I can remember.'

'That's very exciting,' I said. But at the same time, it was dangerous. If Tom fought in the war, there was a strong chance he wouldn't return. And I didn't like the idea of that.

'It is indeed, but not everyone comes back.'

'You are brave, and I wish you luck, although I'll be sorry to see you leave,' I said.

'Thank you, Mags.'

'I never wanted to follow in my mother's footsteps and become a lady's maid. One day, and I know it's a big dream, I'd like to own my own boutique.'

'That's a big dream indeed,' Tom said. 'And I admire your ambition, but women were put on this earth to get married and have children.'

'Is that what you think?'

'It's not just what I think; it's what's right. Women shouldn't get ideas above their station when their role is to look after a family.'

'Oh, well...' I didn't know what to say to this. He'd squashed my dream in a matter of seconds. Was he right in suggesting that my plan would never come to fruition? Weren't things changing for women? While the men were away, women were taking up positions in factories and on farms and doing whatever they could to make up for the lack of men in the workforce. Would these women be satisfied with going back to having such limited options if and when the war ended? I doubted they would be, but kept my thoughts to myself.

When we'd finished our tea and cake, we left Sally's and walked across the fields back to Gatley Hall. The whole time we'd been out, I hadn't thought about Lady Violet and Luca once, but now the vision of them meeting came back to me. All I could do was try my best to shut it out of my mind.

When we reached Gatley Hall it was late afternoon and I needed to check on some of Lady Violet's garments in the laundry room.

Tom opened the door to the servants' quarters, gesturing for me to go first.

'Thank you for taking me out. I rather enjoyed myself.'

'I hope you're feeling more chipper now?' he said.

'I am, thank you. Cheerio,' I said.

'See you later, Mags,' he said.

He headed for the servants' hall and I went to the laundry room, where Sam was polishing boots.

Tom's determination and drive was admirable, and I hoped we'd remain friends for the foreseeable future. Life with him in it would be brighter, for sure. Although, when the RAF recruited him – there was no way they'd turn a man like him down in a hurry, unless he had a medical condition – it wouldn't be long before he left Gatley Hall, and then we'd have to correspond by post. I'd write to him daily to provide moral support, for he was brave, putting himself forward to take part in dogfights with the Hun in mid-air. The thought of him being shot down was terrifying and I'd need to pray for him before I went to bed each night.

Elsie came into the laundry room and threw me a look. I continued to arrange Lady Violet's undergarments on the rack.

'A little bird told me something about you,' she said.

'What's that then?' I replied.

'I heard you met with that Italian prisoner of war down in the village on Sunday,' she said.

'So what if I did?'

'Cavorting with the enemy are we, Margaret?' she said.

Elsie was trying to get a rise out of me, and I wasn't going to give her the satisfaction.

'We just had a sandwich, that's all, Elsie,' I said.

'I bet he tried to kiss you, what with that Latin blood running through his veins,' she said.

My face was warming and I didn't know what to say.

'He'll be sweet-talking you into bed before long, no doubt,' Elsie said with a laugh.

'Well I never, Elsie; how dare you suggest such a thing,' I said.

Glancing across at Sam, I saw he was brushing polish into a

boot as if his life depended on it. So, he had told her. Although I was fond of him, I'd have to be more careful in future. But if Luca sent me messages via Sam, and asked him to write them, what was a girl to do?

CHAPTER 20

CLAIRE

Jim knocked promptly after ten minutes. I'd changed into jeans and a top with a yellow cardigan, finished off with a suede jacket and flats. It was dark outside, and I needed to be practical. Jim used a torch to light the way as we passed through the rose garden. Being in the countryside meant so many stars were visible, and I looked up at them in wonder.

'So, who was that on the phone?' Jim said.

'My ex.'

'What's his name?'

'Miles.'

'Miles,' he said, a hint of disapproval in his voice. 'And why was he calling?'

Did Jim really want to know, or was he just making conversation?

'He wants to bring my post over tomorrow night.'

Jim lifted the latch on the black cast-iron gate as we left the rose garden, and gestured for me to go first as he closed it behind us. We continued to the staff car park, which was dimly lit. He unlocked a pick-up truck with the ATP logo in big capital letters on its side.

'Forwarding post is easy enough. He's realised he shouldn't have let you go, no doubt.'

'He said he misses me, but...'

'Of course he misses you.'

Jim's compliment was a boost and needed, and it made up for our tête-à-tête outside the house. He was probably just being nice because he'd seen how upset I was, but those words *of course he misses you* warmed my insides. They implied that I was worthy of being missed and, currently, I didn't feel worthy of much. That was what the death of a parent, albeit a mostly absent one, and a subsequent break-up did to your confidence, even when only weeks before you'd been a high-flying career woman.

We got into the pick-up truck and fastened our seatbelts, and I inhaled the scent of his aftershave, oaky and musky. Not unpleasant at all.

'Normally I'd suggest we walk or cycle, but we're already running late.'

'What about the environment though, Jim? This truck must be a bit of a gas-guzzler.'

He looked across at me as he started the engine and put on the radio, shaking his head. 'I'll have you know this is the most environmentally friendly pick-up truck there is, and it was my idea to get one. I organised a sponsored 10k run last year in the Surrey Hills to make it happen.'

Impressed, I said, 'Go, you. I appreciate the lift. You won't be able to have a drink though.'

He reversed out of the parking space. 'It's a school night anyway. Why did you and this Miles split up?'

'Can we change the subject?'

'Oh go on, at least tell me who ended it.'

'I did.'

'So why are you so upset then?'

'Well, there were a few reasons,' I said.

'Did he cheat?'

Horrified, I said, 'Don't be ridiculous.' Miles wouldn't do that, would he?

'You cheated, then?'

How could he say such a thing?

'No,' I said.

'Sounds like you grew apart? It happens.'

Yes, people did grow apart when one person stopped making an effort. After Dad's funeral, I'd found myself thinking about the future with a newfound need to make the most of every single moment of the rest of my life. When Miles came home after working late yet again, I put him on the spot. No more dithering or avoiding the question. It was only fair to give me a straight answer. After going round in circles, as we always did – he was a master at making that happen – he admitted finally that he had no intention of having children with me, or anyone else. His teenage son was enough for him. The night he told me, I slept in the spare room, and the following morning I left to stay with Deborah. She'd said, 'You can stay for a few weeks while you sort your life out, but don't overstay your welcome.' In the past, when she'd cast me out, encouraging me to make my own way, I'd thought she was trying to help me become independent. But recently, I'd become aware that she was quite mean. Yes, everyone loved Deborah, the actress who'd once been married to Dickie Bell. She liked to have friends round for dinner and drinks, and usually there would be a jamming session or singalong at the piano. But deep down, she didn't allow people to get close to her, not even her daughter.

Jim pulled out of the car park and onto the drive. It was so dark he had to put the headlights on full beam. We didn't speak any more as he drove, but the silence was a comfortable one. Although we'd only known each other a few days, it seemed like longer.

'You'll be all right here,' he said.

'Do you think so?' Our interaction earlier had made me drop my guard around him, and I wasn't sure if that was a good thing or not.

'I'm sure the answer to your troubles is in that damn drawer,' he said with a laugh.

The flirtatious banter was back.

'You know about the drawer?' I said.

'Everyone knows about the drawer. It's been untouched for years. I can imagine going through it is a real nightmare. 'Would you have taken the job if you'd known about it?'

Rosalind had kept the drawer quiet during our interview but, although it was in a complete mess, Margaret's letter was intriguing.

'Probably. I did find an interesting letter from a woman who worked here as a lady's maid during the war.'

'Interesting,' Jim said. His tone of voice implied he couldn't be less enthused by my discovery.

'I'll probably look into it more, try and help her.'

'Sounds good.'

When we reached the gates, I got out to open them so Jim could drive through before closing them again. He took a left into the village and before long, we'd arrived at the Old Fox, which had a black-and-white Tudor-style exterior – I wasn't sure if it was mock or original. Smoke wisped from the chimney, and I looked forward to seeing what it was like inside. Jim pulled into the car park round the back and took the last space. There was a nice garden with a stream running through it and willow trees glowing blue from the lights placed beneath them. I pictured sitting at one of the picnic tables in the summer with a glass of Pimm's. A group of young lads sat at a table with a heater as they drank pints and vaped.

We went through the back door. The interior was all stone

flooring and wooden beams, so the building was likely to be real Tudor, after all. The Gatley Hall crowd were a noisy lot; they dominated a few tables pushed together near the front door. And there was a roaring fire and gigantic hearth, the mantelpiece lined with jam jars of flowers and tealights. Helen was in deep conversation with some bloke I didn't recognise, and Samantha held court with a couple of women at one end. Joining such a raucous group made me nervous, but it was too late now. Jim approached them and I followed.

'Jim!' Samantha patted the empty chair next to her, her eyes lighting up.

'Who wants a drink?' Jim said, waving a credit card in the air.

This was followed by raised hands and several people saying, 'Me, me.'

He went round the table, tapping orders into his phone, and I went with him to the bar, where he added a glass of house red for me. When I tried to give him a tenner, he shook his head.

'Put it away. This round is on expenses.'

'Oh, great, thanks.'

'Rosalind gives me a budget to spend on team drinks every quarter. She thinks it's important for us to bond, although she isn't actually here herself.'

'Samantha seems to want to bond with you,' I said, the words slipping out before I could stop them.

Throwing me a puzzled look, he said, 'How do you know about Samantha?'

'Helen told me.'

'Well, Helen's got a cheek,' he said.

'Are you seeing each other then?'

He looked away, and then back at me.

'If you must know, casually, yes.'

'A friends-with-benefits kind of thing?'

'You could say that.'

'I tried that once, and it doesn't work. One person usually ends up liking the other one more. And then you've lost a good friend. Does she really have five kids?'

He shook his head. 'Helen knows all the details, doesn't she?'

On the car journey, he'd asked me about Miles, but didn't want to reveal anything about his own love life. This didn't seem fair.

The barman lined up drinks on the counter and Jim thanked him. We carried them over to the table, and Jim took the chair next to Samantha. I was grateful when Helen spotted me.

'Claire, join us,' she said, urging the bloke next to her to move up. I got a chair from a table nearby and placed it next to hers.

'How have you been getting on?' she said.

'The other day I found a letter asking us to help find someone.'

'Ooh, sounds intriguing.'

Maybe this would be my chance to ask for Helen's help. 'It is. I found the lady who wrote it in a photo in the guidebook. She was a lady's maid here during the war.'

'Some of those letters have been in that drawer for years. No one ever had time to look at them.'

'This one was written two years ago. I hope she's still alive.'

'How wonderful. I'm sure you'll uncover a story worth telling. Gatley Hall must have so many stories that people don't know about,' she said.

'True. Would you be interested in helping me if I'm not sure how to find everything?'

'Yes, of course. I'd start with the website; there is some information about the house on there and a few photos of the servants.'

'Thank you, Helen. I'll have a look tomorrow.'

'Oh, and, talking of photos, once the below stairs rooms are set up for the exhibition, you'll need to arrange for our volunteer photographer, Ed, to take photos for the website and new edition of the guidebook. I'll send him over to introduce himself next time he's in. Anyway, I'm glad you came tonight. You didn't seem that keen when I asked the other day.'

I sipped my wine. 'To be honest I wasn't feeling brave enough to come, but then my ex called and I was a bit upset. Jim talked me into coming here with him. He said it would cheer me up.'

'You need to get rid of that ex and move on,' Helen said.

Nodding, I said, 'I know you're right. It isn't easy to make a clean break when you've shared a life together for years.'

'I know, but still, look at you, in a new place with a new job and the opportunity to make new friends, and dare I say it, lovers. Cut all that negativity out of your life. This is your big chance to start again, while you're still young. Get yourself on the right path.'

Although I appreciated Helen giving me the kind of advice Deborah should be dishing out, it was a bit too much too soon. We hardly knew each other. I pulled a face, not knowing what to say.

'Sorry, I might be laying it on a bit thick,' she said.

'Why isn't Ed here tonight, then?' I said, changing the subject. 'Aren't these drinks for the volunteers?'

'He doesn't see himself as a volunteer. He's Wendy's brother and takes photos for the website so he can be on the recommended photographers list for wedding bookings.'

'Gatley Hall does weddings?'

'Yes, in June and July.'

'That must be good business for Ed, then?'

'Very. His usual work involves attending celebrity parties in London, taking photos for magazines. Sometimes, he gets a photo in one of the tabloid newspapers; then' – Helen rubbed her fingers together – 'he makes big money.'

'Impressive,' I said.

'He's quite handsome and he likes to date models, usually, sometimes actresses, if they're up and coming and haven't graduated to dating famous people yet.'

'Oh?'

'He does cause a stir whenever he drops into Wendy's office.' Helen lowered her voice to a whisper and leant towards my ear. 'Had a one-night stand with Samantha once, at the ridiculous divorce party she threw – hence why he and Jim despise each other. Jim wasn't working here then, but when he started seeing Samantha, and he found out about Ed, he wasn't best pleased.'

'Juicy.'

Helen nudged me and nodded in the direction of Jim and Samantha, who were deep in conversation at the end of the table, with her talking into his ear while he smiled.

'Looks like Samantha's whispering sweet nothings,' Helen said.

I laughed. 'Why do you care so much?' I said.

'Once you've had a run-in with Samantha, you'll know why,' she said. 'Nobody has a bad word to say about Jim, but I wouldn't say the same about her. What is he thinking?'

'It might have something to do with the way she looks,' I said.

'Everyone knows she's had work done, and she's quite open about it. Botox, fillers; boob job to celebrate her divorce settlement coming through – you name it.'

'How old do you think she is?'

'At least ten years older than him.'

'So around forty?'

Helen nodded.

'If he was ten years older than her, of course, no one would bat an eyelid,' I said.

'You are right, of course, and, being a bit of a feminist, I should be cheering Samantha on for her cougar skills. It's just that he's wasting his time with her when he could have anyone, what with that lovely smile of his and those kind eyes.'

This was true. 'If I didn't know any better, I'd think you fancied him,' I said.

Helen almost spat out the wine she was drinking. 'Oh, Claire, I'm old enough to be his mother,' she said. 'That really would be taking the age gap too far.'

At that moment, as if he knew we were discussing his love life, Jim looked down the table at me, and I raised my glass of wine and he lifted his drink in return, smiling as if to say, *told you this was a good idea*. Samantha caught him looking and cast a frown in my direction.

'So, you've seen him in a towel. I expect he has a perfect physique?' Helen said.

This wasn't something I could admit to thinking, surely?

'He spends hours rambling and cycling and running and all that, doesn't he?' I said.

'Of course he does. Maybe I'll base my next romantic hero on him. I can't believe that hasn't occurred to me before.' She tapped something into her phone.

The evening flew by, and I consumed more wine than intended for a weeknight. After everyone else had left – including Samantha, to my relief – there remained only me, Jim and Helen, who'd booked a taxi. We waited with her in the car park. The temperature had dropped further, and I pulled up the collar on my jacket and pushed my hands into the pockets.

'Not staying with Samantha tonight then, Jim?' Helen said.

'What's it got to do with you, Helen?' he said curtly.

Her taxi pulled up before she could answer, and she opened the door. 'See you tomorrow, Claire,' she said, climbing in.

We got into the pick-up truck.

'Helen needs to give it a rest,' he said.

'Are you embarrassed about Samantha then?' I said.

'Not at all. I just wish people would find something else to talk about.'

We pulled out of the car park. Then a 4x4 appeared behind us, its headlights beaming through the back window. When we reached the gates at Gatley Hall, I opened them, then Jim drove through and gestured for me to wait for the 4x4 before closing them again.

'Who's in that car?' I said.

'Samantha,' he said.

'You're having a sleepover?'

'I seem to be.'

It was disappointing that we wouldn't be able to chat on the walk back to Rose Cottage. He progressed up the drive and parked and Samantha pulled up beside us. She opened her boot and got out a holdall.

'Evening, Claire,' she said as Jim and I got out of the car.

'Hello, Samantha.'

We all walked along the path behind the Stables, past the bins and then through the rose garden, the pair of them leading, Jim lighting the way with his torch. She reached for his hand, and he took it, and I followed like a third wheel. I longed for a cup of tea and bed.

We stood at our front doors, keys poised, Samantha acting as though I didn't exist as she whispered into Jim's ear and giggled. He laughed and I hoped she wasn't talking about me.

'See you tomorrow, Claire,' Jim said as he and Samantha went inside.

'Goodnight.'

Closing my door behind me, I headed for the kitchen and filled the kettle. Dropping a teabag into a mug, I couldn't shake off why I cared so much about Jim being with Samantha.

I went upstairs and got into bed with the tea and scrolled through my phone. Searching for Jim online, I found he had an Instagram account. He frequently posted photos of Gatley Hall and the surrounding countryside. Samantha had liked the most recent photo, of trees being cut. I scrolled through her grid. There were photos of her children, who looked very sweet, and a few pouty selfies of her as well. Her bio said she'd previously worked in PR in London.

Giggling came from the other side of the wall. Damn that paper-thin wall. This was too much. Getting out of bed, I rolled my duvet into a ball and carried it downstairs with my pillow. It was freezing cold in the living room. After setting an alarm on my phone, I snuggled up as best I could on the sofa and closed my eyes. In the morning I'd talk to Jim about what to do when Samantha stayed. Did he have a spare room? Mine was full of junk and I hoped he wouldn't mind me asking if they could sleep in there next time.

CHAPTER 21

MARGARET

All week, my thoughts were fully occupied with Luca and our next meeting. Despite having seen the chemistry he had with Lady Violet that afternoon, I believed we would continue our romance. I'd think about him when waking up in the morning and before falling asleep each night. Daydreaming about Luca gave me an escape from reality. Lady Violet spent most mornings with him at the gamekeeper's cottage, working on his portrait. The two of them spending so much time in each other's company in such a confined space did not bear thinking about. All I could do was push any jealous feelings away and fill my time with organising and mending Lady Violet's clothes. I counted down the days until my next meeting with Luca by the river. Would he bring egg sandwiches again or would Mrs Marshall use another filling? Would he suggest meeting the following Sunday, perhaps somewhere quieter? What else could he tell me about the magical place called Florence? For I longed to know every last detail about his life and where he was from, language barrier permitting.

On Saturday morning when I entered the laundry room, I had a spring in my step because the next day I'd see Luca again.

Sam was applying polish to a pair of boots and Elsie was folding sheets and placing them into a basket. They stopped talking as soon as they saw me. It was clear they'd been gossiping.

'Did you get the message?' Elsie said.

Had Luca sent another note?

'What message?' I said.

'Mrs Willis said milady wanted you to take her more paints.'

'Oh, did she? Which colours?'

'How should I know?' Elsie said, rolling her eyes and looking at Sam.

'All right, thank you, Elsie,' I said.

Leaving the laundry room, I went upstairs to Lady Violet's boudoir, where a drawer in her writing table contained the tubes I'd bought in the village the previous week. I selected all of the primary colours and black and white. Then I went to fetch my coat from the servants' cloakroom, slipped the tubes of paint into the pockets and fastened the buttons right to the top. The temperature had dropped in recent days, for it was almost October. Before long there would be ice and frost to contend with, and undoubtedly snow.

It was a beautiful day, and the sky was a deep blue with wisps of cloud. A formation of Hun planes passed over and I put my hands over my ears. I was so tired of it all. Entering the bluebell woods, I felt for the tubes of paint in my coat pocket to check they were still there and followed the path to the cottage. Smoke came from the chimney, and I inhaled the scent of burning wood. On reaching the door I was about to knock when, through the window, I saw Lady Violet and Luca, without their clothes, on the chaise longue. They were kissing intensely, and he lay on top of her, his hands running through her hair. She'd taken out the plait I'd spent some time creating that morning, and her golden locks hung loosely around her shoulders. Putting a hand to my mouth, I gasped. The sight of them together like this shocked me to the core. Not only had

Luca said he loved me less than a week earlier, but also Lady Violet, a countess, no less, was committing the act of adultery – and with an Italian POW. What was she thinking? I dreaded to think what action the earl might take if he discovered their affair. Deep down, I'd known this was going to happen, but I had been in denial. I scolded myself for being so deluded. A man like Luca could never love a girl like me.

She wrapped her arms round his neck, pulling him to her, and he ran those beautiful hands up and down the length of her body and they kissed with so much passion, their bodies melting into each other, as they became one. How I wanted to be in her place. Why should Lady Violet have him when she already had an earl for a husband? Fury consumed me right there and then, and I had to stop myself from banging on the door, from interrupting their lovemaking. I wanted to shout out all the thoughts rushing through my mind. *How dare you both do this. I thought you loved me, Luca. What are you thinking, milady?* I considered tapping gently on the door instead, pretending I hadn't seen what they were doing. Would Lady Violet put on her clothes and come to the door as if nothing untoward were going on?

Then a thought occurred to me. Had the message from Elsie been genuine, or did she want me to catch Lady Violet and Luca together? What if Lady Violet had asked for the paints and I was scolded for not bringing them? Would she know I'd been there and seen them? Would she care if I had?

Deciding that I could not allow either of them to be aware of my discovery, I walked away from the gamekeeper's cottage, away from the man I loved as he made love to my mistress. How could I continue to work for Lady Violet with this newfound knowledge? I needed to tell someone, to lessen the pain, but who? I wouldn't want Tom to know about my feelings for Luca and, as Lady Violet's employee, I could not divulge her secret. If only I had a trustworthy friend. Here in Gatley, there was no one to confide in. My only option was to pour any thoughts into my diary when returning to the house. As I closed the gate to the woods and made my way back towards the house, tears flowed down my face so freely they blurred my vision, and I used the sleeve of my coat to brush them away. I stopped by the lake, and the sight of the water was calming. Sitting on a bench, I took a few deep breaths in order to pull myself together. There was no way I'd give Elsie the satisfaction of seeing me in such a state.

Back at the house, I went upstairs to wash my face before returning to the laundry room. Elsie was at the sink, scrubbing an item of clothing with a bar of soap, a look on her face as if butter wouldn't melt. I expected she'd been anticipating my return, eager to see my reaction.

Sam stood beside her. Elsie nudged him and giggled and, doing all I could to ignore her, I undid the rope on the laundry rack and lowered it to remove Lady Violet's blouse. At the ironing table, I pressed the creases out of the fabric. Elsie looked over at me and whispered into Sam's ear. He looked away and I could tell he felt uncomfortable about being part of her attempt to upset me.

'Do you have something to say to me, Elsie?'

'Not at all,' she said.

'I am rather tired of this childish behaviour. If you have something to say, then say it.'

'All right,' she said. 'I just wondered if you saw anything interesting when you took the paints down to the cottage in the woods, that's all.' She shrugged as if she were the most innocent person in all the world.

'What do you mean?' I said.

'Well, a little bird told me that her ladyship is having it orf' – she mimicked an upper-class accent – 'with the POW, would you believe it?'

Now torn between my feelings for Luca and protecting my

mistress, I had to put my fury and hurt to one side and defend Lady Violet.

'I have no idea what you are referring to,' I said.

'Everyone knows they're at it. Sam saw them through the window when he was taking down the firewood.' She hung up the apron she'd been washing. 'And you had no idea, did you? What kind of lady's maid are you, not knowing what your mistress gets up to?'

Sighing, I turned the blouse over to press the other side.

'Didn't you have a thing for him, Margaret? Can't be nice for you, being cast aside like that. And for a countess too.'

Cackling to herself, she opened the door, then closed it firmly behind her as she left the room.

'I'm sorry, Mags,' Sam said. 'I could tell you were in love with him.'

'I can't believe she'd commit adultery,' I said, still not admitting to what I'd seen as it was best not to.

'His lordship has a mistress in London, so she probably doesn't think she's doing anything wrong.'

'Oh, I see,' I said.

Sam left the room and there I was, all alone, tasked with ironing a blouse belonging to the woman who'd taken the man I loved away from me, tears once again streaming down my face.

CHAPTER 22

CLAIRE

The next morning when I left Rose Cottage for work, my head hurt from all the red wine consumed at the Old Fox, and I hadn't slept very well on the sofa. I grabbed a coffee from the Stables and went to my office. Opening my notebook, I reread Margaret's letter. What should my next step be? And how was I supposed to find out where Tabitha was? Perhaps finding out who she was would be a good start.

Picking up an old edition of the Gatley Hall guidebook, published in 1985, I found a section about the servants and their quarters and was pleased to see a floor plan. These rooms included the housekeeper's parlour, where I worked, the kitchen, the servants' hall, the laundry room, the still room and the butler's pantry. The staff and volunteers at Gatley Hall were the modern-day version of the servants from its past, and I tried to picture the house back in the 1940s. Like in all country houses, male servants would have been limited.

Turning the pages, I saw photos of the servants' hall and kitchen in the late 1930s. There were footmen in their livery from 1939 and a housemaid in her dress with apron, hat and black stockings. Gardeners with their tools from 1935. There

were three different housekeepers, including the one in charge
from 1935 to 1945: Mrs Willis, and her husband, the butler, Mr
Willis. I recalled seeing them in the photo of the servants in
front of the Christmas tree. Tabitha Willis had to be their
daughter, surely? But then why did Margaret want to find her?
Mrs Willis looked to be at least in her fifties though, and this
made me wonder if they'd adopted Tabitha. The Willises lived
at Rose Cottage, but from the photo, where they stood outside
the front door my cottage and Jim's were joined together as one.

But there was no information in the guidebook about
Tabitha or Margaret. Then I remembered Helen mentioning
the website and logged on to my computer. There was a photo
of a Spitfire with 'Violet' written on the side, a pilot standing in
front of it, proudly wearing his uniform.

Then there it was: a picture of Thomas and Margaret Bates
on their wedding day, 1 November 1945, at Leatherhead
Register Office. They were both smiling and she held a bouquet
of flowers. He wore a navy-blue RAF uniform with shirt and tie
and wings on the lapel. Her surname had been Anderson rather
than Bates in the letter so she must have married again at some
stage.

The photo was accompanied by an article from the *Surrey
Standard*.

Love Story at Gatley Hall

*Former chauffeur, Thomas Bates, married former lady's maid,
Margaret Bartlett, at Leatherhead Register Office last week.
They met while working at Gatley Hall and she wrote to him
every day while he flew fighter jets over France, Italy and
Germany. Congratulations to the happy couple!*

Could Tabitha be their daughter, conceived before Thomas
went to fight or when he was on leave? And did Mr and Mrs

Willis adopt her because Thomas and Margaret weren't yet married? Would Margaret have lost touch with her if this was the case though? It really was a mystery.

When I got back to Rose Cottage after work, I sat at the table in the kitchen with a glass of wine and looked around the place. I could make it feel more like home. Taking my notepad, I started to sketch a plan of the house and drew out things that could be added – in the living room, a couple of lamps, a rug, some cushions and a throw. In the kitchen, I could buy a cheap sideboard to put a lamp and candles on, and the blind desperately needed replacing. Upstairs, I'd get a new shower curtain, and plants would brighten up the bathroom. In the bedroom, replacing the musty old curtains would make a real difference and an eiderdown would look nice on the bed. Making the house look better would be uplifting and help me get over all I'd been through in the past few months.

Finding myself doodling in the corner of the page, I looked down to see a small flower with petals. I began to colour them in with my biro, one at a time, finding the activity strangely therapeutic. I'd been really into drawing, and painting, once. When I did art at A level, my teacher said I had real talent. The pressure of completing coursework had taken the fun out of it though and I'd lost interest, as it made art more of a chore than something you did for fun.

Jim came through the front door, a towel wrapped round his waist. His appearance made me jump out of my daydream world.

'How are you, Claire?'

'What happened to the dressing gown?' I said.

'Samantha spilled a cup of tea down it this morning, so it's in the wash as we speak.'

'Well, hopefully it will be clean and ready to wear again soon.'

'Did you enjoy last night in the end?' he said.

'Well, you certainly did.'

He ruffled his hair at the front, seemingly unaware of how hot he looked when he did this. 'What do you mean by that, exactly?'

'The wall between our bedrooms is paper-thin and I had to sleep on the sofa because Mike left the spare room in a right mess. There's a tired-looking mattress leaning against the wall and there are random boxes everywhere. We need a plan for what to do when one of us has an overnight guest.'

'Oh sorry, I hadn't thought about that. Mike used to stay at his girlfriend's, and he never said anything about my visitors. To be fair to Mike, I think your spare room was like that when he moved in. You could get a bed to go in there, perhaps?'

'You expect me to move rooms whenever Samantha stays over?'

He shrugged. 'My spare room is set up as an office and there's no space for a bed.'

I could get a bed in my spare room, I supposed, but why should I?

'How have you found your first week here?' Jim said.

'It's taken some getting used to, but I made a bit of headway with the Below Stairs project today.'

'What did you find?'

I told him about the photos in the guidebook and the article about Margaret and Tom's wedding day but there was still so much to find out.

'You'll get there, I'm sure,' he said. Standing up, he tightened the towel round his waist. 'Right, I'd better get on and have a shower.' The prospect of spending yet another evening alone didn't appeal and, as he went upstairs, I considered asking him to have a glass of wine with me. Maybe I could rustle up some pasta with whatever was in the fridge.

Opening the fridge door, I peered into the salad drawer: half a pepper, an onion, a handful of mushrooms. What I really needed was bacon, then I could use the jar of pesto sauce in the cupboard to make my speciality. Jim might have a few rashers in his fridge. The running water above me stopped, and before long he came downstairs.

'Fancy a glass of wine before you go?' I said.

'Sure, what have you got?'

Was he looking for company too?

'A bottle of Australian Shiraz.'

'Sounds good to me.'

He pulled up a chair at the table, and I filled tumblers for us both. I still needed to buy wine glasses. That might be a way to pass time at the weekend. Was there a kitchen shop in Dorking? I wanted to get nice ones though, to invest in this new little home of my own.

'Sorry I don't have wine glasses yet,' I said, sitting down.

'I almost prefer this. In France, they use tumblers all the time for wine.' He took a sip and his appreciative nod and slight smile implied that he approved.

A knock came at the front door, making me jump.

'Well, I have no idea who that is,' I said.

I got up and went to open the door. To my horror, Miles was standing there, a paper bag tucked under one arm from the fancy deli he liked. Oh no. I wasn't up to seeing Miles. This was going to be awkward, especially with Jim dressed only in a towel. Tightening my grip on the door handle, I said, 'What are you doing here?'

'I just happened to be in the area,' he said, throwing me his best smile.

'Sure you were.'

He frowned. 'Aren't you going to let me in?'

'How did you find my cottage?'

'A lady in an ATP fleece was very helpful. Said she knew you.'

'You should have called first.'

'I did, but there was no answer. Have you muted me or something?'

When he'd kept calling the day before, I'd hidden alerts from his phone number and must have forgotten to switch them back on. I stood there, looking at him, not knowing what to say.

He held up the paper bag. 'Brought your favourite.'

'What is it?'

He rolled his eyes. Miles was a keen eye-roller.

'You know. Coq au vin, with mash.'

Although I liked this dish, the sauce and the mash were too rich and salty, and packed with butter and cream. I'd always pretended this was my favourite, because it was his. Looking back, how could I have been so foolish, letting him run my life like that? I'd often wanted to do everything to please him for an easy life as otherwise he could get moody. Miles was one of those people who liked to exercise the silent treatment when they didn't get what they wanted. Now we'd spent some time apart, this was becoming clear to me.

But now he was here, and I could hardly tell him to go home. We might as well eat what he'd brought. Maybe he could have a glass of wine, and we'd work our way towards some kind of closure.

'I'll be off then,' Jim's voice came from behind me.

Damn, this was awkward.

Miles and I moved aside and Jim went past. He gave my ex a polite and unsmiling nod as he unlocked his front door. In return, Miles threw him one of those looks he gave men when they showed any interest in me – it had always irritated him – and stepped over the threshold into my cottage. Closing the door behind him, he scrunched up his face in that way he did when he was not happy.

'Who was that?'

'Jim, the ranger who lives next door,' I said, in an upbeat voice.

'What was he doing here, and dressed only in a towel?'

'He was taking a shower.'

'Doesn't he have his own shower?'

I shook my head. 'His is broken.'

'Well, he needs to get it fixed, and soon. He can't wander into your house half-dressed whenever he likes. Do you want me to arrange for a plumber to go round there?'

Goodness, he was so concerned about another man's presence in my home when he'd allowed me to leave our flat without even helping me to put my things in the car!

'He's got someone coming over next week,' I said, heading into the kitchen.

'It shouldn't take that long to find one, especially somewhere like this.'

'Somewhere like this?'

'There's hardly anyone living in this village, is there? Can't be that much demand in the middle of nowhere.'

After only a few days in Gatley, I found myself wanting to defend the countryside but decided to bite my tongue.

Following me, Miles handed over the paper bag. The coq au vin was presented in beautiful white cardboard trays with matching lids, and I put them in the fridge. Jim would be pleased to see the absence of plastic, although the meal had probably cost Miles a small fortune. Why was I thinking about Jim's potential opinion of my dinner?

'Fancy a glass of wine?' I said.

'I'm driving but will have one small glass.'

He pulled out the chair where Jim had been sitting and looked at me as I picked up the half-empty tumbler and took it to the sink.

'So, he was having a drink with you as well as taking the liberty of using your shower?'

Taking the liberty was one of Miles's favourite phrases, and I hadn't missed it.

'We were discussing a work matter, that's all.' Why should I have to compose a lie and defend myself? Miles and I weren't together anymore. It shouldn't matter who was in my house.

Filling a clean tumbler for Miles, I joined him at the table.

'No wine glasses yet?' he said.

Shaking my head, I said, 'Nope. So, why are you here then?'

He sipped the wine and grimaced. 'What is this?'

He liked expensive wine and it always had to be French. No other country was capable of producing decent wine, apparently.

'Australian Shiraz. Don't complain.'

'Oh. I miss you, Claire.'

He studied me with those brown puppy-dog eyes, a move that used to work but now it seemed kind of pathetic. Emboldened by having consumed a couple of glasses of wine, I said, 'How can you mean that, after everything that's happened?'

He laughed, but I didn't see what was so funny about the way things had ended between us.

'I know. Stupid, isn't it?'

'Are you asking me to come back?' A part of me wanted him to say yes, for the ego boost more than anything else.

Inhaling, he said, 'I wouldn't exactly say that. Yet. Have you missed me?'

'I've missed your company, but moving out was the right decision,' I said, wanting to see his reaction. 'We're not meant to be together, are we?'

'It doesn't feel over though.' He finished his wine. 'I need a few more glasses of this wine so I can't tell how bad it is.'

'Aren't you driving, though?'

He looked me in the eye. 'Can I stay?'

'What do you mean?'

Placing his hand on mine, he said, 'Please, Claire Bear?'

This was what he called me when he wanted something, a

pet name I'd never been sure about. I got up, switched on the oven and removed the coq au vin from the fridge.

He put his tumbler on the counter and came up behind me and put his arms round my waist.

'Can I stay, please?'

He gently pulled me round to face him and leant in to kiss me on the lips. I'd missed this side of being with him. I threw my arms round his neck and he hugged me tightly. My heart had begun to mend since leaving him and sleeping together would open up those feelings again, like losing in a game of Snakes and Ladders. Since being at Gatley Hall, I'd made it a little way up that board.

Refilling his glass, I said, 'Okay, you can stay.'

I put the coq au vin in the oven, and we returned to the table with the rest of the bottle of wine.

CHAPTER 23

MARGARET

After seeing my mistress and Luca in flagrante delicto, my heart was truly broken. Later, while helping Lady Violet get ready for bed, I couldn't look at her and performed my duties as quickly and efficiently as possible, desperate to go to my own room. I selected her dress for the following day and hung it on the handle of the wardrobe.

Picking up on my less than cheery demeanour, she said, 'Are you quite all right, Maggie?'

Putting a hand to my forehead, I said, 'I haven't been sleeping very well and have a little headache, that's all, milady.'

'Oh well, the damn planes don't help, do they? You must get yourself to bed and let's hope you have a better night. Off you go.'

'All right, thank you.'

She dismissed me with a wave, and I went to my room, lifted the mattress to take out my diary and sat at the writing table. Grateful to Aunt Edith for introducing me to a way of dealing with my emotions, I began to write about what I'd seen at the gamekeeper's cottage. All I could do was try to diminish

my anger with them both; life at Gatley Hall was already difficult enough.

On Sunday I didn't go to meet Luca, and was surprised when
Sam brought me a message from him asking where I'd been. So,
Luca wasn't aware that I knew about his affair with Lady Violet.
How dare he expect to court me as well! I didn't reply and that
was that. Not only had I lost the man I loved, but what would
occupy my thoughts now? Luca, with his stories of the magical
place he came from and his supposed love for me, had given me
an escape – and, more importantly, hope. How many women
had he declared his love for, I wondered. Now I had to face the
sheer reality that a war was taking place around me. As well as
the brave men who were fighting on our behalf, innocent civil-
ians were being killed every day.

Because of this war, I was working as a servant. Women in
my family going back generations had been domestics, and I'd
been so proud to break the cycle as a shopgirl. It didn't seem fair
that I'd had to give that up.

Guilt consumed me for having such selfish thoughts, for
there were people far worse off. I didn't have to contend with
food rationing, for a start. And servants beneath me performed
lowlier tasks. Men had no choice but to go and fight. Everyone
was losing relatives, and I'd counted myself lucky until Mother
wrote in November to inform me that Mildred's husband, Jack,
had been killed in action in North Africa. Aunt Edith and I
went to St Andrew's, and we knelt and prayed for my brother-
in-law. They had only been married for a few years and now
Mildred was a widow, and her children would grow up without
a father. This news shocked me so greatly, bringing the war
close to home, and I told myself to count my blessings.

Lady Violet continued to spend a great deal of time at the
gamekeeper's cottage and I did my best to pretend that nothing

was happening between her and Luca. Elsie did not make my life easy, and used every opportunity to bring me down with her snarky little comments, often made in the laundry room. House-maids and kitchen maids would look the other way when they passed me in corridors, for she had turned them all against me. There was nowhere else for me to press Lady Violet's clothes, and so Elsie's treatment of me was something I had to endure. My only friends were Tom, and Sam – when Elsie was not in the same room. I had never felt so lonely in all my life, and would often cry myself to sleep at night. Whenever anyone below stairs mentioned the scandalous affair, I told them it was merely a rumour started by someone spiteful. Despite my broken heart, it was still my duty to defend my mistress.

Christmas came, and Mr and Mrs Willis decided that we should not allow the war to stop us from celebrating. Mr Carter, aided by Tom and Sam, chopped down a pine tree in the woods and placed it in the grand hall. Us servants decorated it with ornaments passed down the Gatley family for generations with the wireless playing Christmas carols. We sang along to 'Hark the Herald Angels Sing' and 'O Come All Ye Faithful' as we worked, and by the time we'd finished, the tree looked rather pretty. The earl arranged for a man from the *Surrey Standard* to take photographs of him and Lady Violet, and all of us servants as well. The photographer arranged us in rows in front of the Christmas tree. I was positioned next to Elsie. We had to stand there for at least half an hour, and she kept nudging and pushing me and whispering things in my ear about Luca and Lady Violet. She was an awful person but I tried not to allow her childish behaviour to affect me.

On Christmas Day, we all walked into the village to attend a service at St Andrew's, and I dropped in to see Aunt Edith before she went to have lunch with her next-door neighbour.

Back at the house, Mrs Downside prepared a goose for the servants, followed by a sumptuous pudding, and we ate like kings and queens in the servants' hall. Even Elsie didn't give me any trouble, and I was thankful. Of course, it was also the day that Tom turned eighteen, and we all sang 'Happy Birthday'. Before too long, he'd be going to fight for his country. I would greatly miss my only ally at Gatley Hall.

After lunch we listened to the king deliver his Christmas message on the wireless, and it was rather sobering. He spoke about all the children who were separated from their parents, some of them having been sent as far away as Canada and Australia. I'd been fortunate to experience a childhood uninterrupted by war, with both of my parents and my sisters, and I scolded myself once more for being so ungrateful about my circumstances. All of us sat quietly as we listened, and his words, 'We must hold fast to the spirit which binds us together now' resonated with me. My only way forward was to do everything I could to face this adversity with all the strength I had inside me. Afterwards, everyone went quietly about their business; the power of the king's words had clearly given us something to think about.

When January arrived, it was a struggle to keep warm. Snow settled, inches deep, in the grounds and surrounding fields, and a thick sheet of ice covered the lake. But the days became longer and, although the snow remained and the temperature was below freezing, spring didn't seem too far away. As we reached the end of the month, I longed to experience Gatley Hall in all its glory, to see daffodils and crocuses and snowdrops and the bluebells in the woods. I'd heard the rose garden was quite a sight when all the flowers started to bloom and their perfume was intoxicating. Oh, to leave the house without a coat, hat, scarf and gloves! And to go for a walk without snow seeping into one's boots, or being at risk of slipping on the ice.

One afternoon, after her nap, Lady Violet asked me to

take a seat in her boudoir. Her face was pale, as it had often been of late, and her mouth was set in a firm line. I wondered if she'd received bad news about a relative. Had something happened to the earl in London? Maybe he was leaving her for his mistress? Was she about to dismiss me for some misdemeanour I'd committed unknowingly? Had she worked out that I knew of her affair with Luca? Since witnessing their lovemaking, I'd found it hard to look her in the eye for some time, but as the days passed my anger lessened. How could she know I'd been in love with him? And why would he choose me over a woman with her status and beauty? My only option was to try to forgive her, and perhaps one day the whole episode would become a distant memory. Mother, a regular churchgoer, had always told me that people who committed adultery were evil. I didn't always agree with her views, but her voice often filled my head, and it wasn't easy to ignore it. I could see why Lady Violet and Luca had become lovers. The earl was continually absent, and everyone knew about his mistress. When he was present, he barely gave Lady Violet any attention. And I knew myself how it would be almost impossible to resist Luca's advances. If he'd asked to make love to me – before marriage being another sin that would horrify Mother – I'd have allowed him to. Therefore I had some sympathy for Lady Violet, who, despite her privileged life, seemed rather lost. And so, I turned a blind eye to what was going on down at the gamekeeper's cottage and tried to carry on as best I could.

'Maggie, I have something to tell you,' Lady Violet said.

Was she going to reveal all?

'I shall no longer be going to the gamekeeper's cottage, for I have rather gone off painting.'

Was the affair over? How I hoped this were true. 'All right,' I said. 'Will that be all, milady?'

'I have rather gone off riding as well.'

'And so what will you be doing with your time, milady, if you don't mind my asking?'

'Doctor Baxter has advised me to get plenty of rest, so I shall mainly be reading and writing letters. I am with child, Maggie.'

Although this was highly likely, I was taken aback by her revelation.

'That is wonderful news. I am sure you and his lordship are delighted.'

'Come on, Maggie. We both know I haven't just been painting down at the gamekeeper's cottage, don't we?'

She made eye contact and I found myself looking away, trying to find the right words. An uncomfortable silence fell between us. I was just beginning to get past the affair, and now this.

'Do we?' I said, finally meeting her gaze.

She sighed and raised her eyebrows. Beating around the bush was no use. Evidently, she wished to have a frank conversation with me.

'So, the child is Luca's?' I said.

'Charles has been married twice before and never conceived an heir. His mistresses have not produced a child either, and so one must conclude that he is not capable in that department, mustn't one, Maggie?'

I nodded. 'One must. Is his lordship aware of this... development?' I said.

'No, he certainly is not, and we mustn't tell him. When I become large enough for people to notice, we shall go to Headley House.' I knew this was a holiday home inherited from her father, on the Suffolk coast. 'It's beautiful there by the sea and I'm sure you'll like it very much. We can properly escape,' she said, her eyes lighting up as if we were going on a grand adventure. 'And once the baby is born, if it's a boy, I shall tell Charles, and try to persuade him to accept the child as his heir. His cousin is an increasing threat and I'm sure he would be accommodating. If the baby is a girl, well, I'll have to think of something.'

'Is that the best plan, milady?'

'Did you think I would become another one of Charles's wives to be cast aside because I could not produce an heir?' she said, her voice steely. 'Do you know that his mother has played a part in him doing so? Would I really allow him to take my money, inherited from my father? If the baby is a girl, I shall keep trying until we have a boy. That's my plan, and I'm sticking to it. And Luca must not find out. The fool thinks I am in love with him.'

From the way she said this, I suspected that Luca was in love with her, and this made me envious indeed. He was not just saying those words to her, as he had with me.

'Very well.'

'We shall leave on the first day of February. My condition may be impossible to hide by then. The servants at Headley House will keep my secret, for their loyalties lie with me.'

Knowing all this, I found it impossible to sleep at night. I was being entrusted with keeping a damaging secret from everyone I knew. I could not even tell Tom. If Elsie found out the truth, Lady Violet would be finished. Once again, the only place I could pour out my thoughts and feelings was in my diary, and I continued to keep it well hidden under my mattress. As Lady Violet put on weight, I added panels into several of her dresses. Towards the end of January the rest of the household was informed that her ladyship wished to take an extended holiday at her house by the sea. She was tired of the sound of the planes and hoped it might be quieter in Suffolk.

A few days before we were due to depart, Tom came to find me in the laundry room while I was removing a tea stain from one of Lady Violet's dresses with a bar of soap. He was beaming from ear to ear.

'I wanted you to be the first to know. I'm leaving, tomorrow,' he said.

'Oh, Tom, I'm thrilled for you, but I shall miss you very much.'

'Thank you, Mags. I've never been more excited. They're going to train me as an engineer. Learning how to fix cars has stood me in good stead and they were impressed with my knowledge.'

He seemed so glad to be accepted, as if he'd won some kind of prize, and I didn't want to dampen his spirits; but it was more than likely that he would be killed. The thought of him dying, and at such a young age, horrified me, but I cast it aside, holding on to the belief that he would return in one piece.

'That is wonderful news,' I said.

'Will you write to me, Mags?'

'Of course I will. Every day.'

And so, not only was I leaving Gatley Hall, albeit temporarily, Tom was leaving too. I'd miss our friendship but hoped one day we'd get to spend time together again. I was glad to be going to Suffolk with Lady Violet, as being at Gatley Hall without Tom's presence would have been even more arduous. Getting away from Elsie and her influence on the other servants would be a welcome break. Nobody at Headley House would be able to resent me for taking their job as she had, and I hoped to find someone there to talk to and spend time with when I wasn't attending to Lady Violet's needs.

CHAPTER 24

MARGARET

We made the journey to Suffolk by train, and I travelled in a first-class carriage with Lady Violet. The seats were more comfortable than what I was used to, and we were served tea and biscuits on our journey. It was a rather enjoyable way to travel. When we arrived at Seamouth station the Headley House butler, Mr Shaw, collected us in a horse and trap and took us to a grand Georgian house, painted white, on the seafront in Seamouth. I went to the servants' hall in the basement and Mr Shaw introduced me to everyone. As it was a smaller household than Gatley Hall, a woman called Mrs Bentley acted as both housekeeper and cook, and she was assisted by housemaid, Louise. A young man called John worked as an underbutler. They all stood up, smiling, and shook my hand; it was a much warmer welcome than at Gatley Hall. At Headley House, it turned out, I was expected to dine with Lady Violet. We were tired and hungry from our journey and Louise brought steaming bowls of broth to the drawing room, where a full-length portrait of Lady Violet's father dominated one wall. Afterwards, Mrs Bentley showed us to our rooms. Mine was next to Lady Violet's and we both had sea views. I seemed to have landed on my feet once again with such luxurious accommodation.

Although Suffolk was milder than Surrey, with no sign of recent snow, the temperature was still fairly chilly. The warmest and most delightful room was the library, crammed with books that had belonged to Lady Violet's father. A large bay window brought light onto the gold carpet, and we were blessed with an uninterrupted view of the North Sea. The cawing of seagulls and the crashing of waves against rocks provided our soundtrack, and we'd sit facing the sea while a fire roared in the hearth.

Before long, Lady Violet and I had established a daily routine of breakfast in the drawing room, a walk along the promenade, and then tea in the library before luncheon in the drawing room. Seamouth was of course impacted by the war and we couldn't go on the beaches because of barbed wire and mines. After luncheon, Lady Violet would have a nap, and then we'd return to the library for the rest of the day. She read novels and I wrote letters to Mother, Mildred, Joan, Aunt Edith and Tom. Tom was at RAF Dunsfold, a base near Guildford, and as promised I wrote to him daily, regardless of whether or not he sent a reply. His friendship had brought me comfort in those early days at Gatley Hall, and I felt a responsibility to do the same in return.

Lady Violet began to put on a great deal of weight, and I added more panels to her dresses. Her demeanour changed and she was no longer the bright and cheerful young woman I'd met when I arrived at Gatley Hall. She was tired all the time, and would no longer go anywhere alone. This meant that I became more of a companion than a lady's maid. We spent most of the time together, and often talked for hours.

One morning, after writing my letters and with no sewing to do, I found myself looking out of the window at the sea, wondering how far away the nearest German submarine might be. Lady Violet was reading and she looked up.

'Are you idling, Maggie?' she said.

'I have run out of tasks, and could go to post my letters, but that can wait until later.'

'I have never seen you read,' she said, lifting up her novel.

Reading was a pastime for those who could afford to buy books, and, although I'd borrowed books from friends and relatives when I was younger, I hadn't read a novel for a while.

'I don't have any books at my disposal, milady.'

She laughed. 'Well, look around you and take any book you like. I recommend you develop a love of reading while we're here, because there are times when it might just save you.'

Was reading doing that for her?

'What do you mean?'

'Getting lost in a fictional world can be an escape, and, if you're like me, I'm sure you have many thoughts rushing through your mind about what we are living through.'

'What do you recommend?' I said.

'I am rereading *A Room with a View*, by E.M. Forster. I lived in Tuscany for a few months when I turned eighteen and it is wonderful to escape there in this novel. Forster is one of my favourite authors and I long to return to Tuscany when this war is over. It's about a group of English people living in Florence, where in fact Luca is from, and I shall lend it to you. In the meantime, I suggest you select a Dickens. You can't go wrong with *Great Expectations* or *A Tale of Two Cities*, I say.'

I got up and went over to the shelves. As the books were organised alphabetically by author name, I soon found *A Tale of Two Cities*, and sat down to read it. The opening line, 'It was the best of times, it was the worst of times', could not have resonated more for me and Lady Violet. Here we were in a room with a wonderful view of the sea but living through a war. Those days in Seamouth were some of the easiest I'd experienced, slow-paced and fulfilling both mentally and physically. Walking along the promenade, tasting the salt on my lips and breathing clean air into my lungs, meant I slept well every night. My love affair with reading began that day in the library, and Lady Violet gave me a gift that would last a lifetime.

As the weeks passed and we counted down the time until the baby was due in July, Lady Violet's stomach grew so large that she looked fit to burst. One afternoon, she received a telegram notifying her of a favourite cousin being killed in action, and she cried every day for the rest of that week. The war had properly intruded on her life for the first time. Being with child, her emotions were further heightened. She seemed more vulnerable, and I empathised, having lost my brother-in-law to the war. My role became that of a surrogate mother on occasion. And the more time we spent together, the more she confided in me.

One morning we were sitting on a bench while Lady Violet rested during a walk along the promenade, and she said out of the blue, 'Does your mother love you, Maggie?'

'Yes, of course she does.'

'Mine doesn't. She's a cold, hard woman. I was brought up by a nanny and a governess, and she had no interest in me whatsoever.'

My parents had been warm and loving, and I was grateful.

'Do you think I'll be a good mother, despite this?' she said.

'Absolutely, any child would be fortunate to have you as their mother.'

'Your words are reassuring, but I hope you're not saying that because I'm your mistress?'

I shook my head. Indeed, I believed that she had much love to give to a child. 'Not at all.'

'I hope you're right. My father was kind to me, but he spent a lot of time in London and then he died suddenly, shortly before I married Charles.'

'Oh, I'm sorry to hear that. My father died a few years ago as well.'

She squeezed my arm. 'Losing a parent is quite a shock to the system, isn't it?'

'Very much so,' I said, feeling awkward. She was confiding in me more than someone of her status usually would, but I supposed she had no one else to talk to in Seamouth.

'I don't love Charles,' she said.

'No?'

'That's why I was so drawn to Luca, well, apart from the need to produce an heir. Who could resist such a beautiful man?'

What could I say?

'The earl is quite repulsive without his clothes, Maggie, and almost twenty years older than me. When he and I make love – if one can call it that – I cannot look at him and it's more of an endurance than a pleasure. Whereas Luca has a physique like the statue of David in Florence, with his broad shoulders and muscular legs. As a young woman, I'm sure you know what I'm talking about, Maggie? Michelangelo could have used Luca as a model for his statue if he'd been alive then, I'm sure.'

While I had to pretend to be unmoved by her mention of Luca, conversations like these brought Lady Violet and me closer, and I enjoyed our time together in Seamouth. One might say we developed a friendship during those weeks while we waited for the baby to arrive.

As the days grew longer and lighter, we'd often walk to the end of the promenade before supper, then sit on a bench by the lighthouse so Lady Violet could rest. She was carrying a great deal of weight now and her ankles were constantly swollen. We'd inhale the sea air and admire the view that lay before us and discuss the books we were reading.

.   .   .

One afternoon, as we walked back to the house, Lady Violet clutched her stomach and cried out.

'What is it?' I said, but then, seeing a clear fluid drip onto her shoes from beneath her dress, I had my answer. Her waters had broken.

She screamed, then took a breath and seemed to wait for the pain to pass.

'These contractions are immense, Maggie, like big waves rolling right through me,' she said through gritted teeth. 'The baby is coming. Get me back to the house, and ask Mr Shaw to call the doctor. Pray for me and let's hope it is a boy.'

CHAPTER 25

MARGARET

Mr Shaw telephoned the doctor, and Mrs Bentley helped me take Lady Violet up to her bedroom and change into her night-gown. Louise brought hot water and towels.

'The doctor is on his way,' she said, before leaving the room.

'I'm scared, Maggie,' Lady Violet said.

Pressing a damp cloth against her forehead, I said, 'Everything will be all right, milady, you'll see.' A knock came at the door, and the doctor entered with his briefcase.

'You may go now,' he said to me, and I left the room, hoping Lady Violet would give birth to the boy she wanted.

Downstairs, in the servants' hall, Mrs Bentley, Mr Shaw, Louise, John and I prayed while we waited.

'I've known her since she was born,' Mrs Bentley said. 'A lovely little girl she was.'

None of us knew what to do with ourselves. After dinner, we played cards into the night. Eventually, the doctor came into the servants' hall.

'It's a healthy baby girl,' he said, with a smile.

'Delightful news,' Mr Shaw said.

'Can I go up and see her?' I said.

'You can indeed.'

Lady Violet's bedroom was lit by a lamp on her nightstand and the curtains were drawn. The wind whistled outside and waves crashed against the shore, and it seemed a storm was brewing. But the baby was here, and so I didn't take this as a sign of anything ominous to come.

Lady Violet was sitting up in bed, propped by pillows, and she held her daughter in her arms. The baby, who was beautiful, had a head of thick dark hair, like Luca, and was wrapped in a blanket. Her eyes were closed, and she was sleeping.

'Congratulations, milady,' I said.

Looking up at me, she gave a faint smile. I couldn't begin to imagine what she was feeling. Exhausted, but also torn between being delighted at giving birth to such a beautiful daughter and disappointed because she'd needed a boy.

'I'd like to call her Tabitha, after my grandmother,' she said, softly.

'All right.'

'Oh, but I need a middle name. It should give a nod to her father – but what is the female equivalent of Luca, Maggie?'

'I'm not sure there is one.'

She thought for a moment. 'It would be nice if it were Italian, don't you agree, Maggie?'

Nodding, and playing along, I said, 'Yes.'

'What about Lucia? That's about as close to Luca as one can get, and after Lucy Honeychurch in *A Room with a View.*'

'A lovely choice. I shall pass the information on to Mr Shaw and Mrs Bentley. Now, you need to get some rest,' I said.

'Put her in the crib, will you, Maggie?'

She handed the baby to me and, carefully, I took her, so very light and small, like a doll, and I laid her down carefully in the wooden crib.

Lady Violet took my hand and squeezed it. 'You must listen to me, Maggie. If I don't make it—'

'What on earth are you talking about? Your work is done now and it's time to get some well-earned rest.'

She shook her head. 'If I die, I want you to do these things for me.'

'Don't be ridiculous,' I said.

'Maggie!' She was almost shouting now.

'What would you like me to do?' I said, humouring her.

'Firstly, ask Mrs Bentley to call Mrs Willis about giving Tabitha a home. Mrs Willis and I talked about the possibility of adoption if the baby was a girl, so I could have her close to me at Gatley Hall.'

'All right,' I said, surprised but also relieved that Mrs Willis was aware of the situation.

'And Luca must not know that Tabitha is his daughter. He wasn't aware of my pregnancy and he has a life waiting for him back in Florence. His father is a baker and Luca is engaged to the daughter of another baker in the city. Their families plan to merge businesses when he gets married.'

I had no idea Luca was engaged. To think his poor fiancée would have no idea about what he'd been up to with Lady Violet.

'Very well,' I said.

'When you get back to Gatley Hall, take my emerald brooch from the safe – you know, the one my mother gave to me on my wedding day.'

'I can't do that.'

'Promise me you'll do it. You must give the brooch to Tabitha on her wedding day. This will be my dying wish and I expect you to adhere to it.'

'You are not dying, milady.'

'Just agree, won't you?'

I nodded, tears pricking my eyes. Surely she was just over-tired and deluded.

Lady Violet closed her eyes, and I went downstairs. Mr Shaw poured all of us a glass of brandy and gave a toast to celebrate the happy news. Nobody mentioned that the earl was not the father and that the baby was not a boy. That would all have to be dealt with the next day for everyone was immensely tired.

An hour or so later, Louise went to check on Lady Violet and the baby, and when she rushed back into the servants' hall her face was pale.

'Whatever is the matter, Louise?' Mrs Bentley said.

'Lady Violet... I think she is dead,' she said.

No, this could not be true. I swallowed and a wave of nausea swept over me.

'Surely she is asleep and you are mistaken, dear girl,' Mrs Bentley said.

'I felt her pulse, Mrs Bentley,' Louise said.

'All right, I'll go and see for myself. What nonsense.' Mrs Bentley went upstairs. She returned a few minutes later.

'Telephone the doctor will you, Mr Shaw. Sadly, I think Louise is right. Her ladyship is no longer with us.'

I burst into tears, and Mrs Bentley handed me a handkerchief. Lady Violet had been right after all and I hadn't believed her. I should have been with her when she took those last breaths.

'This is most upsetting for us all,' she said. 'But' – ever the housekeeper, she continued – 'one must be practical and we shall all need to wear black now this house is in mourning. Tomorrow, we shall all go to St Matthew's together and pray for our beloved Lady Violet.'

I had failed in my duty as lady's maid and guilt consumed me. Why hadn't I listened and provided comfort during her last moments? Mr Shaw refilled our glasses with generous measures of brandy to help with the shock, and I downed mine in one go. All I could do was fulfil Lady Violet's dying wishes: ask Mrs Bentley to arrange for Mr and Mrs Willis to adopt the baby and call her Tabitha Lucia. Taking the brooch from her safe at Gatley Hall could be tricky, especially as my job was now redundant, but it would be my responsibility to get that brooch into Tabitha's hands.

CHAPTER 26

MARGARET

Mr and Mrs Willis were delighted to be asked to adopt Tabitha and Mrs Bentley made all the arrangements. Mrs Willis concocted a story about her niece dying in childbirth and said no one would suspect a thing. Mr Shaw telephoned the earl to inform him that, sadly, Lady Violet had died from influenza. Butlers tended to be good at delivering bad news in an expert way. After the call, Mr Shaw reported that the earl had been practical in his response to the news and they had discussed arrangements relating to the return of Lady Violet's body to Gatley for the funeral. She would be buried at St Andrew's along with other members of his family, as was tradition.

Not only did I have to deal with losing Lady Violet so suddenly after we had become friends, but also I had been left without a job. Once again, I'd need to lean on Aunt Edith and, after informing her of what had happened – sticking to the official line of Lady Violet dying of influenza – I asked to stay while I was working out what to do.

After that, I telephoned Mrs Willis to discuss collecting my belongings from Gatley Hall.

Mrs Willis said, 'But where will you go, Margaret?'

'I'll stay with my aunt while seeking another position,' I said.

'You have been through a great deal, and Mrs Bentley said you performed your role superbly in Seamouth. You were a friend to her ladyship in her time of need, and you should be very proud.'

'Thank you, Mrs Willis. It has been a trying time.'

'I would like to offer you the position of nanny, living in, at Rose Cottage with Mr Willis, myself, Tabitha and a wet nurse.'

Staying with Aunt Edith would mean sleeping on a mattress on the floor in Lilian's bedroom, whereas at Rose Cottage I'd have a bed as well as paid work.

'I'll take it,' I said.

'Jolly good. Mr Shaw will bring the baby here by car, with Mrs Bentley and a wet nurse. I suggest you take the train to avoid arousing suspicion as regards to Tabitha's parentage.'

'All right.'

Before leaving, I went into Lady Violet's bedroom. Her body had already been removed and would be taken to Gatley, as requested by the earl. Seeing *A Room with a View* on her nightstand, I went to pick it up. Should I take it? Would Lady Violet want me to have it? She had said I should read it after her. It would be a keepsake, to remind me of our days in the library; and, as she'd suggested, I would learn more about Florence. Despite what had happened with Luca, I still dreamt of visiting one day, after the war was over. I picked up the novel and went to put it in my suitcase, then descended the stairs. Mr Shaw would take me to the station in the horse and trap and soon I'd be back at Gatley Hall again.

I took the train back to Gatley, via London, the next day, and walked to the village. Thinking back to my arrival that day in

September, I felt as though I'd aged years in the ten months that had passed. Sadness enveloped me and thoughts of dealing with Elsie and the other unfriendly servants consumed me. It would be difficult to bite my tongue while I was feeling such immense grief; who knew what I might say? I wouldn't want to risk losing my new job.

Mrs Willis was in her parlour when I arrived, dressed in black, as all the servants were. They were all sitting quietly in the servants' hall. Even Elsie had the good sense to leave me alone. Hopefully she was done with her troublemaking, and now I wouldn't see her as much. Mrs Willis handed me a key for Rose Cottage and I found my room upstairs at the front, overlooking the Surrey Hills. It was far less luxurious than what I'd become used to in recent months, but, being smaller, it would be warmer at night. What would happen to the servants at Gatley Hall now Lady Violet was dead? Presumably the earl would decide after the funeral.

The week that passed between my arrival at Rose Cottage and Lady Violet's funeral dragged. I shed many tears, always finding a quiet corner to do so. Much of Tabitha's time was spent with the wet nurse, but I still took her for walks in a pram into the village. Getting outside in the warm summer air lifted my spirits. We would pass through the rose garden, walled with red brick. There were beds of roses in different shades of pink and yellow and peach and red, and so many varieties. Often I'd stop and select one to hold to my nose, inhaling its wonderful scent. Many of the roses were in full bloom, some with dry and wilted petals in need of removal. With Tom's absence and therefore Sam's increased responsibilities, Mr Carter would be maintaining the gardens alone, no doubt, and growing vegetables was sure to be his priority.

One morning while I was getting ready to take Tabitha out for a walk, a knock came at the door. It was Sam.

'I have a message from Luca,' he said.

'For me?'

Nodding, he gave me the piece of paper, and I unfolded it.

Please meet me? I need to talk. Luca

Why did Luca want to meet me? Did he somehow know about Tabitha?

'What's this about?' I said.

'I don't know. What would you like to say in reply?'

'Tell Luca I'll meet him tomorrow under the willow tree at one o'clock.'

The next day, I took Tabitha into the village and waited for Luca under the willow tree. I thought back to when we had kissed in this very spot, how I'd been in love with him. Now we were meeting under very different circumstances, and I was anxious to know why he wanted to see me. He arrived promptly at one o'clock on his bicycle and leant it against the wall. He had bags under his eyes and his hair, thick with grease, looked as though it hadn't been washed in days. I was sitting on the bench with Tabitha in the pram next to me. She was sleeping. Luca threw her a glance, seemingly oblivious that he was her father. How I wanted to tell him, to allow him to pick up his child and hold her in his arms. But Lady Violet's words came back to me. He had a life waiting for him in Florence and was engaged to be married. His father's business was dependent on this union of families. Telling him the truth would only bring him pain and sadness.

'Ciao, Mags,' he said.

'Hello, Luca.'

'This is Mr and Mrs Willis's adopted daughter, Tabitha,' I said.

He looked over at Tabitha again and, for a moment, he seemed to be thinking, but then he turned his attention back to me.

'I am very sad about Lady Violet's death. We spent much time together when she was painting me,' he said.

Did he really think I didn't know what had gone on between them? Playing along, I said, 'I shall miss her immensely.'

'Sam said the funeral is on Friday,' Luca said.

Nodding, I said, 'Indeed it is, at St Andrew's.'

'Can I go?' he said.

I wasn't sure this was such a good idea. What if one of the servants spotted him and said something? The rumours had been rife; everyone below stairs knew. There was a chance that the earl may have become aware. How long might it be before someone worked out who Tabitha's real parents were? I thought of how difficult life would be for Tabitha if she were thrown into scandal. We couldn't take that risk.

'I don't think it's the best idea,' I said.

Nodding, he said, 'All right. Thank you, Mags.'

He got up and leant down to kiss me on the cheek, then got on his bicycle and rode off down the high street.

The day of the funeral came, and we servants all walked to St Andrew's. It was a moving service and I found myself sobbing into a handkerchief for most of it. The earl spoke for a few minutes, without expressing a jot of emotion. He announced that he'd bought a Spitfire in Lady Violet's memory and arranged for her name to be painted on the side. This action was clearly for show, and no doubt she'd have been delighted to have her name written on the side of a killing machine.

We stood in the graveyard while the coffin was lowered into the ground and, when I looked up, I saw a man on the pavement opposite, holding a flat cap in his hand. It was Luca. He had come, but kept his distance, and somehow Lady Violet would know this and that he'd always love her even if she hadn't loved him.

CHAPTER 27

MARGARET

After the funeral, I felt a weight lift from my shoulders. Now Lady Violet could be at peace, and I would pray for her every night before sleeping. Rose Cottage was a nice place to be, warm and cosy with plenty of logs for the fires, reminding me of the house I'd grown up in. During the day, while Mr and Mrs Willis were working at the main house, the wet nurse and I had the place to ourselves. I was grateful to be employed and to have a comfortable bed to sleep in, but working as a nanny wasn't the most fulfilling role. My life was on hold, and all I could do was daydream about being a shopgirl again and one day owning a boutique.

One morning, I'd just put Tabitha down for her nap when a knock came at the door. I opened it and there stood Tom, in full RAF uniform. He looked rather handsome.

'Tom, what a lovely surprise,' I said, beaming.

'Hello, Mags. I'm on leave for a day and wanted to come and see you. Will you come for a walk with me?'

'Yes, although I don't have long until Tabitha wakes from her nap.'

I'd written to Tom about Lady Violet's death and my new role as Tabitha's nanny. I hadn't told him who her parents were, and thought it best to keep this information to myself.

'All right, we won't go far,' he said.

He gestured in the direction of the rose garden, and we followed the path.

'I am sorry to hear about Lady Violet,' he said.

'It has been a trying time. The funeral was only last week, and we've all been grieving rather heavily.'

'She could be quite demanding, but still, she was your mistress.'

'Indeed, and we grew closer in Seamouth.'

He lifted the latch on the cast-iron gate and we passed through. Many of the roses were still blooming, but an increasing number were wilting and needed to have their dead petals removed. Still, it was a calming place to be, and I inhaled their perfume as we walked.

Tom led me to a bench in the corner. 'Do you mind if we sit down, Mags?'

'All right.'

'I don't have much time as my parents are expecting me, but I wanted to tell you I'm being sent to Canada to train as a pilot. Who knows when we'll see each other again, but I hope you'll still write to me?'

'I shall miss you, Tom, but of course I'll carry on writing letters to you.'

'And I wanted to ask you something.' He stood up and knelt on the ground and reached into his pocket. 'When this war is over, will you marry me?'

Gasping, I raised a hand to my mouth. I hadn't considered Tom in a romantic way and had no idea he planned to propose to me.

'Really, Tom, are you sure?'

'Yes, I want you to be my wife, Mags.'

The opportunity to marry a man like Tom, who showed a great deal of promise, was not to be taken lightly. Smiling, I said, 'Yes, I will marry you.'

He took my hand and slid a ring onto it. It had a small ruby stone and was rather beautiful.

'This ring belonged to my grandmother, and now it's yours.'

I stood up and we kissed on the lips, and it struck me that I'd made a hasty decision. But saying no would have been a mistake. The pool of eligible men was getting smaller each day as an increasing number were killed in action. I didn't have the luxury of being able to wait a while and choose. Marriage during the war was about who happened to be there at the time. I liked Tom a great deal, and told myself that I could grow to love him.

Mrs Willis informed us that the earl would spend almost all of his time in London from now on. Gatley Hall would become an occasional weekend retreat. He'd take some servants with him to London, leaving Mr and Mrs Willis, Mrs Downside and a handful of staff to maintain the house in his absence.

Summer became autumn and autumn became winter, and my daily routine remained the same, but walking into the village was more of an endurance in colder temperatures. In November, Mrs Willis announced that Lady Violet's mother was sending servants to collect her daughter's belongings and take them back to the family home in Hampshire. And that was when I remembered about the emerald brooch. I still hadn't taken it from the safe, due to my fear of being caught and accused of stealing. But now was the time, if I was to keep my promise and give it to Tabitha on her wedding day.

For days, I dithered over what excuse to use to get into Lady

Violet's former quarters and explored a few ideas when writing in my diary. The best option, I decided, was to tell Mrs Willis I'd mislaid my favourite hat from the previous winter. I asked if it would be possible to go and check my old bedroom. Approaching the house, I felt a gnawing in my gut. What if I were caught and the police were called? I'd have a criminal record and would find it impossible to get another job.

Entering the servants' quarters, I took the staircase without going into the hall, hoping that no one would see me. Upstairs in the boudoir, I opened the drawer in the writing table and pressed the button at the back in order to retrieve the key from under the false bottom. Then I unlocked the safe, and instantly spotted the brooch, standing out in its red box from Ellis and Son. At that very moment I heard the creak of a door opening, but when I turned round there was no one there. Putting this down to my overactive imagination, I slid the box into the pocket of my dress and returned to Rose Cottage. No doubt the brooch would be listed on an inventory somewhere, but, seeing as Lady Violet had been in Seamouth for several months, surely it would be written off? If questioned, I'd say she'd taken the brooch to the house in Suffolk and mislaid it.

The following morning, Mrs Willis called me into the kitchen at Rose Cottage. Her face reflected concern, and it was clear that she was about to divulge news I did not wish to hear. There had been someone at the door of the boudoir after all.

'There's no easy way to say this, Margaret,' she said.

'What is it, Mrs Willis?'

'Elsie came to me last night and said she saw you taking something out of Lady Violet's safe. I am aware that you went over there to look for your hat yesterday. Would you care to explain?'

Finally, Elsie had found a way to get me into trouble good and proper. She had been determined to bring me down all along, and now she had won her little game. How could I deny what I'd done? Would Mrs Willis believe me if I told her Lady Violet had asked me to take the brooch?

'Mrs Willis, I am sorry. You must think I am a thief, but the truth of the matter is that, on her deathbed, Lady Violet asked me to take her emerald brooch, gifted to her by her mother on her wedding day, and worn by her grandmother when meeting Queen Victoria.'

'Why would she ask you to do that?' Mrs Willis said.

'She wanted me to give it to Tabitha on her wedding day.'

'Well, Margaret, I know Lady Violet thought a great deal of you and I am inclined to believe you, but this information puts me in a fix.'

'Because Elsie saw me take it?'

'Yes, and by now she will have told everyone at Gatley Hall. There is no way I can keep you employed here, I'm afraid, whether I believe your story or not.'

'I am sorry, Mrs Willis,' I said, trying to stop my voice from breaking.

'Do you have somewhere to go?' she said.

'I can go to my aunt's,' I said.

'Very well. Get your things and leave as soon as you can.'

'And the brooch?'

'Just promise me you'll keep your word to milady, that's all I can ask.'

'Do you not want to keep it instead, seeing as Tabitha is being raised by you and Mr Willis?'

'Oh no, I wouldn't want to be responsible for such a valuable item. You can worry about keeping it safe until the time comes.'

'And what will you tell Elsie and the other servants?'

'I shall say that you were returning an item, recently found from when you were both in Seamouth.'

'And my reason for leaving?'

'Your aunt is unwell and needs you to look after her.'

'Thank you, Mrs Willis.'

CHAPTER 28

MARGARET

Aunt Edith was glad to have me return to her cottage, as Lilian had recently left to work in a munitions factory. This meant I could have the bedroom previously occupied by Lilian and would not need to sleep on the floor. I helped Aunt Edith by making meals, doing the washing up and cleaning the house, and she provided me with food and board in return. Once again, I wished that I could be working as a shopgirl rather than carrying out such menial tasks, but Aunt Edith needed me. In December a law was passed to say that women above the age of twenty who weren't married or widowed with children were to be conscripted to join one of the auxiliary services. I had turned twenty the previous summer. Aunt Edith fixed me up as a volunteer at the ATS canteen. This arrangement suited her because I could still live in and help out as required.

One evening we were established in the sitting room, listening to the news on the wireless. Aunt Edith was writing up her diary for the Mass Observation and I was darning a pair of stockings.

'Guess who I bumped into today?' Aunt Edith said.

'Who?' I said.

'Sam Maxwell's mother.'

'Sam from Gatley Hall?'

'That's right. She used to attend your Uncle Reg's Sunday service, but she hasn't been to church much lately due to ill health. I saw her in the high street, queuing for meat at Chester's, and she told me something interesting.'

Here was Aunt Edith getting involved in gossip again.

'Oh really?'

'She said that Lady Violet used to meet that Italian POW chap down at the gamekeeper's cottage. Supposedly, she was painting his portrait, but Mrs Maxwell seems to think they were having an affair.'

'Don't be ridiculous.'

'She seemed adamant. And Sam was working at the house, as were you. Did you really not hear anything about it?'

'Not a dickie bird,' I said.

'She said it was all the servants could talk about for months, so I'm surprised.'

'I spent more time with her ladyship than anyone. It's mere tattle, and I wouldn't take any notice.'

'Well I made some calculations. You went to Seamouth for six months. Lady Violet could have been pregnant when you left, just not showing yet. Was she with child, Mags?'

'She certainly was not.'

'I know the official line is that she died of influenza, but it is rather unusual for a woman of her age, and in such good health as well, to die that way.'

'Aunt Edith, what on earth are you insinuating?'

She shrugged. 'Perhaps I'm getting carried away.'

'You are indeed,' I said.

'But if you knew anything, you would tell your aunt, wouldn't you? I can be trusted implicitly.'

'As I already said, dear aunt, it's idle talk, and Mrs Maxwell is damaging the memory of my late mistress. This conversation is rather distressing, actually.'

'I can imagine it would be. Sorry to be so insensitive, Mags.'

Aunt Edith went back to writing in her diary and I hoped she wasn't relaying our conversation. She was writing under a pseudonym but still I hoped she wouldn't go into too much detail if she did refer to her conversation with Mrs Maxwell in some way.

Sam would often pop into the ATS canteen when coming into the village and he kept me abreast of what was going on at Gatley Hall. It didn't take long for the earl to move on with a young debutante in London, Lady Sophia Wootton, the daughter of the Duke of Oxon. He planned to marry her within months. Apparently, her parents were desperate to find her a husband before all the potential suitors went off and got themselves killed. The earl's quest to produce an heir was clearly more important to him than taking a respectable length of time to grieve for his late wife.

One morning Sam told me that Luca had transferred to another farm. I was sad to hear this, and supposed he'd been unable to bear being close to Gatley Hall and the gamekeeper's cottage, filled with all those memories, after Lady Violet's death. The thought of not seeing Luca ever again did not bear thinking about, for, despite all that had happened, I still cared for him. That night before going to bed I said a prayer for Luca and hoped he'd be able to get past losing Lady Violet. If and when the war ended, he'd hopefully be able to return to Florence and marry his fiancée. I'd been reading Lady Violet's copy of *A Room with a View* to help me grieve, as it brought me close to her – it was such a beautiful novel – and I held on to the dream of going to Florence one day. Maybe I'd find Luca's bakery – for I knew his family name was Mancini – and we'd meet again as friends.

Mr and Mrs Willis continued to run Gatley Hall, for such a

grand house needed a great deal of maintenance even in the earl's absence. I would ask Sam for updates on Tabitha whenever I saw him and noticed he'd started referring to her as Lucy. He told me that Mr and Mrs Willis preferred to use her middle name as it suited her better. Of course, I knew that her real middle name was the Italian equivalent, Lucia, but expected they hadn't told Sam this because then it might be obvious that Luca was her father. I considered what Lady Violet might think about her daughter being called Lucy and decided that she'd probably be delighted as it was after Lucy Honeychurch in *A Room with a View* after all. However, I would always think of her as Tabitha, after Lady Violet's grandmother.

Mr Willis started to volunteer for the Auxiliary Fire Service in the village, and spent many a night helping to put out fires created by incendiary bombs. It was difficult to think ahead, as no one knew what was going to happen. Although we did our best to lift our chins and it wasn't the done thing to talk about our doubts in public, there was an undercurrent of fear. What if the Hun succeeded in invading our small island? Aunt Edith had friends around the country who were taking German lessons, *just in case*. She insisted she'd never do such a thing herself because she believed that we would be victorious in the end.

My thoughts often turned to Tom and, when I looked up at the planes overhead, I'd picture him. Would he survive all the dogfights? I continued to write to him every day before updating my diary. As I dropped the letters into the postbox in the village, I would feel a small sense of achievement. There I was, doing my bit by boosting the morale of an RAF pilot. I was fortunate to be engaged to such a man, and I prayed he'd survive the war and return to me. He didn't have Luca's dashing good looks, but his determination to fight for his country was admirable and I was certain that I'd grow to love him with all my heart.

. . .

When the war ended, a party was held in Gatley High Street to celebrate D-Day. It was a joyous day, and the road was closed so we could fill it with tables and chairs and celebrate together, with everyone bringing dishes to share. I couldn't wait for Tom – my fiancé, no less – to come back and looked forward to us finding a home of our own and beginning our life together.

The earl failed to conceive a child with his new wife and, in 1945, he sold Gatley Hall to the Earl of Chiswick, who owned the neighbouring estate, Heybury House. According to Mrs Willis, the earl was in poor health, and didn't want his cousin to inherit the property passed down his family for generations. He made it a condition of the sale that Mr and Mrs Willis remain at Rose Cottage and continue to work as butler and housekeeper. He hadn't forgotten that Mr Willis was his father's batman during the First World War. Little did he know they were raising the illegitimate daughter of his late wife. A few months after the sale of Gatley Hall went through, however, the Earl of Chiswick died after a riding accident, and his son and heir passed Gatley Hall to the Association of Treasured Properties in lieu of paying inheritance tax. Mr and Mrs Willis continued to live at Rose Cottage with Tabitha and they paid rent to the ATP.

Tom and I were married at Leatherhead Register Office. I'd wanted the wedding to be at St Andrew's but, after all he'd seen during the war, he refused to get married in a church. A photographer came from the *Surrey Standard*, and a reporter wrote a few words about us being the love story of Gatley Hall, describing the romance that had developed when a lady's maid wrote to the chauffeur daily while he was in the RAF. This was ironic because, at the time, I still viewed Tom as a friend.

After all we'd been through during the war, Tom seemed on edge that day, and I was overwhelmed with a numb feeling. You couldn't just switch from being nervous and anxious all of the time to feeling joy. Was I making a mistake rushing into a marriage with a man I barely knew? In time, I told myself, we would be happy together. The wedding was a small affair with close family and friends. We had a couple of drinks and a sandwich buffet, and then the best man, Martin Chester, Tom's friend who Lilian had cast aside attached tin cans to the car. The memory still remained of that night at the Old Fox, but I did my best to shut it out and see my husband in the best possible light. For we had our whole lives ahead of us and I told myself it was a one off. We drove away with everyone waving, and spent the night in a run-down bed and breakfast in Brighton.

Tom took a job in a factory in Tolworth that made car parts and we lived in a flat above a newsagent in Dorking. We didn't have much money, and rationing continued; although the war was over, the country still had a lot of recovering to do.

Not long after we were married, I decided to tell Tom about Lady Violet and Luca and Tabitha. As husband and wife, we shouldn't be keeping secrets from each other. We'd conceived our first child on our wedding night in Brighton and I was a few months pregnant. One Sunday, when we'd finished eating dinner, I told him.

'Sam informed me of the affair, but I had no idea about the baby,' he said.

'Well, there you are. I have a brooch that Lady Violet asked me to give Tabitha on her wedding day.'

'Let's see it,' he said.

I went to get it out of the drawer of my nightstand and handed Tom the box from Ellis and Son. He lifted the lid and studied the beautiful emerald brooch inside.

'This will be worth a few bob. We should sell it,' he said.

'What do you mean?'

'We need a new car, and this would help pay for it.'

'But Tom, I made a promise.'

'I'm sorry, Mags, but we're married now and this is a joint decision. I'll take care of it, and don't worry, Mr Dixon will give me a good price.'

'I really think—'

'All those hours I spend working hard to pay our bills, and you're here keeping house. You don't contribute a penny, and you have the nerve to say we'll give this valuable item to someone who doesn't even know of its existence. What did Lady Violet do for you exactly? You don't owe her anything.'

Working for Lady Violet had changed my life. She'd gifted me a love for reading and for that I was grateful. Escaping into books was a way of coping, of getting lost in a different world. And goodness knew, I seemed to need that now more than ever before.

'But I said I'd like to work. In a shop, ideally,' I said.

He looked at me the way he'd looked at Ted that night in the Old Fox, and my gut lurched. His eyes were cold and hard and there was no love for me in them whatsoever.

'Your job is to raise our children, to keep our home spick and span, to provide me with a good meal when I get home from work. It won't be long before you have a Master or little Miss Bates to look after.'

I thought about defending myself further, but it was no use. His mind was made up and I didn't like the way he was speaking to me. Keeping my mouth firmly shut, I cleared the plates and went to wash up, tears running down my face. He didn't apologise or attempt to comfort me. How could Tom take the brooch from me like that? But now I was powerless, with not a penny to my name. There was nowhere to go, even if I wanted to leave, and I was carrying his child inside me. Tom was keeping the roof over my head and, as his wife and future mother of his children, I answered to him. My only option was to find a way to accept this, using books and my diary as my friends.

Tom was ambitious, and determined for his children to have a more comfortable upbringing than the one he'd experienced. He quickly worked his way up to a senior management position, and after that became a director and then a managing director. But this responsibility took its toll. Despite having money for the first time in our lives, and a lovely four-bedroom house in Dorking with a beautiful garden, Tom worked long hours and often travelled abroad.

Due to traumas experienced during the war – he'd often wake up screaming in the night – Tom was a different man. He drank every day without fail, often starting late morning – it was quite acceptable in his company to have a drinks cabinet in one's office at work for meetings – and without a drink to lubricate his mood he'd become grouchy.

We had our daughter, Sophie, and then a couple of years later, a son, Mark. I spent a lot of time managing my husband's temperament. Often, I'd send the children upstairs while he stomped around, shouting and following me from room to room, because something had triggered his trauma – his mother's ill health, Remembrance Sunday, a war film on television. Anything could set him off. He loved our children, but showed it with lavish gifts when returning from business trips, rather than with words. I never once heard him tell Sophie and Mark that he loved them.

He had an affair with his secretary for years, and there was nothing I could do about it. Once, I confronted him and asked for a divorce. He refused to leave, and I didn't have the money to get a place of my own, so had to accept the situation. At least this meant I didn't have to sleep with him, a small compensation, as who wants to go to bed with a man after he's been shouting at you all evening?

Sometimes I'd think back to the moment when Tom and I first met at Gatley station, when he picked up my clothes from the platform. He'd seemed like such a charming, kind chap. Although there were moments early on that I should have taken as warning signs, such as when he almost punched Ted. The temper was always there, simmering beneath the surface, but his wartime experiences brought it out even more.

The children grew up and Sophie emigrated to Australia and married a doctor after she went there to work as a nurse. Mark moved to Aberdeen and worked in the oil industry. I'm sure they both just wanted to get away from their father.

So eventually it was just me and Tom. I tried to look after him as best I could, but he had a big appetite and ate junk food at work and when away on business. He liked his butter and cream and red meat and his heart did not. He continued to drink and smoke too, even though the doctor told him it was putting a terrible strain on his heart.

As the years passed, my dream of going to Florence didn't come to fruition. Tom wasn't keen on holidays because he'd done his fair share of travelling during the war and he went on a lot of business trips. He had no inclination to go abroad with me. My way of coping with this disappointment was to sign up to an Italian class. It took place at a local primary school on Thursday evenings. Our teacher, Signora Mariella Dessi, was a lovely lady and created a happy environment for her students. We'd get into groups and do role-plays about asking where the bank was, buying a coffee, going to the dentist.

It was in this class that I met Nathan Anderson. I was attracted to him from the moment he walked into that classroom. He took the chair next to me and proffered a hand as he introduced himself.

I shook it, and said, 'Pleased to meet you, Nathan. I'm Mags,' as I found myself getting lost in his kind chestnut eyes.

He was married with two daughters of similar ages to my children – we were both in our sixties then. Nathan and I hit it off instantly.

With both of us being married, I had to push any prospect of romance out of my mind. I found myself daydreaming about him quite a lot of the time, though, especially when performing mundane tasks such as ironing and hoovering. We'd all go to the pub opposite the primary school, the Mighty Goat, after class, remaining there until closing time. Those evenings were the highlight of my week and I started to plan my outfits in advance in order to impress Nathan. Sometimes, I'd even book my hair appointment on a Thursday. The classes only ran during termtime and, in the holidays, I missed this opportunity to socialise, and to see him. Nathan and I signed up to the class over and over again. Many students did the same as Signora Dessi was likeable and fun, as well as an excellent teacher.

Nathan and I became firm friends, and then we began what one might call an emotional affair. In the Mighty Goat, we'd always sit next to each other, and he'd buy me a vodka and tonic, always remembering to ask for ice and a slice of lemon, along with his pint of lager. Often, we'd share a bag of roasted peanuts or salt and vinegar crisps. We'd talk to the other students across the table, but mostly he'd ask me about my life, and I would ask him about his. During those hours spent in the pub, we got to know every last detail about each other. His marriage was an unhappy one. He was a history teacher at the local secondary school and his wife taught physical education. Any love they'd had for each other had dissipated long ago, but they remained together, staying out of each other's way most of the time when at home and sleeping in separate rooms. He suspected that his wife had been sleeping with the head of P.E. for years, as they spent a lot of time together on school ski trips and attending away matches together for hockey and football. She would go and stay with her sister, who lived on the Costa del Sol, during school holidays, leaving him alone in the house, and he told me that he was exceptionally lonely.

In turn, I confided in Nathan about my life with Tom and his mood swings, and asked for advice on how I could help him. Nathan had been in the army and fought in Tunisia. He'd been captured and made a prisoner of war, but somehow escaped. Having experienced similar traumas to Tom, Nathan empathised, but he'd found a way to deal with the feelings that at times overwhelmed him: he would write them down in a diary; and he'd been working on a memoir for years. This helped soothe the pain, a form of self-therapy. I'd done something similar myself, of course, during those difficult wartime days. I found it admirable that Nathan managed his emotions in a mature way, enabling him to live more of a normal life than Tom. He liked to have a pint or two of lager in the pub but didn't use alcohol to numb his pain, and he had stopped smoking after the war.

One evening, Nathan told me that he and his wife had separated. She'd upped and left to live with her sister in Spain, and was running exercise classes for expats. And then he said, 'Mags, I've loved you for years, and now Sarah has left I'm available, if you'll have me.'

His words warmed my insides. I'd longed to hear them for some time. However, with Tom's deteriorating health – he'd had two heart attacks by then and a triple bypass – I couldn't exactly abandon him, despite his infidelity. And so, despite the prospect of having happiness within my grasp, I declined Nathan's offer. I told him that, maybe one day when Tom wasn't around anymore, we could make a go of it – if he'd still have me. But for now, I needed to be there for my husband.

CHAPTER 29

MARGARET

Tom died in 1986, of that one last heart attack that had been taunting him for years. Of course I was upset, but his death also brought an unexpected liberating feeling. I did not feel an ounce of guilt, not after all he'd put me through. But I hadn't ever been on my own and so I had no idea about managing the finances for a house. My dear niece, Mildred's daughter Alice, was working in London at the time, and she stepped in to help. I was most grateful. After Aunt Edith died, she'd left her cottage to me. Tom had rented it out, of course keeping all of the money. It was Alice who suggested I sell the house in Dorking and live in Aunt Edith's cottage in Gatley. I didn't need much space, and she helped me move in. Tom left me a substantial sum of money – a bonus after all I'd endured.

One evening, a year after Tom had gone, Nathan said in the pub that he'd bought a caravan on a whim. He wanted to take it on a test run, to see if he might enjoy that kind of life when he retired the following year. I was delighted for him, although quite envious.

But then he said, 'Would you like to come with me?'

'What do you mean?' I said, surprised.

'Mags, we've talked about going abroad together. It's been a year and I feel that's a respectable length of time.'

'Where would we go?' I said.

'Well, firstly, in case it's a concern, there is plenty of space for us to sleep separately at night. But I thought we could go to Florence like you've always wanted to?'

Ever since those wartime years when I met Luca, I'd dreamt of seeing Florence with my own eyes. I'd read the novel, taken from Lady Violet's nightstand, *A Room with a View*, and watched the film over and over again on video cassette. When Alice and I were clearing out the house in Dorking, we found a shoebox in the back of Tom's wardrobe containing a huge wad of cash, some papers and Lady Violet's brooch. When I saw that red box from Ellis and Son, I couldn't believe my eyes. I held the brooch in my hand, running my fingers over the tiny diamonds, and joy filled my heart. Now I could fulfil Lady Violet's dying wish. But then it struck me that I had no idea of Tabitha's whereabouts. She'd gone away the year before, and I sensed she might be in Florence, looking for her father.

I'd kept in touch with Tabitha's two daughters, who were grown up by then, and would send them presents at Christmas. Tabitha herself wasn't good at staying in touch, but I was there if she needed me. Mr and Mrs Willis had told her about her real parents when she turned eighteen and at first she wasn't interested in knowing about them. But when she had children of her own she had wanted to know everything about Lady Violet and Luca. She came to see me and I told her, but then she distanced herself from me. I sensed this was because we'd opened up a can of worms and now I reminded her of the parents she never knew. She married and then divorced when her daughters left home, but started an affair with her boss at work.

Her eldest daughter, Melanie, had written around a year before Tom died to say that Tabitha had fallen unexpectedly pregnant. She didn't want to become a mother again in her forties, but couldn't go through with having an abortion either, so she had the baby – a little boy. One weekend she'd left the baby on his father's doorstep, but didn't return.

She sent her baby's father a letter from Italy, postmarked Florence, saying not to worry about her, but she couldn't spend any more years being a mother. It was time to follow her dreams now. The onset of the menopause was giving her migraines and making her feel low at times. She'd been longing for this chance to go to Italy and do the art course she'd dreamt of doing once her daughters left home.

If Nathan took me to Florence, we could try to find her. We could visit Luca at his bakery – if he were still alive.

'You want to take me to Florence?'

'Why not?'

'When?'

'School breaks up in July and I think we should go then. I have until the beginning of September. We could take our time. Campsites don't cost much. What do you think?'

'I'd be delighted to accompany you,' I said.

At last, I would get to see Florence with my own eyes, and Nathan was going to take me there. I couldn't believe my luck.

Nathan and I set out early one morning to get the ferry from Dover to Calais. I'd stayed at his house the night before and, being a proper gentleman, he'd made up the spare room for me. If anything was going to happen we'd both need to feel comfortable. Neither of us had slept with anyone else apart from our spouses and it would be quite overwhelming to cross the bridge from friends to lovers.

The caravan was brand new and a home from home. I'd never been inside one before and there was everything one needed. A small sitting area with a table in the centre – these seats could be converted into a bed, and that was where Nathan would sleep. A kitchenette included a small fridge and a gas stove with a few cupboards for storage. Nathan had filled these cupboards with tins, including peaches and evaporated milk, Spam, potatoes, soups and carrots and peas. Camping life suited us as we knew how to live on food that wasn't bought fresh. There was a bedroom where I would sleep and a tiny bathroom with toilet, sink and shower attachment.

We sailed at seven o'clock, and by ten o'clock, French time, we were making our way down the autoroute, heading towards Chalôns-sur-Marne. Nathan had done a great deal of research. He was a meticulous person, which made a change from living with Tom, who was always a little haphazard when it came to his home life. Nathan had bought a book and underlined with a pencil campsites for us to stay at all the way to Florence.

We reached Chalôns-sur-Marne that afternoon and, after establishing ourselves, we had a cup of tea in fold-up chairs on the grass outside the caravan. It was absolute bliss. Who would have thought that doing something so simple could bring such pleasure?

Nathan was calm and undemanding company, such a change from being around Tom. I felt so lucky to have found a man like him later in life, and to be given the chance to be truly happy brought immense joy.

We spent the next day on the campsite and bought lots of delicious food at the supermarket – baguettes, Brie, pâté, tomatoes as big as one's hand and so sweet, amongst many other delicious items. Nathan bought a few bottles of Bordeaux and that evening we sat outside the caravan and had a nice meal, washed down with the wine. It was drizzling, so we unwound the awning, and, despite the weather, we still had such a lovely time. Tom and I had rarely eaten together, and when we did that would be his time to be grumpy. The experience of preparing food and eating it with someone you loved was a novelty for me.

. . .

The next morning we progressed to Pontarlier, near the Swiss border. It was surrounded by mountains and very beautiful. We took the Mont Blanc tunnel, arriving in Courmayeur and then progressed to the Aosta Valley, where we stayed on another campsite with great big mountains all around us. After that we drove to Florence. You can't exactly park a caravan in the middle of Florence, and so we left it on a campsite nearby and drove into the centre from there the following morning. I'd told Nathan all about Luca and Tabitha, and he was interested in my story and wanted to do all he could to help with my mission.

Nathan parked in a space by the River Arno with a view of the Ponte Vecchio. I'd seen this bridge in photographs and on television, but being there in person and having this majestic piece of architecture right in front of me was such a treat after all those years of dreaming about seeing it with my own eyes. It was painted in a beautiful shade of lemon yellow and consisted of small buildings in a deeper yellow colour and terracotta, some with deep green or brown shutters. There were three arches in the centre, where tourists could stand and study Florence from a different perspective.

We made our way to underneath one of those arches and looked down the river at the other bridges. Nathan took hold of my hand, and it was a perfect location for a man and woman who were slowly falling in love with each other. I hadn't reciprocated Nathan's, 'I love you', said at the Mighty Goat. After saying it to Tom quite readily when he returned at the end of the war, I was more cautious now. For a split second, I thought Nathan might use this opportunity to kiss me, but he didn't. He did however throw me a sideways glance, as if the thought of leaning in and attempting to kiss me was on his mind. I didn't encourage him because I wasn't yet ready. What if he suddenly switched into some awful version of himself that he'd kept hidden?

We went for a cappuccino at a quaint café before making our way to the tourist office, where a nice young lady circled Luca's bakery, Pasticceria Mancini, on a map. I recalled his surname from that dreadful day he introduced himself to Lady Violet when we were taking a walk. Nathan and I found the bakery in a side street in the centre of the city, a short distance from the Duomo, the cathedral. When we arrived, it was busy with people standing at the counter drinking morning coffees, and there was a queue of customers right up to the door. The aroma of baked goods hit me as soon as I walked through the door and the ambience was comforting and warm. Behind the counter was a wonderful selection of bread, cakes and pastries; my mouth watered just looking at it all. We took a place in the queue, as that seemed the best way to approach the counter and ask for Luca. We couldn't exactly push in. When we reached the front, I asked in Italian – I'd been practising for weeks – 'Vorrei vedere Luca Mancini, per favore.'

The woman behind the counter said, 'Luca, perché?'

I asked if she spoke English, as it was difficult for me to explain further in Italian. She went to fetch a teenage girl with dark hair pulled into a high ponytail and spoke to her in Italian.

The girl turned to me. 'Buongiorno. I am Gina, the grand-daughter of Luca. This is my mother, Maria. She apologises for not speaking good English. Why you want to see Luca?'

I explained that I'd known him during his time spent in England during the war and her face broke into a smile.

'What is your name?'

'Mags.'

'Mags! He has told us about you, Tom, and Mr and Mrs Marshall and Pam and his time on the farm.' She turned and spoke in Italian to her mother, who nodded and smiled. Gina looked at me. 'He and my grandmother, Valentina, live in a house in the country, but we invite you to come here and have dinner with him this evening.'

'Really, are you sure?' I said, not having expected a dinner invitation.

'Yes, you must come. We make delicious Italian food for you to try.'

I turned to Nathan, and he nodded and smiled. It was nice to be with someone who was prepared to socialise with strangers in order to support me.

'We would be delighted to accept your kind invitation,' I said to Gina.

That evening, we arrived at eight o'clock sharp. We'd booked into a boutique hotel round the corner for the night so we could drink wine and not worry about getting back before the campsite gates closed.

Gina showed us upstairs, to a grand apartment that stretched above the bakery. In the entrance hall, she introduced us to her grandmother and Luca's wife, Valentina. She was an exceptionally beautiful and curvaceous woman who looked a little like Monica Bellucci, with thick dark hair, highlighted at the front with streaks of blond, and big brown eyes, enhanced with black eyeliner and long eyelashes. She had won the prize of Luca for life and was very worthy indeed. She smiled at us before promptly disappearing to help in the kitchen. We were then shown into a living room, where Luca sat in an armchair by an open window. It being July, the temperature was hot and the air sticky. Like me, he was now in his sixties, and his hair, of which he still had plenty, was completely grey with white flecks at the temples. Luca remained an exceptionally handsome man and had managed to keep the weight off. He wore a white shirt, undone a few buttons at the collar, and blue jeans cut at the ankle, with brown leather slip-on shoes and no socks. We approached, and he stood up.

'Mags, it is good to see you.'

He leant forward and we kissed on both cheeks. He smelt of cologne with hints of citrus, mixed with tobacco.

'This is Nathan,' I said.

'Pleased to meet you,' Luca said, and they shook hands.

It struck me that he wouldn't know Tom had died, and so I told him in Italian. This was another phrase I'd practised.

'I am very sorry,' he said. 'He was a good man.'

'Thank you,' I said. Of course, Luca had no reason to think Tom was anything other than a good man, and contradicting him would be inappropriate.

Gina brought in a tray of prosecco and we all took a flute and said, 'Cin cin,' as we met each other's eyes and smiled before taking a sip.

Nathan and I sat on the sofa and Gina took a seat opposite, by Luca. It was then that I realised we couldn't just bring up Tabitha, his illegitimate daughter, in front of his wife and family. How on earth was I going to approach this? Would it be possible to get him on his own at some point during the evening? And even then how would I bring up the subject?

Valentina came in, an apron tied round her waist and her hair scraped into a bun. She mopped sweat from her brow with a tea towel, and seemed flustered. She spoke to Gina, who showed us into a dining room where a big fan whirred in the corner. A long table was decorated with jam jars filled with brightly coloured flowers; candles, their flames flickering in the light breeze; and open bottles of Chianti, a local wine I'd read about in the guidebook. The sash windows were pushed up as high as they could go, and we were blessed with a view of the terracotta rooftops and domes of Florence, the River Arno in the distance. It was very *A Room with a View* indeed. Gina gestured for us to take chairs facing the splendid view, and sat opposite us.

Valentina brought in a salad made from enormous slices of

tomato with avocado and mozzarella, garnished with ripped basil leaves. It was absolutely delicious.

'We call this *insalata tricolore* as it is the colours of the Italian flag: green, white and red,' Gina said. 'And these tomatoes are from my grandfather's garden.'

The tomatoes were sweeter and more delicious than those at home; the mozzarella melted in the mouth and Valentina told us, via Gina, that this was because it was made from buffalo milk. Our starter was followed by a bowl of pasta – tubes called rigatoni, the same shape as penne but bigger, served with cold chopped tomatoes, garlic pieces and basil leaves. Such a simple dish, but the freshness of the ingredients gave it an edge. For the main course, Maria served breaded chicken, flattened so it was very thin and tender, with a slice of lemon to squeeze over the top. On the side were bowls of fried potatoes and green beans, cooked until they were soft. Throughout the meal, Maria ensured our wine glasses were topped up, though not by too much, as Gina explained Italians didn't like their glasses of wine too full.

During the break between the main course and dessert, I could see the sun setting. It was a magnificent sight, the sky a mix of purple and orange and blue. Gina brought up a selection of cakes and pastries from the bakery for dessert, along with a tub of vanilla ice cream, which was so refreshing in the heat.

I was glad Nathan had suggested booking the hotel in order to make the most of the experience of dining in an Italian home. Now dark, Florence was lit up with pretty lights and the temperature was cooler. The murmur of people talking came from the street below. After dessert, Luca went out of the room and came back with a bottle of grappa, a very strong spirit I had read about. We drank shots together, clinking glasses and saying, 'cin cin' again as we did so. I hadn't consumed so much alcohol in years, but because we'd had such a big meal it didn't affect me too much. Gina went off to help Maria and Valentina in the kitchen. Nathan helped to clear the table and then said he was going to use the bathroom. No doubt this was an excuse for him to stay out of the way and give me my moment. I was left alone with Luca, and my stomach churned as I realised my opportunity had come. How was I going to broach the uncomfortable subject of Tabitha? He beamed as he took out a packet of cigarettes and offered me one. I shook my head. He struck a match and lit one for himself. Conscious that Valentina, Maria or Gina could reappear at any moment, I decided to exercise discretion.

'I must confess, Luca, that I am here for a reason,' I said.

He drew on his cigarette and turned sideways to exhale the smoke. 'I know,' he said.

'You do?'

Nodding, he said, 'Yes, she came last year.'

Presumably he was talking about Tabitha. 'So, you know that when Lady Violet and I were in Seamouth, she...'

'Yes. I was a little surprised,' he said. 'But then it made sense. You were gone for months. She died from having my child, not from influenza.'

Emotions consumed me as I thought back to everything that had happened, all that Lady Violet, Luca and I had been through. How he'd transferred to another farm.

'When she died, I was very sad for long time,' he said.

'Of course you were,' I said.

'I loved Violet with all my heart,' he said, putting a hand on his chest.

Through the door to the kitchen, I could hear the clattering of dishes as his wife, daughter and granddaughter cleared up, and hoped we had a bit longer to talk.

'So, she came here last year?'

'Yes, she study art. Valentina not happy,' he said, shaking his head, flicking the ash of his cigarette into an empty glass. 'We argue.' He raised his arms above his head to make his point.

Of course his wife would not be thrilled with the news.

'Do you know where she is now?' I said.

He shook his head. 'She came here with Italian boyfriend from La Spezia. She was waitress in a restaurant there. Perhaps she is there with him,' he said. Maria entered the room, carrying a tray with espresso cups and saucers and a silver coffee pot. She tutted when she saw that Luca was flicking cigarette ash into an empty glass, and placed a silver ashtray in front of him. Nathan reappeared and we exchanged a smile.

If only I'd had time to ask Luca a few more questions. Did he recall the name of the boyfriend? How many times had he seen Tabitha and did she intend to stay in Italy?

We drank our coffee, adding teaspoons of sugar, and it cut nicely through all the alcohol consumed. Shortly afterwards, we said our goodbyes, and carried out the Italian tradition of all kissing one another on both cheeks. I thanked the Mancini family profusely for their generous hospitality – they had gone to so much effort to make it a special evening for us. We went on our way, promising to stay in touch, although I doubted we would. What was there to say?

The next day, Nathan and I drove to the Italian Riviera to look for Tabitha. We left the caravan on a campsite and drove into La Spezia, a beautiful town where the streets were lined with orange trees. Sailors walked around in their white uniforms, visiting from the nearby naval base. We wandered for some time, holding hands, but it was hopeless; there were so many restaurants and we had no idea where Tabitha could be working. We went inside a few pizzerias, one by one, and a fish restaurant, asking if they knew of a Tabitha Willis or Dobson. I had no idea which surname she might be using. All of the greeters shook their heads and did their best to get rid of us so they could seat people at tables. And I hadn't seen Tabitha for so many years that I probably wouldn't recognise her. All I knew was that she had dark hair, like Luca, but most Italian girls did, so this didn't help. We tried one last restaurant, an osteria, and the manager told me that an English woman had worked there until recently, but she was called Lucia. She'd got married and moved away. Defeated, Nathan and I returned to the caravan, and I made a pot of tea.

'I am sorry that we didn't find her,' Nathan said.

As I was pouring water from the kettle into the teapot, something occurred to me. I thought back to Lady Violet on her deathbed. 'Do you know something?' I said, joining him at the table.

We sat opposite each other with our cups of tea and a packet of Italian almond biscuits. Nathan squeezed my hand. He was so affectionate, something I'd never experienced with Tom, and I liked it very much.

'What, my dear?'

'I've just remembered that Tabitha's middle name was Lucia, and the Willises used the English equivalent. Do you think she might be using that name instead?'

'It's a possibility,' Nathan said. 'Lots of people opt to use their middle names when they don't like their first name, or when they want a change.'

On her quest to find her father, perhaps Tabitha had decided to reinvent herself at the same time. The manager at the osteria hadn't known which town this Lucia had moved to though, so even if Tabitha was using that name it didn't make a lot of difference. We'd be looking for a needle in a haystack. There was nothing else we could do in the meantime, but I vowed I wouldn't give up, for Lady Violet's sake.

CHAPTER 30

CLAIRE

The next morning when I woke, Miles was facing away from me, breathing lightly. Emboldened by the wine, I'd asked if he might change his mind about starting a family with me one day. When he said he'd consider it, we had fallen into bed together. My head throbbed from all the wine and I needed tea and painkillers. Climbing out of bed, I crept past him and put on my dressing gown. In the kitchen, I made two cups of tea, dipping the bag in his mug for longer as he liked it extra strong, and adding a dash of milk. I popped two ibuprofen out of the packet in the kitchen drawer and washed them down with water. Had I made a mistake sleeping with him?

I carried the mugs of tea up to the bedroom. Miles was sitting up in bed, two pillows propped behind him as he scrolled through his phone, his mouth set in a wide smile.

I placed the mug on a coaster on the bedside table. 'Good morning,' I said.

'Thanks, Claire,' he said, rather formally and without looking up. He hadn't lost the habit of choosing his phone over me. What was it with colleagues getting in touch on a Saturday morning, for goodness' sake?

I climbed into my side of the bed. 'So, what are you up to today?' I said, taking a sip of tea far too soon, scalding my tongue.

He got up and took his jeans from the chair in the corner and my heart sank. Pulling them on, he zipped up the fly.

'I have to go,' he said, reaching for his shirt.

'Why?'

'I'm meeting Toby for lunch,' he said.

He put on his shirt and did up the buttons.

Toby was his business partner.

'On a Saturday?'

'When you run your own business, it's twenty-four-seven, Claire, you know how it is.'

'When will I see you again?' I said, realising as soon as the words left my mouth that I sounded needy.

'I'll text you,' he said, sliding his phone into the back pocket of his jeans.

He studied his reflection in the mirror and I couldn't help thinking Miles was meeting a woman. Toby was married with three kids, and his wife, Madeleine, liked to organise every minute of his weekend life. He spent weekends ferrying the kids to football matches and swimming lessons, and they were part of a dinner party circuit on Saturday nights. We'd been included for a while, and I'd always dreaded going to them. Miles's ex-girlfriend, Natasha from university, would usually be there with some random date. She'd flirt with Miles all night, I'd find it upsetting and we'd argue about her on the way home.

Had Jim been right when asking if Miles had cheated? Did that explain all those nights working late? Then why was he here? To prove he could still have me whenever he wanted, I guessed. And to think he'd lied about the possibility of us having children together one day to get me into bed.

Picking up his watch from the bedside table and slipping it onto his wrist, he said, 'I'd better be off then.'

I lifted the duvet off me. 'Okay, I'll see you out.'

'You stay there, go back to sleep. You always did like your lie-ins,' he said, as if it were a major flaw of mine. Yes, when we were together, weekends were about catching up on sleep. Working at Gatley Hall hadn't left me feeling as tired; perhaps I could do something more worthwhile with weekend mornings now.

'All right then,' I said.

He kissed me lightly on the forehead. 'Bye, Claire,' he said.

His presence and the conversations we'd had would leave me with material to pick through for days. Damn him for tarnishing my fresh start. He went downstairs, leaving the door ajar and his mug of tea untouched on the bedside table.

I reached for my phone, deflated. My mood had been upbeat the night before when I was having that drink with Jim, and now Miles had jostled with my emotions. A key turned in the lock of the front door. Jim, no doubt. Surely he was having more showers than a man needed?

'Hello, there,' I heard him say.

'Back so soon? You must be very clean,' Miles said.

'Indeed, I consider personal hygiene to be most important,' Jim said.

'Hopefully it won't be long before your shower is fixed.'

'Why's that then?'

'I don't like the idea of you wandering in here wearing nothing but a towel whenever you feel like it. It's not fair on Claire.'

'She doesn't seem to mind, but thanks for your feedback, Miles.'

The door banged shut. Jim seemed to give as good as he got, and I smiled to myself.

His footsteps came up the stairs, and he appeared and leant on the door frame, tipping his head in my direction.

'So, he stayed over then?'

'He did. We...' I was about to lie and say we hadn't slept together.

Dismissing me with a wave of his hand, he said, 'That's none of my business.'

'You just asked.'

'I asked if he'd stayed, not if you'd...'

A moment of silence fell between us, and he looked away. He scratched his head.

'If I'd known Miles was still here, I wouldn't have let myself into your house,' he said.

'Okay. But how many showers does a man need?' I said, and instantly regretted my words.

'If you're worried about the hot water bill, I'll make a contribution,' he said, and before I could answer he went into the bathroom, closing the door firmly behind him. The lock clicked into place. What if Miles and I had been at it when Jim walked through the door? A horrifying thought.

Pulling on a pair of tracksuit bottoms and a baggy white t-shirt, I made my way downstairs. While waiting for the kettle to boil, I got a bag of fresh coffee out of the fridge. The kitchen was a mess, as I'd left the washing up the night before, the dirty plates a reminder of how Miles had left me feeling. As the kettle clicked, Jim came downstairs.

'Any coffee for me?' he said.

I looked at him. 'Is your dressing gown not dry yet?'

'Nope. Maybe tomorrow.'

'If you want coffee, you'll have to get dressed first.'

Jim was once again on the receiving end of me being bolshy because of Miles.

'Fair enough,' he said, turning and going out of the front door. I filled the cafetière and put it on the table with mugs and milk. Having company could only be a good thing, I guessed, as otherwise my mind would wander into analysis central territory.

Jim came back through the door a few minutes later. 'Are you okay, Claire?' he said, joining me at the table.

I sighed and rested my head in my hands. 'Not really,' I said.

'Tell me about it, if you want to, that is,' he said.

How much should I divulge? 'I'm just a bit down after last night. He rushed off too quickly this morning,' I said.

'And presumably, he left with no mention of when you'll next see each other?'

'He'll text me, no doubt.'

'Is that what you want, to go back to seeing him?'

'I don't think that's the best idea. I do miss the flat though. The lovely thick carpet and plush sofas and huge TV. The nice kitchen. This place is' – I looked around – 'a bit of a dump, isn't it, really? When did they last give it a coat of paint?'

'And that's why you get to live here for next to nothing. They can't rent it out to holidaymakers until it's refurbished. And then we'll be out on our ears.'

'Oh, are they planning to do that soon?'

He shrugged and sipped his coffee. 'They've been talking about it for years. You don't want your old life back though, do you?'

'I'd like to go back in time to just before my father died, when all seemed okay with Miles, before he admitted he had no intention of marrying me and having children. After leading me on for years, dodging the question. Maybe it's something I did. Perhaps he just didn't want children with me.'

'I doubt that very much. So, you put him on the spot?'

'Yes, losing my dad made me think. I can't waste any more time with someone who doesn't want a future with me.'

'I get that,' he said.

'Last night I entertained myself with the fantasy that we might get back together, when he hinted that he might change his mind.'

'It's not easy to break it off with someone you've been with for a while; someone you thought you'd always be with.' He stared straight ahead, his eyes glazing over, and I sensed he'd experienced this but his vagueness meant he didn't want to reveal more. Not yet, anyway.

'All those years of building a relationship with Miles, thinking we'd always be together. Was it all for nothing?'

'Of course it wasn't,' Jim said.

'What do you mean?'

'It was all part of your journey.'

'What journey?'

'Towards the person you should be with. You needed to be with Miles to know what doesn't work. You're only, how old?'

'Thirty.'

'Exactly. You're still figuring out what life you want. I was supposed to get married last year, here at Gatley Hall. My fiancée called it off the month before, saying she wasn't ready. She was from New Zealand, and wanted to go home, and I didn't want to go with her.'

'Oh, I'm sorry,' I said.

'As I said, it's all part of the journey. I'm glad we had that time together. I loved her, but it would never have worked out. We argued far too much, it was exhausting. She was the kind of person who liked to be busy all of the time – and, as you know, I enjoy a slower pace of life. Perhaps you should give this place a chance, really throw yourself into it and see if you can be happy here?'

'You're probably right.'

'What have you got to lose?'

'Nothing, I guess. How did you end up at Gatley Hall?

'I actually used to work in London, like you, but for an accountancy firm, and commuted every day from Dorking. But the hours were long and the work was intense so I took some time off one summer. I came here one afternoon and remembered my dad bringing me to Rose Cottage when I was small to see a woman who lived here called Hilda – an old family friend. We'd then go off and walk around the countryside, and they were some of my happiest childhood memories. I had some savings and volunteered here as a ranger initially and then got a paid job and the rest is history.'

'So you've managed to change your lifestyle and are happier now?'

'Yes, and I'm so glad I did. That summer when I took the time off, I wasn't sleeping very well as the job was becoming overwhelming. I'd been promoted and didn't like all the responsibility.'

We sat in silence, a comfortable silence this time, the only sound the birds tweeting outside the kitchen window. Jim got up and went to rinse his mug in the sink.

'Right, I'm meeting Samantha for a walk shortly. I'm supposed to be making sandwiches to take with us.'

'Doesn't she need to be with her kids on a Saturday?'

'Her ex has them.'

'Sounds like you have a proper romance going on,' I said.

He laughed. 'Hardly. It was her idea, and so I said yes. Weekends can get a bit boring round here, if you're not working. I might stay at Samantha's tonight. After what you said, I think you'd rather I stay there?'

'That's thoughtful of you. Have fun,' I said, not meaning it one bit.

'Thanks, Claire.'

He put on his flip-flops and left, and I was alone once again.

I went upstairs to shower and get dressed. Jim was right: I needed to throw myself into Gatley. I'd give the cottage the thorough clean it needed, and order some nice things online to make the place feel more homely.

CHAPTER 31

CLAIRE

On Monday, Helen was waiting for me in my office. I took Margaret's letter out of my notebook and placed it in front of her.

'What do you think of this then?' I said.

She read it and looked at me. 'This is the letter you told me about.'

I showed her the photo of Margaret in the guidebook as well as the newspaper article with her wedding photo on the website.

'Photos as well. This love story between the lady's maid and the chauffeur in the RAF would be perfect for the exhibition. Margaret's address is in Gatley, near the church. Shall we go and see her?'

'Do you think we should find out more first?'

'No time like the present.'

'Are you sure?'

'It's a nice day. We can walk.'

We crossed the fields into Gatley and found number fifteen, Church Road, a white terraced cottage, opposite an old

Norman church with a sign saying ST ANDREW'S. The door was red with a semicircle of stained glass above it.

I rapped the knocker. A woman answered the door, but she was much younger than Margaret would be, probably in her fifties.

'Hello,' I said. 'We're looking for Margaret Anderson.'

'She moved out a couple of years ago,' the woman said.

'Oh, sorry to bother you,' I said.

'But, seeing as she's my aunt, I can tell you where she is. What's this about?'

I got the letter out of my handbag and showed it to her.

'Ah, yes, she was upset that no one from Gatley Hall had got in touch. She did try ringing up and left messages as well, but she never heard back.'

'I'm sorry to hear that,' I said. 'My new job at Gatley Hall is to look into letters like this one, so if you're able to tell me where she is it would be lovely to go and see her.'

'She's living at Hyacinth Place, a care home on the road to Dorking.'

'Do you think we could visit her there?'

'You'd need to call and arrange a meeting. I'd come with you, but I'm about to leave for the airport on a business trip. I'm Alice, by the way,' she said.

Helen and I introduced ourselves.

'Nice to meet you both. Do go and see her. She'll be so pleased,' Alice said.

'We will, as soon as we can. Thanks for telling us where she is,' I said.

The following day, I drove to Hyacinth Place with Helen. I'd called the previous afternoon and arranged a time to visit Margaret. A carer showed us into a vast lounge, and we waited at a table by the fireplace. An elderly man read a book in an armchair and two ladies played cards at a table, while another man was asleep in front of the television. It wasn't the most uplifting of places, with walls a turtle-green colour and tired-looking chairs. And the room smelt strongly of disinfectant.

Before long, the carer who'd greeted us brought Margaret into the room. She was very thin and frail with a head of white hair, and she wore a green dress. It was hard to believe that this was the same person in the photos I'd seen.

We stood up and I said, 'I'm Claire Bell from Gatley Hall. This is my colleague, Helen.'

Her face broke out into a smile, and she lowered herself slowly into the chair opposite us. From the way she fixed her eyes on me, Margaret seemed to have her wits about her, and I hoped she'd be able to tell us what we needed to know in order to help her.

'At last! Where have you been? I'm not getting any younger, you know.'

'I'm sorry. I only just found your letter. Do you mind if I ask you some questions?'

'I did ring up and try talking to someone a few times, but no one called me back.'

It didn't seem fair that Margaret had been ignored, and I wanted to make it up to her, to help with her quest. I got the letter out of my handbag and removed it from the envelope. 'Thank you for writing to us. Is Tabitha your daughter?' I said.

Margaret shook her head. 'Oh no. She lived with Mr and Mrs Willis.'

'So, she was their daughter?'

'No, they just took her in.'

'So who was she?' I said. 'And why do you need to find her?'

'Tabitha had a son, later than most women would. He wasn't planned. She already had two grown-up daughters and was divorced, but she was having an affair. He was what one might call a menopause baby. When he arrived, Tabitha couldn't cope with being a mother again at a time when she'd been ready to go and do her own thing. She'd always dreamt of living in Italy and being an artist, like her mother.' Pausing, she tipped her head to one side, a faint smile on her lips, as if reliving a memory.

'But, who is—' I said, but Helen put a hand on my arm.

'Let Margaret say her bit,' she said.

Margaret continued. 'She and her husband had agreed for years that they'd divorce when their daughters left home. They weren't a good fit for each other. Everything was organised, and she'd rented an apartment in Florence, signed up for an art course. She had an affair shortly before leaving and, when she found out that she was pregnant, she had to cancel her plans. When the baby was a few months old, she left him on his father's doorstep with a note. She didn't leave a forwarding address. This was in 1985.'

'A while ago, then.'

'I went to Florence to look for her. She was obsessed with Italy, which was understandable.'

'Why was that then?'

At that moment, Margaret started to cough and couldn't seem to stop, so Helen went to get her a glass of water. She took a sip.

'We couldn't find her in Florence. We went to the Italian Riviera as we were told she might be there. It's very beautiful. You must go there if you ever get the chance. We had a nice time in Nathan's caravan. It was the first time I'd been in a caravan. The first time I'd been abroad. Tom never wanted to take me, you see.'

Margaret seemed to be going off on a tangent, and I expected this was down to her age, and failing memory. I had no idea who Nathan was.

'But it was nice to see Luca and to meet his family. His wife was very understanding, considering. Apparently, she wasn't best pleased when she found out about Tabitha.'

I had no idea who Luca was either, but this information seemed significant.

'Who is Luca?' I said.

'Luca? Oh he was very handsome. I fell in love with him when he saved my life. A German parachutist tried to kill me. I was quite shaken up, I can tell you. Lady Violet painted him in the gamekeeper's cottage.'

Confused by this mishmash of information, I said, 'Did Luca live at Gatley Hall?'

'Oh no, he lived on the farm with the Marshalls.'

'Home Farm, linked to Gatley Hall. It's run by the Marshall family, and they supply the local butcher, Chester's, with meat,' Helen said.

'Oh, that's interesting,' I said.

Margaret started to cough again and took another sip of water. Helen and I exchanged a glance.

'I do apologise, dear. I've had this dreadful cold for some time. They do tend to linger when you get to my age, especially during the winter,' Margaret said.

'Shall we come back another day?' Helen said.

'That's a good idea. I'll make more of an effort next time. I didn't have a chance to put my lipstick on – they didn't tell me you were coming.'

'All right, we'll arrange another visit soon,' I said. 'Thank you, Margaret.'

The carer was standing by the door, and I approached her. 'We'll come back another day. Margaret seems to be quite tired.'

'She's had the cold that's been doing the rounds for a while. And her memory has been deteriorating lately. We did tell her to expect you, but she forgot and was upset because she couldn't dress up. She likes to make an effort for visitors.'

It was disappointing, but hopefully next time Margaret might be able to fill in the gaps. Until then, I'd try to find out who Luca was, and maybe Jim would know whether the game-keeper's cottage was still there.

CHAPTER 32

CLAIRE

The following morning I bumped into Jim when we were both coming out of our front doors. I hadn't seen him since Saturday morning, after Miles's visit, but had heard him return from Samantha's the night before. Here was my opportunity to ask him about the gamekeeper's cottage.

'Morning, Claire,' he said.

'Morning, Jim. Did you have a good time with Samantha?'

He nodded and smiled.

'Do you mind me asking if you know anything about a gamekeeper's cottage?'

'Sure, why?'

'Helen and I went to see Margaret yesterday, the woman who wrote the letter, and she mentioned that Lady Violet did some painting there.'

'It hasn't been used since the war, but I can show you now if you like. It's in the bluebell woods, about a five-minute walk from the lake.'

We followed the lawn down to the lake, the grass, white with frost, crunching beneath our feet. It was quiet, apart from the distant hum of a car, one of those crisp winter days, and the sky was deep blue with wisps of cloud. A sheet of ice covered the lake, and a couple of ducks waddled about, quacking. The trees surrounding the lake were whitened with frost and it looked like a winter wonderland. Being outside in the country-side was uplifting, and I inhaled the clean air.

Jim led me to a stile and took my hand, helping me over. In the field, a group of brown Jersey cows huddled at the other end.

'That big old oak tree is my favourite on the property,' Jim said. 'Over two hundred years old.'

The tree was majestic, with its thick trunk and branches creating a vast canopy. Jim seemed to be truly passionate about his job.

'Wow, amazing,' I said, thinking about all the people who would have walked past it in that time.

'This is Long Meadow,' Jim said. 'And that's the Dairy Field. Beyond you'll find Home Farm.'

Home Farm, mentioned by Margaret, where Luca had apparently been living and working.

On the right was a gate with a sign saying BLUEBELL WOODS. He lifted the latch on the gate, and we entered the woods.

We followed the path, the deep blue sky visible through gaps in the trees above, the sun casting dappled light onto the path. It was so quiet, apart from birds calling to each other and the occasional squawk from a pheasant. Ahead, I spotted a small cottage built from red brick, with a chimney. It was straight out of a fairy tale.

'There it is,' Jim said. 'The Earl of Elmbridge had it converted into an art studio for Lady Violet after the game-keeper went off to fight in the war. It hasn't been touched since she died, I don't think. There isn't a path leading to it as there's nothing for visitors to see.'

This was an exciting development and I caught my breath.

What mysteries could be found there if it hadn't been used since Lady Violet's death in 1941? Would any of her paintings still be there?

'Can we take a closer look?' I said.

'I don't have a key with me, and I'll have a job finding it.'

'Can I have a peek through the window, at least?'

'Okay, go on then,' he said.

He picked up a big stick and used it to bat the ferns out of the way. When we reached the cottage, I peered through one of the windows, taking in the grand fireplace with a Persian rug in front of it. Dust sheets covered a couple of armchairs, and what looked like a chaise longue. Then I spotted the easel. On it was a portrait of what appeared to be a man, but I couldn't make out much. Could it be Luca?

'I need to find out where the key is,' I said. 'But what if you can't find it?'

'If going inside will help with your exhibition, we can always break the lock, if we have to,' Jim said.

His radio buzzed, and he removed it from his belt.

Jim, we've got a ewe stuck in some barbed wire, over in the Dairy Field. Over, came a voice.

'All right, I'll be there shortly. Over,' he said into the radio, then turned to me. 'I have to go, Claire.'

'Okay.'

When we reached the gate, I thanked Jim for showing me the cottage. We parted company, and he headed off towards the field in the distance.

As I walked back to the office, I couldn't get the gamekeeper's cottage out of my mind. Could that really be a portrait of Luca that I'd seen through the window?

Later, I sent Jim a text asking if he'd had a chance to find the key to the cottage yet. After a bit of a search, he found it in a cupboard in the shed, and left it on my desk with a note while I was at lunch. I seized the opportunity to go straight down there. When I unlocked the door and stepped inside, I was met with a damp, musty smell. I switched on the light and the bulb glowed a little, making a light fizzing noise. My eyes were drawn again to the painting of the man I had seen through the window. He was dark, and very handsome, and he wore a white shirt open a few buttons at the neck. The signature said *Violet Grant*: Grant must have been her maiden name as I'd read in the guidebook that the earl's family name was Wentworth. Maybe she'd wanted to use a different surname for her identity as an artist.

The man in the painting looked familiar, and I felt as though I knew him, but couldn't work out why. Perhaps he looked like someone famous. I used my phone to take a photo of the portrait; then, picking it up, I looked on the back, and there it was: *Luca Mancini, November 1940*. Margaret had said he was living with the Marshalls on the farm, but weren't the Italians the enemy? I knew from history lessons at school that they changed sides at some stage, but at the beginning of the war Italians would probably have been considered for internment.

Looking around the cottage, it was as if no one had stepped inside since Lady Violet's death. The guidebook said she'd died while staying at her house in Suffolk in July 1941, of influenza. It did seem strange for someone in their early twenties to have died in that way. Perhaps Margaret would know more about what had happened. On our next visit to Hyacinth Place, would she tell us more?

I opened the drawers in the desk to see if there might be something interesting inside, such as a letter or a journal. But I found they were all empty. Disappointed, I studied the other paintings lined up on the floor, by the wall, one by one, in case doing so gave me any clues to the mystery that seemed to be unfolding. They were all still lifes – one was of a bowl of fruit –

and the only portrait was the one of Luca. Who was he to Lady Violet?

I closed the door, locked up and headed to Jim's shed to return the key. On the way, I spotted Helen with a man taking photos of the house, and I presumed he was Ed, who she'd mentioned that night at the Old Fox.

Approaching them, I said, 'Hello, there.'

'Hi, Claire,' Helen said. 'I was going to bring Ed over to your office to introduce you, but you've saved me a trip.'

Ed continued to snap away, his face scrunched in deep concentration, and didn't acknowledge me.

I told Helen about my discovery at the gamekeeper's cottage and showed her the painting on my phone.

'That's a wonderful portrait,' she said. 'Lady Violet was talented.'

'She was indeed. He seems familiar though, doesn't he?'

Helen looked at the photo again. 'Yes, I know what you mean. Can't put my finger on it though.'

Ed came over and Helen introduced us. He had floppy dark hair and was older than me, probably in his forties. He wore a jumper with a V-neck and jeans.

'Pleased to meet you, Claire,' he said, proffering his hand. I shook it.

'Hi.'

'Claire will need photos taken of the below stairs rooms when they're ready for the exhibition,' Helen said.

'No problem, just let me know when you need me,' Ed said.

'Okay, thanks.'

He smiled. 'My pleasure, Claire.'

There was something about when a man used your name unnecessarily, almost as if to make his mark on a sentence. It was kind of flirtatious.

'Claire recently split up with her boyfriend,' Helen said.

What was Helen doing?

'Oh right,' Ed said.

'You should really do the decent thing and take her on a date.'

What was Helen *thinking*?

'You don't have to do that,' I said with a nervous laugh.

'That wouldn't be a problem,' Ed said. 'Do you like parties, Claire?'

Nodding, I said, 'Yes.'

'Maybe you can come to an event in London with me some time soon?'

'Sounds good,' I said.

'I'll get your number from Helen after and message you.'

'Okay,' I said.

'Well, we need to get these photos up on the website, so see you later,' Helen said, walking away.

'Bye.' I gave them a wave.

'See you later, Claire,' Ed called after me.

Helen had embarrassed me so much, but I knew her heart was in the right place. Ed was probably just being polite, and I doubted he'd get in touch.

I took the key to the gamekeeper's cottage back to the shed. Jim was at his desk, talking on the phone. He looked over his shoulder and winked at me. Smiling to myself, I sat down and waited for him to finish. Jim ended his phone conversation and swivelled round in his chair to face me and said, 'Was it worth the trip down there then?'

I pulled up the photo of the portrait on my phone. 'Look what I found,' I said.

He leant forward and did his best to appear interested. It wasn't his kind of thing but still, I was proud of my discovery and wanted to show it to him.

'You seem very pleased,' he said.

'I can use this in the exhibition and hopefully it will help with my search for Tabitha,' I said.

'Good stuff,' he said, and turned back round to face his computer.

Maybe showing Margaret the photo of Luca's portrait would jog her memory. I hoped so much that it would.

CHAPTER 33

CLAIRE

The next morning, I called Hyacinth Place to book another visit. But Margaret's carer said she still had a cold and it would be better to wait until she'd fully recovered, hopefully the following week. I'd try calling again on Monday. And so instead I immersed myself in putting together a file for the Below Stairs exhibition in June. Although I still had a few months, the time would pass quickly enough, and there was still a lot to be done. The builders needed to finish renovating the below-stairs quarters and I still needed to find furniture and items to fill the rooms we planned to open. I'd look in the basement where they were stored. The best way to make these rooms look as genuine as possible was to look at old photographs.

That evening, I carried on reading *Mrs Field's Diary*. An interesting paragraph stood out to me, from December 1941.

> *Penelope is living with me after effectively being made redundant by her employer's sudden death. She was assigned another role for a short time but is no longer needed, poor thing. However, I am grateful for her assistance around the house as my health has been deteriorating lately. I bumped*

into Mrs M, the mother of one of the servants at a grand country house in the area, today and she alerted me to a scandal. It would be inappropriate to divulge anything more, but it was rather intriguing, I can tell you!

What an interesting paragraph. Could it refer to Gatley Hall? I took a photo and added it to the Margaret folder on my phone. When Helen and I next visited Hyacinth Place, I'd show this information to Margaret and ask if she knew anything about it.

When Friday came, Jim messaged to ask if I wanted to share a Chinese takeaway and a few drinks that evening and, pleased by his suggestion, I replied to say yes. When I got back to the cottage, I changed into Trackie Bs and a cosy jumper and filled a glass with red wine. My phone buzzed on the sofa next to me.

Hi, it was nice to meet you the other day. I wanted to invite you to an event tomorrow night. Officially, you'd be my photographer's assistant, but you'd be able to act as any other guest. It's at a new hotel bar, Swish, in Charlotte Street, London. Let me know and I'll send the address. Ed *smiley face emoji*

What should I say? Here was my chance to dress up like the old days and attend a fancy event. Hadn't I missed doing things like this?

I replied:

That sounds great, thanks. Put me on the list! Claire *smiley face emoji*

He answered straight away with the address and said to be

there by 7.30 p.m. This was a chance to make use of my going-out wardrobe. I replied to thank him.

Jim came through the door, carrying a bag of logs and with a newspaper under his arm. He put it all in front of the fireplace.

'You'll be pleased to hear my shower is fixed,' he said.

'Oh, that's good,' I said, although it was sad that we might not see as much of each other. 'What have you got there?'

'I noticed you weren't using your fireplace and had a few logs to spare, so I thought you could have them.'

'That's kind of you. Thank you.'

'I bet you don't know how to make a fire, do you?' he said.

Smiling, I said, 'Not really.'

He got down on his knees in front of the fireplace and started rolling up sheets of newspaper and making croissant shapes with them.

'So, it helps if you make a few of these and pile them up with the logs, like this,' he said.

I joined him on the floor and made a couple of them with him.

He removed a few twigs from his pocket. 'It's a good idea to use kindling to help get it started,' he said. 'I'll bring some more over. Do you have any matches?'

'Yes, in the kitchen.'

I went to get them, and handed him the box. He struck a match and lit the newspaper, and before long had a fire going.

'That's lovely. Thank you, Jim.'

'It's only a few logs, but I'll bring you some more another day,' he said, using the poker to encourage the flames. The room instantly felt warmer and cosier. He'd done a really nice thing for me.

'Glass of wine?' I said.

'Why not?' he said.

I went into the kitchen and poured us both glasses, and

handed him one. My phone buzzed, and I looked down to see a thumbs-up from Ed. I smiled to myself.

'You look happy. What's going on?' he said, taking a sip of his wine.

'I've just been invited to a thing in London, tomorrow night,' I said.

'Where?'

'Ed asked me to go to an event he's covering. It's at a new bar at a hotel in Charlotte Street, you know, near Oxford Circus.'

'I know where Charlotte Street is, Claire,' he said in a huff.

'What's up with you?' I said.

'Nothing.'

'I'm not sure I believe you.'

'It's just, well... I'm not a massive fan of Ed,' he said.

I guessed this was understandable after what Helen had told me about Ed having a one-night stand with Samantha at her divorce party.

'Where did this come from out of the blue, anyway?' he said.

'Helen introduced us the other day. Ed will be taking photos of the Below Stairs exhibition for me.'

'How nice of him.' His tone suggested it was anything but.

'He is volunteering, unpaid, so he can't be that bad.'

'In return for what will be lucrative work once the wedding season begins. You know that's the only reason he's doing it? To be on the recommended photographers' list?'

'What do you have against him, exactly?' I said, testing Jim to see if he'd tell me the real reason.

He shrugged. 'He seems like a bloke who mixes with the kind of people you're trying to get away from.'

'What do you mean?'

He undid one of the buttons at the neck of his polo shirt.

'You know, pretentious types who go out just to get their photos taken for tabloid magazines.'

'I just miss going out in London. It's not that exciting round here, is it?'

'Suit yourself.'

'Okay. I was going to ask you to help me decide what to wear, but won't after all.'

'That's more of a job for someone like Helen. Who do you think I am, Claire, your male best friend like in one of those cheesy romcoms?'

'I'd like your opinion, that's all.'

This exchange made me feel uncomfortable, and I regretted telling him about the event.

Jim's phone rang. He lifted it from the pocket of his khakis and checked the screen.

'Sorry, I have to take this, Claire.' He answered. 'Hello, yes.' Glancing at his watch, he said, 'Sure, see you in a bit.' He slid his phone back into his pocket.

'Who was that?' I said.

'Samantha's nanny can work tonight after all, and she's invited me over.'

'I thought we were getting a takeaway?'

'Another time. Sorry, I have to go.' He got up and headed for the front door.

'Good job you've only had a sip of that wine so you can still drive.'

'Yep. See you tomorrow, maybe?'

'I'm out tomorrow, at the party.'

'Oh yeah, bye then.'

As Jim walked through the door, closing it behind him, I felt lost. What had just happened? Would he have abandoned me for Samantha if I hadn't told him about going out with Ed?

. . .

The following afternoon while I was reading on the sofa, I heard Jim's front door open and shut as he returned from Samantha's. The pump from his newly fixed shower started humming shortly afterwards. I needed to think about getting ready for London. I had to wash and style my hair, paint my nails, select my outfit, apply full make-up. The whole routine could take ages, and I liked being able to take my time.

While I was running tongs through my hair, a knock came at the door. I went downstairs to open it, still in my dressing gown. Jim was standing there.

'Oh, Claire, I was going to ask what you're doing tonight, but forgot you're going to London, aren't you?'

'I am indeed.'

'Well, I hope you have a good time.'

'Thanks.'

'Do you want me to drop and collect you from the station so you can have a few drinks?'

This was a kind gesture, especially after our exchange the day before.

'Are you sure?'

'Yeah, of course. When shall I take you to the station?'

'Five thirty?'

'Okay, knock when you're ready.'

'Thanks a lot, Jim.'

'No problem.'

At five thirty, I got my wool coat off the hook as I was running late and knocked on Jim's door as agreed. I was wearing a little black dress and gold heels, a matching clutch under my arm containing essentials. When Jim opened the door, he raised his eyebrows.

'Looking good, Miss Bell,' he said.

'Thanks,' I said, my cheeks warming as I pushed my arms through the sleeves of my coat. While he locked up, I did my best to compose myself. Did he find me attractive or was he just being nice?

It was the first time I'd properly dressed up in a while and, although my body was squeezed into my dress so tightly that eating even one peanut might make it difficult to move, I felt good. As I walked alongside Jim through the rose garden, stepping around cracks between the paving stones in my heels, I couldn't help wishing he was my date. It was a bit chilly to be wearing a dress, even with my coat on, and my legs, in tan nylon tights, were cold. We reached Jim's pick-up truck and he drove me to the station.

When I got out of the car, he said, 'Just message me when you're on the train home, and I'll wait here.'

He was being kind, and I appreciated it.

'Okay, thanks a lot,' I said. 'See you later.'

'Bye,' he said out of the car window. I could feel his eyes on me as I walked away from the car towards the ticket office.

As my heels were already rubbing my feet, I took a taxi from Waterloo station to Swish. Before Gatley Hall, I'd attended events like this one all the time, often arriving alone and that hadn't fazed me at all. Now, here I was, afraid to go inside. I took the stairs that twisted down to the floor below, the carpet thick and purple with yellow swirls, nerves engulfing me. What was my problem? Besides my confidence being knocked by all that happened in the run-up to Christmas, I'd forgotten what it was like to be all dressed up and walk into a room full of strangers.

A lady with a clipboard ticked my name off the list and waiters stood at the open doors with trays of champagne. Inhaling and lifting my chin, I took a flute and smiled, saying, 'Thank you,' as I entered the room. It was dimly lit, with a bar circling the centre. Straight away, I spotted Ed photographing a group of women. He wore black trousers and matching polo-neck à la James Bond, and looked very cool, his thick dark hair slicked back. He was a catch, and the women giggled as he made jokes while directing them. When he'd finished, I approached him and said, 'Hi,' and he said, 'Claire, you made it.' We double-kissed, and he looked me up and down.

'Nice dress,' he said. 'So, are you ready to be my assistant?'

'Okay.'

He removed a piece of paper from his pocket and handed it to me along with a pen. 'Here's a list of a few photos I need to get. Can you help me find everyone?'

I skimmed the names and, as someone who'd read *Go You!* magazine every week in my pre-Gatley days, I knew who everyone was. 'Sure,' I said.

'Okay, I can see Smiley Face over there,' I said, spotting the girl band who'd had several hits. I approached them and Ed followed and took photos while they posed, adjusting their faces and bodies to various angles until he was done.

While Ed talked to their manager, someone tapped me on the shoulder and I turned round to see Toby's wife, Madeleine. Toby, Madeleine and Miles had all been part of the same friendship group at university.

'Claire, I didn't expect to see *you* here,' she said.

'Likewise.'

'An old schoolfriend of mine is editor of *Go You!* and so she invites me to loads of events,' she said. 'How did you get an invite?' she said, as though I wouldn't be worthy.

I'd never liked Madeleine much, as she liked to patronise me at every opportunity.

'I'm here with a photographer friend.'

'Between you and me, I am sorry to hear about the baby.' She gave my arm a squeeze. I stepped backwards.

The room was quite noisy, with music coming through the speakers and people talking loudly. Surely, I hadn't heard her correctly? I asked her to repeat herself.

'You must be devastated to hear about the baby,' she shouted.

'What are you talking about?' I said.

'Oh...' She put a hand over her mouth. 'Gosh, hasn't Miles told you yet?'

'Told me what?'

'Natasha is pregnant.'

Natasha, Miles's ex from university.

'What do you mean? Are you saying it's...'

'Miles's yes. Goodness, Claire, I have put my foot in it, haven't I?'

This news was shocking, and all I could do was try not to look bothered.

'Didn't you know they'd been seeing each other again?' Madeleine said.

'No, I didn't. How pregnant is she?' I said.

'Just over three months.'

Counting back to the day I left Miles, it hit me.

'Three months – but that's before...' I thought back to when Dad died in November and I'd stayed at Deborah's for a couple of nights. There had been a dinner party at Toby and Madeleine's, and I'd known Natasha would be there. Had something happened that night? While I was recovering from the shock of losing my father? How could he? And had they been sleeping together before that? 'You held a dinner party that I didn't come to because my father had just died,' I said.

Nodding, Madeleine pulled a face and tried to squeeze my arm again, but this time I took a step backwards before she could.

'I think there might have been what one would call "overlap",' she said.

She was loving this conversation and I needed to get away from her.

'But...' she continued, 'I always thought they'd end up together. You two weren't a good fit, were you?'

Here was my opportunity to put Madeleine in her place for once.

'Well, now you can go on all the double dates you want with your best friend by your side, Madeleine. But just to let you know – and do feel free to pass this information on to Miles – I am living my best life. Breaking up with him was absolutely the smartest decision I've made in years.'

Before she could answer, I walked away, and approached the bar. I ordered a tequila slammer, and knocked it back, and then downed another one. After that, a double vodka and tonic. I needed to drink my way through how Madeleine had made me feel. How dare Miles tell me he didn't want children and then get his ex of all people pregnant? No doubt she'd already moved into the flat I'd spent years making special for what was supposed to be our future together. But what I'd said to Madeline happened to be true. I was living my best life in Gatley, and it had taken her delivering this news for me to realise it. The break-up should have happened sooner. Miles getting someone else pregnant was yet another blow, but I'd just have to get over it.

Once all the photos were taken, guests started to leave and Ed suggested we went to the bar upstairs. He ordered vodka and tonics for us both and we sat at a table in the corner with banquette seating. A man in a tuxedo played big band songs on a grand piano, and the bar filled up with couples and groups of friends out having fun on a Saturday night. We had a few more drinks and, when I looked at my watch, I saw the time was eleven thirty. The last train to Gatley left Waterloo at eleven forty-five. Fifteen minutes was nowhere near long enough to get there.

'Damn, I've missed my last train,' I said.

'I've got a room upstairs. You're welcome to stay, if you want?'

'Really?' I said, studying him. He was handsome but I didn't want to sleep with him. Pulling a face, I said, 'I can't...'

'Look, it's a suite. You can sleep on the sofa. Why don't you think about it while I get you another drink?' he said, getting up and heading for the bar.

I got out my phone, but saw it had run out of battery. Damn, I needed to tell Jim not to pick me up from the station. I'd have to borrow a charger.

Ed brought over another couple of vodka and tonics.

'So?' he said.

'Okay, I'll stay. Thank you,' I said.

'Great, now we can relax.'

The next morning, I woke up on the sofa in Ed's room fully clothed, relieved that nothing had happened. I recalled him asking to kiss me, and I'd said, 'I'm getting over a break-up, sorry.' He'd said, 'Okay, you have the sofa then,' and gone into the bathroom. Ed clearly hadn't understood when I implied this in the bar.

Now, looking over at the bed, I saw he was asleep, his breathing heavy, and my head was throbbing from far too much alcohol for my own good. There was a bottle of water on a table by the window, and I poured myself a glass and downed it. I got my phone out of my bag and only then recalled the battery had run out the night before. Spotting a charger, I plugged my phone in. Instantly, several text messages from Jim popped up on the screen.

I presume you'll be on last train and will be at the station to pick you up as agreed

I'm at the station. See you shortly

You weren't on the train. Where are you?

Are you okay? Do you want me to come and get you from somewhere?

I can't sleep, am worried you might not be okay. Please let me know you're all right

And the messages went on and on, up until four in the morning. My stomach lurched. How could I behave so badly? What a terrible person I'd been, allowing him to think something was wrong. I tapped a message into my phone, squirming as I did so. He'd be furious with me.

Jim, I'm so sorry. My phone ran out of battery. I stayed at the hotel where the event was held as missed last train. So sorry, hope you aren't too angry with me?

The three dots danced straight away. Clearly, he'd been waiting to hear from me.

Glad you're all right.

The full stop – *the* latest way to snub by text – said it all. He was fuming. I caught a glimpse of myself in the mirror above the desk. My mascara had run, and I looked really awful. I went into the bathroom and swigged some mouthwash and did my best to remove the make-up from under my eyes with a cotton bud and some of the hotel cleanser. While I was applying fresh foundation from my clutch, Ed tapped on the bathroom door.

'Are you in there, Claire?'

I opened the door, and he stood there in a pair of boxers,

looking rather fit, his six-pack showing how much time he spent at the gym. He smiled, clearly aware of what a great body he had.

'Morning, Ed. Thanks for letting me stay on your sofa. I have to go now, though,' I said.

He sighed. Yes, he was a catch, but I didn't think much of him as a person. Jim would have offered me the bed and slept on the sofa himself.

'Don't you want breakfast? We can get room service.'

Perhaps he was hoping I'd sleep with him now, but that wasn't going to happen.

'I need to get back.' I put on my shoes and ouch my feet hurt.

'Okay. See you at work then,' he said, going into the bathroom and closing the door firmly behind him.

'Bye,' I said, through the door. 'And thanks again for letting me stay.'

He probably felt I'd led him on in some way, but I hadn't meant to. If Madeleine hadn't told me about Natasha's pregnancy, I wouldn't have drunk so much and would be at home now.

I put on my coat, went to the lift and made my way down to the lobby.

As I left through the swing doors, I spotted a coffee shop opposite. I got myself a large cappuccino, a bottle of water and a cinnamon bun, and consumed everything as I walked to Oxford Circus tube station. There was a chill in the air, and once again my legs were cold, and I could have kicked myself for not bringing blister plasters for my feet. Before long I was at Waterloo, quiet before Sunday visitors descended on London, and I took the next train to Gatley. I nodded off a couple of times on the journey and when I reached the station, my only option was to walk home in my heels. There were no cabs in Gatley and I couldn't exactly ask Jim to pick me up. My feet were so sore by now and I winced with every single step, feeling I deserved it for treating Jim so very badly.

When I reached Rose Cottage, all I wanted to do was climb into bed. As I unlocked the front door, Jim came out of his cottage. His eyes were unusually cold, and they were puffy underneath. I bit my lip, not knowing what to say.

'So, you're back,' he said.

There was no sign of his usual cheeky grin, and I felt miserable, worsened by my hangover and the state of my feet.

'I'm really sorry, Jim,' I said, stepping out of my shoes. I couldn't bear to stand in them any longer.

'You've already apologised, so no need to do it again,' he said with a sigh.

'All right, well I am truly sorry.'

'It will take a bit of time before I can forget about what you put me through last night. I haven't had any sleep. Next time you go up to London for one of your fancy parties, don't ask for my help,' he said.

It had been his idea to pick me up from the station, but that didn't excuse my appalling behaviour.

'I won't.'

He turned his back on me and walked down the path towards the rose garden.

'Jim, I will find a way to make this up to you,' I called after him.

He didn't turn round. I went inside, devastated by what I'd done to one of the few people who seemed to care about me.

CHAPTER 34

CLAIRE

Once inside, I took a shower and slept for a few hours. When I woke the news seemed to hit me about Miles and Natasha's baby, and I found myself sobbing on the sofa for the rest of the day. How could he do that to me? It wasn't just about the baby, but also that he'd been seeing Natasha while living with me, and so soon after my father had died. And then there was Jim. How could I ruin our friendship like that? And what could I do to make amends? Saying sorry wasn't enough. I was ashamed of myself, and would rack my brains to find a way to get him to forgive me.

That evening when I was about to switch off my phone, a message flashed up from Miles.

Maddy just called. I'm so sorry you had to find out that way X

Shaking my head at his pathetic attempt to apologise, I tapped out a reply with my thumbs: 'How could you do that to me? I can't believe...' then deleted it. Then I tried a few variations, trying not to sound too emotional, but couldn't get my

words to work. Putting my phone down, I decided the best reply
was no reply.

The next day, I followed my usual routine at work, but
didn't see Jim. He wasn't at the Stables that morning and I
missed seeing him walk around the property. He could have
been working in his shed the whole time, or be resolving some
ranger-related crisis, but I sensed his absence.

'Have you seen Jim today?' I said to Helen during an afternoon coffee break.

'He's gone to Cleveland House for a few days. There's a flu
outbreak amongst their rangers.'

I knew Cleveland House was down the road, also owned by
the ATP. 'Oh, okay,' I said. So, I'd be alone on the property for a
few nights. Even though me and Jim weren't getting on, it
would still have been reassuring to know he was next door. I'd
have to pull myself together and be brave. Jim could have told
me himself, but I guessed he was still angry about Saturday
night. That was fair enough.

'If I arrange to see Margaret this week, will you come with
me?' I asked.

'Of course, just let me know when,' Helen said. 'How did it
go with Ed?'

'Not that well, really.'

'That's a shame. I was hoping you and Ed might get along.'

Then I told her about letting Jim down badly.

'Oh no, poor Jim. He must be fed up.'

'Yeah, I hope he forgives me,' I said. 'By the way, would you
mind not setting me up on any more dates, please?'

Helen pulled a face. 'I'm sorry, it's the romantic novelist in
me. I just want you to be happy, but can see I've come across as
an interfering busybody.'

I laughed. Helen did seem to want the best for me. 'Thanks,
I appreciate you caring.'

'It's no problem. As I said before, if you need to talk, I'm your woman. Oh by the way, wrap up warm tonight – there's talk of a cold snap on its way.'

'Ah, thanks for the heads-up,' I said.

Helen caring like this gave me a warm feeling and it was nice to know she was there if I needed her.

That night, I had a bad dream about Miles and Natasha and their baby – they were all laughing at me – and woke up sweating. As I lay awake, all I could do was worry about whether Jim would forgive me. Getting my phone from the bedside table, I checked his Instagram account. He'd recently posted a carousel of the big old oak tree he was fond of through the seasons.

Zooming in on his profile photo, I studied it for a few minutes, admiring his kind face and piercing blue eyes. I missed him. When he returned, I'd do everything I could to get him to forgive me. If I bought him a present, what would I get? It would have to be environmentally friendly. Perhaps a thoughtful gesture would work better. Maybe I could make him a nice meal. Putting my phone on the bedside table, I snuggled back under the duvet, hoping to get at least a couple of hours' sleep before the alarm went off.

In the morning, I washed and dressed. With little food in the house, I'd get breakfast at the Stables. But when I opened the front door, a sea of white lay before me. Snow, and lots of it. Stuck in my daydream world while getting ready, I hadn't looked out of the window. The scene that lay before me was truly beautiful, but I needed to find a pair of boots. Would the roads be blocked? And would Gatley Hall be open for visitors? I didn't even own a pair of wellies. But I did have an old pair of fake-fur-lined boots, and it wouldn't matter if they got spoiled. I went back upstairs and changed into jeans, pulled on the boots and took my warmest polo-neck jumper out of the wardrobe.

Putting on my wool coat, I opened the front door, and stepped outside.

I couldn't help smiling. Feeling an urge to record the Christmas-card scene around me, I took a few photos on my phone, in the rose garden, and of Gatley Hall, which looked so pretty with snow on the roof and windowsills. Maybe I'd do some sketches later, get out my watercolours. The path hadn't been cleared and I wondered if whoever was responsible – the gardeners, I expected – would be able to get to work to do it. The snow was inches deep, coming halfway up my boots, but when it thawed the path would be icy and slippery.

When I reached the stable yard, the green door of the Stables was firmly shut. My phone vibrated and I got it out of my pocket. A message from work.

Gatley Hall will be closed to staff, volunteers and visitors today due to the snow. Many of the surrounding roads are closed, and we'll keep you updated when we know more. In the meantime, if your role allows you to work from home, please do so, otherwise enjoy the time off, and we'll be in touch. ATP Senior Management

So, here I was, alone at Gatley Hall, and with hardly any food in the house. Hopefully the snow would thaw so things could return to normal the next day. I'd be able to log in to my laptop from the warmth of the cottage, and so I made my way back there, contemplating working from bed.

When I got back to Rose Cottage, I built a fire with the rest of Jim's logs and made a pot of coffee and two slices of toast with marmalade. Covering myself with a throw, I snuggled up on the sofa with my laptop. After a few hours of work, I made a sandwich for lunch. With little in the fridge for dinner, I considered whether Jim would mind me taking some food from his place.

His key was safely hidden behind the cutlery tray in the kitchen drawer. I tapped out a quick text.

> *Again, I'm so sorry about Saturday night and hope you'll find a way to forgive me. Missing your company. I'm stuck here on my own with Gatley Hall being shut due to all the snow. Would you mind me borrowing some food and milk from your place? Will pay you back obvs *pleading face emoji**

I leapt when my phone buzzed immediately.

> *Help yourself.*

Relieved to hear from him, but sad his message was curt and ending with a full stop, I replied to say thank you and took his key from the kitchen drawer. Leaving the cottage, I went next door. Although I'd been over there before, I hadn't fully appreciated how much nicer his living room was than mine. He had a plush, comfy sofa, fancy glass coffee table, a thick carpet and TV with big screen. A bookcase was packed with novels, including many classics, and biographies, as well as hardbacks about the countryside and the environment. I could have quite a nice time in his cottage while he was away. It was tempting to ask if he'd mind, but it would be a bit cheeky when he was barely speaking to me.

I went into the kitchen and opened the fridge. Half a pack of bacon, six eggs, two pints of milk, a block of Cheddar and in the salad drawer an onion, mushrooms, carrots. In the cupboard, I found tins of beans and tomatoes, dried spaghetti and a bag of large potatoes. I put everything in a tote bag, making a mental note to pay him back. As I was about to leave, it struck me that this was my chance to have a proper nose around and find out more about Jim. I went upstairs to his bedroom. The bed was made and everything was clean and tidy, apart from a pile of dirty clothes on the floor. I picked up one of his t-shirts and held it to my nose and inhaled. It smelt of him – that oaky, musky scent mixed with his hard-earned sweat. I didn't want to put it down. How long could I survive being stuck in this place without his company?

In his office, there was a printout of a book entitled *A Day in the Life of a Ranger*. Reading the first page, I was impressed. His command of English was good, and the words were engaging. He talked about how he'd changed his life after getting fed up with being stuck in an office all day in London and commuting by train. In the winter, he'd go to work in the dark and return in the dark and eat lunch at his desk. I'd been there too. Why hadn't he told me about this book?

Leaving everything as I'd found it, I went back to my cottage, and the silence. Snow made the place seem quieter than ever. I put Jim's food in the fridge. The fire had died down and there weren't any more logs to top it up with. Sitting on the sofa, I looked out of the window at the hills. Perhaps I'd sketch out some of those photos while having so much time on my hands.

That afternoon I worked at the kitchen table, but it started to get very cold, and I went upstairs to find another jumper. I passed the thermostat for the heating and turned it up, but half an hour later the cottage didn't seem to be any warmer. Reaching behind me, I found that the radiator was stone cold. I went round to check the other ones, and they were all the same. Was the boiler broken? At a time like this too. In the kitchen, I looked through the tiny window on the boiler. The flame had gone out. So, no heating or hot water. What was I supposed to do? There was no way a plumber would come out in the snow.

Taking out my phone, I texted Jim again.

My boiler is broken! Hope you don't mind if I keep myself warm at your place in the meantime? *smiley face emoji*

This time, there was no prompt reply. What if he had no signal? The cottage was so cold, my only option was to take a few things over to Jim's and sleep there for the night. Perhaps the snow would clear in the morning, and things could go back to normal. I'd ask Jim for the name of the plumber he had used.

After another hour there was still no reply and I threw a few of my belongings into a bag and went next door. As soon as I stepped inside, it was significantly warmer. For dinner I had a jacket potato and beans, then I lit a fire and set up camp on the sofa. I watched TV, finding the film *The Holiday*, and thought back to Helen and her meet-cute comment that first day when we were talking in the Stables. I pulled the throw over me and fell asleep, waking at midnight, cold again as the fire had gone out.

Would Jim mind me sleeping in his bed? I went upstairs and it did look inviting, and so I climbed in fully clothed and switched off the light and pulled the duvet over me, inhaling the smell of him.

The next morning, I woke up in Jim's bed, at first forgetting where I was. I'd had a dream about me and Jim, walking through the fields in the snow, and I found myself smiling at the image in my head. When would he be coming back? It was now Wednesday. Opening the curtains, I saw the snow hadn't cleared, and checked for any sign of communication from Jim on my phone. Nothing. I fetched my work things from next door and set myself up at his kitchen table.

A message flashed up on my phone.

Sorry for the silence. The WiFi went down and there is no phone signal here. Of course, feel free to stay at mine. Are you okay?

I replied,

Hope you don't mind that I stayed at yours last night as
freezing cold at mine. Also working my way through
your fridge. Am okay, thanks but a bit lonely *sad face*
emoji*. *Although at least now warm*

Glad you're warm, but sorry you're lonely

Thanks. How are you?

I'm stuck in a staff flat at Cleveland House, but we've
been having boozy parties. Bit hungover tbh

I sighed. It was difficult not to envy the people who were
getting to have fun with him.

That night, I slept once again in Jim's bed, and the following
morning I worked at his kitchen table. The weather forecast
showed low temperatures with little sign of the snow thawing. I
was bored out of my mind, and the food supplies were running
low. I pulled up some of the snowy photos on my phone and,
after finding some sheets of paper on the printer in Jim's office
and a pencil on his desk, I started to sketch the view from the
cottage. The walled rose garden and the cast-iron gate on the
left; trees on the right, rolling hills in front of me; all covered in
snow. I was enjoying myself and could feel the act of creating
something lifting my mood.

I was preparing a pot of coffee when a key turned in the
front door.

'Claire?' It was Jim's voice.

I almost ran to the front door, so happy to see him, but did
my best to hide the joy from my face. When I saw him, I wanted
to wrap my arms round his neck and give him a big hug.

'Jim, how did you get here?'

He peeled a heavy-looking rucksack off his back and
dropped it onto the floor. 'I drove into the village and walked

the rest of the way. I was supposed to stay at Cleveland House for a few more days but thought you might need company – and food.'

So, he'd forgiven me. Thank goodness. I wanted to show him some affection, but couldn't. Feeling awkward, I said, 'Well, thank you, I just made coffee. Do you want some?'

'I certainly do,' he said, throwing me a smile as he pulled up a chair at the table.

CHAPTER 35

CLAIRE

'Thanks for coming back, that was really nice of you,' I said.

Jim looked across the table at me and smiled again, and it seemed genuine. He picked up the sketch I'd been working on.

'What's this?'

'I took a photo from the front door and was so bored, I started sketching.'

'It's really good, Claire. You should do more of this,' he said.

My face warming at the compliment, I said, 'Thanks, Jim.'

'Have you been properly out there yet though?' he said.

I shook my head. 'I don't have any wellies.'

'That's no excuse. It's so beautiful and you have to see it all. There are loads of abandoned pairs of wellies in the shed. What size are you?'

'Forty.'

'Okay, I'll go and grab some. Back in a minute.'

Before I could stop him, he went out of the front door. I wasn't desperate to go out in the freezing cold, but he was right.

Ten minutes or so later, Jim returned, holding a pair of black wellies. 'Here you are,' he said, putting them down on the floor.

I wasn't a fan of wellies, but these I approved of. They'd hardly been worn and had buckles at the top.

'I didn't know wellies could be so stylish. Thanks,' I said.

'One of the house managers left them behind when she moved on. I also have something else,' he said. 'Come and see.'

He opened the front door. Outside was an old wooden sledge, propped up against the wall. I'd seen it in a photo in the guidebook, with a male servant sitting on it.

'Oh, a sledge,' I said, half-heartedly.

Jim's eyes lit up. 'Isn't it great? It was at the back of the shed with a few other things from the olden days.'

'And you plan to go on it?'

'We plan to go on it, Claire.'

I laughed. 'I don't think so.'

'There's a massive hill in the Dairy Field, and I want to go down it on this sledge. Imagine how brilliant that would be?'

'We're not children.'

'Didn't you go sledging as a child and love it though?'

Growing up, I'd always envied my friends when they told me they'd been sledging with their dads in the snow.

'Nope.'

'Well, you have missed out.'

'I feel a bit old for it now.'

'But you're thirty, aren't you?'

I nodded.

'That's the same age as me. We're not old, Claire. Come on, let's go and have some fun. You've been stuck indoors for days. And you don't have to go on the sledge if you don't want to. Just come for the walk, at least.'

Rolling my eyes, I said, 'I'll get my coat.'

'That one you've been wearing to the office?'

He was referring to the wool coat I'd worn when commuting into London.

'Yes.'

'I've got a warmer one you can borrow.'

Jim was being quite bossy.

'All right, thanks.'

He went upstairs and returned with a navy-blue puffa jacket. It was too big for me, but I put it on and rolled up the sleeves. It was lovely and warm, and came down to below my knees. And it smelt of him.

'Do you have a hat?' he said.

'Yes, I have my beret.'

Shaking his head, he reached into a cupboard under the stairs and retrieved two bobble hats, one navy blue and one grey.

'This one should fit you,' he said, placing the grey one on my head, pulling it over the tops of my ears, his eyes meeting mine as he did so. 'Perfect.'

'Thanks,' I said.

He wrapped a matching scarf round my neck and tied it into a knot.

'Gloves?' he said.

'I have these,' I said, getting the brown leather pair out of my coat pocket. Deborah had regifted them to me one Christmas.

'Well done,' he said.

He put on a khaki jacket that didn't look as warm as the one he was lending to me, and I appreciated his generosity.

'Let's get those wellies on, then,' he said.

He went out of the front door, and when I was ready I stepped outside. The cold air brushed my face, but the rest of me was covered by everything Jim had provided. He picked up the sledge.

'I'm definitely not going on that thing, by the way,' I said.

'Well, I am. And the walk will do you good. Look at that face, getting rosy already,' he said, adjusting my hat and scarf, and brushing my right cheek with his gloved hand. My gut hopped at his touch, but I shut the thought of us being more than friends out of my mind.

We went through the rose garden, treading carefully around our previous footprints as they'd become sludgy and slippery.

'I'll grit this path later,' Jim said. 'You'd better grab hold of my arm.'

I did as he suggested, using the excuse to squeeze in close to him. We left the rose garden, and took a right down the side of the house. Before us was the most beautiful, unspoilt view. A pretty scene like our very own Narnia lay before us, and the only sign of life was smoke coming out of the chimney at Home Farm in the distance. We passed the lake, covered in ice, and went over the stile into Long Meadow. The snow came more than halfway up my wellies and it was difficult to walk, more of a trudge. And then when we reached the Dairy Field, there it was, the steep hill. The thought of going down it on a sledge was very daunting. We headed for the brow.

'Would you like to go first?' Jim said, winking.

'You go ahead,' I said.

'Okay.' He set the sledge down on the ground. 'Will you give me a push to get started?'

'Sure,' I said.

I tried to push him, but he was too heavy.

'Why don't you get closer to the edge, then it will be easier?' I said.

He used his feet to move forward, and I pushed him, and he was off, and he shouted, 'Woohoo,' as he sped down the hill at some speed. The thought of doing the same scared me, and there was no way I'd do it. He reached the bottom and picked up the sledge before climbing back up the hill, waving as he approached. In that very moment, surrounded by such beautiful scenery and in Jim's company, a wave of happiness swept over me. I was enjoying myself. When Jim reached the top, he held out his hand.

'Your turn.'

'Oh no,' I said, shaking my head. 'I'm just a spectator.'

'But it's exhilarating. You won't regret it, I promise.'

Pulling a face, I said, 'No.'

'How about we go together? The sledge is more than big enough for both of us.'

It was longer than most sledges and I considered his suggestion.

'Well?' he said.

'You promise to take care of me?'

'Yes!'

He placed the sledge on the ground and gestured for me to get on, and said, 'You sit at the back.'

I did as he said, and he took his position in front of me.

'Hold on tight,' he said, pressing his wellies into the snow to shift us forward.

Lifting my feet off the ground, I wrapped my arms round his waist, leaning into him. Closing my eyes, I breathed in the scent of his neck.

And then we were off down the hill, going so very fast. We both screamed like you would on a rollercoaster, my adrenaline racing. A school trip to Alton Towers as a teenager was the last time I'd done anything this daring. We reached the bottom of the hill and I felt a huge sense of achievement.

'What did you think?' Jim said.

'That was fun,' I said.

'Again?'

'Okay,' I said.

We walked back up the hill and, this time, it was even more exhilarating as my fear had dissipated. This was the most exciting thing I'd done for ages; but, as we neared the bottom of the hill, the sledge hit something – a rock, possibly – and turned on its side, and I rolled over into the snow.

'Ow,' I said, as my ankle hit a tree stump, and then I swore under my breath, not wanting Jim to hear how foul-mouthed I could be.

Looking up, I saw him standing over me, his face scrunched up. He sighed.

'What happened?'

'I banged my ankle on that tree stump,' I said. It was throbbing. 'It really hurts.'

Squatting down, he removed my welly and peeled off my sock, and gently ran his hand over my foot and ankle. Despite the pain, I couldn't help enjoying his soothing touch.

'Where does it hurt?'

He pressed the skin around my ankle until I said, 'There.'

'We'd better go and get some ice.'

He helped me up, and said, 'Try not to put any weight on it. Here, lean on me. Let's get you in the warm without making it worse.'

We trudged up the hill and crossed the field, and he helped me over the stile and back past the lake and the house, through the rose garden, and to his cottage, where he unlocked the door and helped me to his sofa. He went into the kitchen, and I heard him open the freezer door and bang the ice cube tray about in the sink. A few minutes later, he returned with a sandwich bag filled with cubes and a rubber band.

'Here, give me your foot,' he said, perching on the edge of the coffee table. I lifted my ankle. It was really throbbing now, any adrenaline having subsided, and he rested it in his lap. He studied my ankle carefully, turning it gently in his hands. His touch distracted me from the pain, and he said, 'Ah, there's a bruise coming out, that's good.' It was turning a purple-black colour and looked terrible.

Sighing, I said, 'Yes. Would you mind getting my bag so I can find some ibuprofen?'

'Let me sort this out first.'

He placed the sandwich bag filled with ice onto the bruise

and used the elastic band to keep it in place. The ice relieved the pain a little. Taking a couple of cushions and putting them on the sofa, he said, 'Right, rest your foot on these.' He propped another cushion behind my head, then brought me my bag and a glass of water.

'There you are,' he said, perching back on the coffee table, his eyes reflecting concern.

'Thanks,' I said.

'I'm sorry, it's all my fault.'

'You did promise you'd look after me,' I said with a laugh.

'True. I hadn't factored in random tree stumps though.'

'Yeah, I know. Thanks for the ice pack.'

'I'm an expert from my days of sports injuries.' He smiled. 'Now it's my job to get you better.'

'That's very kind of you.' I took two ibuprofen with water.

'It's a good job my shower is fixed, at least. I need to have a wash and do some work. I'll go in the office upstairs,' he said. 'Text me if you need anything, and don't move unless you really have to. Maybe take a nap?'

'Okay,' I said.

He threw me a nod and closed the living room door behind him. It seemed he felt bad for encouraging me to go sledging, but it wasn't his fault. And perhaps this was karma for me letting him down that night. The injury had at least balanced everything out. He'd only been trying to get me to break out of my comfort zone and, apart from the injury, the experience had been good for me. Jim brought out a different side of me, and that could only be a positive thing.

CHAPTER 36

CLAIRE

That evening Jim made me spaghetti with tomato sauce, and I ate it on the sofa on a tray. He took his food upstairs and carried on working in the office.

When he brought his empty plate down later, he said, 'Do you want to sleep in my bed again, and I'll crash here?'

He was being a real gentleman, and his kindness was a comfort.

'Don't worry. I'll be fine here, thanks,' I said.

Frowning, he said, 'Are you sure?'

'If I'm struggling to sleep, I can watch TV here,' I said.

He sat on the coffee table and gestured for me to put my ankle in his lap. I'd removed the ice pack earlier, and the bruise had come out more. Most of my ankle was now a purple-black colour.

'This is good progress,' he said. He pulled an elasticated white sock out of his pocket. 'Here, put this on. It will help with the pain.'

He carefully slid the sock over my toes and up my foot, over the ankle. I tried not to show how much I was savouring his touch and said, 'Thanks for looking after me so well, Jim.'

'Hope you manage to get some sleep. Goodnight.'

'Goodnight, Jim.'

When I woke up the next morning I hopped into the kitchen and made a cup of tea. My ankle didn't feel great, and I could barely walk on it.

While the kettle was boiling, I looked out of the window at the back garden, which joined with mine, and thought about filling the terracotta pots with geraniums and roses and lavender. I could plant some herbs too. Deborah had always kept a nice patio garden and I'd helped her with it when I was younger. Miles's flat didn't have a garden, and in the summer when it was hot I'd longed for outside space. My thoughts running away with me, I didn't hear Jim come into the kitchen, and jumped when he said, 'Morning, Claire.'

Turning round, I said, 'Oh hi, Jim.'

'How's the ankle?'

'Not great.'

'Oh dear. You just need to keep off it. The snow might start to thaw this afternoon, and I'll go and grit the path through the rose garden at some point today.'

Not wanting our period of forced proximity to end, I said, 'That's good.'

'Guess you'll have to stay here until your boiler is fixed though,' he said.

'I'll call a plumber on Monday. Can I use yours?'

'Sure, I'll send you the number.'

'Would you like a cup of tea?' I said.

'Yeah, thanks.'

I made tea for us both, knowing by now that, unlike Miles, Jim wasn't picky about how strong it was or the amount of milk used. Jim carried the mugs into the living room and I hobbled back in with him, resuming my position on the sofa. He took the armchair opposite.

'So, do you want to go sledging?' he said.

I rolled my eyes, and he laughed.

'Seriously, I am sorry though, Claire,' he said.

'I appreciate you trying to get me out of the house and have some actual fun.'

'So, you're glad you went, despite the injury?'

How could I not be when it had meant getting to experience him running his hand over my foot so tenderly? I was quite enjoying all his attention.

'Of course I am. And to be honest, it's made me feel better about Saturday night. I was feeling so bad about it and am so sorry.'

'Let's forget it,' he said.

'It's no excuse, but can I tell you why it happened?' I said.

He lifted his eyebrows.

'Go on then, tell me.'

'I bumped into an old university friend of Miles' and well, she told me something...' A tear ran down my face. What was wrong with me?

'What, oh no, are you crying?' He got up and handed me a handkerchief from his pocket. 'It's clean, don't worry.'

It was so embarrassing, but all the events from the past few weeks seemed to have come to a head and I burst into tears.

Jim went quiet while I sobbed my heart out. I wiped my eyes, but I must have looked a right old mess. Somehow this didn't bother me as it usually would. It wasn't like me to cry in front of anyone, but I was comfortable in Jim's presence. He was my friend.

When I eventually stopped, he said, 'What did this person tell you?'

'Miles had been seeing his ex while we were together and she's pregnant.'

Jim shook his head, his eyes filling with fury. 'What?'

'Yeah, she's probably moved into the flat I spent years making nice for her.'

'I'm sorry. That must have been difficult to hear, especially at a party where you didn't know anyone.'

'It was. I went to the bar and knocked back a few drinks very swiftly, missed the last train and my phone battery ran out. I meant to charge my phone and send you a text, but was quite drunk. Ed said I could sleep on the sofa in his room. Nothing—'

'I don't need to know,' Jim said.

'Nothing happened. I'm just telling you that because I want to. In the morning, I plugged in my phone and saw all your messages. Jim, I felt so terrible for putting you through that.'

'It's understandable, and all done now. Let's move on. More importantly, are you okay?'

'Not really, but I will be,' I said.

I was confident saying this. Being in Gatley had brought me strength I didn't know I had.

'If you need to talk, you know where I am. I'll go out for a walk this morning, after gritting the paths, and make a note of what needs doing on Monday. Then, I was thinking I could make us a nice lunch, and we could watch a film?'

'That sounds good to me.'

'Okay. Let's get some more ice on that ankle before I go then.'

Jim went into the kitchen and came back with a bag of ice. He was fitting it round my ankle when the doorbell rang.

'Who could that be?' he said.

He got up to open the door.

'Darling,' a woman said, and it was Samantha's voice. My heart sank.

'Hey, how did you get here?' he said.

'I managed to get the 4x4 down the drive. The nanny is

staying so I thought it might be a nice opportunity to come and see you. Good surprise?'

'You could have texted first.'

'Sorry, I didn't want to do that and not be able to get here. Wanna go upstairs?' she said.

'Err.' He stepped back, and she came into the cottage, clocking me on the sofa. Her face dropped.

'Oh. This looks very cosy.'

'Claire sprained her ankle, and her boiler is broken, so she's been staying here.'

'How sweet of you to accommodate her,' Samantha said, throwing me one of those smiles that doesn't reflect in the eyes.

I reciprocated.

'Well, this is a bit awkward,' she said.

'Isn't it?' Jim said, sliding his hands into the pockets of his Trackie Bs.

As I tried to fasten the ice pack round my ankle, he said, 'Let me finish sorting that out, Claire. Samantha, why don't you get yourself a drink? I'll see you in the kitchen in a minute.'

Dismissed, she flounced into the kitchen, the heels on her tan-brown riding boots tapping the wooden floor.

As Jim sorted out the ice pack, I said in a low voice, 'What are you going to do?'

He shrugged and I sensed he didn't want her to be here. Had he been enjoying our forced proximity as much as me?

'I don't know yet.'

'I'm sure you'd like to take Samantha upstairs, and...'

'Well, I can't do that with you here, can I?' he said.

'Do you want me to go next door?'

He shook his head. 'If she'd messaged, I would have told her not to come over.'

'But she's here now, and after all that effort too.'

'Perhaps I'll take her for a walk.'

'You could always do it in the shed, although it might be a bit chilly in there.'

Grinning, he stood up. 'See you in a minute.'

He went into the kitchen, and the two of them spoke in low voices. I couldn't make out what they were saying but the conversation seemed strained. They reappeared.

'We're going for a walk,' Jim said.

'Okay,' I said. 'Have a nice time. Maybe you should take Samantha sledging,' I couldn't help adding.

She rolled her eyes and shook her head, and they went out of the front door, leaving me alone.

An hour or so later, Jim returned, alone, thankfully.

'Where's Samantha?' I said.

'She's going home,' he said.

'Oh, I'm sorry.'

Was I heck.

'She couldn't really have stayed over with you being here,' he said.

'I feel responsible for depriving you of fulfilling your needs,' I said.

He threw me a look, his lips forming a half-smile.

'Let's not talk about it, shall we?'

'Okay.'

'She's giving me a lift into Gatley to get supplies, and I'll bring the pick-up truck back. Apparently, everything is open as they've cleared the road in and out of the village for the bus route. It's just the driveway that needs to thaw, and hopefully that'll happen soon. Some of the snow has melted already.'

'I'll give you some money.'

He dismissed my suggestion with the wave of a hand. 'Get that ankle rested, and I'll be back in a bit.'

CHAPTER 37

CLAIRE

It wasn't long before everything returned to how it had been. I stayed at Jim's for another two nights but, after Samantha's visit, the bond we'd formed during those days spent together seemed to have broken. She'd reminded us both of her existence, turning up out of the blue like that. The plumber came out on Monday morning and relit the pilot light on the boiler, and I was glad to be back in my own home, to sleep in a bed again. Although able to put a little weight on my ankle, I needed to be careful not to make it worse, so I carried on working from home when Gatley Hall reopened. I texted Helen, telling her about the sledging incident, and asked if she'd be able to drive me to see Margaret at Hyacinth Place on Friday afternoon. We met in the staff car park.

In the car, she said, 'How have you been, apart from the injury, that is?'

I told her about the past few days with Jim, and Samantha's unexpected visit.

'Goodness, you have been through the wringer,' she said.

When we reached Hyacinth Place, we met Margaret in the lounge once again. She was drinking tea and had applied pink lipstick this time. Remembering the photograph of her from the guidebook, I could see her younger face. Her cheekbones were now more defined, the nose slightly larger, the lips thinner. Her nails were painted the same shade of pink as her lipstick, and she wore a navy-blue dress with a floral pattern. It hung off her slim frame, but the colour complemented her pale complexion. I could see she liked nice clothes and had an interest in fashion.

'Thank you for seeing us again,' I said.

'It is lovely to have visitors,' she said. 'And it gives me a reason to make myself look respectable. I'm much better than last time you came. That cold made me feel rather dreadful and sometimes my memory isn't what it once was.'

'I'm glad to hear that,' I said, hoping she might be able to tell us more on this visit. I told her about finding the portrait of Luca and showed her the photo. 'What was he doing here in Gatley?' I said.

'He was an Italian prisoner of war on Home Farm, working as a labourer,' she said.

This explained why an Italian had been in Gatley during the war. I showed her the page from *Mrs Field's Diary* about a servant's mother saying there was a scandal at a country house in the area.

'I don't have my glasses with me, can you read it out?' Margaret said.

I did as she asked, and Helen's eyes lit up.

'Oh can I have a look at that, Claire?' she said.

I handed her the book and she read the paragraph, nodding.

'The house team has been aware of this information for some time and we always wondered if Mrs Field was talking about Gatley Hall. As there were a few country houses in the area, we couldn't be sure,' Helen said.

'Mrs Field was my Aunt Edith. I have a copy of that diary somewhere,' Margaret said.

'Really?' I said.

Helen and I exchanged an excited glance.

'Yes, and Penelope is me. It took all my strength not to tell her the truth when she asked one evening. She was a gossip, you see, and I was being loyal to my late mistress, Lady Violet, but also my intention was to protect Tabitha. It was vital that no one knew her real identity.'

'Can you tell us more?' I said, thrilled with this development, but still confused about who Tabitha was.

'Lady Violet was the Earl of Elmbridge's third wife. He'd discarded the other ones because they didn't give him an heir. She decided to take a lover and get herself pregnant so he couldn't do the same to her and take the money inherited from her father. When my mistress died during childbirth, Mr and Mrs Willis, the butler and housekeeper, adopted Tabitha and I worked as her nanny for a short time. The earl didn't know anything about it as Lady Violet only planned to tell him if the baby was a boy. If Tabitha had been male, Lady Violet would have asked her husband to accept the child as his heir.'

Everything was beginning to make sense now.

'Oh, I see,' I said. 'So, why do you want us to find Tabitha?'

'I have a brooch I need to give to her. After the birth, Lady Violet called me into her room and told me she was going to die. I didn't believe her and thought she was merely exhausted from the birth and all the emotions that came with her situation. She made me promise to take her brooch from the safe when returning to Gatley Hall, and then to give it to Tabitha on her wedding day.'

'So, why didn't that happen?'

'My first husband, Tom, told me he'd sold it as we didn't have much money when we were first married. I was devastated but there was nothing I could do about it. But when he died, I found the brooch in a shoebox. He'd kept it all along.'

'What is the brooch like?'

'It's oval-shaped with an emerald in the centre and

surrounded by diamonds. Lady Violet's grandmother wore it when meeting Queen Victoria.'

This scandalous story was intriguing. And a connection to Queen Victoria would work well in the Below Stairs exhibition. I visualised all the materials I could use to tell this story: Luca's portrait, the photo of the servants, the wedding photo of Margaret and Thomas, the page from Mrs Field's diary, the brooch itself if I was able to borrow it.

'And where do you think Tabitha might be?' I said.

'She must still be in Italy.'

'Italy?' I said.

Margaret nodded.

'The ATP wouldn't pay for me, us' – I turned to Helen – 'to go to Italy, I'm afraid.'

'I'll pay for it. I have plenty of money.'

'We couldn't accept that,' I said.

She shrugged. 'Well, that is a shame. An all-expenses-paid trip to Italy? Are you sure you want to miss out on this opportunity? You'd not only get to see Florence, but also fulfil the request of a dying woman? And just think how wonderful it would be to uncover a secret that changes the history of Gatley Hall?'

Margaret had a point, but how could Helen and I justify going to Italy?

'We'll let you know. Is that all right?' Helen said.

'Very good,' Margaret said. 'Ah, I have something for you, Claire.' She picked up her handbag, took out a hardback book and handed it to me.

'What's this?'

'This is the copy of *A Room with a View* that belonged to Lady Violet. She was going to lend it to me after she'd read it, and I took it from her bedside table after she died, as a keepsake. Reading that book and watching the film has kept me going at times. During my marriage to Tom there was no possibility of going to Florence, but this book took me there.'

What a lovely gesture.

'Are you sure?' I said, a lump in my throat.

'Of course, I want you to have it. I'm passing my love of Florence on to you, and I expect you can use it in your exhibition, seeing as it belonged to Lady Violet.'

'Thank you very much, Margaret. This is very kind of you.'

'I urge you to read it, especially if you can't decide whether to go to Florence or not. And watch the wonderful film too.'

'All right. If I did go to Florence, how would I go about finding Tabitha, exactly?'

'Her surname is likely to have changed. Once it was Willis, then her married name was Dobson. But who knows if she married again? Luca mentioned she had a boyfriend and she might have married him since then.'

'We can have a look on the internet.'

'Do go to Florence. Start with Luca's bakery, the Pasticceria Mancini.'

I made a note in my phone.

'It will be an adventure, and you're sure to regret it if you don't,' Margaret said. 'And don't forget the Italian saying, "Dolce far niente", meaning the sweetness of doing nothing. Luca told me about it. When you're there, you'll understand how it fits so well with the Italian way of life.'

'Dolce far niente,' I repeated to myself. 'How beautiful. How do you know Luca is still alive?'

'After visiting Florence, I wrote to his granddaughter. She sends me a Christmas card every year, signed by him.'

'All right. Thank you, Margaret,' I said.

We got up to leave and she took hold of my hand, smiling.

'If you do this for me, Claire, dear, I will be ever so grateful to you.'

Heading for the door, I felt we had enough information to

hopefully get us somewhere. But also, I was more determined than ever to help this woman fulfil her lifelong wish.

'Wait,' Margaret called after us.

I went back. 'What is it?' I said.

'I've just remembered what I should have included in the letter. Tabitha's middle name was Lucia. Mr and Mrs Willis tended to call her the English equivalent, Lucy, as they thought it suited her better. When my second husband, Nathan, and I went to La Spezia to look for Tabitha, there was an English girl who'd been waitressing there called Lucia. We were never sure whether it was her, but it sounded likely.'

'That is very helpful information. Thank you, Margaret,' I said.

She seemed so determined for us to reunite Tabitha with her mother's brooch. I guessed this was because she'd made a promise that remained unfulfilled.

In the car, Helen and I went over what Margaret had said.

'Do you think we could find Tabitha?' I said.

'I don't know,' Helen said. 'I'd like to go to Florence though, wouldn't you?'

'I'd love to go to Florence, especially for the art and the history.'

'Oh, Claire. You must go. I'm wondering if we even need to tell the ATP about this. Unless we find Tabitha of course. After all you've been through lately, a holiday would do you good. Why don't we book the flights? I could find us a boutique hotel online. We'd have a lovely time, and think of the food and wine. I could expense my half and write a book set there. My publisher has been asking me to write an Italian romance for years and I've never got round to it.'

'You really think we should go?' I said.

The idea of getting away did appeal, and to Florence, somewhere I'd always wanted to visit.

'Yes, Claire. I think we should. Let's strike while the iron is hot.'

'And I'm thinking that if we can reunite Tabitha and the brooch her mother wanted her to have, that would help us get publicity for the Below Stairs exhibition, especially with the Queen Victoria connection.'

'You are probably right. I can imagine Wendy in PR would be very excited if we do manage to reunite Tabitha with that brooch.'

CHAPTER 38

CLAIRE

Helen and I arranged to go to Florence a couple of weeks later, allowing time for my ankle to improve so I could enjoy walking around and exploring the birthplace of the Renaissance, an art history student's dream. During that time, spring came. The trees lining the path leading to the Stables bloomed with pink and white blossom; daffodils and snowdrops popped up all over the place; crocuses grew in circles at the base of trees; and tulips grew in the flowerbeds at the back of Gatley Hall. This spring display was inspiring, and I began to carry a small sketchbook around with me. It wasn't long before I'd filled it with pencil drawings of flowers and views of the rolling hills. Back at the cottage, I got out my watercolours and brushes and began to paint again. I ordered some plants and compost from the garden centre and filled the terracotta pots in the patio garden with geraniums, lavender and pansies. When it was warm enough, I'd be able to sit outside after work with a glass of wine.

As my ankle recovered and the mornings got lighter, I'd get up earlier to walk down to the lake and sit on a bench with my morning coffee – in the reusable cup Jim had given me – before work. I continued to prepare for the Below Stairs exhibition, working out what furniture and objects were needed from storage, and I gathered information for the display about Margaret's story. Photographs needed to be blown up and I arranged for Luca's portrait to be brought over from the gamekeeper's cottage. To make the exhibition extra special, though, Helen and I needed to find Tabitha and persuade her to come back to England to collect the brooch.

Having the Florence trip in my diary was exciting and I bought a guidebook and studied it. Apart from looking for Tabitha, I wanted to go to the Uffizi art gallery and see Botticelli's *Birth of Venus*. And I wanted to see the real statue of Michelangelo's David at the Galleria dell'Accademia rather than just the replica in the Piazza della Signoria. There was the Duomo, the cathedral, with its pink, green and white marble stripes, and of course the Ponte Vecchio, a beautiful bridge crossing the River Arno. I started to read *A Room with a View*, and watched the film, as advised by Margaret, and this made me want to go to Florence more than ever.

Helen reserved rooms in a boutique hotel called Ostello Dolce and booked flights to and from Gatwick online. She had air miles to use and asked me if I minded flying to Milan. This meant we'd need to hire a car. Helen offered to drive, as I couldn't until my ankle was completely better. I googled restaurants, made dinner reservations, booked tickets for the Galleria dell'Accademia and the Uffizi, and put together a two-day itinerary. And I went through my summer clothes, putting aside favourite dresses for dinners out. It was all so exciting.

The night before our flight, I packed and left my suitcase by the front door. We'd be leaving early the next morning, and I wanted to get a good night's sleep. I checked my phone in the kitchen and saw a message from Helen.

Really sorry, Claire. I have a stomach bug, would you believe it? There's no way I can go on a plane in my current state. You could change the name on my ticket to someone else. Maybe Jim can go with you?

My excitement turned to disappointment. I doubted Jim would want to go, and at such short notice too. But how would I drive the hire car?

A knock came at the door, and I went to open it. Jim stood there.

'Now my shower is fixed, I feel the need to knock,' he said, clocking my suitcase on the floor. 'Do you have any milk?'

'Of course, come on in.'

'You're off to Florence tomorrow?' he said.

'Well, I was supposed to be, but Helen just cancelled.'

'That's not good. Why at such short notice?'

'She has a stomach bug.'

'She was fine when I saw her only an hour or so ago.'

'Was she? Perhaps she deteriorated when she got home.'

'Who knows? I saw her chatting away with Wendy in the office. She didn't seem to have anything wrong with her.'

I shrugged.

'You can still go on your own though, right?' he said.

'Helen was supposed to be driving us to Florence from the airport because of my ankle.'

'Oh,' Jim said.

We went into the kitchen, and I filled a small jug with milk from the fridge and handed it to him. Selfishly, I hoped he might feel some responsibility for the sledging incident and offer to drive.

Seizing the moment, I said, 'Do you feel like driving instead?'

Jim laughed. 'I don't think so. Can't you get a taxi or something?'

'It's quite a long way from Milan to Florence, around three hours.'

'Can't you take the train?'

'I guess, although I have no idea how to get a train in Italy. But also it might be fun if you came along?'

'I'm sure you could work out the trains, Claire, although that suitcase does look cumbersome.'

'You can probably change Helen's flight and room into your name?' I said.

'It's a possibility, I guess.'

'Please, Jim? I can't cancel, there's too much depending on this trip. I've mapped out the Below Stairs exhibition and going to Florence will hopefully give me the key to the centrepiece, about Lady Violet's brooch and the story linked to it.'

'All right. Why don't you send me Helen's number.'

Spending one-on-one time with Jim in Florence would no doubt be *the* best experience.

'You're going to come with me?'

'I'm not promising anything but will see if I can get the time off.'

'Oh Jim, thank you!' I picked up my phone.

'Okay, I'll keep you posted,' he said as he left, closing the door behind him.

CHAPTER 39

CLAIRE

The next morning at five o'clock, I added a few last-minute things to my suitcase and sat on it while doing up the zip. When would I learn to travel light? I wanted to dress the part in Florence though. A knock came at the front door and, when I opened it, Jim stood there, a holdall resting on his shoulder.

'Is that all you're taking?' I said.

'It's only three nights,' he said, looking at my suitcase. 'You seem to be travelling as expected.' He rolled his eyes and I smiled.

He'd arranged everything with Helen the night before. Whether he was coming because he felt responsible for my ankle or not, the gesture of support was touching.

Jim drove us to Gatwick airport, and the flight didn't take long. Soon we were in a white Fiat Uno en route to Florence. Despite getting up so early, I felt hugely energised, unable to wait for what lay ahead. Immediately we were thrust onto a busy motorway and we headed south. At a services stop, we bought rolls filled with mozzarella and tomato along with bottles of chilled water and coffees. The temperature was much warmer than at home, and we sat outside at a picnic table in t-shirts. It was so good to feel the sun on my face.

'Are you glad you came?' I said.

'I'm glad to be able to make up for your injury in some small way,' he said.

I thought about how I'd let him down that Saturday night and how forgiving he'd been. And now he felt responsible for my sprained ankle, and that meant a great deal. It wasn't his fault. Sledging with him had been the most exhilarating activity I'd done in years.

We reached Florence mid-afternoon and checked into our rooms. They were next to each other and facing the River Arno, with a view of the Ponte Vecchio. We walked out onto our adjacent balconies with window boxes of hot-pink geraniums clipped onto the railings. It was such a romantic setting and I felt like Lucy Honeychurch out of *A Room with a View*. The warm breeze brushed my face, and at that moment life couldn't be more perfect. Here I was in a place I'd always wanted to visit, staying in a room with the best view – Helen had chosen well – and next door to Jim. We were neighbours, like in Gatley.

He leant on the railings and looked ahead. 'Well, Helen seems to have done me a favour,' he said.

'It's worked out well for you, hasn't it?'

Part of the itinerary I'd put together was a plan to go to Luca's bakery and ask about Tabitha the following morning. But for now, my urge was to explore this magical place and use the tickets I'd bought online.

'Shall we go out for a wander?' I said.

'Why not?'

The hotel was located in a small square with a gurgling fountain, complete with smiling cherubs set in a circle. From there we headed for the centre along a quiet, narrow street with cobblestones and tall old buildings in yellow and terracotta, some of them with shutters. We reached the main drag with its shops and cafés. The street bustled with tourists in shorts and t-shirts and hats, some wielding cameras with big lenses, and most of them moving at a snail's pace. We made our way around a group of Americans, a tour guide leading the way with a flag attached to a stick.

We reached the big square, the Piazza della Signoria. It was dominated by the replica of Michelangelo's statue of David, a man with a very fine physique, sculpted in white marble. He was surrounded by tourists taking photos.

'I have tickets to see the real David at the Galleria dell'Accademia,' I said.

'I hadn't realised you'd booked me in for a cultural tour. Is there any point when we have the replica right here?' Jim said.

'Well, I'm going, and you can choose to come with me or not,' I said. 'Tomorrow, we're going to the Uffizi to see Botticelli's *Birth of Venus*.'

'Can't wait. Why don't we get an ice cream first?' Jim said.

'Good idea.'

It didn't take long to find a gelateria and I chose pistachio flavour in a cone, and Jim selected chocolate. We ate our ice creams on a bench near the Duomo with its beautiful terracotta dome and marble facade in white, green and pink.

'Margaret told me about an Italian saying that fits this moment,' I said.

'What's that?'

'Dolce far niente.'

'Meaning?'

'The sweetness of doing nothing.'

'That's my kind of saying,' Jim said.

Although tourists were bustling around us, I still felt a sense of calm. There was no pressure to do anything apart from enjoy ourselves.

We walked to the Galleria dell'Accademia and saw the real statue of David. Although we'd seen the replica, it was so good to see the original, sculpted by Michelangelo himself, and tick it off my list.

When we went back outside, I said, 'There's one more thing on the itinerary for today before dinner, I'm afraid. You don't have to come with me, but I think you might like it.'

'What's that?' Jim said.

'You'll see,' I said.

I took him to the Duomo and we climbed the narrow, spiral staircase with many steps, 463 of them according to the guidebook, which led to the Brunelleschi dome. The climb made my ankle ache, and I wondered if it was such a good idea. But when we reached the top, I'd timed it perfectly; the sun was setting, the sky purple and orange and pink and blue. We were rewarded with a view of the terracotta rooftops and domes of Florence, the gentle Tuscan hills as a backdrop. We found a quiet corner and there were no words as we studied the spectacular view together. As we stood beside each other, it struck me that I wouldn't have wanted to experience that moment with anyone else. Jim meant more to me than I'd been admitting to myself.

'You know I prefer the countryside to cities, but this is very impressive,' Jim said. 'You were right to bring me up here.'

'It wouldn't have been the same without you,' I found myself saying.

He looked at me, his eyes meeting mine, those blue eyes like the Med on a hot day, and my gut lurched as I registered he was about to kiss me. He hesitated, as if waiting for me to give him the nod, to lean forward a little and show that any move would be welcomed. How I wanted him to kiss me right then – but was it such a good idea? Was I totally over my relationship with Miles? The last thing I wanted was for Jim to be a rebound guy – he was too good for that. Was being colleagues and neighbours such an issue? And what about Samantha? As I debated the pros and cons in my head, taking far too long about it, Jim's phone rang. He took it out of his pocket and checked the screen and sighed.

'Who is it?' I said.

'Samantha,' he said.

Of course it was.

'Aren't you going to answer it?'

'I'll call her later,' he said, putting the phone away.

The moment was ruined. We weren't going to kiss now, were we?

'Does she know you're here, with me?' I said.

'I haven't had a chance to tell her yet,' he said.

'You should,' I said.

'I know, and I will,' he said, curtly.

As we walked back to the hotel, I thought about how much the tickets for the Duomo had cost me: a small fortune. What a waste of money and an opportunity. If only I'd made it obvious that I wanted him to kiss me. That was what I wanted, wasn't it? But Samantha would still have interrupted us, so perhaps it was for the best. Would I get another chance? Her call would have reminded Jim of her existence. Even though they weren't in a relationship, he might feel guilty for starting something with me before ending their arrangement.

We returned to the hotel, exchanging few words en route, the mood a little tense. In my room, I showered and changed for dinner. Feeling a need to look my best, I selected what I believed to be my most flattering dress, made from lemon-yellow linen. I slipped on a pair of kitten heels before checking myself in the mirror many times. If any dress was going to encourage Jim to try to kiss me again, this was the one. I knocked on his door, and he opened it wearing a pair of boxer shorts. I went inside and sat on the bed while he dressed. Being present while he put on his clothes felt rather intimate and I scrolled through my phone, watching him out of the corner of my eye. He put on a crisp white shirt and jeans, sliding his phone into a back pocket.

It was dark when we left the hotel and we walked along the pavement by the river with old-fashioned streetlamps lighting our way. We crossed the Ponte Vecchio to the restaurant I'd booked, and ordered Florentine steaks with chips and salad, and shared a bottle of Chianti. The walls were crammed with old black-and-white photographs of the city and the ambience was romantic with white tablecloths and tea light candles and soft music played. While taking a photo of our surroundings to post on Instagram, my phone rang. It was Miles. What did he want?

I declined the call, but Jim said, 'Who is it?'

'Miles.'

'Why would he be calling you?' Jim said.

Shaking my head, I said, 'I don't know.'

A message flashed up, followed by several others.

Are you there?

Can you pick up?

Natasha lost the baby.

I need to talk to you x

Oh no. I took a glug of my wine and looked across the table at Jim. 'I think I need to call him.'

Jim sighed. 'Okay.'

I went outside and called Miles.

'Claire.'

'Are you all right?'

'No.'

'When did it happen?'

'A couple of weeks ago, but she's just moved out, gone to live with her mother. She doesn't want to be with me any more.'

The loss of a baby was a terrible thing and, despite my feelings towards him and Natasha, I felt bad for them both. But he'd almost destroyed me with his selfish behaviour and now he expected me to be there for him. His call couldn't have come at a worse time.

'I'm sorry,' I said.

'Will you come over?'

'I'm actually in Florence.'

'You're in Florence. Who with?'

'Jim.'

'The man in the towel. I knew he fancied you.'

'No, that's not why he's here. He replaced my colleague when she dropped out last minute. We're here for work.'

'Yeah, sure.'

A moment of silence passed between us.

'So, why are you calling, Miles?'

'I just felt this need to hear your voice.'

'How would I help?'

'I miss you, Claire Bear. When Natasha got pregnant, I came round to the idea of having another child. I wonder if we ought to talk about giving it a go.'

He must be joking. I'd spent the past few months getting over him and now this, especially after the way I'd found out about Natasha's pregnancy.

'I'm sorry about your situation, but that's not going to happen.'

'What, you won't even consider it?'

'We're done, Miles. You can't expect to come crawling back after the way you treated me.'

'Fair enough.'

'Can I go now?'

'Yes, whatever, you go and enjoy yourself.'

'Thanks, I will.'

Back inside the restaurant, Jim was scrolling his phone. He looked up when I sat down.

'What was all that about?'

I relayed the conversation to him.

'Obviously I wouldn't wish that on anyone, but at the same time, what a cheek, expecting you to be there for him,' he said.

'I know.'

'Well, you can forget about him now and move on.'

Jim looked across the table at me. Did he still want to kiss me? I wondered if he'd called Samantha back, and how the conversation might have gone. For some reason I couldn't bring myself to ask.

After dinner, we walked back to the hotel and the temperature had dropped. Jim gave me his grey jumper and I pulled it over my head, inhaling his oaky, musky scent. The streets were filled with the murmur of people ambling to and from bars and restaurants, all dressed up. The moon was full and shone brightly like a giant lamp lighting our way. I took it as a sign that something significant was about to happen and I hoped Jim might try to kiss me again.

Back at the hotel, we took the lift, just us, and the tension as we studied each other in the mirror was off the scale.

'You look very pretty in that dress,' Jim said.

'Thanks,' I said, smiling to myself.

The lift reached our floor with a bump and, as we got out, Jim said, 'I feel we wasted an opportunity at the top of the Duomo earlier.'

'It was a beautiful setting,' I said, rooting around in my bag for the room key. What did he want me to say? Yes, you should have kissed me before Samantha called. You should have had your phone on Do Not Disturb so it wouldn't happen. You shouldn't have answered. You shouldn't be seeing someone like Samantha in the first place as she's all wrong for you.

'Can I have my jumper back?' he said.

'Oh yes, of course.'

I peeled his jumper over my head and handed it to him, still inside out, and we laughed as he said, 'Thanks.'

We stood there looking at each other. 'How about we raid my minibar and have a drink on the balcony?' he said.

'Okay.'

He scanned his key and we entered his room. My feet were sore from the walk, and I slipped off my shoes. Squatting down to open the fridge, he produced a few miniatures of vodka, whisky, brandy, gin, and lined them up in a row on the desk.

'What do you fancy?'

'What are you having?'

'Claire, I must admit, I don't need anything else to drink. I just wanted an excuse to carry on where we left off earlier.'

'Oh.'

'If that's what you want, of course?'

I nodded, and he leant forwards and kissed me on the lips, and then gently pushed his tongue into my mouth. He was such a good kisser and I just wanted to get completely lost in him. We fell onto the bed, and he reached for the zip on the back of my dress, and said, 'Is this okay?'

I'd never wanted to be with anyone so much, and perhaps that was because we'd got to know each other slowly over the course of a few months. And I really fancied him. But then it struck me – what was I doing? He was still seeing Samantha, and I didn't want to be competing with her for his attention when we got home. If he wanted to start anything with me, he needed to end it with her first.

'I think we should stop,' I said.

He rolled off me and stood up.

'You're right. What was I thinking? It's too much, too soon.'

'Obviously, I want nothing more than to carry on, but if

anything is going to happen between us you need to end it with Samantha first.'

'Samantha and I aren't exclusive.'

'Yeah, but that's not really my thing.'

'Claire, I can't launch straight into a relationship with you. After what happened with my fiancée, I'm not ready for any of that. I'm not sure I will be for a while, if at all.'

'Well, there you go. I just made the right decision then.' I sat on the side of the bed and put my shoes back on.

'So, you'd want the real deal?'

He seemed surprised by this.

I got up and walked to the door. 'Jim, I'm not looking for something casual, I'm afraid. I'm sorry if I led you to believe otherwise.'

'We seem to have got our wires crossed,' he said.

'Well, no harm done. See you in the morning?'

'Okay. Goodnight, Claire. I hope this doesn't change anything, and we can still be friends?' He ran a hand through his hair, in that way he did.

'Sure, of course. Goodnight.'

I went to my room and got in the shower and let the water run over me, attempting to process what had happened in Jim's room. Had I done the right thing, turning him down like that? I'd wanted him so much but didn't want him to end up breaking my heart.

CHAPTER 40

CLAIRE

When I woke up the next morning, thoughts of Jim were running through my mind. Should I have stayed? Although I'd wanted to more than anything, it had seemed like the right decision at the time. I wasn't going to compete with Samantha for Jim's attention. Perhaps he might change his mind about starting a relationship with me once he'd had a chance to mull it over. That was the best I could hope for, but, in the meantime, we'd have to go back to being friends. All the Chianti from the night before had given me a headache and I needed caffeine. Getting out of bed, I pulled back the curtains. Before me was a blue sky, wispy clouds tinged with pink, and it was the most incredible sunrise I'd ever seen. Grabbing my phone, I took a few photos, planning on painting the scene when returning home. Selecting a pod for the coffee machine, I made an espresso and slid open the door leading to the balcony. Pulling up a chair, I sat down to appreciate the view with my coffee. The way the rising sun reflected in the river was truly magical, and in that moment, I thought again of Margaret's saying: 'Dolce far niente'.

Unable to wait until after breakfast to explore, I showered and dressed and went down to the lobby. It was only seven o'clock and there was no one around. I went outside and walked along the pavement bordering the river with the Ponte Vecchio ahead of me. It reminded me of Venice, with the little buildings running along it in lemon yellow. I approached the bridge and a man poured a bucket of water onto the pavement outside a jewellery shop and swept. The swishing sound of his broom was soporific. When I reached a gap between the buildings, I studied the river and a long narrow boat glided along as its crew pushed oars through the water. All was quiet and still, the calm before the storm, when tourists would overrun the city for the day.

It was easy to get lost in the beauty of Florence, but I mustn't forget my reason for visiting. That morning, I needed to ask about Luca at the bakery. Perhaps Tabitha had been in touch since Margaret's visit, and he'd know what surname she was using. Margaret had mentioned Luca telling her about a boyfriend in La Spezia in 1986. Perhaps they were now married.

The walk had made me hungry, but it was still too early to wake Jim to have breakfast with me. Perhaps it would be better to have some space from each other anyway. When I returned to the hotel, I found the dining room. Only a couple of tables were taken and I sat in a corner. The buffet was impressive, and I selected slices of orange melon, a bowl of muesli and a croissant. The waiter brought me coffee and I sat there and ate without feeling the need to scroll through my phone. Instead, I got *A Room with a View* out of my bag and read.

When I'd finished eating, I texted Jim to say we should meet later, after I'd visited the bakery. Using Google Maps, I went to find Pasticceria Mancini. It was only a ten-minute walk from the hotel, down a side street. Florence was starting to wake up and a few locals looked as though they were making their way to work. The doors to the bakery were open and the room bustled with customers, standing at the bar, drinking espressos and cappuccinos, and eating sandwiches and delicious-looking pastries. The smell of coffee fused with bread and cakes baking in the oven was wonderful. Customers queued right up to the door, and I could see why. Behind the counter there was a variety of delicious-looking bread, with loaves in all shapes and sizes, and then there were pastries and cakes arranged neatly under a sheet of glass. The woman behind the counter served quickly, pushing goods into paper bags before moving swiftly on to the next customer. I wanted to eat just about everything. Not knowing how to go about asking for Luca, I joined the queue, thinking I should buy something in order to start a conversation with the woman serving.

When it was my turn, I said, 'Do you speak English?'

'What you want?' the woman said.

'A pastry,' I said, pointing at what looked like a giant croissant dusted with icing sugar.

'Questo?' she said.

I nodded, and she used tongs to put the pastry into a bag before handing it to me. I tapped my card on the machine.

'And I'm looking for Luca – Luca Mancini.'

'You want to see Luca? Who are you?'

'I'm...' I didn't know what to say.

She pointed to the ice cream counter. 'You wait there,' she said.

Nodding, I said, 'Okay, thank you,' and did as she'd asked. While waiting, I studied the ice cream flavours, wanting to try all of them.

A few minutes later the woman came over, wiping her hands on the apron tied round her waist. She lifted a phone to her ear and spoke in Italian before hanging up.

'We wait some more,' she said.

I nodded. 'Thank you,' I said.

Before long, a door opened and a younger woman appeared, dressed in jeans and a t-shirt. She seemed familiar, but I had no idea why. They spoke in Italian before she turned to me.

'My mother's English is not good, so I translate,' she said.

'Ah okay,' I said.

'I am Gina and Luca is my grandfather. This is my mother, Maria.'

'Hello, I'm Claire.'

'Why you want to see Luca?' she said.

'Is he here? Can I talk to him?' I said, excited at the prospect of this.

'Yes, but he is old and gets tired. Who are you?'

I explained that I worked at Gatley Hall in England and that Luca had lived on its Home Farm during the war.

'I wanted to ask him some questions for an exhibition we're having.'

'He talks about his time in England fondly and we met Mags when she came here.'

'Can I see him?' I said.

'Come with me,' Gina said.

She spoke to her mother in Italian. Their conversation seemed a little heated, but I wasn't sure if this was how they spoke or whether there was a problem. Gina gestured for me to follow her through a door and up a few flights of stairs. We reached a flat on the top floor and she unlocked the door. Inside, she took me into a kitchen. It was a bright and airy room and through the tall windows was a view of terracotta rooftops. A light breeze lifted the curtains. In the corner a frail-looking elderly man sat in a chair, his eyes fixed on the television in front of him.

'He is watching his favourite programme, *La Donna in Giallo*,' Gina said with a smile.

Looking at the screen, I saw the programme was *Murder She Wrote*, dubbed into Italian.

Luca didn't seem to have noticed us enter the room. Gina said, 'You want coffee?'

Nodding, I said, 'Yes, please.'

She approached a machine and prepared an espresso in a tiny cup and handed it to me.

Gina spoke to Luca in Italian and he looked up, but didn't smile. He studied me with suspicion.

'Could you ask if Tabitha has visited recently?' I said.

'Don't you mean Lucia?' Gina said.

Of course, Margaret had said Tabitha might be using her middle name.

'Yes, has Lucia been here?'

Luca picked up the remote control and paused the television, clearly understanding. And then he spoke to Gina, slowly, his voice raspy, and she nodded along before turning to me.

'A few years after Mags visited, Lucia sent a letter and they corresponded for a while. My grandfather is illiterate, but his friend from the bookshop across the road read the letters to him and wrote the replies. They met a few times in secret as my grandmother would not have liked it.'

'When did your grandfather last hear from Lucia?'

'They had an argument around ten years ago. He said she shouldn't have abandoned her son in England, but she said he'd done the same to her. His situation was very different, and he told her this.'

So, Luca knew about the grandson Margaret had mentioned.

'Does he know where she is now?'

Gina spoke to him again and he replied.

'Somewhere in Liguria, a small town but he cannot remember the name. She came to Florence to study art and to see him, then she fell in love and married an Italian man, and they moved to the Italian Riviera, somewhere near La Spezia.'

'Do you know her married surname so I can try and find her?' I said.

She said something to Luca, and he shook his head.

'No, he cannot remember.'

But then he raised a hand, and said, 'Aspetta.'

'Wait, he says,' Gina said.

He pointed to a vase on the table filled with tulips, and then he said something else: 'Was a flower,' he said, in English; then he spoke in Italian.

'He says he can't remember which one,' Gina said.

Nodding, I said, 'That's helpful, thank you.' How many surnames with flowers could there be? I'd do a Google search. 'Can I give you my phone number in case he remembers?'

'Sure,' she said, unlocking her phone and handing it to me. I keyed in my number and gave the phone back to her.

'Thank you, Gina,' I said.

'You are welcome. Good luck.'

'Would Luca mind if I took a photo of him? You see, there is a portrait of him that we want to display, and it would be wonderful to include a photograph of him taken now to go next to it.'

They had a brief exchange, and Gina said, 'Certainly. My grandfather remembers sitting for that portrait in the small house in the woods.'

'Yes, we only discovered it recently.' I pulled up the portrait on my phone and showed it to her.

'That is amazing,' she said. 'Can I have a copy?'

'Of course.' I sent it to her phone, then went ahead and took a photo of Luca, who raised a smile especially.

'My grandfather is tired now, I'm afraid,' she said.

'You've both been very helpful, thank you.' I said goodbye to Luca, who gave me a nod.

Gina showed me out, and I went downstairs and through the bakery and made my way back to the hotel. I sat by the fountain in the square to think everything over. The water cascading from the cherubs was soothing and I ran through my conversation with Gina and Luca. I needed to find out Lucia's surname and go to Liguria to find her.

CHAPTER 41

CLAIRE

On the way back to the hotel, I messaged Jim to ask when he wanted to meet. After our last conversation, I was worried about it being awkward, but also couldn't wait to tell him about my visit to the bakery. We agreed to have lunch in the hotel bar, and I waited there for him. I ordered a bottle of water and read.

'Hi, Claire,' he said, and I looked up.

He had bags under his eyes and his voice was weary. Had he been lying awake thinking too?

'Hi,' I said.

We ordered sandwiches, and I told Jim about what Luca had said.

'Well, it sounds like you're not far off finding her,' he said.

'It's very exciting,' I said. 'I'll google surnames with flowers later. And I'll look on Facebook and Instagram too. Surely it won't be that difficult?'

'That's true,' he said, nodding.

'Thank goodness Mags told me she might be using her middle name. To think, I could have been looking for Tabitha all along and that would have led me nowhere.'

'Did she?' Jim said, studying the bill, and signing it.

'Yes, apparently when Mr and Mrs Willis adopted her, they preferred to call her by the English version of her middle name, Lucia instead.'

'Which is...'

'Lucy.'

He frowned. 'Lucy? And what was her surname?'

'Dobson but, as I said, it's probably one of those flower surnames now. Why?'

'Her name is Lucy Dobson?' He sat up in his chair.

'Well, when she came to Italy she starting calling herself Lucia.'

Jim swallowed. 'I don't believe this,' he said.

'What?'

'Tabitha, Lucy, Lucia – whatever you want to call her – has to be my mother.'

How was this possible?

'*What?* Jim, what do you mean?'

'How did I not put two and two together before? Remember, I told you my dad used to take me to Rose Cottage to see an old family friend called Hilda – she worked at the house during the war and adopted my mother when she was a baby.'

This was a shock. Hilda must have been Mrs Willis. What must Jim be feeling? Then I remembered Mags talking about Tabitha having a son during our first visit to Hyacinth Place, when she'd started going off at a tangent. She'd said Tabitha left him with his father so she could go to Italy and follow her dream of studying art. Could Jim really be that baby?

'Oh Jim, I don't know what to say.'

He picked up his glass and sipped the water, his eyes glazing over.

'Dad always said my mum had gone to live in Australia.'

'He must have thought it was kinder for you to believe there was no chance you'd see her again, to manage your expectations?'

'The last thing I want to do is see her now.'

'I can understand that, of course.'

He stood up. 'I need to call my dad.'

'That's probably a good idea.'

This was a huge crisis for Jim, and I needed to give him space.

He left the bar, and I took out my phone to check the photo of Luca's portrait. Finally, I knew why he'd seemed familiar. Luca and Jim's faces were the same square shape with a strong jawline. Jim's eyes were blue rather than brown and his hair was a lighter brown colour, but otherwise they looked unmistakably alike. And Gina had looked a little like Jim too, and that was because they were also related.

Luca and Jim should meet; but it didn't seem the right time to make such a suggestion.

When I got back to my hotel room, I sat in bed with the French doors open, a breeze lifting the lace curtains, and searched for Italian surnames with flowers on my phone. There was the word flower itself, Fiore, and della Rosa, and I searched for Lucia Fiore and then della Rosa on Facebook. Then, trying Instagram, I found an account with the name Lucia della Rosa. She owned an art gallery on the seafront in a fishing village on the Italian Riviera near Portofino, called Camona. This had to be Tabitha. There was a photograph of her sitting outside painting at an easel. She looked as though she'd be in her seventies, and her hair was bleached blond. Her Instagram account showed coastal scenes, still lifes and portraits and it was clear she was really talented. I needed to find her before returning to England. The rooms in Florence were booked for another night, but we ought to leave a day early and call in at Camona, especially as it was only a slight detour from the route back to Milan. Searching for hotels online, I saw there were plenty of rooms available and they were much cheaper than in Florence. But how would Jim feel about it?

Still tired from the early start the previous day, I decided to have an afternoon nap. When I woke up, it was too late to go to the Uffizi, but it hardly mattered in the circumstances. I checked my phone and there was a text from Jim.

I'm sorry about leaving the bar like that. The news was a bit of a shock as you can probably imagine. I've spoken to my dad who confirmed that Tabitha/Lucia is indeed my mother and he apologised for making me think she was in Australia all this time. I never thought she'd come back into my life and am a little confused. I don't feel like company at the moment so see you tomorrow?

Jim didn't even know about my plan to go to Camona and was probably thinking we'd have another day and evening before returning home.

I replied.

I'm really sorry about how you found out and hope you are okay. I'm here if you decide you want to talk. I've done some research and Lucia della Rosa is in a fishing village on the Italian Riviera called Camona. She owns a small art gallery on the seafront. I feel bad asking this of you but I promised Margaret I would try to find her. Would you mind very much if we cut our stay in Florence short and went to Camona tomorrow morning? I can book us a hotel for the night and we can go to Milan from there the following day for our flight home. Please say yes. You don't have to go anywhere near her, of course

The three dots danced while I waited for Jim's answer.

No problem.

Torn between being pleased that he'd agreed to go to Camona and deeply upset for him, I tried to imagine how confused and devastated he must be. I felt as though it was my fault. What if I hadn't found Margaret's letter? Jim could have spent the rest of his life thinking his mother was in Australia and that he'd never see her again. And then he wouldn't have to deal with the possibility of a reunion and all the emotions it would bring. But was this what he needed? Had her abandoning him as a baby wounded him in some way, making him feel rejected? I'd read enough self-help books to know it made sense for him to have the opportunity to speak to this woman, while he still could.

CHAPTER 42

CLAIRE

Jim and I were in the car on the way to Camona, speeding up the motorway in the fast lane. Over breakfast at the hotel Jim hadn't said much, and so I didn't press him to talk about the situation, instead doing my best to remain supportive. I'd tried calling Tabitha's art gallery, Camona Arte, that morning, using the number on her website, but no one answered, and the answer machine had been full. I hoped she wasn't away and that we weren't wasting our time.

When we arrived in Camona, Jim parked by the sea. It was a pretty village with pastel-coloured houses and maritime pine trees and fishing boats. Although I'd loved the buzz and hum of Florence, and the art history and architecture, it was good to be somewhere calmer, and also to experience the Italian coast.

As it was too early to check into the hotel, we went straight to the art gallery. Camona Arte was on the seafront, tucked amongst cafés, an ice cream parlour and a shop selling buckets and spades and beach umbrellas. The front door was open, and I said to Jim, 'Do you want to go and get a coffee or something?'

'Yeah, I'll do that,' he said, heading for the café on the other side of the shop selling touristy things. I saw him take a seat with a sea view. He hadn't even attempted to catch a glimpse of Tabitha, if she were indeed inside. I ran through what to say in my head, and there was no way I'd mention the son she'd abandoned was sitting at a table only metres away.

Inside the art gallery, paintings similar to those on the website hung on the walls, and there were more canvases on the floor, propped against the wall. And then I saw her. She stood at the till, writing in a notebook, and looked up as I stepped over the threshold, the ding of a bell announcing my arrival.

'Buongiorno,' she said.

'Buongiorno,' I replied. 'Do you speak English?'

'Yes,' she said. Putting down her pen, she studied me. 'I am English, actually,' she said. 'Where are you from?'

'Surrey.' I hadn't been prepared for the purpose of my visit to be obvious by me revealing where I lived.

'Oh, so am I. Whereabouts?'

'Well, currently, I'm living in a village between Guildford and Dorking.'

She lifted her eyebrows, her interest now clearly piqued.

'It's called Gatley.'

'You live in Gatley?' she said.

'Yes.'

'I know Gatley very well. I grew up there, in fact.'

'You did?' I said, continuing with the charade I'd started.

'Yes. I'm Lucia.' She proffered a hand, and I shook it.

'Claire Bell.'

'Do you fancy a cup of tea, Claire?'

'Yes, please.'

She gestured for me to take one of the white plastic chairs outside the gallery, and I sat down. A few minutes later, she brought out mugs of tea and a plate of biscuits, placing it all on a table with an umbrella.

'So, clearly you're here to see me. May I ask why?' she said.

'Well, I've been working at Gatley Hall for a few months.'

She nodded and took a sip of her tea.

'And I found a letter from a woman called Margaret.'

'Oh yes, good old Mags.'

'And she's been looking for you for a really long time.'

'She has?'

'Yes. She wants to give you a brooch that belonged to your mother.'

'Oh really? That's very kind. How old is she now?'

'In her early nineties. Would you be interested in coming back to England to see her?'

'I'd have to think long and hard about that. There might be another reason why she wants me to return, although I don't see Mags as the interfering type.'

This must be a reference to Jim, but I acted as though I didn't know of his existence.

'Do you have a card or something?' she said. 'You turning up like this out of the blue has kind of bowled me over, to be quite honest.'

'Absolutely, I understand,' I said. I handed her my business card.

'Thank you for coming all this way, Claire, although it does seem to be a waste of your time.'

'All right. Don't hesitate to email me if you'd like to come over. I can arrange for you to stay in a hotel nearby, if you like.'

She smiled, but said nothing as she slipped the card into the pocket of her trousers. Feeling dismissed, I got up and made a thing of pushing my chair under the table while thinking about what to say. Should I mention that Jim was here? Would I regret it if I didn't? But he wouldn't be happy about that. All I could do was hope Tabitha and Jim would find their way back to each other. She got up and gave me a small wave as she went back inside the gallery. My visit must have stirred up a lot of emotions and I needed to give her time to mull everything over.

Putting my bag onto my shoulder, I went to find Jim in the

café. He was staring at the sea, an Americano on the table. He'd arranged a chair beside him and our view was of a small bay with a sandy beach. To the right was a harbour with fishing boats and pastel-coloured houses, reminiscent of Cornwall.

'This is a nice spot,' I said, sitting down.

'How did it go?' he said.

'Okay. She was quite friendly at first and even made me a cup of tea, but once I told her my reason for visiting, leaving you out of it, of course, she wasn't interested in talking further.'

'It was bound to be a bit of a shock, you turning up like that.'

'Perhaps she just needs a bit of time. I gave her my card and hopefully she'll get in touch. I've done what Margaret asked of me, and fingers crossed she decides to come over to England.'

He nodded and looked straight ahead, out to sea.

A waiter approached the table, and I ordered a cappuccino.

'Let's make the most of being here and try to enjoy the rest of the day,' Jim said.

'It would be a shame not to.'

'After this we'll check into the hotel, and I might have a nap. Then out for early drinks and dinner, seeing as we didn't have lunch?'

'Sounds good to me,' I said.

Once we'd checked in, I took a long bath with the orange-scented oil provided by the hotel and then went down to the bar. Jim sat at a table outside in the courtyard, under a tree. It was a lovely setting, with trees providing shade during the day and tall terracotta pots filled with red and pink flowers. Someone splish-splashed in the pool at the far end of the garden as they swam lengths up and down.

Jim scrolled his phone with a bottle of beer by his side. When I approached, he looked up and said, 'Hi.'

He studied what I was wearing – a knee-length pink dress with cap sleeves that clung in all the right places.

'Another nice dress,' he said.

My face warming, I said, 'Thanks.'

Now we'd kissed, he was making no secret of being attracted to me, and I wondered if we might have a future together once he'd worked through all of the Tabitha and ex-fiancée stuff. I sat down opposite. A waiter approached, and I ordered a glass of Pinot Grigio.

'Well, this is a lovely spot,' I said, selecting an olive out of the bowl on the table.

'Isn't it,' he said, putting his phone away. 'I kind of wish we could stay for longer.'

'It does feel a bit rushed, doesn't it. Camona is lovely.'

'We'll just have to make the most of the evening,' Jim said, raising his bottle of beer.

'Definitely.'

The waiter placed my wine on the table. Picking it up, I clinked Jim's bottle and we said, 'Cheers.'

'So, after this drink, dinner?' Jim said.

'Sounds good to me.'

I felt it was my duty to at least try to persuade Jim to meet Tabitha while he had the chance. He didn't need to reveal who he was. Maybe it would help him in some way.

'Jim, I have to ask... do you want to meet your mother while we're here?'

'I don't see her as my mother, so could you not call her that, please?'

'Sorry.'

Here we were in this perfect setting, and I'd ruined the mood.

Attempting to recover the situation, I said, 'I shouldn't have brought it up.'

'No, you shouldn't have. Before coming to the bar I walked

to the end of the promenade, and there's a nice-looking restaurant called La Rotunda. Do you fancy going there?'

'Sure.'

I recalled from the website that the gallery would still be open, and it struck me that we'd be walking past it on the way to the restaurant. If Tabitha and Jim were supposed to meet, it would happen then.

'Shall we go now?' he said.

'Okay.'

The waiter appeared, and Jim asked for the bill. I checked my phone, and there was a message from Helen.

How's it going? Enjoying alone time with Jim?

I replied:

Oh you. Hope you're feeling better (if you are in fact unwell)

I have no idea what you're talking about *winking emoji*

So, she had faked the stomach bug. How very Helen. I'd become a character in one of her books.

Had a feeling you were making it up

Was it a good idea?

I wanted to tell Helen about the new development, but it wouldn't be fair to Jim.

I think so.

Well, good luck.

Thanks. See you soon.

I put my phone away.

'Who were you talking to?' Jim said.

'Just Helen.'

'Is she feeling better?'

'A little.'

'I don't think she was really ill,' he said, standing up.

'Oh, I'm sure she was,' I said.

'Hmm,' he said.

We left the table and he gestured for me to go first into the hotel lobby. We crossed the white marble floor and went outside. There were people milling about, all dressed up for the evening. As we walked along the promenade, there were still people on the beach. A dad built a sandcastle with a small boy and a group of teenagers sat in a circle with a speaker playing music. We passed Camona Arte, and sure enough it was open, and Tabitha was sitting in a chair outside.

'Claire,' she said, beckoning me over.

'What do you want to do?' I said to Jim through my teeth.

'I don't know,' he said.

'I need to say hello. Come with me, and I'll introduce you as a friend?'

'She knows my name though,' he said.

I pulled a face. 'We can make one up.'

We walked over.

'Hello,' I said.

'This must be the friend you mentioned?' she said.

'Yes, this is J... John,' I said.

She held out a hand, and said, 'Lucia.'

Jim shook her hand, giving her a slight nod and without

looking her in the eye. He seemed so wounded, and I felt bad for him.

'Nice to meet you, John,' she said.

'Likewise,' he said.

She studied him, as if sensing he was familiar. If she'd seen Luca's portrait, she might be putting two and two together. Did a mother know when she was looking at her child, even if she hadn't seen them since they were a baby?

'We're heading to La Rotunda for an early dinner now,' I said.

'All right. Nice to see you again, Claire. And I am sorry about earlier. It was a bit of surprise you turning up out of the blue. There is more to it than meets the eye, you see.'

Nodding, I said, 'I understand.'

We exchanged a look, and I said, 'It would make Mags so happy if you got in touch. Perhaps email me when you've had time to mull everything over.'

'Okay,' Tabitha said.

'Bye,' I said.

As we crossed the road back to the promenade, I looked at Jim. His shoulders were hunched, and he seemed greatly affected by meeting Tabitha. Perhaps I'd made a mistake taking him past the art gallery. I knew about having a mostly absent parent, but at least my dad had taken me out for birthday lunches. I desperately wanted to make Jim feel better.

When we reached La Rotunda, a waiter showed us to a table on the veranda with a view of the bay. The sun was setting, creating the most beautiful sky, a vast canvas painted in pastel pink. A fishing boat pulled out of the harbour and I watched it disappear into the distance. I looked across at Jim, who was studying the menu.

'I'm sorry,' I said.

'It is what it is. Let's get some wine. A bottle of Pinot Grigio?'

'That would be great,' I said.

While Jim ordered the wine, I had a thought. Shouldn't I encourage him to go and see his mother, to try to bring about some kind of reconciliation? Was it my responsibility to do that? Would Mags want me to do that?

The waiter went to get the wine and Jim continued to look at the food menu.

'Jim?' I said.

'Yes.'

'Do you think you should go back to the gallery?'

'No,' he said from behind his menu.

'Are you sure?'

'Claire, please can you stop this? I already feel quite annoyed by the whole situation. Obviously if I'd have known she was my mother I wouldn't have agreed to replace Helen on this damn trip, would I?'

'You wouldn't?'

'Of course not. Why would I want to see her after she abandoned me as a baby? She's already made it very clear that she wants nothing to do with me.'

'Oh Jim.'

'What?'

'How do you know she doesn't regret what she did?'

'Wouldn't she have got in touch if that were the case? Tried to see me?'

'I guess you're right.'

'I know I'm right.'

And then I saw to my surprise, over Jim's shoulder, Tabitha approaching our table. Oh no, had she overheard our conversation? And how was Jim going to deal with this?

She came up to the table and Jim threw me a look.

'Hi,' I said.

'Hello, both,' she said, pulling her pashmina around her

shoulders. 'I'm sorry to interrupt your dinner, it's just, well, after you left, I realised something.'

'What's that?' I said, already knowing the answer.

'Your name isn't John, is it?' she said to Jim.

He shook his head.

'Should we offer Lucia a seat?' I said to Jim, using her preferred name.

'I can't do this,' he said, getting up. 'You can sit here.'

'Where are you going?' I said.

'For a walk.'

'Can't you stay for a minute and listen to what I have to say?' Tabitha said as he walked away. But he went down the steps onto the pavement and crossed the road to the promenade.

'Why don't you sit down?' I said.

She took Jim's chair. 'When Luca and I spent some time together,' she said, 'before we sadly had a falling-out, he showed me some photos of when he was younger and, well, I saw the portrait that brought him and my mother together at the game-keeper's cottage. Mrs Willis took me to see it.'

'I don't know what to say,' I said. 'After I came to see you I tried to get Jim to introduce himself, but he's hurt by you leaving, understandably.'

'Yes, I know. I can't expect a good reaction from him.'

'He only found out who you were yesterday.'

'It must be a shock for him,' she said.

'He'll come round,' I said.

'How long are you in Camona for?' Tabitha said.

'We're flying home tomorrow.'

'Well, now the cat's out of the bag, I'll have to seriously think about coming to England, although it would be an emotional trip.'

'I'm sure it would be. Well, you have my details,' I said.

'I'd need to arrange for someone to look after the gallery.'

'The exhibition is the first week in June, if you'd like to

come for that, and I'd love for Margaret to be able to give you the brooch soon. Time isn't on her side.'

'All right. I need time to think,' she said, getting up. 'Goodbye, Claire, and thank you.'

Tabitha had completely ruined any chance of us rescuing the evening by interrupting our dinner, but I still hoped she might come to England and try to talk to Jim.

I said, 'Goodbye,' she left and then I messaged Jim to say she'd gone, and he should come back and eat with me. He didn't reply and so I ordered a pizza margarita and ate alone, then took the rest of the bottle of wine back to the hotel. While I was getting ready for bed, Jim sent a message:

I'm sorry about walking off like that. This is all a bit much and I just need to be alone. I hope you understand. I'll see you in the morning.

All I could do was give him time.

CHAPTER 43

CLAIRE

Jim and I didn't talk much on the flight home. I read *A Room with a View*, and he watched some football match on his phone. While he was waiting for me to collect my suitcase from the carousel at Gatwick airport, he went to sit down and scrolled his phone. When I approached him, wheeling my case, he looked up and threw me a smile. But it was a smile that didn't show in his eyes, and I sensed something was wrong.

'What's the matter?' I said.

'What do you mean?'

'You look as though you just found something out on your phone.'

'The big oak in the Dairy Field was blown down during a storm last night.'

I knew how fond he was of that tree.

'Oh, I'm sorry. That's a real shame.'

'It was over two hundred years old. A real beauty too.'

'I remember you telling me that day we went to the game-keeper's cottage.'

'Also, this means I'll be thrown straight into getting it sorted out first thing tomorrow.'

'Not the best end to our trip.'

'It wasn't the best trip anyway,' he said. I looked at him, and he pressed his lips together.

'I know.'

Soon we were driving through the gates at Gatley Hall. Jim parked, and wheeled my case back to Rose Cottage, and we nodded and said, 'Goodnight,' outside our front doors.

I took a shower and went to bed with a cup of tea. In the morning I'd email Tabitha, and do everything I could to persuade her to come over and see Margaret.

When waking up, I felt at home for the first time at Rose Cottage. Being away from Gatley Hall had given me a chance to appreciate my new life. Leaving my job at the Frampton Gallery had been the right decision. Breaking up with Miles had also done me the world of good. Living a slower life and tapping into my creative side with the sketching and painting and taking photos was helping me to grieve for my father. And, although I knew the pain of losing him would never truly go away, it was beginning to lessen. I was grateful to have found a way to alleviate the grief in some small way.

There was still the matter of me and Jim. I hadn't expected anything to happen in Florence, and hoped that one kiss hadn't ruined our friendship. He was almost self-sabotaging by continuing his situationship with Samantha, because there was no future in it. I'd made it clear that with me it was either all or nothing, and that would mean dealing with his emotions. Jim didn't seem ready for any of that. And perhaps I wasn't either after being with Miles for so long. Although I'd loved him, deep down I had known he was wrong for me for the last year or so of us being together. On a subconscious level, I knew he wouldn't provide me with what I wanted – the family I'd never had when growing up. I'd envied my friends at school and university for having siblings and a father who wanted to know them and a mother with maternal instincts. Maybe I'd delayed leaving him because I was afraid of uprooting my whole life. Dad dying and what happened subsequently had pushed me into making the changes I needed.

All I could do was wait for Jim to decide what he wanted. If it was meant to be, it would happen. In the meantime, if he needed a friend to talk through the Tabitha situation with, I'd be there. I would always be there for him and couldn't imagine not having him in my life.

I got out of bed and put on jeans and a t-shirt. The weather wasn't as hot as Italy, but warm enough for short sleeves. Did I really need to wear smart clothes for work every day? They didn't really fit with the laid-back environment at Gatley Hall. Perhaps I'd wear my old work clothes one day a week, just to keep my hand in.

When I stepped outside, I saw the roses had started to bloom and they rambled up the trellis on the wall between the front doors. They were a pastel-pink colour and I leant forwards to inhale their sweet scent. Standing back, I admired how beautiful the cottage looked and took a photo on my phone. It would make a lovely painting. As I walked to the Stables, I noticed that the roses were also blooming in the walled garden. At the Stables, I ordered a takeaway coffee along with a croissant, then went to the office and called Helen.

'Hello, Claire,' she said.

'How's it going?' I said.

'A bit hectic here this morning as I'm dealing with the PR for this oak tree. It's over two hundred years old so it's getting some attention, from the national newspapers as well. I'm writing a press release as we speak and need to update the social media channels. Ed is out there taking photos for us.'

'Oh, okay.'

'How was the trip?'

'It was good, thank you.'

'A success, then?'

'Well, we found Tabitha, and I gave her my card. I'm hoping she'll come to England so Margaret can give her the brooch.'

'I'll message you when I've sent this off and we can meet for lunch?'

'That sounds great.'

At lunchtime, I went to meet Helen and we bought sandwiches and coffees.

'Spill the beans then,' she said.

'Well...' I told her about what had happened with Tabitha, leaving out the part about her being Jim's mother.

'And Jim?' she said.

'He's dealing with the tree, obviously, and—'

'Did anything happen?'

'What do you mean?'

'I was really hoping you two might get together in Florence. You're a much better fit for him than Samantha. He needs a woman like you in his life.'

'Oh thanks. It's a bit complicated though.'

'Why?'

'We're both working through a lot of stuff.'

'What do you mean?'

'Well, I'm dealing with my father's death and the split with Miles, and—'

'And what has he got to deal with?'

'He split with his fiancée, didn't he?'

'That was last June, almost a year ago.'

'I know, but—'

'He should be over that by now.'

'I'm not sure if he's ready for a relationship. I'm not sure I am either.'

'There's something you're not telling me, I can see it in your eyes.'

Sighing, I said, 'If I tell you this, it can't go any further.'

'My lips are sealed.'

Helen took a sip of her cappuccino.

'It turns out Tabitha is Jim's mother, the woman who abandoned him when he was a baby.'

She abruptly put down the cup she was holding and some of the coffee spilt onto the table.

'What! You're kidding?'

'Nope.'

Helen blotted the coffee with a napkin.

'I remember Margaret talking about the menopause baby. And that's him. Wow, I can't believe it.' Helen tipped her head to one side as if she was in deep thought. 'But that's such a coincidence, isn't it? He's living in the house where his mother grew up. Surely, he must have had an inkling?'

'His father used to bring him to Rose Cottage to see an old family friend, Hilda who worked at the house during the war. I'm assuming that's Mrs Willis?'

'Yes, Hilda was Mrs Willis and she continued to live at Rose Cottage until she died in the late 1990s.'

'I thought it had to be. Afterwards, Jim and his dad would go for walks through the countryside. He developed a love for Gatley Hall and so it's not such a coincidence really.'

'Ah, I see. His father was trying to bring him as close to his mother as he could by spending time in the place where she grew up. But where did Jim think she was all this time?'

'His dad said Tabitha had emigrated to Australia so that Jim wouldn't ever expect to see her. As you can imagine, he's quite upset by it all.'

'But why didn't he cotton on when you told him you were looking for Tabitha?'

'Because it's only Margaret who calls her that. Mr and Mrs Willis preferred Lucy, the English equivalent of her middle

name. She's been using Lucia in Italy. As soon as I mentioned
that, he worked it out.'

'Oh.'

Helen tapped her fingers on the table, a writer's mind at
work, I guessed, as she processed all the information.

'I can understand why he's being weird with you at the
moment after all of that.'

'Yes, it's a lot to work through, isn't it?'

'He needs time.'

'That's the plan, and, if he needs a friend to talk to, I can be
there for him.'

'I have a hunch you two will work it out. I've seen how you
can't take your eyes off each other.'

'Really?'

'Yes. You don't always catch him watching you, but I've
seen it.'

My face warmed. Did Jim like me more than I'd previously
thought?

'I guess what happens happens.'

'Only time will tell,' Helen said. 'Right, I have to get back to
work, but call me if you need me.'

'Thanks. I need to get on with organising this exhibition,
and I'm hoping Tabitha will come over and get the brooch.
Maybe then she can talk to Jim too.'

'Okay, keep me updated.'

We cleared our plates and went back to our respective
offices. I felt bad betraying Jim's confidence, but had needed to
talk to someone. And I trusted that Helen wouldn't let it go any
further.

At the office that afternoon I carried on preparing for the
Below Stairs exhibition, adding information to my file. It was
coming together nicely, and I was excited. The photo I'd taken
of Luca in Florence would look really good next to the portrait.
With only a few weeks to go, I needed Tabitha to visit soonish

and provide an ending to Margaret's story. Before leaving for the day, I sent her an email.

Dear Lucia,

It was nice to meet you in Camona. It would be lovely if you're able to visit Gatley for a couple of days. You could stay at the Old Fox, a nice local pub with rooms and I'd take you to see Margaret – it is her lifelong wish to give you the brooch belonging to your mother.

Best wishes,

Claire Bell

On the way back to Rose Cottage, I went to find Jim in the shed. He was at his desk, tapping away on his keyboard.

'Hi,' I said.

'Hi, Claire.'

He continued to look at the screen as I sat in the chair next to him, waiting for him to finish.

'How have you been today?'

He sighed. 'I'm very sad about the tree, obviously. It's heart-breaking, really.'

'I know, and I'm sorry,' I said.

He turned to face me. 'They need me at Cleveland House because a couple of trees were blown over there during the storm too. So I'll probably be gone for a few days.'

'Oh, okay.'

'Claire, I hope you don't mind but I have a few emails to send before packing to go over to Cleveland House tonight. I want to be there first thing in the morning to make an early start.'

Dismissed, I got up. He didn't seem to want to talk to me at all. 'All right. Well, I'd better get back. Let me know if you need anything,' I said.

'Thanks, Claire,' he said, rather formally.

I didn't say goodbye as I closed the door behind me. Walking through the rose garden, I felt immensely sad. We'd been so close in Italy and now it was as if we'd never known each other at all. I'd miss him while he was at Cleveland House but hopefully he wouldn't stay there for too long. Back at the cottage, I'd do some sketching of my photos from Florence. I just wanted to think about nothing for a while.

CHAPTER 44

CLAIRE

Jim stayed at Cleveland House for the rest of the week, and he didn't get in touch. I missed him. One morning, I typed out a message on my phone.

How's it going?

He didn't reply until the evening.

Okay. How are you?

When are you coming back?

I'm covering someone now who's gone on annual leave so don't know. Maybe next week.

Oh, it's not the same without you

He didn't reply.

I carried on preparing for the exhibition, but I didn't hear from Tabitha and so started to put together a display that wouldn't need her to visit Margaret. It was disappointing, but if she didn't want to come over I couldn't make her. I'd written to Margaret to tell her not to get her hopes up, but that I was still working on persuading Tabitha to visit.

Jim came back on the Friday, and I heard him unlocking his front door. Would he come and see me? Should I go and say hello to him? He seemed to be avoiding me and there wasn't a lot I could do about it. I decided to leave him to it. If he wanted to see me, he would. The weekend passed with me hearing him move around next door. One night, I heard Samantha's voice and went to sleep downstairs on the sofa. The thought of them seeing each other again grated, but he'd made his decision.

He didn't knock to ask for milk, or whether I wanted to have a drink with him or a takeaway. I continued to immerse myself in my art by painting the sketches I'd drawn in Florence – one of the Ponte Vecchio, and another of the view from the top of the Duomo. And I spent some time in the garden, watering and deadheading the flowers with a new pair of secateurs I'd treated myself to, and I planted some herbs: basil, mint and rosemary, three herbs I used often when cooking. I removed the limescale from between tiles on the bathroom wall and around the sink. I put some plants on the windowsill and bought candles to go round the bath, and started to take long baths every night before bed. I was living my best life, remembering the saying, 'Dolce far niente', and I didn't need Jim or anyone else to make it better. I couldn't help missing him though.

When Monday came, I still hadn't seen Jim, so I went to find him at the shed, but he wasn't there. I sent him a message. It was time we talked.

Hello stranger. Hope you're okay?

The three dots danced.

Hi, I meant to tell you, I'm working at Cleveland House until further notice. I need to take a break from Gatley Hall.

This was gut-wrenching. Who knew when I'd see him next? I'd just have to hope he'd come back to me when he was ready.

It was a lovely time of year at Gatley Hall with all the flowers blooming, and I started to take longer walks before breakfast and at lunchtimes, and after work too as it was lighter later. I'd sometimes take my dinner down to the lake and sit on a bench by a rhododendron bush, its hot-pink flowers in full bloom. Then I'd feed the ducks with stale bread. Sometimes, I'd take photos and do some sketching. The time alone was therapeutic, and I could feel myself healing from those awful weeks in the run-up to Christmas and changing into a future version of myself. I was beginning to enjoy a simpler life. I bought a cookery book and taught myself how to make bread and pasta. And I made healthy salads. In the evening, I'd often sit in the patio garden with a glass of wine and a book, or I'd do more sketching. I was beginning to build a small following on Instagram as I posted my photos, drawings and paintings and got to know other artists and photographers online.

One morning I saw an artist post a photograph of Florence, saying she was doing a month-long art course and how wonderful it was. This made me think. Could I do one of these courses? I felt as though I wasn't done with Florence yet. The thought of spending a month there, painting all day and enjoying the city, seemed self-indulgent. But why not? Miles and I had spent money on holidays in hotels where we just lay by the pool all day and ate there in the evenings. We'd rarely explored the local towns and I'd always found this kind of holiday unfulfilling. And it seemed a waste not to find out more about local culture and to see the places that were only minutes away from the hotel. I googled the course and the price was more affordable than expected. I looked at the dates available and there was a course in June, after the exhibition had opened. Would Rosalind give me the time off? I'd probably have to take two weeks unpaid so as not to use all of my annual leave at once, if she did agree to it. I decided to mull it over some more, and pluck up the courage to ask.

The week before the exhibition, months of hard work came to fruition at last. The builders had done a fine job, repainting the servants' quarters in magnolia, and the flagstone floors were gleaming. The below stairs rooms were almost ready to go on show, and I just needed to add the finishing touches. We weren't opening all of the rooms to visitors, as it was too expensive – some would open the following year, and I'd be charged with managing that project too. For this exhibition we'd open the servants' hall, the laundry room, the housekeeper's parlour, the still room and the kitchen. I'd arranged for furniture and objects to be brought from storage, and the copper pots looked especially beautiful and shiny, all lined up on the kitchen counter. As the servants' hall was the biggest room, that was where I arranged the display about Margaret's story. I'd sent Tabitha a follow-up email the previous week, but still no reply. Like Jim, she had obviously made her decision.

That week, I also set up Luca's portrait on its easel. I displayed photographs of Luca in Florence, the servants by the Christmas tree, Margaret and Tom's wedding. And of course there was Margaret's letter. I added Lady Violet's copy of *A Room with a View*. Without Tabitha's visit, though, I couldn't include the brooch or any mention of Jim being her son. And even if she did come over, Jim would need to give me permission to include information about him. I wasn't sure how he'd feel about that, but how I'd love to include a photo of him next to Luca. Jim and I hadn't stayed in touch during his time at Cleveland House and it felt as though our friendship was over and done. I would just have to get over it.

With only a few days until the exhibition started, an email from Tabitha popped up on my phone.

Dear Claire,

Thank you for your emails and sorry for taking so long to reply. I've been thinking a great deal since your visit and have decided to come tomorrow. I'd like to see Margaret, and also to try and talk to Jim. I'll keep you updated.

Regards,

Lucia

I was so happy about this, and I immediately called Hyacinth Place and left a message for Margaret. There was a chance I'd fulfil Margaret's wish before the exhibition started and that was an exciting prospect. As soon as I knew more, I'd arrange for Tabitha and me to visit her.

CHAPTER 45

CLAIRE

Tabitha travelled to Gatley the next day, as promised, and booked a room at the Old Fox. After some dithering I decided to tell Jim, and sent him a message.

Hey. Just to let you know Tabitha will be staying at the Old Fox tomorrow and the following night. She's coming to see Margaret and get the brooch and would like to see you as well, if you're around? Of course I understand if you'd rather not, but thought I should tell you

The three dots danced and for a few seconds, I was hopeful. Was he going to say yes?

Thanks for letting me know.

Maybe when Tabitha arrived he might change his mind. All I could do was keep trying to get through to him.

When Tabitha arrived, she messaged me, and I went to meet her at the Old Fox.

'Thanks so much for coming,' I said.

'Is Jim not with you?' she said.

'I told him you were here, and that's all I can do. Perhaps he'll change his mind before you go back?'

'Oh, I was hoping he might have had a chance to come round already. Let's hope he does. Shall we go and see Margaret then?'

I drove Tabitha to Hyacinth Place. When we arrived, Margaret was waiting in the lounge, elegant in a green dress and a string of pearls round her neck. Her nails were painted bright pink and she wore lipstick to match. Her hair was in a bun, and she looked fabulous.

Tabitha approached her, and took her hands, and said, 'Dear Margaret. I want to thank you for persevering with your search for me.'

'It is good to see you, Tabitha.'

'I'm sorry for everything.'

'My dear,' Margaret said. 'I know you had your reasons for leaving, but all that matters is you are here now.'

Margaret took a red box with Ellis and Son written on top in gold letters out of her handbag and placed it on the table.

'Here is your brooch.'

Tabitha looked at the box, shaking her head.

'I can't believe this is for me,' she said.

'Open it,' Margaret said.

Tabitha opened the box, and there lay a beautiful oval-shaped brooch with an emerald in the centre and encrusted in diamonds.

'I don't know what to say,' Tabitha said.

'Your mother wanted you to have it. She asked me to take it out of the safe at Gatley Hall and give it to you on your wedding day, but I thought my husband had sold it. When he died, I found it had been in a shoebox in the back of his wardrobe all along.'

'Thank you, Margaret,' Tabitha said, closing the box. She

wiped away a tear with her hand. I felt privileged to witness such a special moment between the two of them.

'I know it's taken many years for Margaret to track you down and give you this brooch, Tabitha, but what would you think about me borrowing it for the exhibition?' I said. 'I could arrange for it to be returned to you in Italy – I could even bring it over myself, if necessary.'

Tabitha laughed. 'So, I've come all this way to get it, and you want to keep it for longer?'

Nodding, I said, 'Yes, it would mean the exhibition is complete, and then we can get lots of press attention for Gatley Hall, meaning more funding for the preservation of the estate.'

'That sounds good to me. All right.'

Tabitha flew home the next day without getting to see Jim. He remained at Cleveland House, and I wondered if he'd ever come back. Perhaps he would arrange to be transferred there. We'd stopped messaging each other, and every time my phone vibrated, I hoped it might be Jim. I wondered if I'd even see him again.

CHAPTER 46

MARGARET

JUNE 2015

It was a warm afternoon and I sat in the lounge at Hyacinth Place, the television showing an old black-and-white film. The room was occupied by very old people like me, all waiting for their time to come. My days consisted of eating rather bland meals and swallowing a range of pills to keep me alive. My life could not be more dull. After Tabitha's visit, all I could think about was whether I'd lived a good life. To be mulling over regrets and chances not taken would be sad indeed. I was fortunate to have led a better life than most. I never did return to London to work as a shopgirl, and I never fulfilled my dream of owning a boutique. If I'd been born a few decades later, those opportunities could have been open to me, and I might have had a husband who wasn't so closed off to my having anything of my own.

Despite my unhappy marriage to Tom, I was thankful for my children and grandchildren, and for my niece, Alice, who had done so much for me over the years. And most of all, I was glad that I had the courage to sign up for that Italian class on

Thursday evenings. Tom hadn't liked it one bit when I told him I was going, but by then the children had left and the menopause somehow emboldened me, my hormones no longer focused on putting others before myself. I became quite selfish and discovered a more confident version of me existed. Tom made such a fuss that first evening when I was getting ready to leave for the class, and started an argument about my not having made him a proper dinner – I'd made fish fingers with oven chips and frozen peas rather than a home-cooked meal. He tried to stop me from going and having just one thing of my own. But I walked out of that door and got into the car and drove with dogged determination, putting myself first for once.

Meeting Nathan at that class gave me twenty happy years – the happiest I'd ever known. After being with Tom, I had thought love was a myth and that all men were like him. But Nathan was so warm and so kind, and interesting. We would talk for hours about all sorts of things. He had a sense of adventure that made life exciting. We returned to Italy many times in his caravan and those days and nights spent on campsites together were the best days of my life. Who would have thought one could derive such joy from living so simply? All that time spent in the big house in Dorking did not compare.

And then there was Luca. I'd thought I loved him at first sight, but in time I realised it was merely infatuation, for he was a beautiful man with film-star looks. We could barely hold a conversation, for goodness' sake. Over the years I came to believe that he and Lady Violet were meant to have that time together, to bring Tabitha into the world. And in turn she brought her own children. I was so glad to get Lady Violet's brooch into her daughter's hands. Not only had I fulfilled her dying wish, but also I realised my own, and in the process reunited Tabitha with her son.

With my failing memory, I couldn't always recall what I did yesterday, but was able to describe every last detail of those days during the war, of when I saw Taylor and Stone in flames before my eyes, of getting the train to Gatley – I could even still picture everyone in my carriage – and of meeting Tom for the first time, before knowing what he was really like. I could visualise that day Luca saved my life as if it were a film playing at the pictures. And how seeing Luca make love to Lady Violet on the chaise longue broke my heart. But I couldn't tell you what I had for breakfast that morning.

Marjorie, the carer, came over. 'Claire is here to see you, Margaret,' she said.

'Oh, Claire from Gatley Hall?'

'Yes, you asked us to call her and arrange a visit.'

'Oh? All right.'

After she and Tabitha went home that day, it struck me that I had one more thing to give her.

'Would you mind bringing me the carrier bag on my dressing table, Marjorie?'

'No problem, Margaret.'

Claire came to sit down and smiled at me. I was grateful to her for all she'd done.

'Hello, Claire.'

'Hello, Margaret.'

Marjorie came back in and handed me the bag.

'Since you came in with Tabitha, I've been thinking about the exhibition,' I said. 'When you asked if you could borrow the brooch, I thought about what else I could give you to display.'

'Oh yes?'

I handed Claire the bag and said, 'Look inside, I think you'll be pleased with what you find there.'

* * *

CLAIRE

I opened the bag and took out a black leather notebook.

'Look inside,' Margaret said.

I turned the first page, and saw that it was a diary, beginning with the words:

> *A few days ago, a very handsome man called Luca saved my life. Mrs Willis asked me to go and get supplies from Home Farm as Sam's brother was home on leave and as I walked through the fields...*

'Oh Margaret, this is your diary from the war?'

Nodding, she said, 'Yes, it is.'

'This is wonderful. Thank you very much.'

She took my hand and gave it a squeeze.

'You are welcome, my dear. Thank you for all you have done for me, Tabitha and Jim.'

'It's been a real pleasure. Would you like to come to the exhibition and see everything for yourself?'

'I'd be delighted,' she said. 'As long as you can get me there.'

'Helen will come and get you, I'm sure. We'll arrange it.'

'All right. Thank you, Claire.'

On the first morning of the exhibition, I went to speak to Rosalind, who was glued to her computer screen. She threw me a glance.

'Morning, Claire. The brooch story is causing quite a stir,' she said. 'I've got a couple of local journalists coming down later today. One from the *Surrey Standard* and one from *What's Up, Surrey!*'

'Brilliant,' I said, anxious to get on with what I had to say before I chickened out. 'I have something to ask you.'

She swivelled round in her chair to face me.

'I'm all ears,' she said.

'I was thinking that now the Below Stairs exhibition is done, and I haven't started work on my next project yet...'

'You're looking to take some annual leave?' she said.

'Yes.'

'How much?'

'Well, it's longer than usual as I haven't had a proper break since my father died, shortly before I started working here.'

'Yes, I am sorry and do feel that perhaps it wasn't fair of me to pressure you to start here so soon without taking any time off,' Rosalind said.

'Coming here was exactly what I needed, although it took some time to realise that. Anyway, I've got back into drawing and painting recently – something I used to love doing when I was younger – and it's really helped me to grieve.'

Rosalind nodded. 'Go on,' she said.

'I've found an art course in Florence, similar to the one Tabitha did – when I was there, I felt so inspired by the art and the history, and the only thing is, it's a month long, but I was thinking I could take two weeks' annual leave and two weeks unpaid.'

'Done,' Rosalind said.

'Really?'

'Of course. We're all so impressed with the work you've done here already, the way you reunited Tabitha and Mags and the brooch. And you uncovered a wonderful story that we can now use to promote Gatley Hall and get some real press attention. When does it start?'

'Next week.'

'All right.'

'Thank you, Rosalind.'

'That's fine. Submit the paperwork and we'll get it fast-tracked, okay?'

She turned back round to face her computer screen and I left the room, amazed that she'd agreed. I hadn't expected her to, at all, and felt quite pleased with myself for plucking up the courage to ask.

The first week of the exhibition was a huge success, and the *Surrey Standard* wrote up a fantastic piece that got picked up by some of the national newspapers. Helen brought Margaret and she beamed as I took her round, her arm linked with mine. She was delighted to see all the work we'd done to bring Gatley's wartime era to life. I felt as though I'd done her proud.

CHAPTER 47

CLAIRE

I rented a flat in an old medieval building, painted yellow, with a view of the River Arno. It was compact and cosy and felt like home. I could hear traffic and the voices of passers-by and would sit in the chair facing the window for hours, savouring the view, the Ponte Vecchio on my left. The day before, I'd met Tabitha for a coffee and returned the brooch to her. She told me that she'd emailed Jim but hadn't heard anything.

I'd been in Florence for a week and was enjoying myself. I had a routine that worked well. There was no way I could waste the opportunity to see as much of the place as possible while I was there, and so I'd get up at half past six every morning, without fail, and by seven o'clock I was ready to wander around the city while it was still quiet. I'd walk by the river, where there would usually be rowers out for their early practice. Often, I'd stand on the Ponte Vecchio and just be present, remembering 'Dolce far niente'. I'd visited the Uffizi many times, and stood and admired Botticelli's *Birth of Venus*. I'd climbed the steps of the Duomo at sunset and replayed the almost-kiss with Jim over and over in my head.

Jim was still on my mind, and I missed him. He'd sent me a

message on the day I left, wishing me luck and asking where I'd live on my return. For we'd both received notice to leave our cottages in July so the ATP could refurbish them for holiday-makers. Helen had kindly offered me her granny annexe for as long as I wanted it. I'd gratefully accepted and would move in on my return to England.

One morning when I got back to the flat and checked my pigeonhole in the lobby, there was a letter addressed to me. I opened it.

Dear Claire,

I didn't want to tell you this in a text message, but Margaret died a few days ago. She had a cold that developed into pneumonia and passed away peacefully during the night. It is very sad, but I guess that after you helped her fulfil her greatest wish, she didn't need to stick around any more.

The other reason I'm sending a letter is because it's time that I told you how I feel. I couldn't bear to write it in a phone message and go through the pain of you leaving me on read while anticipating your reply. I'd rather kid myself that if I haven't heard from you, it's because you haven't read the letter yet or it went missing.

Anyway, I love you, Claire. And I loved you from the moment I barged into your cottage in my towel. The look on your face was one I'll never forget. I could tell you liked me too, despite the way you glared at me disapprovingly, and it was as though we'd always known each other. They say that you know you've met the right person when you feel like that, a familiarity as if you've met them before. And of course, I think you are the prettiest girl in all of Surrey. Oh, and by the way, I broke it off with Samantha a few weeks ago.

So, there you are. Perhaps write back and tell me what you think about us going out for dinner when you get back from Florence. Or, better still, how about you send me a message, because I'm going to Camona to see my mother – yes, I feel able to call her that now – for the week your course finishes. I could drop in and see you in Florence if you'll let me, and our first dinner date can be in some lovely restaurant with a nice bottle of Chianti. Maybe you can come with me to meet Luca too. Anyway, let me know your thoughts.

And I am sorry to deliver the news about Margaret. But just remember that you did a wonderful thing for her and should be proud of yourself. And by doing that, you have reunited me with my mother and after spending a great deal of time thinking (and I'm sorry it took so long) I am grateful.

Love, Jim xx

As I finished reading the letter, I tried to make sense of the mixed emotions that consumed me. It was very sad that Margaret had died, but at least I'd managed to fulfil her wish in time. And hopefully she'd now be at peace. And then, there was Jim: at last, he'd told me how he felt. Tears ran down my face, but also I found myself smiling as it struck me: the wait was over. We could be together at last. Taking out my phone, I tapped out a message.

Hey you, thanks for your letter. I just read it now. That is so sad about Margaret, but hopefully she is now at peace. I'm so glad that you're visiting your mother, and of course I'd like to go out for dinner. And you still need to go on the second day of my cultural tour – don't think you're getting out of the Uffizi visit that easily. I love you too, by the way. Claire with an 'i' xx

After the last day of my art course I went back to the flat, hardly able to stop thinking about Jim's visit. He should be arriving soon. I went into the kitchen and made a cup of tea and sat in the living room with the French doors open. At that moment, with the anticipation of Jim's arrival, I couldn't have been happier. Mopeds buzzed past, telling me I was in Italy, and I closed my eyes. I must have fallen asleep because the sound of someone shouting woke me up. I couldn't make out what they were saying, but it seemed to be coming from outside.

'Claire,' the voice shouted again. It was Jim.

I got up, rushed onto the balcony and looked down below. And there he was, standing there with a huge grin on his face.

'I don't think your intercom is working,' he said.

'You always did like to make an unconventional entrance,' I said.

He laughed. 'Are you going to let me in then?'

'Okay.'

I went to press the button for the main door downstairs, and then I opened my front door, and leant on it and waited for Jim to come up all of the stairs, for there were many of them, me being on the fourth floor. Finally he reached the last flight and, as he came towards me, I was so happy to see him. Jim, my Jim, here to see me. As he got closer, my gut hopped and then he cupped my face, and said, 'Can I kiss you?'

'Yes, you can.'

He leant in and pressed his lips to mine, and we kissed for what seemed like forever while leaning on my door. And then we went inside, and he picked me up and carried me to the bedroom. There was no more time to waste.

A LETTER FROM ANITA

Dear reader,

I want to say a big thank you for choosing to read *The Florence Letter*. If you did enjoy it, and want to keep up to date with all my latest releases, just sign up at the following link. Your email address will never be shared and you can unsubscribe at any time.

www.bookouture.com/anita-chapman

I hope you enjoyed *The Florence Letter* and if you did I would be very grateful if you could write a review. I'd love to hear what you think, and it makes such a difference helping new readers to discover one of my books for the first time.

I love hearing from my readers – you can get in touch via my website, and follow me on social media to see updates about my books and everyday life as a writer.

Thanks, and best wishes,

Anita Chapman

KEEP IN TOUCH WITH ANITA

www.anitachapman.com

facebook.com/anitachapmanauthor

x.com/neetschapman

instagram.com/neetschapman

tiktok.com/@neetschapman

ACKNOWLEDGEMENTS

Thank you so much for helping to make this book happen:

My editor, Jayne Osborne, who has been an absolute joy to work with and the rest of the fabulous Bookouture team. Thank you especially to Peta Nightingale, Myrto Kalavrezou, Kim Nash, Jess Readett, Imogen Allport, Jen Shannon, Mandy Kullar; Debbie Clement who has designed an absolutely beautiful cover; Jacqui Lewis for doing a very thorough copy edit; and to proofreader, Anne O'Brien who picked up so many important things.

Thank you very much to readers who read advance copies via NetGalley and for the blog tour. I really appreciate you taking the time to read *The Florence Letter* and write reviews.

To my social media followers, especially all those who continue to cheer me on and share news about my books.

To my family and friends who always support me, and to my writing retreat pals: Jules, Donna and Liz.

To Lorraine Mace, who read an early draft of *The Florence Letter* and who has really helped me to develop my confidence as a writer over the past few years.

To Evelyn Ryle, who once again helped me enormously with information relating to hereditary titles.

To everyone who bought, read, spread the word about and wrote reviews for my debut, *The Venice Secret*. Thank you for encouraging me to write more books with your lovely words.

PUBLISHING TEAM

Turning a manuscript into a book requires the efforts of many people. The publishing team at Bookouture would like to acknowledge everyone who contributed to this publication.

Audio
Alba Proko
Melissa Tran
Sinead O'Connor

Commercial
Lauren Morrissette
Hannah Richmond
Imogen Allport

Cover design
Debbie Clement

Data and analysis
Mark Alder
Mohamed Bussuri

Editorial
Jayne Osborne
Imogen Allport